Y0-DOL-641

The Rapture Syndrome

by
Dennis Knotts

Front Cover by
Ronald G. Patterson

Strategic Book Publishing and Rights Co.

Copyright © 1978 Dennis Knotts.

Final version 6/23/2013. All rights reserved.

No part of this book may be reproduced or transmitted in any form or by any means, graphic, electronic, or mechanical, including photocopying, recording, taping, or by any information storage retrieval system, without the permission, in writing, of the publisher.

Strategic Book Publishing and Rights Co.
12620 FM 1960, Suite A4-507
Houston TX 77065
www.sbpra.com

ISBN: 978-1-62857-869-0

Design: Dedicated Book Services (www.netdbs.com)

Dedication

To Jim Baxter, who started this whole crazy thing by playing Larry Norman's "I Wish We'd All Been Ready" for me years ago. And who didn't know any better than to let me move in for a week while his father was gone so we could check out this Rapture thing for ourselves. See where all of this led?

Table of Contents

Introduction

(Some Common Sense About The Rapture)

Ever since the Jesus People Movement of the 60's, the topic of the Rapture has been on believers' lips at one time or another. Perhaps we do not see it as widely discussed or looked for as we did in the 60's and 70's, but this does not mean it isn't coming. However, too much attention on the Rapture can be unhealthy for believers. Let me share an incident with you:

I received a call from a former co-worker and close Christian friend who was very excited. He had been telling me about a book that was on the market which predicted the date of the Rapture. In fact, the date was the very next day. He wanted me to take off at lunch and meet him at the local Christian bookstore because they had the book on sale for half-off. I told him, "Why don't you wait until the day after tomorrow, and you can get it for free from the dumpster in back of the store?"

He wasn't happy with my sense of humor, but what do you want from a puppeteer? Having a foam and fur character as your alter-ego does affect your mind from time to time.

It was then that I first considered this editorial, but never got around to writing it. Now, as I'm about to tackle THE RAPTURE SYNDROME once more, I thought it would be good to put these thoughts together.

First of all, I am a devout believer in the Rapture. Does this mean that at least once a day I step outside, shout "Rapture Practice!" Leap into the air, and hope I don't come down? No (although I still cherish the thought of that happening.) Will the Rapture take place in my lifetime? I can't say. The way my luck seems to run, Jesus will announce, "Rapture at three o'clock tomorrow afternoon!...Oh, by the way, Dennis, you die at two o'clock today."

We were at a surprise birthday party for the same friend who wanted to go buy the book. While we were waiting for him to arrive, several friends from his Church saw this as a perfect opportunity to witness to his parents since they were a captive audience. Every topic, every subject was geared to drive the point home to the parents who were sitting on the sofa trying to ignore all the fanatics around them. The friends kept bringing the topic around to the Rapture as if this topic was sure to lead the parents to salvation.

Finally we were hiding in the hallway waiting for my friend to come through the door. They had to take one last shot at winning the parents to Jesus, and they tried to bring me into the conversation. "Hey, brother?" (No, they didn't even know my name; it's kind of dangerous to recruit an unknown into the witnessing program.) "Do you believe in 'pre,' 'mid,' or 'post'?"

Now for those who are untrained in the topic of the Rapture, they were asking me if I believed the Rapture would take place before the Tribulation Period, during the Tribulation Period, or at the end of the Tribulation Period. I was just tired enough to be ornery - yes, my parents' families do come from hillbilly country. In response to their question, I replied, "It doesn't matter what I believe, God's gonna do what He wants to do, even if I disagree with Him."

Well, that kinda dampened the mood real fast. The Christian friends were looking up the Scriptural references about "excommunication" and "turning a brother over to Satan for the destruction of the body but the preservation of the soul." However, I have found that people are more than willing to listen to you concerning Christianity when they don't feel like they're a notch on your Bible, or that you won't beat them into submission and drag their senseless body off to Church against their will.

These, and other events in my life, made me realize that it was time for someone to use some common sense about the Rapture and put it into perspective. Not that I am an expert on the subject, but I did have to do a little bit of research on the subject. I'll discuss the research I did when you get to AUTHOR'S NOTES. [No fair jumping ahead or it will spoil the surprise.]

First of all, the word "Rapture" is not found anywhere in the Bible. (Okay, get the smelling salts, and revive the women folk and the wimps who couldn't deal with that thought.) Does that mean there is no Rapture? No. It just means that it isn't mentioned by name. "Rapture" is a word variation of the Greek word found in the Scriptures. The Greek word is in the Scriptures and scholars used it to refer to the concept of God removing believers from the world in a world-wide, instantaneous fashion. Paul spends quite some time discussing it in his letters to the early Church. He tells us that it's a "mystery." He tells us that not all of us shall sleep (die). He tells us that some of us will be caught up to meet Jesus in the air. So even though the word Rapture is not specifically mentioned in the Bible, the concept is clearly discussed, taught, and endorsed by the Bible.

The next point is that Jesus tells us that no one knows when this Rapture is going to take place. It is something that only the Father knows. This would imply that even Jesus did not know the date of the Rapture. This gives me a great deal of comfort when people start trying to set dates, times, seasons, etc to predict the Rapture. We need to stop and realize that Jesus was the greatest Bible scholar of all...after all, He is God the Son. He did write the Bible through others. Since He wrote it, inspired others to write it, was quoted as the basis for four books in it (the Gospels), and the remainder of the New Testament is made up of books written by others who took His teachings and tried to analyze them; it seems that if it were possible to discover the date of the Rapture by studying the Bible, then Jesus would have known. However, Jesus says that even He doesn't know the date. That is something only God the Father knows...and He ain't telling.

So, why do we spend a lot of time, energy and effort trying to figure out the date of the Rapture? I guess we just like to be on the inside track. Jesus understood this, and He gave us some signs to look for in order to know when it was getting close. Matthew Chapters 24 and 25 cover this topic in some detail. Does Jesus give any dates? Nope!

The most important clue that Jesus gives is that it shall be like it was at the time of Noah. Everyone was going on about their lives up to the point when Noah went into the ark, and God closed the door. The world, as a whole, was ignorant to the major event.

Now, there is an important point to consider here. The Bible also tells us that Noah was a preacher of righteousness. He was always telling people about God, and the need to obey God. Yet, after one hundred years, when the ark was sealed shut by God, the only ones who were inside were Noah, his wife, his three sons, and their wives. For all of Noah's preaching, no one changed their minds, repented, or was added to the ark's passenger list.

If things are going to be the same as it was in the days of Noah, I would tend to believe that this means everyone who can be saved under the current system, will be saved. Those who are not saved will have heard the message, thought about it, and said, "No thanks! Not interested." They will not reconsider the message of salvation unless God does something drastic to wake them up. The drastic thing, I believe, will be the Rapture. We will have shared with our loved-ones, begged them, pleaded with them; they know, but they won't believe. Then the Rapture takes place, and everyone who had been holding off, wake up and realize what they've missed. We see that there will be, at least, one hundred and forty-four thousand believers after the Rapture. They missed it. They had hard hearts, and now they aren't taking a chance on missing out again.

This brings me to point out that the Tribulation period (as harsh as it will get) will actually be a seven-year period of God's grace. Remember at the time of Noah? Once the door was shut, the rains fell, and everyone was wiped out. There was no second chance in Noah's time. Now we will have seven years to change our minds.

Yes, from the above statement you will deduce that I believe the "pre-tribulation" Rapture doctrine. Am I 100% sure? No. I recognize that there are other arguments for each time frame for the Rapture, and God will do what He wants to do. I've just checked my phone messages, and He hasn't called to ask my advice on anything yet.

Now, what is the Rapture? It's simply that point where God removes His Church (the people, not the buildings) from the world. He has allowed us to be in the world as a kind of preservative. The Holy Spirit, living in each believer, has been able to keep Satan's influence in check...at least to some degree. Many people right now would love to see all the Christians disappear because we are the ones who hate gays, beat our kids, judge others, and are basically party-poopers. We are not tolerant of sin. The big push in the world today is to love one another and be tolerant of the flaws. But it's not going to happen until they get rid of us. Once we are gone, the world will be free to do what it wants; and no one will give them any grief about it. And that's exactly what's going to happen.

Now, how do we look at the Rapture? The Rapture is like working at an office. You're sitting at your desk working, the boss comes along and says, "Okay! That's enough work for today. Take the day off with pay!" Now, take this analogy a little further. You've heard that you might be getting off early today. Some say ten o'clock, some say noon...one even says two o'clock. So what do we do? We slow down production. Not because we are lazy, but we're waiting for the boss to come in and send us home. We don't start new projects. We don't pull out projects which will take a long time to complete. We don't answer the phone because we don't want to be stuck in the office handling an emergency when the boss sends everyone home.

Ten o'clock comes around, and the boss is wandering through the office. You've got briefcase in hand, with the computer logged-out and ready to go. He passes by and goes to his office. Noon shows up, and the boss comes out of the office. You've even got your phone on voice-mail this time so you can leave right then. The boss passes by, and goes to lunch. By two o'clock, you're angry at the boss. Keep in mind that no one said for sure we would be going home early. We may be one of those who spend our entire life working for God, and the Rapture takes place after we die.

When a believer is focused on the Rapture, and it is the most important thing in his/her life, then he/she becomes less productive. They may deny it. They may tell you that they witness that much harder to friends because they believe the Rapture is about to happen any moment, but I still disagree. They may be active. They may be busy, but they are not productive. Someone who is looking to leave any minute only does the small jobs, the quick jobs. They don't commit to the long-term projects. They don't go in for the long-term investments. So lots of quick easy jobs are getting done, but the real work, the big work is still undone.

Lastly, as closing this discussion about common-sense regarding the Rapture, let me point out that the Rapture is not the topic which wins lost souls. The love of God is what draws people to Jesus. The Rapture is an advanced doctrine. Paul wrote about it to believers. He didn't tell them to share it with non-believers. It was something we use to comfort one another.

The latest Rapture flop was not the first Rapture Scare the world had to face. When I worked at one office back in the early 1980's, we were told that the Jupiter Effect was coming. This was when all the planets in the solar system would be in a straight line. Some predicted the greatest earthquake we had ever seen. In response, many Christians in the office saw this as a sign that the Rapture would take place that day. They told everyone in the office not to be surprised if all the Christians just disappeared that day. I took a look into the Jupiter Effect, and found that it took place every two hundred years. I then asked Christians in the office why we would have an earthquake this time, and not on any previous lining up of the planets?

If stoning was still an option, I'd be a pebble patty in the back parking lot. They said I was destroying their witness to the others in the office. I needed to get on the bandwagon and start sharing. Being the non-conformist that I am, I chose to disassociate myself from the others over this one issue. When the big day came, the big earthquake didn't. Further, nobody disappeared except a few believers who couldn't take any more teasing from co-workers. The credibility of most believers in the office suffered that day. We had taken pearls, and cast them before swine. (Sorry co-workers) They trampled the pearls into the mud, and then attacked us. Jesus told us that was what would happen. So, as exciting as the Rapture doctrine is, it's something we keep among ourselves.

So yes, I do believe in the Rapture. Is it important? From a personal stand point, it depends on if I'm still here when it hits. Is it taught by Scripture? Definitely! Now there were some interesting things about the book, and some of the ideas which I used. However, my wife tells me to put those at the end of the book so I don't spoil the story line. So enjoy the book, and I'll meet you on the other end for a few closing comments in AUTHOR NOTES.

April 11, 1998 Dennis Knotts

Prologue

Rescue At Midnight

The Arab supervisor motioned for Amir to bring his truck. He field-stripped his cigarette, climbed into the large dump truck; and fired up the diesel engine. It belched black smoke from its throat as it roared to life. Amir slammed it into gear and it rumbled across the area near the backside of the Temple Mount. A bulldozer began to dump debris into the bed of his truck. The weight caused the entire cab to shake and rock. After several deposits, the supervisor motioned for him to move out.

As Amir headed out the back route and onto Route 417 Derech Jericho between the Temple Mount and the Mount of Olives he watched the rear view mirror to make sure he was not being followed. The supervisor and employer had been very clear about this.

"Those damned Israelis will stop at nothing to get their hands on this." Hassad told him during his job interview.

"It's all debris. Why would the Israelis care?"

"Don't ask questions. Just haul it to where we tell you and turn it over to the man at the gate."

Amir nodded and kept his mouth closed. He needed this job. No one knew how much he needed this job. For three miles Amir monitored the roads behind him. It was dark and the traffic once he was out of the Mount of Olives area became thin. There were no longer any headlights behind him. He looked for any evidence of dark shadows crossing between him and the lights of the city in the distance. After a few more miles he was sure no one was following. He came close to the rendezvous area. He flashed his headlights twice and turned the truck to the left. Another truck, identical to his own, also filled with debris, pulled onto the road he had been traveling and took his place.

About another mile down the dirt road Amir came to a factory. He stopped before the gate and a woman came out to greet him.

"You're right on time, Amir."

"Of course I am." He flashed his best smile and his white teeth stood out in the midst of his deeply tanned face. She opened the gate, and Amir pulled the truck through and around to the docks.

***

Several miles away and about ten minutes later the identical truck pull up to a different gate down a different road. A rough Arab guard came out with his rifle trained on the cab.

"You're three minutes behind schedule!"

Amir flashed his best smile and his white teeth were all the guard could see in the darkened cab.

"You told me to make sure no one was following. That always adds time to the trip. If you want on time, I'll be on time. If you want safe; I might be a little late."

The guard grumbled and pulled opened the gate. Amir pulled the truck through and headed to a place off to one side where an industrial grinding machine was located. It was the kind of grinder used on freeway construction sites. All the concrete and rock debris would be dumped onto a conveyor belt; hauled up to the mouth of the massive maw and dumped into the steel teeth as it would be ground up into gravel and sand which could be used to cut construction costs.

This time, however, the debris in the truck represented material dug out of the chambers beneath the Temple Mount. The Jews had been doing careful excavations under their area of the Mount. The Arabs were pulling out tons of material and sending it to this secret site to be ground up before it would be disposed of.

As Amir dumped his load and pulled forward to empty the last remnants of the load onto the ground for the bulldozer to scoop up and deposit on the conveyor belt; he climbed out and lit up a cigarette. Several guards had become friendly with Amir over the last few months of the project. He offered each a cigarette. As the bulldozer scooped up its second load, rock and pottery fell to the ground. Amir picked up one of the pieces. It was from the Roman Era. It had probably been a water jug. He turned it over to examine it, showed it to the guard closest to him and they both laughed. He then tossed it back onto the heap to be ground into gravel with the rest of the debris.

"Why would the Israelis want this junk?" he asked the guard. They were co-workers and not management. They spoke freely and ignored the covert operation status.

"They keep trying to find evidence of their Temple. They keep trying to prove they were here first. They take junk like this and make claims to the world that they own the land, that their God gave it to them. If their God is so great, then let him give it back to them." The guard spat before taking a drag on the cigarette.

"There is no God but Allah, and Mohammed is His messenger." Amir replied. The two guards grunted in agreement.

When the bulldozer came back, Amir crushed his cigarette with his foot, climbed back into the cab and brought his steel steed to life. It plodded over the rough landscape back to the gate, down the dirt road; and then onto the main highway. When he came back to the rendezvous an identical truck to his own flashed the headlights. He returned the signal and the other truck, also driven by Amir turned back onto the main road and headed toward the City of Jerusalem and the Temple Mount for another load. This Amir turned down the dirt path to the factory.

At the gate the same woman came out to greet him.

"You just missed Amir."

"I flashed my headlights at him on the main road." He climbed out of the cab and lit up another cigarette. He offered one to the guard.

"Those things will kill you one day."

"But not today." He flashed her his white-teeth smile.

"It's the one difference between you and your twin brother." she noted.

"What's that?"

"You crush your cigarettes out with your foot and grind them into the dust. Your bother Amir always field-strips his. Someone is going to notice."

"My brother and I are both Mossod; but this is hardly the kind of operation when anyone will notice those kinds of details. We drive a truck. He goes to the Temple Mount and picks up all their artifacts. I take our junk from other excavations with worthless pottery and deliver it to the Arab's grinder to replace what they have found."

"It's a strange rescue mission." the guard admitted.

"No guns, no suicide pills. The worst that could happen is we could get fired."

Yosi began to call them from the factory loading dock. His excitement was obvious even from this distance.

"What do you think, Miriam? Another sword handle? A piece of jewelry? Maybe some Roman money?"

"If it's money, Shmuel; you're buying the drinks tonight." the guard replied as they headed off to the loading dock door at a trot.

Yosi ushered them into the factory where dozens of archeologists were carefully sorting through the debris. Where Shmuel had dumped his load in the dirt and it was hauled by bulldozer to the grinder, Amir had carefully eased his load out so it could be sorted and picked through by hand to avoid any further damage than the Arabs had already inflicted upon the Temple Mount debris.

Several of the archeologists were huddled around a marble box that had been found in the load. They had worked the lid off and begun to examine the items inside. They were scrolls—obviously from centuries ago. Already the head archeologist was preparing a chamber to treat the parchment and reintroduce the time-lost moisture so it would be possible months from now to eventually unroll the scroll and through x-rays and scans eventually read what was written there. It was the same process their scientists had used a few decades ago to preserve and salvage the Dead Sea Scrolls. Inside the marble box a portion of one scroll had broken off due to the rough handling and dumping of the marble box into the truck bed by the first bulldozer. One of the supervisors with surgical gloves on used special tweezers to carefully lift the fragment just enough to slide a protective clear plastic support under it. Now protected he slowly lifted it out of the box and took digital photographs of it before putting it into the chamber. Since it was already separate from the scroll and exposed, procedure called for immediate photographing and preserving in case further damage might be done.

The group with Yosi, Shmuel and Miriam huddled around the large LCD Screen as the smaller fragment was now displayed on a theater-sized screen. Naphtali began to translate, at first to himself and then out loud.

"It's from Malachi! We may have a copy of Malachi!" His excitement was suddenly contagious. He used his laser pointer and read the Hebrew from right to left:

> Behold, I will send you Elijah the prophet before the coming of the great and dreadful day of the Lord.
> And he shall turn the hearts of the fathers to the children, and the heart of the children to their father, lest I come and smite the earth with a curse."

"That's from Malachi?" Shmuel asked.

"The very last verses." Naphtali replied. The scroll was rolled in reverse so the outer portion was the end of the scroll and contained the last few verses."

"So we rescued something of greater importance than old sword handles tonight?" Shmuel confirmed.

"Much more important." Yosi was bubbling. "Tonight you and your twin brother rescued the Word of G-d."

CHAPTER ONE

Discovery In Space

Fred Galley reached over and stabbed the button to kill the monitor. The redness inflaming his eyes added to the dark circles under them. He rubbed them with his gloved hand and the rough material of the space suit actually felt good as he scratched at the itching eyes. In the reflection of the TV screen he saw his three day stubble of growth, and then noted that his hair was standing up on end. He spat out an expletive as he tried to press the rebellious hair back down.

"How long has my hair been like this?" he complained to his two companions. Rob Hamilton floated to him and patted his head.

"I told you to keep it cut short." Rob's own bald head glistened in the cabin lights. Fred shoved him back, and the biologist/communications officer did two flips in the air before landing feet-first on the far wall. Jim Silvers, meteorologist/electronic specialist, refused to respond as he sat hunched over his computer screen scrolling through hundreds of read-outs.

"You're a lot of help." Fred observed. In response to his commanding officer's comment, Jim raised a single finger in Fred's direction without looking up from the screen.

All of the above was recorded by Houston. Several psychologists were huddled around the wall of monitors.

"You're sure they don't know they're being recorded?" Fran Oakney asked, scribbling several notes on her clipboard.

"We've programmed the cameras to record without activating the red recording light. So far it appears that no one has noticed." Major James Hiller checked the console to confirm the computer commands. Of all those stationed in the room, only he still wore the air force uniform with his major insignia proudly displayed. The others had slipped on lab coats as these had more pockets to carry pens, calculators, cell phones and other personal equipment.

"Captain Galley still isn't getting much sleep?" Lieutenant Daniels asked. He was pulling up several screens of bio-data on the commanding officer of the Freedom II team.

"You don't need read-outs to tell that." attacked Oakney, the only civilian consultant on the team.

"But we still don't know why he's not sleeping." Lieutenant Daniels retorted.

"What's to tell? The mission is a bust!" observed Nick Wong.

"We don't know that!" snapped Hiller, causing several in his vicinity to cringe. "The mission is only in its third month."

"Major..." Fran interrupted. "Look at these men. They've given up on discipline. Their personal hygiene is shot. They don't sleep. They fight instead of communicate. They're going through the motions; but they don't believe the mission has any chance of success."

"You're here to evaluate their mental condition, not to address the success or failure of the mission. That is a military decision. Until authorized, the mission is off-limits as a subject for your team." Hiller challenged.

Fran slammed her clipboard on the console. "You can't divorce the two! You sent three highly-trained, over-achievers into space on a top secret mission. They've failed. That's what's driving them at this point! You have to discuss their mental attitudes in relation to the success or failure of the mission."

"We sent up three specialists who have never worked together. Each one was trained on his own, and the parameters of the mission forced us to send them up prematurely. They know their jobs. They're trained to do those jobs. We just got a bad mix of personalities. That's where you and your team come in." Hiller countered. "Now, I am not about to write off this mission before we're through."

"Is it that vital, Major?" Daniels asked.

"It's that vital." Hiller struggled for long moments considering his options. Finally he nodded to Fran and would only say, "Fill them in." He then thought for a second, looked at his constant companion, and added, "About everything." With those words Hiller spun about, and stormed out of the room; his companion at his heels.

"Well, that went better than I expected." Fran quipped once the commanding officer was gone. "Kill the cameras. What I'm about to say is classified. No recording equipment of any kind. Nothing leaves this room." Peter Strauss, their basic go-fer, scanned for any evidence of broadcast signals from the cameras inside the control room. He then nodded the all-clear to Fran.

"I know you were ordered here to address only the mental condition, but their mental attitudes are related to the results of the mission. These men have no sense of motivation. They are going through the motions just to get us off their backs. In short, we are dealing with extreme depression and an over-all sense of failure. In order to treat these crewmen, we need to re-establish some sense of hope in them."

"If the mission is a failure, what's the back lash?" Nick asked.

"If this mission fails, then life on earth only has a short time left to live." Peter announced. Although he was the lowest in rank of the team, and he was sent mostly to run the errands, Peter Strauss had a knack for picking up bits of information through unofficial channels, even the most classified bits of information. Fran shot an icy glare in his direction.

"It can't be that bad!" Daniels challenged, a hint of fear in his voice.

"Even though Peter seems to know more than the rest of you, let me give you the unofficial version. Remember Black Tuesday?" Fran asked. Daniels shook his head. "Back when England used coal as their main source of energy. The burning of coal created a high level of sulfur in the air. This created a different kind of smog. When London had a heat wave in 1952, an inversion layer held it close to the ground, it mixed with other pollutants using heat as the energy to trigger the change, and thirty-five hundred to four thousand people died. England changed from coal as a major source of energy. However, another six hundred died from air pollution in England in 1962. India, 1984, thirty-three hundred died from air pollution and another twenty thousand became ill..."

"Black August: one hundred, twenty-five thousand dead; another half million ill from air pollution. I read the papers." Daniels interrupted.

"That was the entire basis for this mission." Fran added.

"I thought the mission was about placing and monitoring weather satellites...a kind of weather control experiment." Nick challenged.

"That's the official version." Fran announced. "There's been a lot of damage to the ozone layer...a lot more than anyone is aware of. After decades of public denial of any green house effect, the administration couldn't change its position."

"Yes, and Vice President Gore declared Global Warming, and that fell flat in the first decade of the century. Now we're chasing sunspot cycles, solar flares and every other kind of theory to explain what we're seeing in our weather patterns." Daniels stole the spotlight. "The Indonesian quake and tsunami at Christmas and the Japan quake and tsunami shifted the earth's axis; the Iceland Quake. Our weather patterns became more severe starting that far back."

"So far the general public has been speculating, just like Mr. Daniels here." Fran cut in regaining the floor. "Secret meetings in Geneva produced evidence and test results that could no longer be discounted. Thus, Congress was briefed on the sly, appropriations for Freedom II program were pushed through at over five billion dollars. The space shuttle program was shut down in 2011. The economy forced other countries to down size their space efforts. The International Space Station went into mothballs by 2020. Those billions of dollars went mostly to pay for the extra crews, over-time, and expense refurbishing of the Freedom II shuttle. Most people believe it was a brand new shuttle. In reality it was the Atlantis being brought out of retirement."

"I thought the Atlantis was destroyed in the fire…" but Fran cut Peter off.

"It was the most reliable. We needed it. That was all a cover story to steal it away. Time has been of the essence."

"So that explains why we went back to the Centaur rockets—speed not safety" Nick noted.

"The Centaur rocket was the workhorse of NASA." Fran suggested.

"And when it failed it took out the Challenger, the team and the mission in one fireball." he countered.

"So we were the first to go back to the International Space Station. How come the other countries haven't joined us?" Daniels interrupted to stop the coming debate.

"All of the space programs have been gutted by budget cuts. Cosmonauts, astronauts; all gone. We pulled up these three because they are our best experts in the areas of air pollution, storm engineering, and meteorology. And because they were the closest things we had left to anyone in the military with any astronaut training."

"Storm engineering?" Nick echoed.

"Weather control. The mission of Freedom II was to create thunder storms in the high atmosphere…lots of them. Thunderstorms have lightning, and lightning produces ozone." Fran explained.

"Thus, by increasing the number of storms in the upper atmosphere close to the ozone layer, we would create ozone and replace the lost ozone in the ozone layer?" Nick suggested.

"Exactly, but after three months it doesn't look promising." Fran confirmed. The briefing lapsed into an awkward silence. Daniels stared blankly at the documents on the table in front of him. He was obviously disturbed. Fran knew it was not an easy concept to assimilate.

"How long do we have?" Daniels finally asked. Fran could detect the panic in his mannerisms.

"We figure ten years, fifteen on the outside."

"But we can't die! We've always found a solution. Now you're telling me that no matter what we do the human race dies in fifteen years?"

"Get hold of yourself, Daniels. I need you on this project. I can't be counseling you and them at the same time."

"But we need to do something." he ranted as the reality of the situation crashed upon him. "Maybe we should bring in others. Tell the press. See if someone has any other ideas..."

Even as Daniels spoke, Fran hit the red button on her console. Two guards burst into the room. She motioned towards Daniels. Before he was even aware the guards were in the room, one guard drew his pistol from its holster, pressed it against his head, and discharged the bullet. His body fell like a marionette with its strings cut. Several of the staff cried out, dropped charts, or turned away.

"Let's get one thing clear. This information does not leave the room. When you leave this room, each of you will have a 'shadow.' That shadow has only one function. If, at any time, they believe you may be revealing what you've learned in this room, both you and the person you are speaking to will be dead before you are aware of the shadow's presence. There will be no trials, no appeals, and no resignation. Anyone wanting to leave this project will leave the same way Daniels left." Fran nodded in the direction of the limp form being dragged out of the room by the two guards. "Any questions?"

The team leader studied each face. Most could not make eye contact. Terror now guaranteed their loyalty—or at the very least—their obedience. "Good! Let's get to work."

***

As Captain Galley floated past the observation window in the cabin, he caught a glimpse of Lieutenant Hamilton jerking his head in the direction of camera seventeen. They had begun to notice that the camera lens moved and focused even though the red broadcasting light was off. It had been a soft whirling sound which tipped Lieutenant Silvers to the action. He had been smart enough to position himself out of all camera angles when he checked on the camera.

The commanding officer found it ironic that the one thing that had brought them back together—at least for an uneasy truce—was their home base. Silvers had scribbled a note to Hamilton telling him the cameras were on and watching them. Hamilton had checked it out for himself. The pair then lured Galley away from the monitors for a confrontation. When it became obvious that Galley knew less about the monitoring than they did; the three found a common enemy.

The trio of astronauts had mapped out every angle in each cabin where a "blind spot" was located. In these "blind spots" they were hidden from any camera in the cabin. They had even developed a crude sign language to communicate so Houston wouldn't know what they were saying.

"I'm getting the feeling they're on to us." Lieutenant Wong suggested as he kept moving the camera to follow Captain Galley until he passed out of camera seventeen's view. The officer had flipped the switch for camera twelve to pick up Captain Galley as he continued to float, but the commanding officer never came into range.

"What makes you say that?" Fran asked, coming to his station to look over his shoulder. Wong was sure the temperature at his station had dropped three or four degrees just from her presence.

"Just a feeling. Whenever we activate a camera, they seem to move out of view. They stay out of view for several minutes before floating back into the camera's view; and they seem to be working very hard at not doing anything." the lieutenant reported. As he spoke, Captain Galley finally floated into camera twelve's field.

"We've also had three cameras and five microphones damaged or knocked out." Peter added.

"How?" Fran shifted to his console, and hovered like a spider about to pounce. Peter flipped a replay switch, and the first tape ran. It showed Silvers and Hamilton yelling at each other. Hamilton picked up his tube of green peas and squirted it at Silvers who ducked at the last minute. The green paste hit the camera lens and coated its entire surface.

"Did you tell them to clean the lens?" Fran inquired.

"Yes, ma'am. However, this was their response." Peter flipped another switch and the monitor shows the now-trade-mark finger Silvers used to respond to most command directives. "Then this happened..." The new monitor showed Galley confronting Silvers, and Silvers slamming him hard against the wall. The screen displayed the cracking and shattering glass before the camera went dead from Galley's left shoulder.

"These could be accidents; but keep a tab. If they know they are being monitored it can corrupt all the data on their behavior." She let out one of her own trade-mark expletives; and left the lab to consult with Major Hiller.

Silvers gave a thumbs up sign as he completed his last splice job. While the others had kept Houston watching, he had slipped up next to each camera, popped open the panel, and slipped in a small light which clipped directly onto the power line to the last camera. The small razor edges of the alligator clip dug through the insulation and embedded into the metal of the wire. Whenever power was passed through the wire, the make-shift small red light would glow. There was no way to operate any of the cameras or microphones in the cabin without illuminating a red indicator light.

"So how long are we going to be able to pull this off?" Hamilton signaled as he coasted through the air to the point where they had created a "safe zone."

"How much longer are we going to be here?" Galley whispered in reply.

"Look, everything we've tried has failed. We can't reverse the damage to the ozone. The environment is collapsing. There's nothing else we can do up here. Why don't we tell Houston so we can go home?" Silvers whispered back.

"Daniels is dead." Hamilton announced.

"Dead?" Silver's voice was almost loud enough for a microphone to detect.

"Nick told me during a session this morning." Rob revealed.

"Those sessions are monitored. How could he tell you something like that and not get fired?" Fred challenged.

"He needed to talk to someone, too. He couldn't talk to anyone outside the center, and since we've known each other since before the project..." Rob let his voice trail. "Turns out, the center is the only place they can talk about the project and what happens on it. Nick's fearful for his life. Daniels wanted out, and they killed him; right there in the control room."

"So when we finish our mission; we won't be coming home." Fred observed.

"They're going to let us die out here?" Silvers realized, panic creeping into his voice.

"Not in the space station. They'll dupe a few other experts to come up and take over. We'll die returning to earth or once on the ground some accident will happen. The station is too valuable to endanger. It's the last hope for earth." Hamilton speculated.

"So what are we to do? Are we trapped up here?" Silvers' terror was now obvious in his eyes.

"We'll think of something. We've beaten them this long. We just have to be a bit more careful. Any ideas?" Fred's attention was focused on Hamilton. Finally the once-hard-bitten face softened.

"You're going to think I'm crazy...Well, you already think that. But my wife slipped something in my pack before we lifted off. She told me it might help. She had been acting differently several weeks before we took off. I figured she was having an affair or something. She kept taking off different nights of the week. She would come back acting more friendly than ever before."

"Yeah, yeah." Silvers interrupted. "We all know your marriage is on the rocks. What's the point?"

"I finally went through my pack, when all of this started happening." Hamilton motioned with one arm to include the entire station. "What I found was this..." He unzipped his leg pocket, and pulled out a small Bible.

"Don't tell me she found religion." Galley spat out. His contempt was mimicked by Silvers.

"Yeah. She's a believer now. Ain't that a kick in the head?" Hamilton fingered the small book with its onion paper thin pages. His wife had even torn the cover off the book to keep it under the regulation weight limit. "But I've read some of this. She even high-lighted some sections. You'll going to laugh at me, but some of this stuff makes sense, and even more so, some of this talks about the problem we're trying to solve up here."

That had been the hook. The trio took turns passing the book around over the next few weeks. Rob had pointed to the first high-lighted passage his wife had referred him to. As they went through the book, they found other passages about the condition of the world during the "End Times."

The change in the astronauts' personalities had been noted by Houston. The psyche-team was now more at ease dealing with them. Major Hiller was sure they had everything back on track. Then Silvers slipped during one session with Fran and mentioned the Bible.

"What are you doing with that?!" she was all-but-screaming. Her professional calm was torn away.

"I've been looking at it." Silvers lied. He thought it best to keep the Bible exposure to just himself.

"Get rid of it!" Fran shouted at him.

"But it's just a book..." he began to defend.

"It's a pack of lies! It can undo weeks of counseling. It corrupts hours of careful monitoring. Get rid of it now!" Fran was screaming. The others on the team backed away from her. When she was in such a mood, things were broken, beaten, or damaged...including co-workers.

"What?" Silvers reverted to his flippant personality. "You want me to just walk over to the air lock, open it up and toss it out?"

"Exactly! Do it now, and keep in view of the cameras when you do it." Fran had let too much out. Her ranting had announced to the astronauts that they knew there were "blind spots" on the station, and that the control center had been monitoring them. When the official indicator lights were on, none of the three left the viewing area. The only way Houston could have known about the "blind spots" would have been monitoring when the official indicator lights were off.

Silver let out a few choice expletives of his own, floated to the air lock, and opened the inner hatch. He tossed the object in his hand into the lock, closed it; and then hit the outer lock mechanism. There was a "whooshing" vibration felt through the walls since there was no longer any air in the air lock to transfer the sound. The small object that had been in Silvers' hand was now sucked out into the frigid cold of airless space. Silvers hit the controls once more closing the outer hatch.

"Satisfied?!" he spat at the camera. As Fran began to talk, he turned his back on her, displayed his one finger response; and moved out of the camera range. He stayed out of camera range for over an hour as Fran screamed, ranted, raged, and ordered him back to the camera for the rest of his session. Finally, she ordered Hamilton and Galley to drag Silvers back into the camera's view, and hold him there so she could counsel him. Both refused.

The control room doors burst open, and Major Hiller stormed inside. "What are you doing, Oakney?"

"We have a problem with one of the crew. He's not obeying orders."

"It's more than a problem. You've got a full-scale rebellion on your hands. What's this all about?"

"Silvers had a Bible..."

"A Bible?! This is all about a stupid Bible?"

"It's more than a Bible. It's a pack of lies. It brainwashes people. It could undo weeks of counseling..."

"It seems like you've undone weeks of counseling! If they want to have a Bible; let them have a Bible. For God's sake, woman! I don't care if they have a Bible or a Ouija board; so long as they work together and complete the mission!" Hiller turned to the others and shouted, "Carry on!" He then set his coldest gaze on Fran Oakney, "In my office, NOW!" The two stormed out of the room together. An hour later Lieutenant Wong was named team leader; and Fran Oakney was never seen again.

★★★

"You had to tell her about the Bible?" Hamilton chided."

"I didn't think it would make her go ballistic." Silvers defended.

"So what do we do now?" Galley asked. He did not realize that he had come to find the Bible such a source of comfort and inspiration. It had helped him refocus his life; put things into perspective. Now he felt like someone had cut his tether line and had cast *him* adrift out in space.

"Maybe we can slip out and find it?" Hamilton suggested.

"It's gone. Remember your basic physics. The blast of the air escaping the air lock will have it moving away from us faster than we can follow. Plus, open any air lock and Houston will know."

"We don't have to go after it." Silvers said with a strange smile in his eyes.

"What do you mean?" Hamilton asked. In response, he reached into his suit and pulled out the Bible he was to have thrown into space.

"How were you able to pull that one off?" Hamilton asked.

"Slight of hand. As I was turning around, I traded the Bible for a book I had in my suit."

"So what did you throw out?" Galley asked.

"That? Oh that was our book of regulations...Not like we're going to need them since we've mutinied against Houston."

"So now what do we do?" Hamilton asked.

"When the monitors are on we go back to hating each other and being surly." Galley declared.

"I can do surly." Silvers announced.

***

"Baruch Ah taw Adoni Eloheinu" the patriarch of the family began. Those gathered round the Seder table began to repeat in unison:

"Blessed art Thou, O Eternal, our G-d, King of the Universe, Creator of the fruit of the vine."

It was the fourteenth of Nisan—the Passover; and before the small family were the elements of the Pesach meal: the salt water representing the tears of the Children of Israel, the parsley that represented the new life G-d had created for them, the roasted egg reminding them of the sacrifices and burnt offerings performed so many years ago in the Temple, there were the bitter herbs to remind them of the bitter life they had when they were slaves in Egypt, the charoset made from cinnamon and apples but which was to remind them of the mortar they used to build with bricks back in Egypt. Missing was the Z'roa—the lamb shank bone to remind them of the original Passover Lamb whose blood was smeared over the door posts to cause the Angel of Death to pass over them as he went forth to kill all the first born of Egypt. It was gone because with the Temple complete and fully operating, an actual family lamb had been sacrificed according to Mosaic Law and was now the centerpiece for the awaiting meal. Finally there was the silver cup that would be filled four times during the meal.

***

"Why is this night different from all other nights?" the youngest at the table recited. "Any other night we may eat either leavened or unleavened bread; but on this night only unleavened bread..."

Those at the table smiled as the question continued. When it was done, the Patriarch smiled and began, "Because we were slaves unto Pharaoh in Egypt..."

**

The Patriarch began and the others followed along, "Blessed art Thou, O Eternal, our G-d, King of the Universe who brings forth bread from the earth."

The head of the home reached for the Unity—the three loaves of the unleavened Matzah bread positioned in the center of the table. It had been baked the way it had been baked for thousands of years. It was without leaven—yeast— and it had to be baked in such a way so that it was pierced and bore stripes upon it from the baking. This was a picture of their long-awaited Messiah. He, too, would be without sin. He would be pierced. By His stripes they would be healed. The prophet Isaiah had predicted that ministry of the Messiah. The elder pulled out the middle Matzah. He wrapped it in a linen napkin, and broke it.

"Blessed art Thou, O Eternal, our G-d, King of the Universe, who hast sanctified us with Thy Commandments, and commanded us to eat Unleaven bread."

In the distance the scream of jet fighters roared overhead. The nation was on high alert. The threat from their neighboring countries was still real even though they had stopped to remember all G-d has done for them. The Patriarch made eye contact with several. They nodded in agreement.

"It seems the Angel of Death is passing over us once more." he observed at another jet's scream. Several laughed at the analogy.

They knew he would not dismiss them until the meal was done. They all agreed with that decision. They would eat the Passover meal—the Pesach—as his father had done. As his father before his father had done. As his people had done for thousands of years. The enemy would not cause him to break tradition with his ancestors. They were Israel. They were One. This meal reminded them of the power of their G-d. It bound them as no other ceremony could bind a people.

***

The child ran back to the Seder Table with the broken Matzah wrapped in linen in hand. Those at the table applauded the success of the child in finding the Afikomen they had hidden during the meal. The elder produced a coin for the child as reward. He poured the fourth cup of wine as the eldest child rose from the table. He was nervous from the sounds of the jets screaming overhead. The Patriarch nodded for him to continue. The boy opened the door to look for Elijah as they had done for more years than they had been alive. Each generation had looked and waited with the hope of "Next Year Jerusalem" on their lips and in their hearts. The youth suddenly stepped back from the doorway as a man walked boldly into the room without waiting to be asked. He passed the child and those at the table rose in protest. He raised a hand to silence them.

He was dressed in black slacks, white dress shirt, black vest and black dress coat. He wore a yamaka over what was obviously a bald spot in his long white hair. His prayer shawl was tucked and wrapped around his waist. His short, well-trimmed white beard still carried some hint of his original black hair color. He was a Jew—one of their own; and so those at the table waited to see what this unexpected guest would do.

He made his way directly to the place set for the long-awaited prophet Elijah—the one whose return had been promised before the coming of Messiah by the prophet Malachi. He slid into the chair as if it were prepared for him. He took the fourth cup of wine and drained it in one gulp. Then he reached for the Matzah bread wrapped in linen and took it from the child's hand. He held it up to the room for all to observe.

"Afikomen!' he declared; and then he translated from the Hebrew: 'I AM come!'"

The Matriarch of the family dropped her dish as she realized what was being fulfilled before her eyes, in her humble home. The china shattered on the floor. The guest who sat in Elijah's seat rose and declared. "Messiah has come."

With that he walked back out through the still-opened door.

***

Six months later Galley watched as the Freedom II fired its retrorockets, tearing the shuttle from the docking bay of the International Space Station. A faint wisp of air and now-frozen water vapor signaled their last contact with the orbiting station. Several satellites had been deployed to continue the work.

"So what are the chances?" Galley asked as they settled into their pilot and co-pilot positions.

"For all our technology, it isn't feasible to create lightning this high in the atmosphere; at least not enough lightning to create sufficient ozone to heal the ozone layer." Silvers was the best on storm engineering. If anyone could have made it work; he was the one who could do it.

"And how much time have we bought?"

Hamilton calculated several factors from the numerous experiments. "By my guess, we may have bought the earth another two or three years. That would put it between fifteen to twenty years. But already the chain reaction has been triggered."

"Chain reaction?" Fred queried.

"The infrared and ultra-violet bands have increased along with x-rays and other forms of solar radiation. The first to feel the effect will be the more sun-dependent life forms."

"Plants?" Fred asked.

"Plants, several micro-organisms, plankton. Basically any life form that uses photosynthesis as all or part of its food source. If we were able to stop the damage to the ozone today, all we would do is stop further damage; we wouldn't undo the damage already begun."

"You're the biologist, what's your calculation?" Silvers added.

"One third of the pant life, currently on the earth, has been affected. It may take another year or so to realize the full effect; but by my calculations we're going to lose one-third of the plant life on earth."

"Irreversible damage?" Fred probed.

"I've given the figure to Lieutenant Wong. They're trying to put together some programs on the ground to undo the effect. They can create greenhouses to protect some areas. Israel has done great things with their use of sheet plastic to create makeshift greenhouse coverings. That can help. It can slow things down. However, to deal with this world-wide and stop the damage; right now we're at a loss. One third of the more sensitive plants have already suffered irreversible damage. They will be dead in a matter of months. We've already lost a lot before we even started."

"What about the rain forest?'" Silvers suggested.

"It would take another three or four rain forests to pick up the loss. The United Nations has already sent in secret armies to stop the destruction of the rain forests and force the South American and African countries that have such vegetation to stop cutting them down. News agencies were not advised, and a black-out was kept over the entire operation. A lot of killing. A lot of mass unmarked graves."

"Is this going to be the worse of it? The plant life?" Galley returned to the conversation.

"No, that's just the beginning. Keep in mind that we joke about the food chain and where we are on it. With one third of plant life, and plankton gone; one third of the fish and lower land animals will starve. You then move it up the food chain. Everything depends on the members of the food chain below it, so..."

"One third of mankind will starve to death." Galley concluded.

"If we could stop the ozone deterioration today. But we haven't. Somehow the greater radiation pouring through the ozone layers adds to the damage. The greater heat and radiation create more energy, and the ozone is not stable. The greater energy causes it to break up, combine with other gases which won't protect the earth as effectively." Silvers added.

"Zero Population Growth." Fred quipped.

"You think they have the solution?"

"No. It's just something I read a long time ago. One of the proponents of Zero Population Growth said we needed something like the Black Plague every generation to weed out the population. They've taught for decades that the earth can only support a population of a certain size."

"So they might be right." Silvers noted.

"That's not what worries me. Given the desperation and the lack of morals on the part of those in charge; what if they decided to create their own methods of weeding out the population?"

"All I can say is, let's just hope we aren't the weeds." Hamilton added.

"Which brings us back to our own personal problem...how do we get out of this alive?" Galley asked.

"From the isolation they have us in; I suspect it's going to be pretty hard. We're sealed in here. We can't get out before landing. When we land it will be at a military base on full-alert to keep us quarantined..." Hamilton let his voice trail off.

"If this had been like the Gemini and Apollo Missions we would have dropped into the sea and waited for the rescue teams. It might have given us a chance to blow the hatch and try to escape." Galley suggested.

"To where? We would be in the middle of the ocean with only a life raft." Hamilton reminded. He opened the contraband Bible. He began to read:

"The Lord is my shepherd; I shall not want...'"

Each man listened in silence. They lifted up their silent prayers to the One they had discovered outside of the earth—in the heavens which were the threshold of His realm. When their peace had been made with their Creator, Silvers noted to no one in particular,

"I would have liked to have seen my daughter one last time, to tell her what we found in space."

"Yes, I think my wife would have liked to have heard about our discovery." Hamilton added.

The intercom from the cockpit crackled, and came to life. "Freedom II, do you copy?"

"Freedom II Houston. We copy."

"Good thing we decided to bring you home a little early."

"What's happening Houston?"

"Didn't want to shift your concentration off the mission, but now that we ready to shift to the debriefing phase, seems that all Hell is breaking loose in the Middle East."

"How so?"

"Israel announced a major oil discovery two days ago. Seems it's big enough to give OPEC a run for its money."

"Great. I'd love to pay less for a gallon of gas." Fred mused.

"Well it may take a while for the oil to make it to market. This morning Russian, Syria, Iran, Libya, Ethiopia, Hamas and Hezbolla invaded Israel en masse. It looks like a major war, with Israel being caught completely off guard due to everyone celebrating Succoth throughout Jerusalem and around the new Temple. There are more visitors to Jerusalem for this Holy Day than ever before. You can't even move on the streets from all the booths and tents that have been built. They are everywhere; in open fields, on roof tops and filling hundreds of streets in and around the city. The nation is almost at a stand still for any ground vehicles in that area. They haven't been able to mount a single defensive position. All military planes are still on the ground. Odds are that by evening Israel will cease to exist."

"Houston," Silvers replied, "Say again on those countries?"

As their contact on earth recited the list of countries attacking

Israel, Silvers flipped their worn Bible opened to Ezekiel; and pointed to chapters thirty-eight and thirty-nine.

"Russia, Syria and Iran. Hezbolla crossed over the boarder between Israel and Syria with thousands of Russian tanks. There's also a massive cavalry riding with the tanks. They have already pushed south to the Sea of Galilee. Hamas joined with Iranian, Ethiopian and Libyan forces that had gathered in Egypt; and they crossed the Gaza strip a few hours ago. Our satellites are showing them long past Masada and probably within an hour of Jerusalem itself; maybe closer."

The three astronauts exchanged knowing glances among themselves.

"Houston? Any word on that weird guy who showed up at the Passover Meal a few months back?" Silvers asked.

"Nothing more than what the news said back then. Some guy showed up. Barged into some family's Passover Meal. And took off."

"No one's seen him since?" Galley pressed.

"Not a word. Looks like it was a one time thing. Why the sudden interest?"

"Just adding it to the list of strange things going on over there. That's all." Silvers added.

The radio crackled once more. "Okay gentlemen. You'll be coming into the sunrise on the west coast. Break out your sunglasses and buckle up. Contact with atmosphere in five, four, three, two, one..."

And then it happened.

CHAPTER TWO

Crisis

Major Brown tossed a quick salute to the guard at the entrance as he raced to the waiting jeep. The CNN news feed on the television mounted on the office wall still showed swarms of tanks and ground soldiers advancing toward Jerusalem. The tickertape reading at the bottom of the screen read: Arabs rejoicing over fall of Israel. United Nations refuses to come to aid of Israel. Tel Aviv under attack.

Jim's mind was controlled chaos, a turmoil of thousands of thoughts, facts and concepts; all spinning wildly about to be acknowledged or discarded in only a nanosecond so that the next could be evaluated. The invasion of Israel was on everyone's lips all morning. He had put the base on high alert. The Arabs had made no bones about the fact that America and Israel should be cursed with the same breath. Any attempt to attack Israel would suggest that terrorists were probably already activating their cells inside the United States. Russia, although neutral toward the U.S.; was now clearly allied with the Arabs. It wanted the new oil deposits for its own survival.

The CNN cameras shifted to Egypt, near a mosque. Two elderly men were shouting something about the Messiah. Egyptian troops tried to close in. Major Brown turned from the screen and headed out the door just before the camera caught the scene of fire plunging out of the sky and consuming the Egyptian troops before the intense heat caused the news camera lens to crack and die.

Every alarm on the base was sounding. No one was giving him anything reliable to go on. Something was wrong; and no one was responding to his questions. He needed to check on this himself. Four dozen M.P.s and guards were slamming magazines into their weapons and flipping the safeties to the off position. They poured out of the buildings and into transports to fall in behind Major Brown's jeep. The major breathed a sigh of relief as he recalled no nuclear weapons or devices were stored on the base.

His team was responsible for security, any breech and he would have to give an account. For twenty years it had been his responsibility. For twenty years he had used friends, broken enemies, sacrificed family. At the thought of family, several scenes came unbidden to his mind. For a brief moment he ceased being Major Brown and was only "Jim" or "Daddy." All the thousands of times when he had seen the look of disappointment in his three children's eyes when work forced him to break another promise. With the same cold efficiency, and in less time than he had given to other matters churning in his mind, he pressed the thoughts of family down, ignored the weight that hung in his heart; and barked directions to the driver of the jeep, gunning it across the compound.

"Report!" he snapped as he burst through the doors of the building where the alarm had been triggered. The four dozen guards poured in behind him, securing the building inside and out.

"Seven men missing, sir!" the guard stationed in the building shouted and saluted at the same time.

"Seven men missing? This is all about soldiers going AWOL?" his anger was obvious and the guard bristled with the fear Major Brown's reputation had created.

"No sir!" the man blurted out, more out of fear than discipline. "There were seven men in this lab, and they suddenly disappeared."

"They left?"

"Not exactly sir!"

"What do you mean not exactly?" Major Brown's temper was boiling; and the guard was his victim. He was about to order the guards with him to stand down when the door to the lab suddenly flew open and Colonel Jackson interrupted the tirade.

"Before you skin the guard, come take a look for yourself." The guard let out a long breath as soon as Major Brown bolted from the room. As they were about to leave the entrance area the senior officer shouted back to the new troops: "Secure the area. No one gets in or out."

The pair stormed down the hallway to an observation area outside of a lab. Colonel Jackson held up a hand to block entrance into the lab, and motioned to the observation station to the left.

"It's a 'clean room', major. We've got a team already suiting up to go in and investigate." As they came into the observation area, Colonel Jackson motioned to the large picture window of triple-pane glass. Next to the lab bench, crumpled on the floor were two piles of clothes. The inquisitive look on Brown's face was the indicator for Colonel Jackson to continue.

"This is the camera we have running of the 'clean room'. I'll just play back the last fifteen minutes until we get to the right place." Jackson pushed the button, and the overhead monitor began to playback the activity in the "clean room" in a fast motion. Several technicians were moving around the lab, two were looking into microscopes, three were mixing chemicals, and another one was writing notes on a computer print-out. The Colonel hit "play" on the console; and the movement resumed its natural speed. For a second all looked normal; and then suddenly several figures were simply no longer in the room. Their clothing and personal items clattered on the floor. Those still in the lab began to scream and charge for the exit. Several guards blocked their escape, and at gun point herded them into a quarantine area.

"Wait a second. Back it up, slow." Brown requested.

"I can freeze frame it for you if you'd like. There's no other information there." To prove his point, Colonel Jackson reset the digital counter on the camera controls, moved it ahead at super slow motion. At the right point, he froze the scene; did a single frame advance. At frame number three there was a room filled with technicians. At frame number four, several sets of clothing were hanging empty in the air. In frame number five the clothing was beginning to drop. Even when the colonel used computer enhancement on one subject, there was no other way of explaining the phenomena. In one millisecond the subject was there, the next the subject was gone with only their clothes and personal items hanging in the air, about to fall. If this had been a normal camera with film, the disappearance would have taken place between one frame and the next; but with digital there was no frame spaces involved. Literally, in less time than the eye could blink; the lab workers were gone.

"That can't be!" Brown declared.

"My point exactly, but that's what happened. One second they were there, the next they weren't."

"What about the others?"

"We have then in quarantine, but they're about to crawl out of their skin. Never saw anyone panic to this degree. We want to check them out, but we can't risk opening the lab and letting out whatever caused the disappearance."

"You think it was a germ or organism?" Brown inquired.

"They work with some pretty lethal stuff in there. Any one of a number of organisms could mutate without warning."

Brown flipped open his cell phone, punched in his personal code. "Seal the base. No one comes in or goes out. No overhead air traffic. This entire sector is now under quarantine. I also want complete blackout. No messages out; and no one calling in until we...What?" Brown's face went pale.

Colonel Jackson's cell began to ring. He snatched it up and answered.

"What was that?" The voice on the other end was stammering, but the information got through. "How many?" He waited for the response. "Where were they?" When the last bits of information were relayed, Colonel Jackson added. "I am up-grading this level of quarantine. This is now a lethal exposure. Anyone trying to leave the base is to be shot on sight. No questions asked, no warning given. All bodies stored at a central location away from the gates. No one, under any circumstance leaves this base. I want an immediate lock down. I want all personnel accounted for. There will be a meeting of all commanding officers at the mess hall in fifteen minutes. I want a complete report on all incidents and all data. No exceptions. MPs are now to have live ammunition and all safeties off until further notice."

"How many?" Jackson stammered putting his cell phone away. He, too, was in a state of shock.

"My source says thirty-five. Yours?"

"Twenty-one in the Mess Hall"

"They're all over the base." Colonel Jackson noted. "A panic is starting. Already three people have tried to force their way off the base. Two were apprehended. The third was killed by guards."

Jackson punched the intercom to the quarantined area. "Captain?"

A trembling, high-pitched voice cracked on the other end. "Greenly here, sir!"

"I need a complete report on all experiments that were running in the 'clean room.' I also need a listing of all organisms stored here, what their effect is on humans, and a list of all events leading up to the disaster. I need it yesterday!"

"How sir. We're in quarantine?"

"Use the computer console." He pointed on the screen motioning behind the Captain. "Type it out and transmit it to my office. I have a meeting with all command personnel in fifteen minutes. I need your report in ten. Get to it." He cut off the connection without waiting for a response.

"It got out?" Jackson suggested.

"Only possibility. Only question now is how far it's going to get, and how long we have. We have to shut this down fast before it spreads."

"It would have to be air borne, that would be the only explanation..."

"Not exactly. Nothing gets out of that room. It's sealed. Even the air is re-cycled and never released into the atmosphere.

There might have been a leak somewhere, but we have half-a-dozen alarms systems to announce it if it did."

"Then how could it get out of the room and strike the others?"

"I'm also concerned about why it hit some and not others. Our survivors on this base may be the key to a defense against this. We need to get moving on this. If we have to recommend sterilization of the base and surrounding area, I want it done before the organism gets too far from here."

"'Sterilization'?" Brown echoed. He didn't like the sound of that.

"That's the order. If something gets out, we activate the nuclear destruct, and take it out before it spreads."

"But wouldn't the radiation mutate the germ, and the blast simply spread it further and faster?"

"That's what we have to determine before too much time passes."

Shots suddenly caught their attention. Jim spun on his heels, crouching with gun drawn and bullet in the chamber before he even realized he was responding to the sounds. Two soldiers hit the ground as he watched. Two more were charging the gate and the soldiers opened fire a second time. Jackson tapped him on his shoulder and motioned him to follow.

"The sooner we contact command the sooner we can resolve this." The pair broke into a run to the communications building. Jim noted several piles of clothing and personal items crumpled on the ground as they worked their way across the compound. He felt his skin beginning to crawl as imaginary microbes leaped from the clothing to him. He knew if that was the problem, he wouldn't be able to feel it; but his mind was running a mile-a-minute right now. Adrenaline was pumping through all of his muscles and his mind was looking for some kind of release.

As they burst into the communication center, another pile of clothing blocked their path. Jackson kicked it out of the way.

"Is that safe, sir?" Jim asked.

"If it's a germ; then we all have it. No sense in beating around the bush. He punched up the secure line code to command. A few moments later the screen flickered to life. The scene that greeted them was a mirror-image of their own. Panic was barely under control. Terror was reflected in each face. The serviceman who answered their call was obviously more concerned about his own emergency than theirs.

"We may have a contamination." Jackson replied.

"Join the club." the serviceman snapped back. He hit a switch, and another face replaced his. This time it was an officer.

"Location?" the voice was monotone. Jim was amazed that the officer's face was a mask of non-committal.

"Base 793." Jackson replied. Jim then realized how calm Jackson was being in response. He was about to be told whether or not he and the entire base was going to be wiped out in a nuclear fireball, and neither one seemed the least bit interested.

"Situation?"

"We may have a biologic."

"Symptoms?" the voice showed some concern for the first time.

"None we can track. One moment the victim is standing there, the next all that's left are their clothing and personal items. There's no body left to examine."

"How many?" At this point Jim had to fight down the urge to step in and scream at the man. He showed all the emotion of someone reading off a grocery list.

"No final count. We did have seven at first. Thirty-five others from another source and another twenty-one from a third source. We've seen a dozen others on the way to command." his commander replied.

"Is it on-going?" Here the voice broke enough to show genuine concern and interest.

"We don't know. We haven't seen any new cases. It may have happened all at once, but no one discovered them until later. We've sealed the base. Recommend sterilization before it gets out."

"Request denied." came the reply.

"Sir! I don't think you understand. This is something we can't control. We've already had several incidents of people trying to get off the base. I don't know how long we can contain it."

"Containment is no longer an issue in this matter. You and your officer need to report to command as soon as possible."

"Sir?" came Jackson's reply. The response he had been given was completely unexpected. "I told you that we may have a biologic. The last thing we need now is for one or more of us to leave the base, and take it with us."

"I heard you, colonel, now hear me. You and your security officer report to command immediately." Without any further response the connection was broken.

"Sir?" Jim asked of Jackson.

"Those are the orders. Let's go."

CHAPTER THREE

Meeting In Hell's Penthouse

An hour after the order was given; a two-man super-sonic fighter was touching down in what appeared to be a deserted air strip in the Rocky Mountains area. Brown and Jackson climbed out of the cockpit, removing their flight helmets.

"Are you sure this is the place?" Jim asked kicking at a clump of grass growing up through a crack in the concrete.

"Careful. It costs the government twenty thousand a year to replace those things." Jackson cautioned. The runway was suddenly alive with fifty troops coming out of various camouflage locations. Jim noticed that no one had their gun on "safety."

"Okay, maybe it's not as deserted as I thought. Should I put the grass back?"

"Jackson, Randall T. Colonel. Base 793, Biological Research. We were sent for. This is Brown, James R. Major. Head of security. Base 793. He was also asked to attend."

The soldier who appeared to be in charge motioned with his rifle barrel toward a section of the run way. As they stepped forward, it slid back to reveal a set of stairs. Major Brown and Colonel Jackson descended without another word being said. Several of the guards followed, the rest faded back into their posts. At the foot of the stairs, the wall parted to reveal an elevator. The commanding officer stepped inside. Major Brown and Colonel Jackson joined him. The others assumed guard positions outside. With a faint whisper, the doors slid closed and the car began to descend—a little too fast for comfort—Jim thought. He cast a look at their guard who gave no indication of being friendly. He then looked at Colonel Jackson.

"Hell's Penthouse." Jackson offered.

"Hell's Penthouse?" Jim had heard a vague reference to such a base, but could never get more than its unofficial name.

"Probably our third most secured base in the states. It's build so deep in the mountains someone made the comment it was low enough to be the penthouse of Hell. Once the comment was made, the name stuck. However, something must be very wrong. They've gotten sloppy."

"Sloppy?" Jim echoed, and made sure the guard heard the insult. Their escort showed no change of emotion.

"They've already violated about seven security procedures since we've landed. Whatever is going on must be bigger than we thought." Jim began to think the soldier who named the base was right. He could tell they were descending faster than several amusement rides. It wasn't a free-fall, but close to it. By his calculations they had dropped a mile or more into the mountains. After a minute-and-a-half more of descent at this rate, he stopped counting and tried to focus on his stomach and keeping his meal in it.

When the doors finally parted, a long corridor lay before them. A man in a military-style golf cart was waiting. Jackson and Brown climbed into the cart. Their escort pressed the button that closed the elevator doors and carried him back to the surface. Their driver never said a word; but once they were in, he turned the cart around and moved it full speed down the sterile tunnel. Jim noted that the corridor sloped gently down, and their half-hour trip took them deeper into the belly of the mountain range. Except for the row of lights in the ceiling, no other change marked their passing. Jim actually let his imagination take over to ease the boredom, and let the lights "flit" pass the way he had followed old telephone poles out the back seat window of his father's car when he was young.

Jim wasn't "spacing" enough to be obvious, but he had created the illusion of the lights in the ceiling moving, and he was sitting still. He liked the mind games. It was an exercise in mental discipline that he had used for many years to hone his thinking skills. "Everything is just a point of perspective." he would tell himself; and then he would pick a situation or philosophy, and dissect it based upon various points of view. It had earned him the reputation of being able to see all sides of an issue; and this aided him when he had to investigate some crime or breech of security. His approach had helped him solve several mysteries that had baffled others on the case; and had quickly moved him up in his career.

The cart reduced speed, and Jim brought himself out of his thoughts. There was a turn in the corridor that wasn't visible until you were upon it. The design of the sloping and curving hallway had created an optical illusion that the hallway still went on until the last part of the turn where they found themselves in front of a massive entrance. The door to the entrance reminded Jim of a giant bank vault. He searched his memories of several bits of classified information he had collected without proper authorization, pieced them together; and asked Jackson, "The vault?"

"That's the more official name, but Hell's Penthouse seemed more glamorous. Let's go." As they climbed out of the cart, the entire wall swung open on silent hinges powered by various hydraulic systems. The door was easily five feet thick, with locking bolts as big in diameter as his body. Another escort was waiting for them on the other side. This time their journey was shorter: down three doors, a turn to the left, five more doors, and inside.

"...These are satellite photos taken thirty minutes ago." The briefing was already in progress, and so they slipped into two empty chairs closest to the door. Jim picked up the packet in front of him. It didn't have all the fancy security seals or declarations; but he knew it would be of the highest classification. That told him the packet must have been prepared on such a rush basis that no one wasted the time for the official versions. A long whistle of surprise from one of the other members in the meeting caught his attention, and he looked up to see the slide everyone else was watching. He almost replied in kind. A vast crater was all that was left of one base.

"Enemy attack?" came a voice to his left.

"No. This was a self-destruct device. The commander gave the order without proper clearance. The same here, here, and here." As the speaker paused between each word, a new slide was presented with similar results.

"I take it that our experiences are not confined to just one or two bases?" Jackson asked. Jim was surprised at how fast his traveling companion picked up on information.

"The experiences you've all had are not limited to just one or two bases. Nor are they limited to military targets. In fact, they are not limited to just United States territories. From what we have been able to piece together, this is a world-wide event."

"Event, you make it sound like some kind of Olympic meet, or get-together! This is a disaster!" bellowed a voice off to the right. Tempers were raw among some of the members.

"I've lost fifty-seven personnel, three of them were some of my closest friends." came another voice.

"Do we have any numbers, yet?" Jackson asked, taking the subject off the personal to the professional before things got out of hand. Jim had to admit that Jackson was a cold one, all business. The officer presenting the data showed visible signs of relief to move back onto such an impersonal topic.

"No final figures, yet. We have personnel collecting everything they can from news stories, computers, and other sources. Our best source has been internet web sources. Echelon scans of E-mails sent to various contacts were intercepted using several key words we would expect to find and this calculation puts the current loss at over twenty-five million world-wide. Silence crashed on the room. Finally someone gathered enough strength to ask,

"Is it still going on?"

"We don't know. From all indications it hit all at once. No one has had any reports of additional personnel missing after the first hit."

"Is it connected to the Middle East?" one of the calmer voices in the room asked. The presenter switched programs and suddenly they were seeing thousands of bodies strewn across the landscape.

"Iran has been declaring that the 12th Imam has returned. They even blamed him for the unrest, the Arab Spring; and the overthrow of several Arab governments recently." Several nodded their agreement. Islamic Eschatology was part of Anti-Terrorism 101 in the Department of Defense. You could not understand the radical Muslims apart from their religious views of the End Times. The 12th Imam was the last direct line blood descendant of Mohammed who was reported to have disappeared centuries ago; but was expected to return to unite the Arab world. Iran's claim that he had returned made everyone nervous because the next phase was the Final Jihad that would plunge the entire world into fire and blood. When it was over the entire world would be under Islamic control.

"When Israel announced their discovery of oil a few days ago and their find was about to break the OPEC monopoly; it sent chaos into the Arab financial world. Several Arab powers saw their wealth and power begin to collapse overnight. Immediate action was needed to restore OPEC to power. When Iran announced the appearance of the Mahdi yesterday this leader rallied other nations to attack as part of their Final Jihad. It was predicted to be the last upheaval in the Middle East. Prophecy declared Islam would conquer the entire world. Despite the United Nations vote on a Palestinian State, and the treaty to allow Israel to rebuild their Temple, peace still had not been achieved with Israel. Iran has continued to promise to wipe Israel off the map."

Several in the room snickered at the thought since Iran had never even printed a map with Israel on it. "How can you wipe out what doesn't exist?" one officer dared to joke.

"Last week Zion Oil claimed they found one of the largest oil deposits in the world. The Arab armies rallied to the Mahdi who led them into battle against Israel this morning during the last day of the Jewish Celebration called the Feast of Tabernacles. You might remember this as the anniversary of the beginning of the Third Temple Age." Jim recalled it was also on the last day of the Feast of Tabernacles that militants took the Temple Mount by force and began to lay the foundation for the current Temple.

"Russia, Iran, Ethiopia, Libya and Syria moved their armies into Israel at 06:37 this morning. It was a lightning raid. They pulled out all the stops. Russia had been preparing with light-weight plywood tanks that moved faster, used less fuel; but were just as durable as the strongest metals. Arabs were using cavalries with several thousand horses. We're seeing everything from swords to hand guns to portable missiles and then some. Hezbollah joined in with an impressive arsenal. Seems the missing weapons of mass destruction from Iraq had been transported to Syria."

There was a ripple of laughter across the room as the "open secret" had been known since President Bush took the hit for the intelligence community not being able to find them after the Iraqi Invasion. Jim had seen the videos filmed in military night vision of the convoys being loaded and moved out of Iraq to Syria by trucks. Then it switched to air lifts. Even one of Hussein's top generals had written a book about their weapons of mass destruction program, and how he had convinced Saddam not to launch against Israel.

It was an open secret among the intelligence community that the weapons of mass destruction had been there, they had been moved; and the U.S. could not touch them without going to war against Syria—and that meant Russia, too. Unfortunately, it had been the battle cry for the Iraq War and so intelligence reports were falsified, careers were destroyed, a president disgraced; and the government had even funded a major action movie to make the disappearance of the weapons look like a political mistake rather than an on-going threat.

"Syria had built its own weapons research program in the desert. Russia was supplying the yellow cake. The Iranians had paid three million dollars for the radar defense system to protect it; but the Israelis blew it out of the ground in the Fall of 2007. They were kind enough to drop one of their fuel tanks at the site to tell Syria that they had been there.

The Jewish state had sold defective materials, infected thousands of computers, corrupted years of research; and kidnapped or killed nuclear experts in Iran to hinder its nuclear weapons program.

"Israel has basically ticked off every one of its neighbors and given the opportunity the armies moved into Israel from all directions. We haven't seen action like this from so many since the 1948 Arab-Israeli War. They spread out across the entire landscape. By 08:00 this morning the Golan Heights, Galilee, and most of the agricultural lands were overrun. Hamas slipped in Iranian, Libyan and Ethiopian forces through Egypt and the Gaza. Thousands of tanks. Air support, cavalries and ground troops were almost to Jerusalem. The Israelis were caught completely off guard. Here is what satellites showed at 08:32 this morning."

The pictures showed thousands of tanks and ground troops moving across the southern wilderness and into position around Jerusalem. As the film unfolded, the Dome of the Rock exploded in a ball of fire. Debris rained down and several chunks struck the Temple, but there was no visible damage. Suddenly there were explosions everywhere, but these were all outside of Jerusalem. Vapor and smoke trails were streaking across the skies.

"Here are the same satellites at 08:47."

With the exception of one or two tanks here or there moving aimlessly, and handfuls of troops running; the scene was the same as the first one the presenter had flashed on the screen earlier. Thousands of Russian, Syrian, Hamas, Hezbolla, Ethiopian, Libyan and Iranian troops were lying motionless on the ground. Flames were everywhere. Extreme zooms on the satellite images showed the corpses were little more than mummified skeletons.

"Neutron?" someone asked.

"Although these corpses look like the result of a neutron bomb, there is no evidence of the radiation residue that a neutron bomb would have generated. From all appearances, something hit almost every troop. Our first thoughts were a meteor shower; but NASA and tracking systems tell us there was no shower. Also, there was an actual pattern to these hits. The one strike inside Israel, which took out the Dome of the Rock on the Temple Mount, completely missed the Temple next to it. After that everything fell outside the cities and among the invading armies. Nothing hit any of the homes, businesses or Israeli military installations. Even the booths set up for the Ceremony seem untouched. It was almost like some kind of controlled precision bombing taking out only the invading forces. Sulfur bombs are what one source is calling it; fire, possibly gas and intense heat were used. Most of the invaders were dead before they hit the ground. Their eye sockets are hollow. The skin almost completely fried off their bones."

"It looked like survivors." a voice in the darkness noticed.

"We don't have the numbers. Those who were not wiped out by the attack must have become confused. They began turning on each other. Even the handful that survived the firestorm were quickly reduced in number. A quick count put the estimate as two-thirds to three-fourths wiped out. The fact that there were survivors suggests it was not a neutron bomb. If it had been, there would not have been any survivors."

The slides scene now shifted. High altitude satellites captured most of Russia in flames. Iran was a massive smoke cloud from orbit. Libya was in flames. Ethiopia was smoldering. Syria showed thousands of fires across its landscape—each one believed to be a terrorist stronghold. Damascus appeared more of a crater than city. The last scene showed Egypt in what could only be described as some kind of nuclear mushroom cloud spreading across its surface.

"A CNN news crew in Egypt caught this scene before they were taken out."

The scene shifted to a mosque in downtown Egypt. Two men were standing in front of the mosque. They were dressed in black slacks, white dress shirts, black vests, black dress coats and yamakas—the traditional attire of modern rabbis. They were shouting in an Arabic language—probably Egyptian. The voice of a translator had been added.

"*The Messiah has come. Yeshua Ha Ma Sheach is the Anointed One. He is the Son of the Blessed One; the Son of the Most High.*" The translator interpreted. The same cry began again with the same message. The interpreted added, "They are crying out in Egyptian, but they are blending in Hebrew terms. *Yeshua* is a proper Jewish name. In Hebrew it is *Joshua*. In Greek it is *Jesus*. *Ha Ma Sheach* is a Hebrew term for *Our Messiah*. They then recite several terms for the Messiah in Egyptian."

"So it looks like this is Israel's doing?" someone called out from the back of the room.

"Wasn't that the message that kook announced when he broke into that Jewish family's home during Passover a few months back? I thought he declared the Messiah was here or something like that." another voice challenged.

"Are they related to that guy? Is it an Israeli terrorist cell starting up?" Still someone else added his two cents to the debate.

"You might think that, but keep watching. The one on the left does match the description the family gave of the intruder; but it's still too early to be sure. That description fits about half of the Jews world-wide." the presenter noted. The two figures continued to shout and their cries inflamed the crowd. Egyptian soldiers charged them with guns drawn. It looked like fire fell from above and consumed the soldiers in an instant. The burning figures flailed wildly and squirmed in the intense heat before collapsing. The fire grew closer toward the camera. Whoever was holding the camera dropped it. It fell on its side on the ground. The flame hit the camera lens, causing the lens to crack; and then the scene went dark as the camera was also consumed by the flames.

"Here is the satellite film of this area at the same moment." Here the scene showed a flash of fire forming in the upper atmosphere and falling on the area. A few moments later the fire moved toward the mosque. At that point the room was filled with brilliant white light as several nuclear devices detonated in the mosque. The satellite camera captured the billowing mushroom clouds on the scene. The room fell into shocked silence. The presenter shifted the satellite images on the screen.

"What you are seeing are the entire oil fields and reserves of Iran now a complete loss. The black smoke rising there is nothing short of thousands of oil fires. Our experts are telling us that these are—for lack of a better term—sulfur bombs. Large blocks of sulfur burning as they fell. However, it was not a natural occurrence. There are no reported deposits of sulfur in our orbit. It would have burned up once it entered the atmosphere. It fell with precision only on the armies and countries that invaded Israel. Everything else was left untouched. Even Israel is claiming this was not their doing."

"It's the only explanation." someone in the back of the room offered.

"They've taken our technology for years and altered it." someone suggested.

"But even we do not have anything like this."

"Let's add this to the mix." The presenter added. "At the precise time of the invasion, just moments before the hail of sulfur bombs, a massive earthquake hit in Israel and several other countries. Some are blaming this on Elenin's alignment once more with the earth and the sun. That makes four major quakes conspiracy theorists are crediting to this comet. However, for all the damage to buildings around the world, Jerusalem and cities in Israel were undamaged by the quake. Other countries cannot make the same claim."

"Maybe a dormant volcano erupted and spewed sulfur into the air?" a voice to the right countered. The satellite camera pulled back showing the entire country of Israel.

"Anyone see any active volcanoes there?" the presenter asked.

"Here's another piece of information. These sulfur bombs dropped with precision and began hitting mosques throughout the Arab world at the same time they fell on the invading armies. Thousands have been wiped out. The fireball that hit the Egyptian mosque was more for fire than sulfur. It was generated about one and a half miles above the mosque. There was nothing on the satellite camera to burn at that altitude or cause the fire. It fell outside the mosque to protect the two Jews, but then spread to the mosque itself. Seems the terrorists were storing one or more bombs in the mosque to use as a last ditch effort if the invasion failed. Obviously, those Jews were also suicide bombers or victims of their own technology."

"I know we joke about Israeli Intelligence being good; but no one could coordinate something on this scale; with this precision." an officer to the left of Jim conceded.

"Could whatever did this in Israel have mutated? Could it have been released world-wide?"

"We are looking into that possibility. However, this took several minutes and left bodies. We can trace it to sulfur bombs. The events we have in the rest of the world were instantaneous and left no bodies. Anything organic on the victims was gone. Eyeglass, surgical implants, dental fillings, pacemakers, cosmetic implants, joint replacements, stints; these were all left behind. Whatever hit, wiped out everything of an organic nature all the way down to the cellular level. We could not even find any DNA or residue on any of the remains. It might be connected. It might not. It's too soon to tell."

The door opened, and two more figures slipped quietly into the room. However, this time the speaker chose to notice the addition. As the pair dropped into the last empty chairs he interrupted himself. "It seems that everyone is now here. At this point, I will start the 'real' briefing you have all been called here for. Allow me to present the President of the United States."

Instead of a screen flickering to life, a door at the other end of the room opened, and several figures entered. The entire room was on their feet and at attention as the President of the United States walked physically into the room. Several secret service operatives surrounded him, but three other figures with the President monopolized all the focus. Directly behind the President were three powerful figures. They almost glowed with a light of their own. They were over seven feet tall, and moved with a grace that seemed impossible for their size. A power flowed from them and touched everyone in the room. The amazing thing about them was how they did not seem to have any features one could remember. If asked to describe them, they would be faceless, or their eyes would be the dominant feature. They had eyes, nose, mouth, ears and hair like anyone else; but there was something "*more*" about them. Jim came to realize that "*more*" was the word he was looking for.

They seemed more human, more alive, more...real. That was the description he was trying to find. Compared to these three figures; he felt like only a shadow. They were so much more than he could hope to be on all levels, that he was drained by their presence. He could easily fall face-down on the ground before them. They were too much for him to stand in their presence. They were too great for him to recall any details of their appearance. It was more than his mind could store in his memory. If someone were to put wings and a halo on each one, he would have no objection.

"Be seated." came the President's voice; but everyone in the room was transfixed on his companions. One of them spoke... *sounded* may have been a more appropriate description, like the silver strings on a harp or the chiming of a golden bell.

"Peace" came the melodic tone. Jim felt it in his mind more than heard it with his ears. The lead figure held up his hand, lowered it; and everyone in the room dropped into their chairs. The three companions looked at the officers; then stared at each other. One nodded as if in agreement to some unspoken decision; and for all intents and purposes the three *"turned down"* their presence. They became less *"more"* than they were a moment before. Jim was finally able to function in their presence. Everyone was shaking their heads to clear them and focus on the events around them. One of the three motioned for the President to be seated; and as if some obedient servant, the most powerful man in the world complied.

"We are guests here...Visitors" came the voice of the one who took the podium.

CHAPTER FOUR

Revelations

"Aliens?" asked someone gathering what little courage he could. Even as he spoke, his voice was filled with awe.

"Not in the sense you understand. Allow us to brief you on events." He motioned and the screen began to display scenes that could not have been captured on any slide in the computer.

"We have always been visiting your world; from its most early beginnings we were there." Several scenes of early man struggling with survival were displayed. In one a "*visitor*" was showing how to use tools, another showed how to plant crops, another showed how to use plants to heal an illness.

"We have taken you under our wings to guide you and protect you. You are our children in a sense. Without our help and guidance, you would have died with the first ice age; but we were there." Again scenes of "*visitors*" showing how to use fire, make clothing from animal skins, build shelters, and hunt were displayed.

"In more recent years, we needed to take a more active role or your own flaws would drive you into extinction." Here scenes of various primitive wars, and then more advance wars began to unfold. In each scene, a "*guest*" was present. During the scenes of the Second World War, several scenes showed "*guests*" advising Hitler. The officers began to whisper and mumble among themselves. The speaker paused the scenes to address the concerns.

"We were not guiding him to victory, but we needed for him to make inappropriate decisions. We were the ones who guided him into fighting a war on more than one front. We paused his attack on Britain until they had time to prepare a defense. If we had not made him insecure regarding naval warfare; he would have crossed the channel and swept across Great Britain with no one to stop him. We convinced him to end the Battle of Britain before the last planes in the Royal Air Force were destroyed.

"At each point in the history of your world there have been sudden changes, poor decisions from those who seemed above such flaws, equipment that did not work, or supplies that did not arrive. We have been constantly involved in the preservation of your race."

"Angels?" came an observation more than a question from the far side of the room.

"That is one name we are known by. We are not extraterrestrials as you have come to call us. We are beyond this realm of existence. We call ourselves extradimensionals, EeeDees for short; as this is a more accurate description of our nature. Our world is superimposed upon yours, but you lack the ability to perceive it. Just like the various dimensions of a cube are obvious when you are on the same plane of existence as the cube; but if you are a line that makes up a square that is part of the cube, you are unaware of the entire cube. You could not see us. You, however, are obvious to us; and so we have reduced our reality to the point where your senses can see and hear us."

The screen came alive once more. This time it was showing several atomic explosions.

"When you came to this level in your evolution, we could no longer simply influence. We had to take a more active role. Our appearances were more obvious and sightings became more common. Again, because your technology could not capture our existence, no reliable documentation was available. However, we made our presence known to various leaders in a more open fashion. In the previous scenes you could see us clearly; but those we were influencing only knew us in the form of an inner voice, a dream, or a suggestion.

With the dropping of the first atomic bomb; we began to move among the leaders of the world openly."

Here the scene shifted to show leaders of Russia, Britain, China, Japan, America, France, Spain, Italy and other countries that were pivotal in the history of the world in conference with one or more "*angels*."

"When these leaders followed our suggestions; we were able to guide them into security and prosperity. When they did not listen; we found it necessary to remove them. This leader was disgraced and removed from office." The scene showed a ruler of Russia beating his shoe at the United Nations. "If they could not be removed by political means; we had to take more direct action."

Now several scenes of scandals, illness, and assassinations were displayed. The last was a motorcade through Houston. Several objections were expressed around the room. The President was motioned to come to the podium and take over.

"In 1963, America went through a coup. The president in office at that time would not back down, nor follow suggestions and recommendation of our guests. America was in serious danger of upsetting the balance of power established by our guests and plunging the entire world back into war. In order to preserve world peace; the government followed the suggestions of our guests."

"We brought a hit squad from Cuba." The first EeeDee interrupted. "They were led to believe they were going to make an attempt on your president's life, but were instructed to miss so it would be only a warning not to send hit squads into Cuba to remove Castro from office. However, we took control of events and moved it from a failed attempted assassination and made it successful so it removed him from office."

"'Removed him from office'?!" bellowed one voice. "That's the president you've killed. That's an Act of War!" Tempers were rising around the room. As someone stood to protest, one of the guests motioned toward the figure; a Secret Service agent drew his gun, and executed him where he stood. He dropped like a sack of wet concrete spilling the chairs around him. Suddenly each officer in the room became very aware that no one else had a weapon in the room other than the Secret Service; and they were there to follow the orders of the "*guests*."

The President was trying to find some diplomatic way to explain what had just happened and restore some semblance of order, but the lead "*visitor*" brushed him out of the way and took control of the podium. He increased his "Presence" until it was painful to those in the room.

"Make no mistake about who is in charge. This is the message we give you. It is the same message that has been given over the last several decades to each political and world leader. Follow and prosper, resist and die." came the voice of the guest who had ordered the officer's death. Although it was still the melodic sounding, it was cold and unemotional. He then reduced his "Presence."

"This was the message we gave your rebellious leader many years ago. He chose to ignore us. He thought that he was in control of his own destiny. He was not...neither are you. We have been the power behind your country, and other countries for many years now. We have left your political structures in place so your populations would not be aware of the change in power; but we have worked behind the scenes to ensure our objectives.

"When it came time to vote on leaders, we chose who would rise to power and who would fall by the way-side in disgrace, defeat, or scandal. It was a simple thing to ensure that only those who would comply with our directives were the choices your citizens had to choose between in elections. When someone slipped through our evaluation process, rose to a position of influence, or passed laws that hindered our progress, we found 'loop holes' to ignore the law, tied it up in legal battles, or removed the politician from office. Even when consolidated efforts were made by parties, we were able to expose their secrets and nullify their efforts."

"We have controlled your country through many means." began another of the guests. The President stepped awkwardly away from the speakers as it was obvious he was no longer important. "It is a simple thing to inspire writers to present various points of view; to show the horror of certain thoughts or beliefs. Your country and the entire world, has been carefully programmed and orchestrated to bring it to this point in its history. No one in this room will be allowed to alter that course. It is the right course—the necessary course—in order for your world to move along its evolutionary path."

"Did you cause this current disaster?" came one voice off to the side. Jim was surprised that someone had the courage to ask the question they were all thinking.

"The one in Israel was our doing. The nation of Israel is the one nation that has rejected our influences. They have refused to comply. Even when we arranged to restore their Temple as a way of gaining power over them; they refused to submit. A plan is in the works to remove that nation from the face of the earth permanently. Unfortunately, these other countries this morning tried to put their own greed and needs ahead of the world order. We sent a warning to stop them." At this point the slides appeared with what looked like real-time ground level video. It was physically impossible to have captured these images. Each army was attacked by swarms of bees and wasps. The entire army came to a halt. Numerous troops would turn and run only to be shot by their fellow soldiers. Flame throwers wiped out the pestilence that threatened the army. Then the advance began once more. The ground began to shake. Soldiers lost their footing, but tanks continued to move forward. At that point the sulfur bombs fell and obscured the video.

"Each has now been removed as a world power. They will be unable to influence or alter our future plans. All nations will come under a single world order. All nations will work for the good of the entire population of the world. Not for their own good; but for the good of all. Earth will become a community—working together for the common good.

"However, the loss of twenty-five million lives at the same time we were chastising our rebellious children this morning was a different event; and it was not of our doing." As if suddenly remembering the President, the guest stepped back and motioned to the national leader. Here the President came back to the podium to speak; looking to the guest for permission before beginning.

"We had been made aware that this was something that would eventually happen. Our guests warned us about a defect in our genetic make-up. A portion of the inhabitants of the world had defective genes; certain genes are missing from their make-up. These defective genes would make their hosts susceptible to organisms in space. This is why we had down-sized our space program. We stopped going to the moon, but earth had the desire for space. So we gave them the International Space Station to wean them off manned space flight. In 2011 we retired the shuttle program; then eventually abandoning the International Space Station, and leaving planetary exploration to unmanned craft that did not return. We knew the organism was out there, and it was just a matter of time before this disaster struck. If it did not happen the way it did, we believed a meteor or some other object falling to earth would have brought the organism into our atmosphere. We have been preparing for this; but it still caught a lot of us off-guard."

The President nodded, and slides from the computer program were displayed on the screen. "This is Project Olympus. Named after the legendary home of the gods." Jim had an involuntary flash of the "guests" in the room being the topic of such legends. He pushed it back from his mind, and focused on the briefing the President was giving them. "Zeus was known for his lightning bolts, and this project was designed to place into orbit numerous satellites that would be used for weather control and storm engineering. The theory was to create enough lightning storms in the upper atmosphere to create and replace the lost ozone in the ozone layer. The damage to the environment necessitated moving higher than we had deemed safe given the threat of the space organism.

"This morning the astronauts completed their assignment with the placing of the last satellite. They left the International Space Station in Freedom II and were returning. This is the point of entry with the atmosphere." A satellite photo showed the shuttle dropping away from the station. "We have calculated that it was the exact moment when their craft made contact with the atmosphere that our current disaster struck. Our specialists show that the organism brought back by their craft hit the oxygen-rich atmosphere and exploded into a plague that hit all the earth at the same moment. From our sources, this organism attacked as predicted all of those who had the genetic defect. It struck at each cell at the microscopic level, disrupting the bonds that hold the chromosomes together. The result is that every chromosome lacking the protective gene dissolved. As each chromosome in the body had the same basic code, they all lacked the gene necessary to fight off the organism. Thus, one second a person would be standing before you. The gene hit every chromosome in the body, broke the cellular bonds; and before you could blink, the entire body, every cell, whether skin, organ tissue, bone or blood was disassembled. The outward appearance was that the person simply vanished, and left behind their clothing and other non-organic personal items."

"So it's not the 'Rapture'?" came a voice to the right.

"'Rapture'?" several echoed the strange word. The "guests" murmured among themselves and resumed the briefing.

"We created the story of the 'Rapture' to prepare your world for this event. We inspired early writers of your various religious documents. It is unfortunate that they twisted the message we gave them and presented it as something of a supernatural event, a prelude to judgment. It was never intended that way. When we first revealed this to them in dreams, they wrote about the organism coming from the sky, and removing a portion of the entire world population. They did not understand space travel, germs, or genetic make-up. They put it into what terms they could understand. When others came after them years later to translate the original works, they changed the concept even more, and turned it into a judgment from God. Look at one of the few passages that was not changed in later versions. It says to *'comfort one another with this information.'* We had revealed the information to these writers to keep everyone calm when it happened. It has just been distorted over the centuries."

"So this would be the '*Rapture*' in the Bible, but it's not what we think it is?" came the voice once more.

"Yeeessss..." came the long response as if saying it slowly and over a longer period of time would add to the credibility of answer.

"I heard reports that this was mother earth expelling those who could not be retrained or conform. Others are claiming you kidnapped these twenty-five million people." someone suggested near the front of the room. The "*visitors*" seemed to be growing tired of the discussion. The head "*guest*" took up the topic once more.

"Short of making ourselves completely part of your plane of existence it is difficult for us to communicate openly with your species. Those who are "*spiritual*" –keeping their minds in tune with the universe and the various forces of the universe—are most open to our normal means of communication. This is why we transmitted messages to your early religious leaders. When our message of the "*Rapture*" was misinterpreted and twisted; we began to contact other spiritual leaders in recent years. Their minds were opened to us. They listened and taught what we revealed to them. They tried to put it into a positive light. The loss of twenty-five million people is a double blessing."

Here the audience began to challenge and protest, but as the Secret Service officers stepped forward the crowd grew deathly quiet.

"The loss of your twenty-five million people is a double blessing. First of all, the results of Project Olympus will reveal that your efforts to repair the ozone layer have failed. Events have been set into motion that will eventually lead to the starvation of one third of your world's population. The loss of these twenty-five million will buy life for others with their deaths.

"The second blessing is that these modern preachers are correct. Mother earth, through us would have eventually been forced to expel these twenty-five million people. These genetically defective people were holding your world back from reaching its true potential. Our modern messengers knew that we would have to remove them by force at some point to jump start your evolution into a one world government, and a Golden Age for earth. So their predictions and teaching are true; but this organism solved the problem for us. It acted before we were forced to do so.

"Perhaps it is best to think of this new plague as the 'Rapture Syndrome.' It would best describe the effects, and seeing that it is caused by an organism, and not some supernatural judgment, should help to calm the panic taking control of the world right now."

The "visitor" stepped back and motioned for the President to continue with the meeting.

"In response to the 'Rapture Syndrome,' I have declared Marshal Law. Congress has been disbanded until those who are victims of the syndrome can be replaced. However, new elections will not be held until we get this country back in order. That will take more than a few weeks, even months. We may be under Marshall Law for a year or more. FEMA has faced numerous natural disasters over these past few years. Between floods, tornados, hurricanes, earthquakes and fires, the American treasury has been hit hard above and beyond the damage to the economy to the housing market collapse and other industry collapses. We will do what we can for disaster control, relief for those who need it..."

At this point the lead visitor interrupted to correct the President. "That will not be the case. As mentioned before, one third of mankind will die. Zero Population Growth is a program we inspired many years ago. Our students recognized that the resources of this world can only support a limited number of people. For the good of the whole; those who are not strong should not be allowed to drain the weakened resources left to us. FEMA will not be involved."

"I understand." The President cleared his throat. Skimming the notes he picked up where he had left off. "... We will begin rebuilding what has been lost; but right now we need to control the panic. We will eventually release all of this to the public; but for now no one outside of this room must know."

"Unfortunately, the panic may be even more intense that you realize, Mr. President." The head guest had actually interrupted the President and bumped him from the podium. "These are scenes that are taking place even as we speak."

The projector came to life on its own; and the skies over numerous cities throughout the world were filled with space crafts. It looked like a world-wide UFO invasion. Several officers were on their feet.

"It's an invasion." one of the officers shouted. Those next to him pulled him back to his seat and calmed him before action was taken.

"It is not an invasion. It is a revelation. We have chosen to reveal ourselves to your world. They need some way to explain what has happened this morning. It is time to reveal who we are. However, our true nature will remain a secret. Consider this a rescue mission. This is how it will be presented. Your entire world is in a state of panic. Governments are about to collapse. War is eminent along various boarders. As your President noted the resources of this world have been taxed beyond their ability to cope.

"These..." pointing to the thousands of ships filling the air, "... are our people. We do not need ships. But this is how your people perceive us. They are looking for aliens; extraterrestrials you called us—or ETs. Let the world now know of us; but they will know us as ETs, and not what we truly are. We had already begun this preparation through television, books and movies. The general population has long believed that there was life out there. Various religious groups were created and influenced to provide an alternate story concerning the Rapture. You, yourself, recited one of the rumors running wild right now. Mother Earth was predicted to be dispelling its rebellious children in preparation for a Golden Age. We were hoping to slowly slip these thoughts and concepts into everyone's beliefs and thought processes so when this plague hit; it would be seen as a positive thing. Unfortunately, the Rapture Syndrome took place before everyone was prepared. We have communed among ourselves and we feel the best action at this time is to disclose our existence; but not our identity. To give it the encouragement it needs; we have created these images of ships to signal our coming to your world in a manner most will be able to accept."

The "*guest*" had interrupted the President to address the group. The President's face took on the appearance of a child who had spoken out of turn. The "*guest*" now permitted the President to continue his presentation.

"Our first priority is damage control." The President looked toward the EeeDee for confirmation. "We must get the people calm."

"Your President, and each of the world leaders will hold a press conference in half-an-hour." the EeeDee seemed to be getting new information as if some plan were being created on the spot. He had cut the President off once more. "Each leader will have one of us at his/her side as a sign of unity and support. During the conference, we will show the remains of Freedom II."

Here another slide showed the crash site of the space shuttle.

"Apparently they not only brought the organism back from space; but they all had the genetic defect. No one survived to land the craft. Your mission will be to collect and destroy all references to the '*Rapture*' so that people will have to face reality. Once they realize that this is a space organism, and not the wrath of God; they can focus on rebuilding and getting on with their lives." The EeeDee stepped aside and allowed the President to take the floor once more.

"I have already shut down all radio and television stations through military action. Several were beginning to broadcast '*Rapture*' messages that were pre-recorded to the public, and would have added to the confusion. Some cable stations had computer-controlled programs that automatically sent the broadcast from their satellites. I have had the satellites destroyed to stop the messages. All such messages, videos, transmission, tapes, books and documents are to be collected and destroyed. No exceptions!"

"Weren't the people who paid for these transmissions around to stop their own broadcasts?" Jackson asked.

"No." came the "*guest's*" reply.

"Doesn't that seem odd to anyone else in this room?" asked the Colonel. Jim was beginning to think he had better get ready to dive for cover before another bullet came in his direction.

"It should not. We have not told you about the genetic defect. Perhaps now is the time to address the issue. As your race evolved, the complete genetics, or 'CGs' as we called them, were evolving faster than the defective genetics or 'DGs.' The DGs were more hostile. Lacking the gene in their make-up, testosterone produced violence and aggression. When testosterone was present in those with the complete genetic make-up, it did not create hostility, but creativity. The CGs were moving at a more advanced rate towards their evolutionary goal. They even created some early cities where they gathered at our suggestion. By concentrating the CGs together in a society, we had hoped to increase their numbers. However, their civilization was feared by the DGs. These other races used their violence and hostility to conduct animal sacrifices that we outlawed in the CG communities. Finally, the DGs attacked, put the cities to the flame, and nearly wiped out the CGs in this part of the world."

"Sodom and Gomorrah?" asked Jackson.

"Yes. Those were the cities." the *"guest"* acknowledged. "There is a kind of genetic memory, something that occurs on the subconscious level. DGs react with hostility when they encounter a CG. On some subconscious level both species recognize each other. They either group with those of their own kind, or attack those who are different."

"So you're saying that the gene for homosexuality is what is lacking in the genetic make-up of those who were hit by the Rapture Syndrome?" came an incredulous voice which Jim couldn't pin point.

"Yes. As a matter of self-preservation, the CGs have hidden their differences. Some knowingly, some without conscious effort. We have worked over the years to change public opinion to accept the CGs without jealousy or hostility. In some areas of the world we were able to encourage them to openly express their differences, to take pride in the fact that they were genetically complete, superior to those around them. It has been a gradual process, but now it must be sped up."

"Wait a minute!" someone challenged on the other side of the room. "If we're still here; then we've got the homosexual gene in our make up?"

"Yes."

"Impossible!" declared several at once.

"You resist the idea; but it is true. Imagine how the entire world would feel if this information was thrust upon them before they had been prepared for it. You have been conditioned by the DGs to think it is wrong. Those who have produced these messages of doom and gloom were following a centuries-old genetic response to attack CGs, and try to destroy them as they did at Sodom and Gomorrah and other locations. This is why those who attacked the CGs are now gone. They knew their doom was coming. They knew only the CGs would survive. It was just a matter of time. This made them jealous at the subconscious level. This jealousy made them lash out."

"But gays are sick!" someone blurted out. There was almost a panic in the voice; the same panic Jim was feeling crawling up his own spine.

"The ones you refer to were not sick. Homosexuality is not a sickness. It is the natural condition of your race. It is the completeness of the genetic code. The ones you are referring to were dysfunctional. They were dysfunctional because they could not reconcile the teachings of the DGs to their own inner feelings. In an effort to fight what they were, they became unbalanced. This was not the fault of the homosexual gene they carried, but of the DGs trying to destroy them."

"But, once the entire world turns to homosexuality, won't that mean the end of our race?' Jim asked. He couldn't believe he was calling attention to himself. "I mean, same sex relationships do not produce offspring. If there is no offspring; then the race dies out after one generation. The system you are suggesting would imply that those with the homosexual gene would not seek to reproduce. If they don't reproduce; then they die out after a generation. How can 'CGs' as you call them be a superior race if they won't survive past the first generation? You need 'DGs' for the race to survive."

The "*guest*" set his eyes on Jim, and Jim wished he could unspeak the words. It was not the kind of attention he sought. "You are right." the "*guest*" answered, "If the preservation of the race depended on reproduction."

"Now I'm confused." Jackson retorted.

"Long ago, when the CGs were a dominant species, reproduction was not vital to the preservation of the race because the race had near immortality. Those long ago lived hundreds of years, had no illness or disease. They were involved in living life to its fullest. However, a coming planetary disaster, in the form of a comet crashing into the Earth nearly wiped them out. A DG had been living pretty much as a hermit. He had been outcast by the world as a sexual deviant because he had a heterosexual relationship, and continued to create offspring. He had even encouraged his children to follow his deviant behavior. Because he was not permitted to associate with normal society, he turned his attention to the stars. He drew star charts, discovered the comet; and calculated its path. He built a shelter for himself, his family and livestock. His hostility towards 'normals' led him not to warn the others of the coming danger; and so the world's population was nearly destroyed when the comet struck the earth, broke the tectonic plates, shifted continents, flooded the land, and drowned everyone who wasn't in his shelter."

"Noah?" Jim whispered more to himself than others.

"Yes, Noah. He was a DG. All CGs would have been wiped out except for the fact that the three wives of his sons had CG chromosomes. They preserved the race; but since Noah was a DG, his sons were DGs; and it polluted the strain. It would take many generations to sort out CGs with enough of a pure strain to set them apart from DGs. However, now that only CGs are left, there is a process we will show you to 'trigger' other genetic codes to increase healing, and prolong life."

"An immortality gene? I saw that on the news some time ago." someone suggested.

"Yes, the contamination with the DGs in the genetic pool made it difficult to isolate the immortality gene. This is simply a gene in the embryo stem cells that is active in the womb. As the embryo develops, the immortality gene produces a steroid—a chemical—that activates various chromosomes to grow a hand, a leg, a brain, a nerve, or some other body part. With the activation of the immortality gene, this process can take place upon command outside of the womb. If someone were to lose a hand in an accident, the immortality gene would activate the chromosome blueprints already in the wrist, 'trigger' the growth process, and grow a new hand. As you can see, reproduction in a society of immortals would create greater problems. It would tax the resources of the ecosystem to sustain a specific level of life. Thus, it is perfectly natural for an advanced society to exist where reproduction is unnecessary, and even looked down upon. The homosexual gene works in connection with the immortality gene to balance each other out."

"But we don't even know that there is a homosexual gene. Scientists haven't been able to find it, and they have looked for years. How do we know it even exists?" Jackson demanded.

"You're still here…What more proof do you need?"

"One of our own demonstrated the immortality gene centuries ago." one of the other "*visitors*" revealed.

"How?" a voice near the front asked. The concept of being able to live forever was catching hold of the group. Gone were the fears demonstrated just a few moments before.

"He was able to heal with a touch, restore sight to the blind, let the lame walk, raise the dead…"

"Are you talking about Jesus?" one man suggested. The shock was obvious in his voice. "He was one of you?"

"Yes. He was a rebellious member of our race. One of the few who did not follow the Plan. He stepped into your plane of existence; and revealed himself openly. Rather than working behind the scenes with suggestions, or dreams; he gathered crowds to him with demonstrations of his abilities. He would touch people who were deaf, blind, lame or disfigured. He would send a command into the genetic code via his physical contact with their bodies. Once activated, the immortality gene would do the rest. He was always given credit for the supposed miracles."

"You mean the immortality can even bring someone back from the dead?"

"If the damage to the central nervous system is not too extensive, the brain can send the signals to the immortality gene and activate the healing process."

"And Jesus?"

"He taught lies and half truths to his followers. They became confused. They misdirected the human race. We inspired various leaders to take action and shut him down."

"Crucify him?"

"Yes. That should have gotten his attention and let him know that his actions were no longer to be tolerated. Others before him accepted the warning and returned to our plane of existence. However, Jesus was stubborn. He activated the immortality gene in his body and resurrected the physical form he had assumed. For forty days after his 'resurrection' he continued to corrupt the human race with lies and falsehoods. We had no choice but to physically remove him from your world.

"Remove?"

"Yes, when he was meeting with his followers on the Mount of Olives we levitated him; and pulled him up out of sight of his followers where one of these ships imprisoned him. He has gone through retraining now. He is sorry for the damage he caused to your world. He grieves over the years of death and suffering his followers have caused. He refuses to have any further contact with them; but still they misquote him, and do things in his name that he would never condone."

"Why doesn't he come and explain it to them?"

"He has tried; but each time he tries to manifest in your world and correct his mistakes; they refuse to listen because the things he is teaching are not the things they wrote down centuries ago. They reject him and the truth over and over. Their minds are clouded."

"Just one more question..." Jackson trailed off. The extradimensional nodded for him to continue. "When is 'Wormwood' coming?"

Those at the conference table stared with blank expressions. It was obvious that Colonel Jackson had touched on a topic none of them had heard of before. However, the looks the "guests" gave each other, and exchanged with the President told everyone Jackson had hit a nerve...a big nerve.

"Wormwood will be here in about three years." the "guest" replied.

"And what have we been doing to get ready for it?" Jackson pressed. The "guests" motioned for the President to fill in the others.

"We first spotted Wormwood several years ago. It was called to our attention by our 'guests' here. Our own scientists did the calculation, and they confirmed that it will strike the Earth." The sudden comments and whispers caused the President to stop. He thought for a moment; and backtracked. "Wormwood is the name of an asteroid that has never been recorded previously. We do not know where it came from, but its course brought it from outside the orbit of Pluto. We know that it is going to hit. We know it will do a great deal of damage. We have several scenarios in place trying to find a way to knock it off course, break it up, or destroy it; however, we have to consider the possibility that all plans and efforts may prove to be ineffective. We have been in conference with world leaders. They have all been made aware of this impending disaster by other *'guests'* who are advising them. In fact, it was this warning of the approaching asteroid that brought an end to our cold war, turned Russia toward democracy, and led both our countries to stop stockpiling weapons of mass destruction, and start working together."

"Who came up with the name *'Wormwood'*?" someone asked from the other side of the room.

"When we first saw the asteroid, no one knew what to call it. Normally it's named for the one who discovered it. In this case, that would be our *'guests;'* but they declined the honor in order to remain anonymous. As we started putting together our defense plans, someone noted that the mountains of the world would soon look like wormwood because of all the tunnels and chambers. We then called our efforts *'Project Wormwood.'* Once the project had a name, everyone started referring to the asteroid by the same title.

"I am not sure where the security on Project Wormwood broke down, and how you learned about this asteroid, but we have been preparing for years without calling any attention to it. Hell's Penthouse, its only one of hundreds of tunnels and complexes we have dug out and built in our deepest mountain ranges. Those along the eastern coast, those in the Rockies. Other countries have been working on similar projects. We have been storing provisions to help us through the disaster. We have been copying technology, history and all other knowledge known to man so it will not be lost. We have been conducting testing in schools and colleges to earmark those we want to bring into the shelters. Every country in the world has been preparing. Given the long-range warning provided by our 'guests' we believe that even if the worst scenario happens, most of us will survive.

"As you can understand, this information has the greatest secrecy, and is classified for only those directly involved with the project. It must not go beyond this room. If information is released prematurely, the upheaval and panic can undo years of preparation. I am calling upon you to keep this among yourselves. You will be briefed further when we need the military to become involved."

All those in the room nodded their agreement even though their faces were drained of blood and pale from the shock of what they had just heard. Only Colonel Jackson's face showed any semblance of what Jim might call a smile.

CHAPTER FIVE

The Empty Home

Little was said on the return flight to the base. Jim navigated the two-seater fighter jet through opened skies. In truth, the skies had little traffic other than military. The fear of a recurrence of the Rapture Syndrome caused all civilian air traffic to be grounded until the FAA cleared flights once more. The ETs' ships were scattered throughout the country; and this made flying large aircraft unsafe. The attack on Israel and the subsequent retaliation raised the Home Land Security to its highest level since 9/11. America—and probably the entire world—was at a standstill.

Jim had the impression that Colonel Jackson wanted the silence. They both had a great deal to consider. With one meeting, their entire world had crashed, burned and been rebuilt. Earth had been run by extradimensionals for decades. The American people were not in charge. Homosexuality was the standard for life on planet earth. Immortality was now possible; and Christianity was exposed for a sham and its founder discredited. It was a lot to take in. The earth was no longer the center of the universe and the American way of life just ceased to be in the same breath Jesus was dismissed.

Jim wanted to discuss the information, try to put it all into perspective. It had been a lot to absorb in one sitting. He assumed that his commanding officer wanted to assimilate it in silence first before they would debrief each other. The silence was broken only long enough for Colonel Jackson to resend the order of shoot to kill anyone trying to leave the base. He advised his aide that Major Brown would give the all-clear order when the base would be opened once more.

The silence then followed them into Colonel Jackson's office. The colonel closed the blinds so no one could see inside, and locked the door. Jim was about to say something, but Jackson motioned for him to be quiet a moment longer.

It was then that Jim saw something he never thought he would see. His commanding officer reached into a desk drawer, pulled out a small item, pressed it to his lips, squeezed it tightly, lowered his head, and appeared to be praying. It only took a few seconds. When the prayer was over, Jackson laid the relic on his desk, and Jim could see that it was actually a small unassuming metal cross.

"My wife gave that to me years ago. She told me I might need it some day. She told me a great deal of things." Jackson paused for a moment; and then seemed to change the subject. "The first thing you have to remember, Jim, is that even if you are alone, you may not be alone. Don't take anything for granted."

"I don't follow you sir." Jim admitted. He found it rather odd that his commanding officer referred to him by his first name. In the ten years he had been serving under Colonel Jackson, he couldn't recall a single incident where that had been the case. Jackson had always been all business.

"Do you want to know how I found out about 'Wormwood'?" Jackson asked dropping into his chair, and motioning for Jim to be seated. Jim followed the recommendation.

"That was one of about three thousand questions I now have."

"My wife told me about it."

"But how? She wouldn't have access to classified information, would she?"

"Normally, no. She also told me about the existence of EeeDees…"

"But that's impossible!" Jim insisted.

"She also told me about the Rapture Syndrome." Jackson finally admitted.

"Sir, I've been in charge of security for a number of years. Even I couldn't pick up all the information your wife has…"

"Had." Jackson corrected him.

"Had?" came Jim's shocked response. "I don't follow."

"She gone now." the colonel admitted.

"She's left you?" Jim stammered suddenly awkward. The wife of an officer, especially as high as a colonel would never leave her husband no matter how bad things got at home. It was an unwritten law of the service. An officer did not go up in rank unless his wife was the proper military-issue.

"Not in the way you think. I haven't been home since the Rapture Syndrome struck, but I don't have to go home to know she was one of the victims."

"How sir?" Jim sought for some kind of words to offer comfort, but this was an area he wasn't good at. At the same time the fear that his own family may have been hit was creeping up his spine. He tried to fight it down and focus on just one disaster at a time.

"Did you miss everything the EeeDees were telling us?" Jackson asked with anger in his voice. Jim knew the colonel was hurting, and he was the closest target for the pain; but it surprised him how restrained his commanding officer was acting.

"I'm not following you, sir." Jim admitted.

"How well-read are you?" Jackson asked.

The question caught him completely off-guard. When the colonel realized Jim didn't have an answer, he continued. "There's a lot of literature out there. You may have been required to read some of it to get out of high school. Some of it deals with government cover-up. That's the kind I always found interesting. I was fascinated by how the government would take the obvious, give it a new definition, and then make it say exactly the opposite."

"And you think that's what happened in the meeting?" Jim asked.

"I *know* it happened in the meeting!" The anger was building. Jim wasn't sure if the anger was because of the disaster, the meeting, the colonel's wife, or some other source.

He also wasn't sure who the victim of the colonel's anger was going to be. "They took terms we always used in common, everyday conversation. They put them in a different light, gave them a new meaning, and then suddenly, the entire world is turned upside down; and you're on the underside wondering how you got there."

"I admit, colonel. I find it hard to believe that either you or I are closet gays..." Jim confessed.

"It's more than all of that. Do you know where my wife picked up that information?"

"No sir."

"Church!" Jackson declared.

"*Church?*" Jim echoed in disbelief. "But how? No one at Church would reveal government secrets."

"They weren't government secrets. They were verses from the Bible."

"The Bible? Sir, are you sure you're feeling all right?"

"I'm your superior officer, man! My mental condition is not the subject of this discussion." Jackson snapped. It was the old Jackson Jim was used to...almost. Even in his anger he seemed somehow subdued.

"My wife was always going to Church. I wouldn't call her a Jesus freak, but she was pretty serious about her religion. She never made it an issue in our marriage, but she was always talking to me about it. She was always posing questions, issues, concepts to me; and then we would debate them at dinner or breakfast. That woman had a mind like a steel trap. She could always give me a run for the money.

"She told me about a passage from the Bible just a week ago. It was from the last book in the Bible...'*Revelation*' she called it. It was supposed to be written by one of the apostles when he was stranded on an island as a kind of imprisonment. While there he claimed to have a vision, wrote about it, and early believers turned it into a book of the Bible."

"You mean someone two thousand years ago knew that this asteroid was coming?"

"Even more so, they knew the name of the asteroid."

"Wait a minute. It didn't even have a name until after the project was underway."

"Exactly. It's hard to do that kind of thing...at least on your own."

"The EeeDees?" Jim suggested.

"No. They didn't have a name for the asteroid, either. Doesn't it seem strange to you that the subject of God never came up in that meeting?"

"It was a military briefing, sir. Not a Church service. I wasn't expecting anyone to talk about God."

"Why not? We talked about Sodom and Gomorrah. We talked about Noah and the flood. We talked about the Rapture. We talked about angels. We talked about every damn religious topic but God in that meeting." Jackson's right arm swept the contents of his desk onto the floor.

"Sir? Maybe you should take some time off."

"And do what? Go home to an empty house? Go home and discover that everything my wife was telling me, warning me about for years was true? Go home and realize that this wasn't a biologic. The people who disappeared weren't genetically defective. They were Christians. Hell! They were more than just Christians. It was more than some label someone stuck on them. It was more than going to Church on Christmas and Easter. They believed! They believed what the Bible said. They believed so much that they modeled their lives after its teachings. Everyone who's left didn't believe. We're not here because we're queer. We're here because we didn't believe!" Jackson dropped his face into his hands. His frame shook for several moments with sobs, but then he composed himself.

"The only way the apostle could have known the name of the asteroid was if God had told him."

"But the EeeDees said they inspired people to write the Bible, and it all got turned around."

Jackson's fists slammed on the empty desk top. "Damn it, Jim. Listen to yourself. It wasn't twisted, turned around until that meeting we were in. Haven't you ever heard of demons?"

"I put them up there with the boogie man." Jim replied.

"Then what do you think you met today in that meeting?"

"Them? No, they couldn't be demons. Angels, maybe; but not demons."

"How can you accept one and deny the other? Demons *are* angels. They are those angels who broke away from God. They rebelled, and were driven out of Heaven. They were cast down to the earth with Satan..."

"Satan? The devil? You're telling me that you believe in the devil?"

"Open your eyes, man!" Jackson bellowed. "You can't have one without the other. My wife told me something years ago. It didn't sink in until the meeting. She told me about demons. She told me that they were fallen angels, and that they could still appear like creatures of light. They could still make themselves look beautiful, awe-inspiring. She also told me that in the last days men would give heed to the doctrine of seducing spirits...demons! If it were possible, even believers would fall for their lies! Doesn't all of this sound a little familiar or were you in a totally different meeting than I was."

Jim thought for long moments. He wasn't sure what he believed. "I'm not sure."

"Then think about this. EeeDees are from another dimension. They have always been here. They have been able to influence everything we do in one way or another. Doesn't that sound like angels? We all have our guardian angels. Now if they are angels, then documents that tell us about angels are probably true. That does follow doesn't it?"

"Yes, I suppose so, sir." Jim stammered.

"It also makes sense that the earliest writings about angels would also be true since it was our first knowledge of them. It was put together before anyone else had the chance to twist things, add to it, corrupt it with science and pre-conceived ideas about angels not being real. It would be an innocent account of angels."

"Yes sir." Jim admitted. He wasn't sure where the conversation was going, but felt it best to follow along.

"The earliest account of angels is the Bible."

"But aren't there other works older than the Bible?" Jim offered. He tried to recall what some of his instructors had said in a philosophy class he had taken many years ago.

"Maybe older than the Gospels, but I'm talking about the oldest books of the Bible...Job, Genesis. These were the oldest books we have. They're older than any other religious books around. And what do they tell us?"

"I've never read them for myself, sir." Jim confessed. He wasn't sure why that made him suddenly embarrassed.

"They tell us about Satan coming before God. He made a deal with God to torment Job. The oldest book ever written is about God and Satan. Genesis has Satan in the Garden of Eden. But Satan has to get God's permission. He isn't as strong as God. He's a subject of God. Keep reading. My wife pointed all of this out to me years ago. Satan leads the demons. These are angels who swore allegiance to him and were part of a rebellion in Heaven. They were driven out, cast out of Heaven. They came to earth, and now they are trying to destroy everything God does here. So if EeeDees are angels, are they heavenly angels or fallen angels?"

"I would imagine Heavenly. You can't look that majestic and be evil..."

"They can! The Bible warns us about them. It tells us they can pose as messengers from God. Don't let the looks deceive you. Listen to the message they give us!"

"Their message was..."

"Their message was," and here Colonel Jackson had a string of expletives to describe exactly what he thought of the EeeDees' message. "Their message was that the Bible was a pack of lies. Have you ever heard about any angel in the Bible claiming the Bible was a pack of lies?"

"No sir."

"So if they were heavenly angels, why didn't they tell us about God? They are God's messengers. Every passage my wife showed me for the thirty-five years we were married always had the angels talking about God. These never even acknowledged His existence. In fact, they implied there was no God by the way they presented themselves. It's all part of some dimensional structure. We're from the lower dimension; they're from the higher dimension. They're above us, but nobody ever mentioned if anyone was above them."

The office fell silent for long moments. Jim was confused by what he had heard. He was also uncomfortable with this side of his commanding officer. This had been a hard-bitten military career man. He had ordered his own soldiers' death before they took that flight to Hell's Penthouse. He had even been there when some of them were killed. He was asking permission to nuke the entire base and kill all four thousand, two hundred and thirty-seven troops. The blast would also spread to the housing area, and would have kill thousands of other women and children. No, this was not the same man he had served under before the meeting. However, Jim did have to admit that some of the points his superior officer raised had made sense.

Jim then thought of his own family, and wanted to run home to make sure they were okay; but, before he could do that, he had to discharge his own orders.

"Sir, shouldn't we be collecting the material we were ordered to secure and destroy?"

"Be careful what you ask for, Jim. You just might get it..." Jackson paused for long moments. He rose from his desk, stopped in front of an outside window, and pried the blinds apart to look out. "Do what you think you need to, Jim, but keep one thing in mind: remember that if I'm right...Hell, if the EeeDees are right, they can always be around us even when we can't see them. You may not be alone, even if you are alone. However, if I'm right, then that little piece of metal," Here Jackson pointed at the cross still on his desk. "That, and silent prayers will keep them away. What I've said today, in this room, would be ground for court marshalling. If the EeeDees heard what I said, I would be removed from command and never be heard from again."

"I won't breathe a word of this to anyone else, sir." Jim offered.

"I'm not worried about you, son. The point I'm trying to make is that I'm still here. No one has broken down the door to arrest me. Think about this. EeeDees can be anywhere, just like guardian angels. They can sit in on any conversation. They can be in the room. Hell, the entire room can be filled. *'How many angels can dance on the head of a pin?'*" Jackson quoted the old riddle. "If I had just briefed a room-full of officers, given them information we didn't want out, and I could follow each one of them around to make sure they didn't tell anyone; don't you think I would have done it? You're a security man. Every one of us in that room is now a security risk. I now give you the unlimited resources to bug every conversation they ever have, to tap every phone conversation; to bug their offices, homes, bedrooms. You can even put *'shadows'* on them twenty-four hours a day. You can re-program all of our spy satellites to record their every move. You can have Echelon scan for each of their conversations. As a security officer, wouldn't you want to do that?"

"Yes sir, as a security officer, I would...if I had the personnel, the resources, and the authority."

"These EeeDees control the President! They don't need authorization. The EeeDees ordered Major Barton executed during the meeting, not the President. Secret Service agents obeyed the EeeDees, not the President. They have the power. They have the resources. They have the funding, the personnel, and the authorization to do it. If you would do it, wouldn't they?"

Jim thought for long moments. He raised several possibilities in his mind, but they all failed to counter the colonel's point. "Yes sir, they would."

"Then why am I still in command? Barton was a good friend. He simply spoke out of turn. He voiced what we were all feeling; and he was shot without a moment's hesitation. I've said more things in this meeting than he did. I attacked their entire concept. If I had done that in the meeting, do you think I would be alive when it ended?"

"No sir, I don't" Jim admitted.

"So we have left the meeting. We've come back here. You've sent your companions along to make sure we don't do anything we aren't supposed to do...such as ask these kinds of questions, make these kinds of accusations. Your agents are watching the entire thing. It's been ten minutes since I finished making my treasonous remarks. It's been half an hour since I started. You don't think they can drop the dime on me and have someone here by now taking me out... Probably taking you out as well?"

The thought that he might be killed because of what the colonel had done struck Jim hard. He was angry, but there was nothing he could do about it. "What's your point, sir?"

"The point is this. Before this meeting started, I did what I saw my wife do hundreds of times. I grabbed that cross she gave me years ago. I had all but forgotten about it. She made me promise to keep it here. I threw it in the desk drawer years ago and forgot about it...until I came back in. I grabbed that cross, and I prayed. I prayed for God to forgive me for what I'd done, and for God to protect me. I prayed for God to bind the demons, and to cast them out so they couldn't be here. Then I began to talk about this."

"And you think God kept the EeeDees from being here while you vented about this?" Jim asked.

"To quote one of the EeeDees, 'you're still here aren't you?'" Jackson paused to let the thought sink in. "I'm not asking you to believe...Well, maybe I am. But I do want you to think about it. I made the wrong choice, and I'm still here. It's going to get really ugly before it's all over with. I don't want to make any more wrong decisions. Think about what I've said. You've got a sharp mind. You do investigations. You have to test the credibility of witnesses, weight evidence. Use those skills now before you make any more wrong decisions."

"With the colonel's permission, I'd like to complete our assignment and go home to check on my family. I can't do that until we've completed our orders." Jim wasn't sure what he thought; he just wanted to find out about Kelly and the kids. Everything Jackson had said made sense in some twisted sort of way. If Jackson was right about all of this, Jim feared for his family. His wife had been fanatical about Church. She always took the kids, too. It had been a point of contention between them. He needed to know. He'd call first, but if they didn't answer; he would have to go home. He couldn't do that until all material concerning the Rapture was collected and destroyed. He couldn't do that until he was out of this meeting. He would take everything one step at a time.

Jackson nodded permission as he dropped back into his chair, picked up the cross, gripped it with both hands, elbows on the desk. He dropped his head onto his hands as he added, "Close the door on your way out."

Jim had collected what personnel were left. Most had been shaken by having to fire on their own troops. The latest count had been two hundred and seventy-three killed trying to leave the base. Another five or six hundred were wounded and sent to the base hospital for treatment. Two hundred and fifteen had been struck by the Rapture Syndrome. Jim relayed orders to all of his men. They began the systematic sweep of the entire camp. Several trucks were sent along to help collect the material and destroy it.

As Jim sat in his office, Corporal Jenson knocked softly on the door frame. Jim looked up, and motioned for his aide to come in.

"I just wanted to turn this in before I got in trouble. I haven't read it or anything." As he spoke, the corporal handed Jim a battered Bible.

"What's this all about?" Jim asked taking the Bible from his aide.

"You gave the order to turn in everything about the Rapture. I wanted to get rid of this before I got in trouble."

"This talks about the Rapture?" Jim asked.

"Well, I don't know sir. Perkins, he's the 'Holy Joe' in the barracks, gave it to me. He was always talking about the Rapture and trying to get me to read about it in here."

"Where is Perkins?" Jim asked.

"I haven't confirmed it yet, sir. However, someone said he has hit with the biologic. I figured he wouldn't want this back. I sure don't want it; so I figured I'd pass it on to you to have it destroyed."

"Thank you corporal. That'll be all..." Jim caught himself and added, "Oh corporal, any word on my wife?"

"No sir" Jenson replied, and then quickly added, "But the phones are really screwed up right now. Most people can't get through."

"Corporal, pass the order along. Since the biologic is not confined to the base, and we pose no threat of further spreading it, once all the material has been collected and destroyed; those not on duty can leave the base to check on family and friends. However, I want this done orderly! Officers will have to reassign soldiers to replace those dead or wounded. I won't have this base jeopardized at this point. If their commanding officers issue passes, they can leave; but anyone who doesn't come back will be considered AWOL, arrested, and charged with desertion. Given the condition of the nation, that may be grounds to be shot. I'll be at home."

Major Brown scooped up the Bible, dropped it into his briefcase unseen by Jenson. He snatched his cap and darted out of the office.

When Jim pulled into the officers' housing section, he could see from down the road that his house was dark, even though it was already late enough to use headlights to drive. He fought down the fear; telling himself that Kelly must have taken the kids and gone to neighbors or something.

The front door was unlocked, another bad sign. Kelly never left the door unlocked when she left. He kept telling her that this was a military base. It was too secure to need to lock your door; but she always did any way. It must have been the panic, he thought. He pushed the door opened, turned on the light, and was confronted by four piles of clothes scattered around the room as if they had all been sitting in the living room when the Rapture Syndrome hit. Jim dropped to his knees, scooped up the clothes. His wife's clothing still carried the hint of her perfume. God how he loved the way she smelled. He buried his face in the clothing, and did something he thought he had forgotten how to do...he cried, and cried, and cried until he cried himself asleep.

CHAPTER SIX

Reunions

Amir stood in the crowed marketplace of Jerusalem. The open stalls were covered in wares from clothing, to fruit and trinkets that tourists would appreciate. There were few tourists these days. For years the tour guides had kept the tourists from the Arab vendors and stores out of fear the money from the sales would go to fund terrorism. Many of the store owners were driven into poverty. Several had closed up and moved to other countries where they could sell their wares. It did not matter that they had no ties to terrorism, the religion made them suspect; and so they went hungry.

Now the Israeli and Christian vendors were facing the same specter. Few came to Israel. It was not just due to the invasion by Russia. There were still many dead bodies littering the landscape outside the city, and throughout the country. Israel had used their army and drafted retired soldiers to search for all the bodies before it polluted the land. One team would travel by foot and find the various bodies. They would plant a small flag near the body. Those in hazmat suits would come later and begin the process of burying the dead. With so many bodies, the Jews could not offer anything better than mass graves. The men and women in the hazmat suits would try to recover dog tags or some kind of identification and map where the bodies were being buried. These would be shipped back to their countries to be given to their families and relatives, but they could not do much more than this.

No one knew why the bodies dropped in their tracks. It might have been some kind of radiation, but Israel did not use any nukes. It might have been a biologic. Many were not accepting that this was the hand of G-d. Despite the length of time these bodies were left lying in the fields, they did not stink, and there were no diseases coming from the bodies. G-d was watching over them once more.

Amir rubbed his hand over the short stiff bristles of his hair. It felt good to his scalp, but that was not why he was doing it. A shopper off to his left performed the same motion. He waited and the person who had mirrored his action slowly moved toward the Lion's Gate. When the figure was passing St Ann's Amir began to move slowly in the same direction. Once outside the gate, he looked for the other person who had been in the crowd. The Lion's Gate still bore the pot marks from bullets created when Israel regained the city in the Six Day War of 1967. Moshe Dayan, Yitzhak Rabin and Uzi Narkiss made the gate famous as they strode through on foot claiming the city.

Amir had not even been born on that historic day, but his father had placed Shmuel and himself on his knee and pointed to the picture. He had been one of the troops that reclaimed the city that day. They had not intended to take the city, but G-d was with them. His father's face would light up as he spoke of that glorious day. It made possible the Passover declaration: "Next year in Jerusalem!"

Someone bumped his shoulder. He cursed himself for letting himself get distracted. In his line of work, it was a fatal flaw. He spun quickly; reaching for the gun nestled in the small of his back under his jacket. The figure was quick to block his arm so he could not retrieve his weapon.

"You were careless Amir." The familiar voice reprimanded. The figure pulled off his head covering and it was like looking into a mirror.

"Shmuel!" Amir cried out; and then caught himself.

"Where have you been?" Shmuel asked.

"In the desert, near Ein Ghedi."

"What would bring you to that forsaken place? You got a thing for goats and conies, now?"

"I've seen them." Amir's face lit up as he spoke.

"Seen who?"

"Elijah and Enoch."

"You're crazy!"

"Remember the last mission?

"Rescuing artifacts from the grinder. Why?"

"The Jeremiah Scroll. The Malachi Scroll."

"I remember. You couldn't shut up about them. All of Mossad worried you would start babbling to your co-workers. We were afraid you would blow the cover. You were becoming a risk to the operation."

"I wasn't *that* bad…" The look Shmuel gave him challenged his memory of the events.

"Look, there was that fragment. '*I will send you Elijah…*'" he quoted.

"You're not believing that crazy Yenta, are you. She says he came to their Passover. He drank the cup. He then disappeared into the night. It was probably some homeless drunk looking for a free meal—or glass of wine. Once he got it; he was gone."

"I've tracked him down."

"You found the wino?" Shmuel mocked.

"Shmuel, I'm serious. He's been out in Ein Ghedi. He and Enoch. They were at the Mosque in Egypt. They called down fire from Heaven."

"They set off nukes in the mosque. They're terrorists. Stay away from them. Mossad does not work with terrorists, PERIOD!"

"They're the witnesses promised by the prophets."

"Amir, look at you. This isn't Shul. We aren't in synagogue. We're in the real world. Get hold of yourself. You're talking like a zealot, a fanatic. You were always so solid in your beliefs. I could trust you to have my back."

"I do have your back. I've found them. I want you to meet them, too."

"Amir, don't. Don't make me report this. You're already on suspension. Don't make it permanent."

"Shmuel, three days. That's all I ask. Come with me for three days. You can tell your boss. Make it a fact-finding mission. Put together a report on them. Mossad needs to know more about them. They're going to be moving outside of the country. Humor me."

Shmuel pulled out his Blackberry. He punched in the access code, and turned away from his brother as he spoke in soft tones. His eyes were darting around him taking in the entire scene. He needed to know who was watching them. He needed to see if anyone was using tech to track or monitor. He caught movement off to his left. Someone was lifting a cell phone up even as Shmuel made contact. He pressed a button and the signal scrambled. He used the reflection in a car window to see if the man continued speaking or cut the connection. The man continued to speak and a moment later a woman joined him. He had been making contact with his wife so she could find him in the crowd.

"Paranoid." Amir whispered. He had watched the entire scene play out and knew what was going through his brother's mind.

"Paranoid, maybe. Alive, definitely." Shmuel pointed out. Once he felt secure that no one had thought them any more than two brothers meeting outside the gate. He finished his discussion and ended with "Shalom" and then shut down the tech.

"Three days. And only three days. And I am there not as your brother. I am there as a representative from Mossad. I'm making a full report, and if I deem them a threat, I'm taking them out."

Amir studied his brother's face. Gone was the joy he had shown just a few moments ago at their meeting. He was all business now. That was ok. He had gone in as a skeptic, too; but they had convinced him. They would convince his brother as well. He smacked his brother on the left shoulder and both pulled their head gear back over their hair and covered their faces as Amir led Shmuel in the direction toward the south and Ein Ghedi.

***

Ted Brown passed the six-foot poster of the ET standing between members of two races. The ET rested a protective hand on a shoulder of each minority type. The word "Unity" flashed and changed colors as he passed as part of the holographic printing effect. Several other similar posters were spread out across the airport. Each encouraging people to *Embrace the Change*, and *Prepare for the Golden Age*.

"It's amazing. ET Pelton was at the opening. He was just amazing. We had quite a crowd due to him being there" the news monitor running the cable channel blared in the background. The celebrity was filmed leaning against the impressive figure, both her hands on ET Pelton's shoulder, her left leg bent and her head on his chest.

"The ETs have made their presence known not just in the political circles, but they have been appearing at charity functions, movie openings, art centers and dinners for fundraisers…"

The New Alliance officer moved away from the monitors; and found a vantage point to spot his brother when he came down the escalators from the secured gated area. Ted adjusted the major insignias on his stiff upright collar. It still took some getting used to. Several travelers stole glances at the new uniform. The black material looked more impressive than the old green or brown uniforms he had been used to. Knowing that he was on display as one of the New Alliance representatives made Ted stand a little straighter, create a more imposing figure. The news telecasts and papers had carried pictures of the new uniforms along with the announcement of a new European Alliance which had previously been the European Union. The Alliance had been forced to make drastic changes to deal with the current political, economic and military demands. The ink on the new treaties was barely dry, and this was the first day when these uniforms were worn. He knew people would be looking, and he determined to put on a good show.

"Ted!" came a cry from across the terminal. The major for the New Alliance resigned himself to having to break the image he had tried so hard to create in order to respond to his brother.

"Jim! Over here!" He hated to wave his arm like some tourist; but it was the only way to get his brother's attention among all the travelers. Ever since the attack on Israel, and the disaster in Egypt, Iran, Russia and other countries all the terminals were flooded with people from various countries either relocating, or afraid to go home.

His brother let a long whistle escape. It was loud enough to attract further attention, and to further destroy his carefully-groomed image. "Boy! Aren't you the poster boy?"

"Good to see you, too." Ted replied extending a hand to shake and then completing it with a manly embrace for his younger brother. "How was the flight?"

"About as well as can be expected. Sardine airlines everywhere you go. I thought there were regulations against over-crowding planes."

"Normally yes, but these times are anything but normal. Everyone who's afraid is on the move, and everyone's afraid. Airlines are taking chances, cutting their safety margins. If they can't move this many people faster; then the terminals will be pure chaos."

"Worse than this?" Jim asked looking around him at the pushing, shoving, demanding mob.

"This is one of the better days. The New Alliance is making its presence known everywhere. The new treaties and agreements are supposed to calm the people." Ted observed.

"They don't seem too impressed if you ask me." his brother noted as a small crowd nearly stumbled against them and moved on without a word or back-wards glance."

"Let's get out of here. I have to get you back to the base. Why the civvies?" he asked, rubbing the cloth of Jim's wind breaker between his thumb and index finger."

"You know how people feel about the U. S. military. We're the ones who brought the Rapture Syndrome back. Unless you're on duty, you don't dare fly the colors. And if you do, you keep your gun loaded, and the safety off."

"That bad?"

"Yeah. Six guys in my unit were beaten to death in separate incidents. The town people recognized them as being from the base, even out of uniform. By the time my team got there, there wasn't much left to save or bury. Just a minute. I need to get my luggage." Jim broke away from his brother, and forced his way up to the luggage drop. As soon as he hefted his bag off the carousel, screams broke out around him; people fled or fell to the floor as seven men surrounded the U.S. military officer with weapons trained on him. Slowly he released the bag, and let it drop to the floor.

"What's going on here?" Ted demanded, barging his way to the center of the commotion. The senior agent saw the uniform, and the insignias.

"Sorry sir. This is a civilian matter. We don't need the military here. We've got a terrorist here." The agent never took his gaze, or his aim, off of Jim the entire time he spoke.

"Seeing how this is my newest aid, fresh from the American Union, I believe this is a military matter, and falls under my jurisdiction." Ted pressed.

"He's one of yours?" the agent asked, daring to look Ted in the face.

"He's just been assigned here from the AU. What's this about being a terrorist?"

"Our security detected two hand guns in his bag." the agent replied.

"They're military issue, declared and unloaded per regulations." Jim announced.

"Yes they are, but we didn't know you were military." the agent admitted.

"If the world hates you for the Rapture Syndrome, would you go around announcing who your employer was?" Jim retorted. The agent nodded to his team, and they lowered their weapons. As they moved past, one of the security men slammed hard into Jim from the back, nearly knocking him off his feet. Ted had the man in an instant, slammed him to the ground, and had his weapon out, barrel pressed hard against the man's temple.

"Sir!" the team leader was begging. "It was an accident."

"You know the law; assault on any member of the New Alliance is a capital offense. Your man knew he was one of us, and he assaulted him anyway."

"It was an accident!" the leader pleaded.

"Ted. Let it go. No harm done." Jim suggested.

"The law is the law. He needs to be taught a lesson." Ted spat back.

"How can he learn if he's dead?" Jim inquired. The tension mounted; finally Ted released his pressure against the man's head with his gun. As the man started to get up, Ted's foot slammed his head back to the ground and pinned it there. While holding the man on the floor, Ted ground his boot into the man's ear, and turned to the security team leader ignoring the cries of pain.

"This is going on your record." his hand pulled up his communicator and flashed the leader's picture. "Anything...I repeat, any thing like this ever happens again, from any one of your men, and *you* go up against the wall and catch the bullet. I want this man to apologize, and to be disciplined. As security, he should know better. He had better act better!"

After the incident was over, and the security men had faded into the background. Jim retrieved his bag. "Rather harsh response, wasn't it?"

"You should have let me blow him away. The New Alliance wants to make it clear that we're hard on criminals."

"But that wasn't a criminal. That was some guy angry at the United States for messing up the entire world."

"You might be in the military still, and on special assignment here; but you are not from the United States. Break all alliances and drop all references to that government. That country is gone—forever. Don't ever forget that. If you do, you'll be dead. The freedoms and rights you had on the other side of the Atlantic were left on the other side of the Atlantic."

"This is all a backlash from the Israeli thing?" Jim asked as they walked out of the terminal. Where once before they had to push their way through the crowds, people were now giving them a wide berth, and unobstructed passage.

"Israel and the United States. Two of the most hated countries in the world. Israel refuses to work with the ETs to bring about a Golden Age for the rest of us. The U.S. brings back the Rapture Syndrome. The U.S. was the only ally Israel had until the ETs restructured the world governments. Anyone who clings to the good old USA is automatically associated with Israel—the terrorist nation."

"That's the feeling over here?"

"You figure it out. The world is sick of terrorism. You think of 9/11; but over here we had the London trains, the planes, the Spanish and the French incidents. Germany lost nearly six thousand, and the number of schools and buses attacked; and children killed are frightening. You've got one incident. We've had hundreds. We live with terrorism every day; so people are sick of dealing with it. The ETs are going to shut it down world-wide. Enough is enough. Terrorists have been using their religion and their mosques to collect money to fund terrorism, to recruit and convert new radicals, and to hide their weapons all under the guise of religious freedom. Hell, they even had nukes in Egypt."

"So why is everyone mad at Israel for what the terrorists did?" the younger brother countered.

"The terrorists had the nukes. But it was the Israelis who set them off. *THAT* makes a big difference."

"It wasn't the Israelis. It was two men who looked Israeli. They acted on their own."

"One fits the description of the guy who stormed into a Jewish family's Passover meal over a year ago. The family members confirm his identity. He and the other Israeli were on CNN video. We have their pictures. Somehow they did not die when the nukes went off. They've popped up in Russia, London,

Spain, New York, Los Angeles, Mexico City. They're popping
up all over the world and threatening everyone. They must be
clones because you can't travel around the world that fast. That
sounds like a Mossad operation to everyone—even me."

"They're not threatening. They're predicting. They're
predicting droughts all over the world."

"And what about that new weapon they have? The one
that generates balls of fire falling from the sky? That's not a
threat?" Jim did not have a response for that, and so he chose
to hold his peace.

"The Israelis set the nukes off and took out the entire
country...the entire country Jim! Those who weren't part of
the fireball, and the shock wave, are dying by the thousands
from radiation burns and infections. The world has sealed
off the entire country, and is letting them all die. It'll be forty
years before anyone can live there again. Forty years. Even
the animals are keeping clear of the area. It's too big a disaster
for what's left of our world's resources to handle. There's a lot
of Egyptians who were out of the country and survived; and
who don't like us leaving their countrymen to die. There's a
lot of Arabs who are siding with them."

Jim dropped his bag into the trunk of the car. Ted unzipped
the bag, pulled out Jim's handgun, slammed in the ammo
clip, and passed it to his brother.

"Don't leave home without it!" he warned. Jim tucked it
under his belt in the small of his back and pulled the wind
breaker over it. He climbed into the passenger side of the
back seat of the car. Ted slipped in on the other side, and
motioned for the driver to pull out into traffic.

"And Israel gets blamed for all of this?" Jim asked.

"They've always been a problem. The old United Nations
voted on Palestinian autonomy, gave them their own county.
Made them a member. The world tried to turn Jerusalem into
an international city like our Vatican. They refused. The world
let them rebuild their Temple to get them to comply with the
mandate. They ignored the agreement. The first thing they did
was to start those damned sacrifices. Animals everywhere,

blood everywhere. Animal rights groups protesting. It made the situation over there an even bigger powder keg. The Vatican stepped in with the *Rapture Syndrome* and the *Israeli Incident* and shut down the sacrifices, appeased the animal rights people. As one religious group to another they agreed to stop the daily stuff; but they made it clear come the Holy Day Festivals, and it will be back for that. The Israelis refuse to work with us. They have blood on their hands and they keep getting blood on their hands."

"I was surprised when the Israelis let the daily sacrifices be shut down."

"They normally wouldn't; but they all turned into Jesus Freaks on us."

"I thought that was just a rumor. They hated Jesus."

"Right at the time of the *Israeli Incident* it's like the entire country woke up and suddenly realized that Jesus was the Messiah Moses had predicted. It wasn't like any other religious movement. It didn't pop up in one place and spread to the rest of the country. It was as if the entire country all came to the realization at the same time."

"I thought our two world-hopping Israeli suspects started all of that. Didn't they declare Jesus was the Messiah everyone had been waiting for several times when they were in Israel and in the Temple area?"

"That has been one of their messages; but people have been trying to tell the Jews that for centuries. Why now? What's different?" Ted really didn't want an answer. He did not pause long enough for Jim to reply. "For the first few weeks after the *Israeli Incident* people were afraid to reveal what had happened. They all kept silent for fear of being disowned. Then as they started to open up; seems like everyone had the same revelation at the same time."

"So what's happening over there now. America...the American Union pretty much lost all contact with a lot of the rest of the world after the *Rapture Syndrome* struck."

"Israel should have been hit pretty hard by the quake...7.9. And a lot of buildings should have been damaged or toppled; but it was like there was no quake as far as Israel was concerned. That quake was centered in Israel, but it hit other areas around the world and did a lot of damage. Tsunamis ranging from three to eight feet tall slammed into shore towns washing everything and everyone away. The Israelis are claiming that God came to their rescue. At least that's the official position out of Tel Aviv. We don't believe in God, so we don't believe their explanation. You can't blame what you don't believe in; so people turn their anger toward Israel."

"But why?" almost letting slip what he knew from Hell's Penthouse; but then catching himself because his own brother had to be kept in the dark.

"Because it's there. The same reason so many radicals hated Israel. They hated it because it survived. It didn't roll over and die. And then to have the Dome of the Rock turned into melted slag…It's one of the holiest sites of Islam. You can't rebuild that."

"The Russian invasion did a lot of damage."

"But people don't think of it as a Russian Invasion. The Press are calling it the '*Israeli Event*.' "

"So people associate the fall out with Israel and not Russian or Iran."

"It's the Samson Complex. We have to deal with that over here."

"Samson Complex?" Jim asked. It was a new term to him.

"Yeah. Israel used to have what they called the Masada Complex…"

"That's another new term for me." Jim admitted.

"Masada, if you didn't read the history books, you should have at least seen the movie on television. Back when the Roman Empire was conquering the world, a small plateau in southern Israel held out. Zealots were hold up there, and Rome spent years trying to get them out. Had to build a ramp to get to the top and break in. When they got into Masada, everyone was dead. They had chosen to die rather than to go into slavery. That's the Masada Complex. '*I'll die before I let someone conquer me again!'* A lot of people had no problem with that. It's like the old *'You'll never take me alive!'* Bang!" Ted imitated pulling the trigger on a pistol. "Not a problem."

"Seems pretty pathetic. Instead of fighting back, they kill themselves. Saves the invaders a lot of work."

"Well, they wised up to that problem. They then turned to Samson. When he died, he killed everyone in the temple with him. He took his enemies with him. That's the Samson Complex. If Israel is going out, they're going to take out their enemies...all of them."

"And so people think the Israelis set off the nukes in Egypt because they thought they were going to be taken out by Russia?"

"Back in the seventies, when the Three Day War was on, Russia almost invaded then. However the US got involved. Israel told the President that if Russia got involved, they were going to nuke the Arab oil fields. They would send the world back to the pre-Industrial Revolution unless we kept Russia out. Everyone in the Middle East knows the story...They also have very long memories."

"But the invaders were wiped out. Israel is still burying all the bodies. Sulfur bombs lit up the Iranian oil fields. How is Israel getting the heat for that?" Jim demanded.

"We've long suspected Israel had nukes. We even suspected they had neutrino-bombs capable of wiping out all life with intense radiation, but leaving the buildings and technology intact."

"But Israel still insists they didn't do it."

"But over here people know that Israel is dirty. They're blaming God for what they did. Bull! They've long been considered in the same light as the Taliban, Al Qaeda, and Hamas. They're as much a terrorist group as the ones they fight. It's government-sponsored terrorism just like Libya was. We're just caught in the middle here. They're a problem, and they need to be taken care of. It's about time. The new American Union has pulled back its support of Israel. That little nation is pretty much on its own in this great big world.

It's not a safe place for them. They had better learn to play nice or it could get worse."

"What was the final count of losses?"

"Can't tell. They're still finding bodies all over the place there. Estimates are about five out of six dropped in their tracks. That's based on those who made it back to their headquarters. Russia had all that new steel-wood hardware and tanks. Made it easier to travel over the mountains and desert areas. They lost so many troops; no one could bring them back. Israel's got one full time team looking for bodies. Another full time team doing the burying."

"Hasn't Russia asked for their weapons back? That plywood construction for steel-wood is pretty expensive."

"Of course it's expensive, but it's lighter than metal, stronger than steel, and it cuts down on gas consumption. Oh yeah. Russia wanted their weapons back."

"So what happened?"

"Israel told them they were the spoils of war. Then to add insult to injury, instead of using the weapons, their people are cutting them up for fire wood."

"Will that stuff even burn?"

"That's the beauty of steel-wood. It cuts like regular wood, but you can't punch through it with bullets or shells. Put a hot enough fire under it and it burns long and slow. The glues used to hold the layers together make it burn pretty hot, too. Some experts estimate that there's enough firewood in the abandoned tanks and trucks to keep Israel in firewood for at least seven years.

"They had a perfect opportunity to try and undo some of the damage from the *Israeli Incident*, and what to they do? They spit in Russia's face. They kept blockades on Gaza for years leaving them struggling to feed their own. Their raids into Syrian, Lebanon, and Gaza show a complete disregard for international law. Their drone missile attacks blowing up homes they claim held terrorists. Right now most of the New Alliance thinks Israel is more of a terrorist state that Libya or Saddam ever were. '*Terrorist*' and '*Israel*' are dirty words over here; probably generating as much hostility as 'American' does these days. All the countries are on highest alert. If you have been touching down in an airport closer to the Middle East, they wouldn't have arrested you for having the guns. They would have shot you as soon as you touched the bag."

"I'll remember that when I travel in the future."

"We need to get you into uniform as soon as possible. The New Alliance has the fire power to keep everyone in place. Once you're wearing one of these..." here Ted tugged at the coat lapel of his uniform. "...Once you have one of these on, people keep out of your way, and no one gives you any problems."

"Some place we can get something to eat around here? The airplane food was terrible, what there was of it. I also need to exchange some money."

"Won't find anyone to exchange your money around here. New Alliance has everyone using one of these." Ted handed Jim a credit card. His picture was already impressed in hologram on it along with his signature and thumb print.

"These babies have several EMP-shielded micro-computer chips embedded in them. It's better than the magnetic strips we used to use. Several countries were really in a bind when the electro-magnetic pulses from the nukes in Egypt hit their cities. None of the credit cards, ID cards, or computer records would work. One pulse; and everything was erased. These were in the works, and after the bombing of Egypt, we sped up production. This thing not only accesses your bank accounts, it has you whole medical history on it, military records, personnel records, driving records, dental records. Hell, if there's a record on you, it's copied into here."

"So if I lose this, someone will know everything about me?" Jim held the card up to the sunlight coming through the window. The card actually looked like clear plastic when held one way, was a hologram picture of him and his signature when light struck it from a different angle, and when he held it another way, he could see an LED screen with small contact buttons to input information along the bottom edge under the LED display.

"That's the beauty of it. Each time you use it, you have to place your thumb over this box. It scans your thumb print to make sure you're the one using it."

"And if someone kills me, steals my card, cuts off my thumb to use it...?" Jim asked.

"You've got a sick mind." Ted declared.

"I don't have a sick mind. I'm in security. If someone can steal something, they will."

"Only a sick mind would think of something like that." Ted repeated.

"So what do they do?"

"Well, just so happens that the people who dreamed this thing up also had sick minds. Each time you use the card, you have to scan your thumb print before the transaction. After the transaction, you have to sign the plate. It scans the signature. It can't be an exact copy of any previous signature you've done so someone can't just use an old one. It has to be a new signature, and it has to meet certain criteria of the handwriting program in the data base. If it doesn't match; then the card doesn't work."

"How many tries do I get before the card shuts down?"

"Two, so don't make too many mistakes." Ted cautioned.

"And if I get hurt, have to sign with my other hand, then what?"

"Then you go hungry. Like I said, the minds that designed this were sick, not sympathetic. It's designed to keep everyone out who isn't allowed in. If you have a problem; it keeps you out, too."

"You said people were allowed in. Does that mean someone other than me can get in here?"

"They can't take money out or make purchases, but the government has access to everyone's card. They can pull up any information stored in there. That's why you have to keep this with you at all times. If someone needs to check you out, they scan the card. The card tells them what they need to know. If you're clear, then you move on. If not, you're in jail. Since you're military, there's a GPS tracking system in there. We can find you no matter where you are."

"Hello Big Brother!" Jim said to the card as he slipped it into his shirt pocket.

"You used to say that to me." Ted chided.

"You were never able to keep this close an eye on me, even in boot camp."

"How many times did I save your keester?"

"How many times was I in trouble?"

"Oh!' Ted added. "I heard Jackson retired. I thought that guy was heading for general."

"I don't think retired is the right term. After the *Rapture Syndrome* hit, he took it pretty hard. Lost his wife. They never had any children, and so she was everything he had. One day he just walked off the base, and never came back. No one was ever able to figure out where he went to."

"Speaking of wife..." and here Ted was obviously uncomfortable and unsure what to say.

"I know. It's been eight months. You'd think I'd be over it by now."

"Eight months? Hell, you were married twelve years. That's a lot of memories to get over."

"Yeah, but that's all they are now are memories." Jim dropped off into silence, and Ted cursed himself for bringing the subject up and ruining their reunion. The driver navigated the car onto the main Autobond, and out of the city, heading for the base that would now be Jim's new home.

CHAPTER SEVEN

Assassination

"Here's the problem." Ted announced as he flashed the imagine of a man on the wall. The figure looking back at them could not be more than twenty-five years old...thirty at most. His steel blue eyes seemed to pierce and hold you, even though it was only a computer-generated image and not the actual person. His curly, black hair was cut close, and his face held only a glint of stubble. It was the expression that caught Jim's attention the most. It was as if a permanent sneer had been etched onto the face.

"So what's the problem?" Bryan asked from the back of the room.

"The problem is this: Since the *Rapture Syndrome*, there has been a lot of unrest throughout the New Alliance. Several of the old European Union representatives were victims of the Syndrome. Obviously they need to be replaced. The other members have sent new ambassadors to represent them in the Alliance, but Italy is the problem.

"You might remember Ipileno as the head of the unauthorized negotiation committee that secured Israel's right to rebuild their Temple in Jerusalem. When the leaders of Italy fell victim to the Syndrome, Jason Ipileno stepped in and took control, also unofficially. He returned to Israel shortly thereafter as the head of Italian and the Vatican's joint team to stop the sacrifices. He seems to be a no-nonsense, get the job done kind of personality. That image has served him well. He not only assumed the leadership of Italy; but word has it that even the Catholic Church has recognized him as the official head until they can recover from the Syndrome's damages..."

"Wait a minute" Carter interrupted. The briefing sessions had been informal enough to allow all members of the security team to speak their mind. "Ipileno? Wasn't he the one who broke into the Vatican, stole some of their treasures, hocked them for some fast money; and then gave it to the poor several years ago?"

"Head of the Class, Carter. Yes, this is our modern day Robin Hood. His actions would have led him to jail, but the public outcry was too great at the time. The Pope thought it best at that time to drop the charges since his efforts fed so many of the poor in the slums of Italy."

"I hear the Pope was afraid the poor in Italy would rise up and physically attack the Vatican if they didn't drop the charges." Grant added.

"Well, regardless of the true political story, Ipileno is now the head of Italy, and the unofficial head of the Catholic Church. He's the first to hold such a position in centuries." Ted continued.

"I thought the king of Spain was the proper defender of the Catholic Church?" Simmons asked.

"Not after Ipileno took office. Everything he does just makes him that much more popular with the common people. His shutting down the daily sacrifices in Israel made him a hero of the Animal Rights Groups."

"You mean he arranges to have the Temple get built; and then he shuts it down? That's a lot of political clout. So what's the problem?" Simon echoed Bryan's original question.

"The problem is this: All other countries have appointed ambassadors to the New Alliance, Italy wants to send Ipileno as their ambassador."

"Nothing like being a control freak." Jim observed.

"Hold on! The guy who runs the country, and the church, wants to represent his country in the New Alliance?"

"Now you see the problem." Ted agreed. "Several other leaders have voiced protest over this, but Ipileno is adamant that he has the authority to appoint himself to the New Alliance council."

"To add to the problem, he's expected to arrive tomorrow, and there have been rumors running everywhere. We have everything from a hit squad coming after him to people claiming this is going to be a coup for Ipileno, and he will take over the New Alliance."

"Which is where security comes in." noted Jim.

"Which is where all of you come in. We have his itinerary. We know where he's going to be from the moment he leaves Italy, until he gets back to Italy and comes off the plane. Italian security will handle everything regarding his leaving and arrival, but from the moment he touches down here, until his plane is airborne again; he's our responsibility."

"If he's so damned important, why aren't the ETs covering this? They've got their hands in everything else." Shepherd asked. As if on cue the air shimmered for a second, light filled the room; and two ETs were now among them.

"Our ways are not your ways." The first ET sang to the group. Carter had drawn his weapon the moment the air began to shimmer and when he saw who they were, holstered it before anyone could see his reaction.

"We could over-see security, but this honor has been bestowed upon you. You must assume responsibility for your own." The second vibrated in their minds. With a flip of a wrist in the officer's direction, Shepherd slammed against the back wall. "Do not seek to criticize us again." he added.

Suddenly the first ET motioned and Carter was crashing into the book case on the side wall a moment later.

"Do not raise a weapon to us again." He cautioned.

Just as quickly as they appeared the shimmering returned and they were gone. Shepherd was pulling himself up off the floor. Carter still lay groaning where he fell. Jim was closest and helped him to his feet. Ted tried to suppress his look of fear as he scanned the room; and then resumed the briefing. There was nothing he could do, and so he chose to ignore the invasion.

"We've been through the drill before. Check all routes to and from the airport, remove all mail boxes, check all cars, weld all manhole covers, no over-head flights along the route, check all sewage and access tunnels."

"But, how do you deal with the fanatic? If someone is willing to trade his life for Ipileno, how do you stop it?" Jim asked.

"The age-old question which has plagued security men for centuries." Simmons noted.

"We'll have security with him at all times. There won't be a corridor he walks down, a sidewalk he crosses that isn't lined with our people." Ted declared.

"But how do you know that everyone can be trusted? In most major assassinations, there has always been someone on the inside. It's always been the weak link. Even though it was never proven in the Kennedy assassinations, or the King assassination; it has always been suspected that someone on the inside set it up, or at least gave access to the assassin. What kind of precautions have we taken with our own?" Bryan asked.

Jim fought down the urge to share what had been revealed concerning the Kennedy assassination. Given the quick response by EeeDees to improper comments, he knew he would never get the chance to slip and say anything.

"Anyone who has any credit problems, anyone with a family member who is ill, anyone whose family member is not in the city, has not been cleared to guard the route. We've tried to find the weaknesses that the enemy always exploits: family members, money, vices, and questionable loyalties..."

"What about replacing one or more of our people at key positions?" Carter interrupted.

"We have identification cards on everyone—the newest kind which are all-but-impossible to duplicate. We have passwords and ID checks for our people on a regular basis. If anyone fails the password, or if someone doesn't check in at the appointed time, the ball drops; and that person becomes suspect. Within three minutes of a missed check-in time, or a failed ID check or password, the person missing is targeted, and any area where his ID card or name is used is sealed off." Ted added.

"So four minutes after we've been popped by the assassin, you'll know about it and arrest the guy."

"Or the woman." Jim added.

"Well that should make Ipileno more comfortable, but it won't do a hell of a lot of good for the guy who gets popped." Simmons noted. Ted handed out the packets of the additional information, assignments, positions, and route to the various team leaders of his security staff. As they were threading out of the door, Jim held back with Ted. Once they were alone Jim added,

"You still realize that for all of our efforts, the danger we have to watch out for is the lone gunman who doesn't have a power base, isn't part of any known terrorist group, and doesn't mind dying to carry out his mission."

"We try to prepare for everything, but when you're dealing with '*crazies*,' there's no way you can know everything."

"So fill me in on this guy. Seems that he's better known to the natives; than to those of us back home." Jim suggested. Jim had almost slipped and mentioned the states; but he was working hard to avoid any comment that tied him to his home county.

"Not a lot to tell. He's Italian, catholic on his mother's side, but his father was Israeli...if you believe he has a father. According to records, his father disappeared just after the mother got pregnant, never married which is why he has an Italian name. They lived most of their lives in poverty. Ipileno was trouble from the start. Had a lot of anger inside. He broke into the Vatican when he was thirteen, stole some of the lesser works of art, fenced them; and used the money to help the poor. It gave him the name of the Italian '*Robin Hood*.' When arrested he declared he had simply taken back the money the church had stolen from the poor.

"He was part of a militant gay movement in Italy; and between the gays and the poor, there was a near-riot when they tried to bring him to trial. The entire community began a boycott of the church, withheld their offerings, stopped the volunteer work. It began to spread outside of Italy, and when the church saw the drop in income, the Pope did the politically correct thing and dropped the charges."

"Sounds like we have a real sweetheart in this one." Jim noted.

"He's been in the spotlight ever since. He's got a knack for computers, hacked several systems, but INTERPOL could never prove it was him. He turned his attention towards reform, and his ideas were revolutionary. He had a total disregard for the current political power structure, crushed anyone who got in his way, pushed his programs through, and won the hearts of the people. His slogan was 'people not power.' He claimed the entire political structure was corrupt, and it was the back-scratching and palm-greasing that made the entire government dysfunctional. Whenever he rose in power from city to province and up, he disbanded all existing political power bases, and set up new ones which he claimed couldn't be bought or corrupted.

"When the *Rapture Syndrome* hit, he was in the right place at the right time. His charismatic personality, his support from the common people, and his ideas on reform made him the only candidate to lead when the power vacuum was created. What surprised everyone was when the people voted him into office, and then he declared himself the head of the church. The archbishops and cardinals all protested, but the people began another wave of counter-actions. The average person on the street believed he would bring the same levels of reform to the church that he had brought to politics. They wanted someone like him in charge to make sure their tithes and offerings weren't being abused or used to pay off child molesters. He was accepted, but not given the title of Pope since he wasn't a priest who had worked his way up through the ranks. The first thing he did was to remove the protection of the Church from child molesters. He turned records over to law enforcement. Every suspected priest or nun was thrown out of the Church, sent to prison and has been ordered to stand trial for their charges. After his appointment, people were more than generous towards the church, and their treasury was nearly bursting. Ipileno began some sweeping reforms, and turned the money around to feed the poor, heal the sick, and make sure the elderly were being taken care of. He changed the function of the church from evangelical to social, and the people loved it."

"And the sacrifices?"

"The Vatican was on equal status with Jerusalem. Two cities that appear to be above ties to countries or governments. Seems the Vatican arranged for Ipileno to meet with the High Priest in Israel. It was a show of power. Ipileno had some powerful negotiating chips. No one knows what they were, but when he finished his meeting; the High Priest announced that the Daily Sacrifices were no longer needed. He spoke of the Messiah having dealt with sin; and so all the sacrifices for sin were ceasing. He made it clear, however, that the Holy Feasts: Yom Kippur, Pesach, Shavuot and Succoth. Day of Atonement, Passover, Pentecost and Feast of Booths" Ted added to Jim's blank expression. "Those are Holy Days with prescribed sacrifices and rituals. They won't give those up; but they were willing to give up the daily sacrifices. It was a compromise; and made Ipileno more popular than ever with the animal rights people. He came up out of nowhere, but now that he's on the scene; everything he get involved with, he takes over."

"And now he wants to bring all that to the table here in the Alliance?" Jim asked.

"That's the point we have to watch. Our orders are to protect him, but we also have to make sure he doesn't establish a power base in the Alliance."

"Wait a minute! We have to keep him out of power here? What measures are we talking about?"

"For your ears only..." Ted cautioned. He studied his brother's eyes carefully before continuing. "If we see him as a threat to the structure of the Alliance, I have orders to recruit those I can trust, and those I will need to take him out."

"Take him out?!" Jim fought to keep his voice to a whisper. "So the assassin we might have to deal with is ourselves?"

"The Alliance is still gaining power, Jim. It's too weak to allow anyone to usurp its power base. Ipileno is the kind of man who could do that. Our loyalty is with the Alliance. Even the AU sees that. If, in my opinion, Ipileno poses a threat to the Alliance, I have orders to see that he doesn't take over."

Jim tried to take it all in as they left the briefing room. As security, he would have to be willing to give his life to save Ipileno; but then may have to turn around and be one of the ones to pull the fatal trigger. *This* was why he hated being in security.

CHAPTER EIGHT

Sacrificial Lamb

Shmuel checked his gun. The clip was full. The safety was off and one bullet in the chamber. Amir frowned as he looked at him. "You won't need that."

"Standard operating procedure when dealing with terrorists."

"They're not terrorists."

The brothers made their way up the path into the national park of Ein Ghedi. "*Ein Ghedi*" was Hebrew for "*the goat.*" It was an oasis in the wilderness just north of the Dead Sea. Although you drove through barren rock for hours to get there, there was a stream of water that formed several pools. Years ago there was more water, but up-grades to the park had kept the water in the stream and pools to a minimum. There was a group of tourists off to one side in a clearing next to the path. A tour guide was talking about the account of David hiding out from King Saul in one of the caves in the area. Several conies were sunning themselves sleepily on flat rocks off to one side. Several wild Nubian goats were on the other side of the clearing. A tourist was ignoring the tour guide and offering a branch filled with fresh leaves to one of the younger goats. It was slowly inching closer and nibbling at the leaves. The tourist found himself in the uncomfortable position of having the goat close enough for a great picture, but unable to raise his camera for a shot without scaring the goats away. He chose to be satisfied just feeding the young goat. As they walked by the other tourists noticed the action with the goat and one by one they slipped away from the tour guide's lecture to get close enough to photograph the goat and tourist without scaring the goat. The tour guide looked at the two bothers as they passed and nodded.

He was Mossad. Tourists rarely knew that. Many tour guides were nothing but covers to protect tourists and to dispense information they wanted the tourists to take back to the outside world. Some of it correct, some of it designed to make the world think the small country was stronger than it truly was. Each of the tour guides and drivers were "packing" and each tour guide constantly checked their Blackberry or tech to get the latest security information. It was only last week that one of the operatives had to abandon their bus in the Arab sector of Jerusalem and convince their tourists that he knew a short cut and they could run after him, rather than revealing they were in serious danger of being cut off by the locals as they passed through. None of the tourist picked up on it; but it was something all the guides feared.

The narrow path up into Ein Ghedi crossed over the stream several times. There were pools down below where young students in uniforms played and explored. Three men with automatic weapons stood guard. One with the children and two on the high points above the stream. There was probably a fourth either protecting the van or in the brush standing guard. Israelis did not take chances with their children.

They continued to climb for half an hour. The air was thin as Ein Ghedi was elevated. If you had gone to Qumran several miles away where the Dead Sea Scrolls had been discovered, you would be high enough to be at eye level as fighter pilots would scream by on the way to Gaza.

The brothers had left the park behind. The tourists were far behind them. They came to a grove of carob trees. One figure had his back to them. He was dressed in casual clothes. Blue jeans, sneakers and a t-shirt. He probably had a yamaka on, but he had pulled out his prayer shawl and it covered his head as he prayed. The other figure sat on a large stone eating a handful of carobs from a local tree.

Shmuel had his gun out instantly and alternated between the man with the prayer shawl and the other on the rock.

"Hands up!" he demanded.

"Shmuel!" Amir shouted and tried to knock the gun down, but Shmuel hooked his brother's knee from behind with his foot, swept the limb out from under him; and he hit the ground hard. Before he could catch his breath Shmuel's foot held him to the ground pressing hard on his throat.

"What are you doing?" Amir gasped trying to breathe and speak as his wind pipe was being compressed enough to make him helpless.

"I told you: terrorists. Standard operating procedure. I wasn't sent here to gather information and report. I was sent to take them out. They have become an embarrassment to the government." Without batting an eye, he squeezed off one bullet at the head covered by the prayer shawl. The second shot less that a heartbeat later was screaming to the point between the eyes of the man on the rock. Neither one flinched.

Shmuel was suddenly aware that the temperature of the surrounding area had grown hot, very hot. He dared to look up and about thirty feet above him hung a massive fireball churning in the air and thrusting against the force that held it there so it would not fall on the Mossad operative.

Shmuel could not move. It was not fear that held him to the spot. His body would not respond. Then something in his mind told him to move his foot and let Amir up. His foot moved against his will. The hand that held the gun went limp and Amir snatched the weapon before it could fall. Amir stepped back, took a bead on his brother and started shouting at him. Shmuel was able to move his eyes and head and no longer stare at the heaving ball of fire. The heat had already made him break out in sweat and his eyes were stinging as it streaked down his face.

The man with the prayer shawl pulled the shawl over his shoulders and stood up. Shmuel noticed the bullet that had been speeding towards his head fell to the ground. The man touched Amir's hand and lowered the weapon. The man on the rock stood up. Took a second to study the bullet hanging in the air and flicked it away. It resumed its original speed but on a new course and embedded in a nearby tree trunk.

"What did that tree ever do to you?" the prayer shawl man asked.

"Quite right." the other seemed to realize. He motioned and the bullet removed itself from the tree, fell to the ground and the bullet hole in the tree trunk disappeared.

"It's alright, Amir." The prayer shawl man said. "Give him back his weapon. I don't think he will try to use it again."

"We are not, to use your term, 'terrorists.'" The man from the rock added. "I am *Eliyahu*" the man from the rock began. "This is "*Chanowk.*"

When Shmuel only gave a blank look, Chanowk added, "I am Enoch. This is Eli."

"It seems that your superiors wanted to make you a sacrificial lamb." Enoch added pointing to the roaring ball of fire still hanging in the air.

Shmuel found his voice but is was raspy and dry. "How...?"

Eli passed his hand over Shmuel's eyes. It created the effect of another world being superimposed upon this one. Thousands of beings of light filled the carob tree grove. They spread out on the hills throughout Ein Ghedi. Shmuel fell to his knees. His legs would not longer support him. Eli touched his head and the vision faded. Shmuel blinked. He looked around. The next second he fell flat on his face.

"Well," declared Enoch as he helped Amir drag his brother over to the rock and prop him up, "That wasn't part of the plan."

Eli motioned and the fire ball consumed itself and disappeared without ever touching the ground.

✶✶✶

Jim took one last look at the wrist monitor. It flipped between ten additional cameras that had been mounted in preparation for Ipileno's visit. Each hallway, passage, stairwell and doorway was clear. He tapped the clear button with his left index finger. His ear piece picked up Ted's voice.

"Keep a constant watch. We're bringing him in now." The ear piece used his own head bone to pass the audio sounds onto his inner ear. No one could hear the command, but it was clear to the one wearing the state-of-the-arts communication. He clicked his teeth together twice, and the microphone caught the vibration and passed the acknowledge signal back to his brother.

Jim kept his gun primed and in his left hand. He held his right wrist so that he could see any change in the image as the micro-computer flipped systematically between its ten signals. Jim had practiced to keep one eye watching the wrist screen, and his other to scan his territory. He trusted the "eyes in the back of his head" to pick up what his other senses were missing. He wasn't sure why, but there was a nagging doubt in the back of his mind. He scanned the hallway. Ipileno would be there in one minute, fifteen seconds. Everything looked clear, but something wasn't right. He couldn't put his finger on it, and he didn't want to blow the whistle; and have it all be for nothing. Finally he cleared his throat.

"You got something?" came Ted voice. He had been monitoring for any unusual sounds that might serve as a signal.

"Nothing I can put my finger on. Something doesn't feel right, but I don't know what it is."

"Sure it isn't first assignment jitters?" Ted suggested.

"I've had too many first assignments to have any jitters left." He kept his voice to a very soft whisper, but the ear piece was tight in the ear, and picked up the vibration through the bone.

"Should we hold?" Ted asked. Jim was glad that his brother was giving him the benefit of the doubt.

"Send up two men. Have them check with me. I'd rather mess up the time table than get our visitor shot."

"Sanchez! Frisco! Move to corridor three. Meet with Jim for a final sweep." came Ted's orders to the men with him.

"Have we done an infrared sweep?" Jim asked.

"About thirty minutes ago. It was clear."

"What about an audio scan?"

"Just a couple of mice in the building. Nothing else." Ted offered.

"Mice?" Jim asked. "In this kind of building?"

"It happens." Ted offered.

"Where were they?"

"Up in the air conditioning vents."

"How do you know they were mice?"

"You're getting paranoid, Jim. We did the audio scan, picked up what sounded like small claws on metal, and fur rubbing. The only thing in there are a few mice."

"Where was the target...Specifically?" Jim demanded.

"Just ahead. At the intersection of our corridor and yours."

Jim looked in the direction Ted had identified. He then realized what was bothering him. It was slight, ever so slight that you wouldn't notice it unless you were specifically looking for it. It was also above normal eye range so you wouldn't detect it by accident, but his "sixth sense" must have seen it and been trying to get his attention. The tile in the ceiling wasn't quite back into place. It was obvious by one edge having a little wider crack than the others in the ceiling around it.

"Get Ipileno out of there! Get Him Out NOW!" Jim was shouting as he ran. He gave up the pretense of stealth.

"What is it, Jim? Jim?" When Jim did not respond, Ted began shouting. "Get him back. Cover him, now!" Jim could see the tiles in the ceiling were falling and clattering on the floor. Five people dropped out of the air ducts.

"Stealth suits!" Jim yelled. "Take 'em out." Three of the figures began to open fire in the direction of Ted and Ipileno. Another discharged a blast in Jim's direction. The fifth knelt to cover any other attacks from other directions. Jim began to dive for the floor and began to roll. A "shimmer" filled the air for only a brief moment. Something pushed him hard and sped up his descent. It was only there for a millisecond and then it was gone. There came the burning in his shoulder, ribs and thigh. Even with whatever pushed him; he was too slow. He came up and opened fire in return. The target staggered, but was already getting back on his feet.

"Body armor!" Jim shouted, and aimed for the face. The assailant's head snapped back from the impact, and he dropped in a heap on the floor. Other shots were coming from the hall where Ted and his team protected Ipileno. Jim struggled to his feet, staggered when he tried to put weight on his leg, caught himself against the wall. The fifth assailant was turning his way. Jim's laser sight rested for a heartbeat on the attacker's forehead, the last heartbeat the man would ever know.

Ted and his team had picked up the battle plan, and all but one had been dropped. The last attacker had been disarmed, and over-powered by the sheer weight of the onslaught. Jim, leaning heavy upon the wall, rounded it just in time to hear additional shouting. There, on the floor of the hallway was Ipileno, his head lying in the center of an ever-growing pool of blood.

CHAPTER NINE

Playing God

"D.O.A.? So why are you still here?" Jim asked as his brother continued to position his men around the hospital via a headset. Several ETs were also making the rounds and checking various positions. Jim tried to shift his weight on the gurney to get a better look at the activity taking place around him. He sucked in air to fight off the pain that tore through his ribs and shoulder. It reminded him that the shock of the bullet wound was wearing off, and the pain killers hadn't kicked in yet.

"Doctors said Ipileno was dead on arrival, but they still want to try something." Ted retorted, pushing his brother back onto the gurney as he followed it into the emergency room.

"Ted, the guy took a bullet in the brain. Half of which was blown away." Jim observed.

"Had him on life support almost immediately." Ted countered and motioned to one of his men to move to another exit.

"What good is life support if the guy's dead?!" Jim rebutted.

"I thought the same thing, but they showed up and took over." Ted motioned to the ETs. At the movement in their direction several ETs appeared around Ted and his brother.

"You were there." Jim challenged. The ET looked down and replied.

"No."

"Yes you were." Jim continued.

"Do you challenge us?" The melodic voice was dripping with threatening tones.

"He's on drugs, sir. He's fine." Ted tried to position himself between his brother and the ET. He found himself flung to the other side of the corridor.

"Don't lie to me" Jim confronted. "I saw something. I felt something. It was one of yours right when the shots were being fired."

The ET stopped for a moment. Jim could tell that he was communicating with the others. He returned his gaze to Jim.

"You are wrong. I checked and none of our people were there when this happened."

"None of them? Then…"

The ET cut him off. "It was not one of us."

Before Jim could press the question, all the ETs in the building increased their light, shimmered and were gone.

Ted was back to his brother's side. "Are you crazy challenging an ET? What kind of drugs do they have you on?"

Jim was about to comment, but he felt a warning in the back of his mind to drop the subject for the time being. "So why the life support for a dead guy?"

"The doctors here want to try something completely experimental. Say it just might work. They've got the equipment, the specialists, and the materials they need, so the Alliance gave them the 'go-ahead.' My job is to make sure nothing else can go wrong."

"I hate to rain on your parade, but the guy is dead. How much more wrong can it go for us?"

"Probably not much, but if this works, things might start going right."

Jim gave up on trying to get any more information out of his brother regarding the procedure. It was obvious no one wanted to talk about it, and so he shifted his line of questioning. "Who were those guys? They had some pretty high-tech stuff there."

"Before the survivor took his own life, he made a few comments, mostly political. Looks like this is a splinter group from some ultra-conservative group."

"Took his own life?" Jim echoed.

"Seems they were on a suicide mission. The stealth suits were to keep them hidden from our scans until it was too late. The body armor was to keep them alive long enough to finish the job. Once Ipileno was dead, they were to either die in combat or take their own lives. We searched, and each body had three or four techniques available for self-termination."

"Sacrificial lambs." Jim mumbled.

"Got that right. Once the hit was done, no one was even trying to go home. We've got some info on them. We should pin-point their operation within two or three hours. Then we move against the others in the group."

"I doubt if you'll find any of them...at least not alive." Jim noted.

"That was pretty quick thinking on your part about the ceiling. What tipped it off?"

"The description. I was part of an operation back home that used stealth suits. The small plastic clips on the zippers made sounds just like little claws on sheet metal. The fabric rubbing on the head across the hair makes sounds like fur rubbing on fur. They must have been up there for some time, but so long as they kept everything covered in the stealth gear, no infrared would pick them up. I wasn't sure, but when I saw the tile slightly out of place, I felt it best to act. I just wish I had acted a few seconds sooner."

"So these suits are part of A. U. technology?" Ted asked.

"No, it was a joint mission with Israel. They made these suits for anti-terrorist activity."

"Well, now they're considered terrorists. Maybe we can get them to use their high-tech on themselves. Not a word about who makes the stealth suits until we clear it." Ted cautioned. "The last thing we need now is more fuel for the fires." Ted broke away from Jim and they wheeled him into surgery. Jim felt a slight stinging on his neck and everything went black.

***

When Jim came to in the recovery room, he started to move and found several IV tubes running out of his arms, and support boards strapped to keep him from using either hand. Another tube came from his nose and he could feel it going down his throat.

"Damn! You look worse now than when you went in." It was Ted's voice to one side. He turned his head and was struck with a wave of nausea, but there was nothing in his stomach.

"Careful!' Ted cautioned and came closer to the bed to help him. "You were in pretty bad shape there. That bullet that went in through the ribs took a little trip around inside before stopping. Couple of organs were hit. You shouldn't have been able to stand, let alone take out those two hit men."

"Always wanted to be the hero." Jim was surprised at how weak and hoarse his voice sounded. It couldn't be him speaking.

"Well, now you are. Front page headlines, ten o'clock news, and a couple of magazines are running stories on you. They've been interviewing me almost non-stop while you were in surgery.

"I thought that to be a hero, you had to save someone. If memory serves me correctly, Ipileno died." Jim noted.

"Yeah, that's the strangest part. He was dead, but not any more."

"What do you mean, 'not any more'? Dead people don't just get up and walk around. You don't have to graduate medical school to know that."

"Oh, he's not up and around, at least not yet. Seems there was a conference taking place in town. Some of the top research people, and surgeons who had been working on some pretty experimental stuff."

"Define 'experimental stuff.'"

"Partial brain transplants."

"Brain transplants?! Maybe you should go get one. We can't do those kinds of things."

"I spoke with the surgeons who were on the treatment team, seems like we can...and we did. Of course, this is the first time it's been done on a human, but it's been a big thing in the research field since the 1970's."

"How so?" Jim was tired. He was starting to fade in and out. He had to use all of his energy to focus on Ted's words.

"You remember the old Sci Fi movies of the 70s?" Ted asked. Jim nodded. He and his brother had spent many a weekend hold up in a dark theater stuffing themselves with popcorn, candy and soft drinks. Every monster, alien, space travel movie they could find was on the agenda.

"Remember when they did those first movies on cloning and they had to educate the audience on the subject?"

"Yeah, pretty impressive the first time you saw them; but when they came out on video they looked pretty lame having to explain what everyone already knew."

"Same thing here. Three days ago nobody ever considered the idea of a partial brain transplant. Now it's headline news. Everyone knows about it; and it's already old news."

"Well, I've been out of the loop. Fill me in."

"Started out as an experiment to transfer memories from one lab rat to another. They took a rat that had run this maze successfully hundreds of times, took out part of his brain that had to do with memory, and put it into a rat who had never run the maze. The new rat could actually run the maze as if he had done it hundreds of times before. He knew where to turn, which corridor to use, and which ones to avoid."

"But how? You can't just stick a piece of a brain into somebody's head. You've got to hook it up, neurons, blood vessels..."

"That's the beauty of it. If you use the right tissue, the transplant tissue actually seems to know where it should grow and attach itself. Some doctor named Krieger did a paper on it back in the 1980s. They took a chunk out of one mouse's brain and dropped it into an opening in another mouse's brain. Then they stepped back and let it do its thing.

"Turns out that it's easier to replace part of the brain instead of all of it. They had everyone in the world right here in town who had any kind of experience in the process. The guy who pioneered the lightsword..."

"Don't you mean light saber?"

"He couldn't use that term. It was already copyrighted by Star Wars."

"So what's it do?"

"It's a laser. They used lasers for the surgery. It's commonplace now, but the guy who first started doing it years ago jokingly called it his 'lightsword.' It's amazing what they can do with that thing now. And it's all controlled by computers. You have to be more of a computer nerd than a doctor to make it work; but I watched, and Damn! It's impressive."

"I think I read something about Special Forces getting some kind of laser or plasma tool for emergency field surgeries."

"Yeah. That's the thing."

"So, does Ipileno have this sudden urge to run through mazes?"

"No, he hasn't been out of surgery long enough to find out exactly what changes he's going to have, but he's breathing on his own, and his heart is working...Hell! Everything seems to be working, except for his right arm. However, since he's had one of the biggest strokes in history and lived through it, that's not unusual. The team is with him now and running a lot of tests. Getting him ready for rehab."

"You're serious about this! He's had a fatal head wound and has come back from the dead?"

"I've never been more serious. You remember the guy who got shot in the head when Reagan took the bullet? Then there was the Senator from Arizona. Lots of people with serious head wounds are surviving and getting on with their lives."

"Hell! There's going to be no stopping him now. How do you control someone like that?"

"You don't. Right now our superiors are re-thinking this whole situation. It's a hands-off policy from here on in. Once the doctors get done, we make sure he has round-the-clock protection. The public is calling him another Lazarus or Jesus Christ for coming back from the dead."

"If memory serves me correctly, they both were dead for days, not hours; and they came back without any medical help."

"Doesn't matter. The people are desperate for someone to lead them. They're all collecting in the streets around the hospital, chanting his name. Helped or not, he's come back from the dead, and that's enough to make him a man of miracles to them."

"Sounds like sheep to me." Jim retorted.

"People are always sheep. Take one person, and he does the right thing. Put him in with a crowd, and he becomes an idiot every time. That's what the rulers of the world have always counted on."

"Rulers of the world?! Aren't you getting a little carried away here? He's an ambassador. He's in charge of one country. That's a pretty big leap to make."

"All I know is that the people in charge are starting to talk about things, strange things. It's like they're following orders from someone else...someone even higher up. "

"EeeDees?" Jim asked without realizing that his brother had not been part of the earlier meeting.

"ETs?" Ted snapped misquoting his brother. "What do they have to do with all of this?"

Jim closed his eyes for a moment. Ted thought it was the pain hitting once more; but Jim needed protection. The EeeDees had confronted him once already. He could not chance another meeting. When he felt it was safe, he opened his eyes.

"More than their publicity blogs are telling us."

"That's all we have from them. Anyone who seems to have any real knowledge about them is either tight lipped, or dead."

"In case you didn't notice, I was almost the latter." Jim looked around. He was tired, too tired to carry on such an intense conversation. Further, he needed all his mental powers to discuss the topic with any sense or clarity. "Later, Ted. Just remember one thing, even when you're alone, you may not be alone."

He closed his eyes to rest for a second, but drifted deeper than he had intended. Ted watched him for another few minutes. Noted he was deep asleep, and went out to direct security on how to deal with the army of press gathered in the lobby, and the mass of believers now growing large enough to disrupt traffic around the hospital.

CHAPTER TEN

An Issue of Faith

Shmuel shook his head to clear it. He glanced to the sky to look for the ball of fire. He scanned the grove and the hills for these beings of light. Amir noticed him first. "They are still there; you just can see them. Not yet."

"Can you?"

"They gave me the vision when I first met them, but not now."

"How do you know it's isn't hypnotism, drugs?"

"It's an issue of faith." Eli added from the side of the grove. He had been praying and was now removing his prayer shawl from his head and wrapping it around his waist and tucking it in. His head bore the traditional yamaka.

"Faith?" Shmuel almost spat the word out as if it left a foul taste in his mouth.

"Yes, faith." Enoch added coming to join them. "Look at this…"

Enoch touched a point in the air between them. It began to ripple. Figures seemed to be moving, but they were a blur. After a moment the picture became very sharp and distinct. Shmuel reached up and poked his finger through the display. It formed a ripple where his finger entered. He did not feel anything. When he pulled his hand back the picture resumed.

"Two years before the *Israeli Incident;* two years before the *Rapture Syndrome…*" Eli began. '*Succoth,* the Feast of Tabernacles. One of the three feasts where G-d mandated every Jewish male to appear before Him in Jerusalem."

"But Succoth is different." Enoch pointed out. "For Passover and Pentecost, converted Jews and Gentile men can participate; but this Feast. This feast is only for the Jewish-born male. No one else."

"A seven-day feast that lasts eight days. Did you ever wonder about that?" Eli asked. Shmuel shook his head "no."

"Eight is the number for new beginnings. Noah and his family numbered eight when they came out of the Ark for the beginning of a new world. On the Seventh Day YHWH rested, so eight would symbolize a new work for G-d."

"At Passover, the Messiah revealed Himself, was offered as a sacrifice for the sins of the world, was buried and returned from the dead."

"Wait a minute. Are you trying to tell me Yeshua was the Messiah? Have we been blind all these years that we missed it?"

"Actually you have." Eli commented. "King David pronounced the curse for rejecting the Messiah, 'Let their table become a snare before them; and that which should have been for their welfare; let it become a trap. Let their eyes be darkened that they see not.' Our people really ticked King David off when they rejected the Messiah."

"Pentecost the Holy Spirit was given, the beginning of the harvest, a spiritual harvest. Now, Succoth," Here Enoch pointed to the display in front of them.

"The prophet Zechariah spoke of this day, 'And I will pour upon the House of Israel, and upon the inhabitants of Jerusalem, the spirit of grace, and of supplications; and they shall look upon Me whom they have pierced, and they will mourn for Him as one mourns for his only son...'"

"How could we have known?" Shmuel began to protest. Eli continued.

"Again the prophet Zechariah, 'And one shall say unto Him, "What are these wounds in your hands?" Then He shall answer, "Those with which I was wounded in the house of my friends."'"

"Amir?" Shmuel turned to his brother for help. His mind was churning. He could not think straight.

"Don't you remember the *Awakening*? That morning we all woke up and it all just made sense?"

"Not me. Never me. I am Jew. I am Israeli. I am not Christian. I will never be Christian. I would die first!"

"No one is asking you to be Christian. We are all Jews; but we are Jews who had discovered and found our Messiah."

"You and your brothers that day…Oh that day. Many Arabs wanted to kill you." Eli pointed to the display and it began to play out the scene from a few years ago.

"Rabbi Gobbles has declared the red heifer fit. Prepare the sacrifice." It was a younger Amir, holding the rope of the red heifer with Rabbi Gobbles next to him. A cheer began to break out in the crowd. Suddenly Shmuel was next to him.

"Leave the sacrifice."

"I can't leave the sacrifice." Amir protested.

"Others can do the sacrifice; we must do what we can do. Get your crane. Get it now before the Arabs get wind of this."

"What are we going to do?"

"Get the crane and meet me in ten minutes at the base of the Temple Mount."

"Temple Mount? Are you crazy?"

"No, inspired. Now is the time. We must move before they can build a resistance."

The brother vanished from the display, but then the image sharpened once more and Amir was lifting one of two large stones from off the ground onto Shmuel's flatbed truck. Other Jews were beginning to gather. In a matter of minutes the two stones were on the truck. Shmuel slammed it into gear and shouted for Amir to follow. He barreled up the Temple Mount. The Muslim guards were shouting and coming out with rifles. Shots were fired, but Shmuel dropped the two closest to the truck and drove the others out of the way. Amir was close behind them, but a throng of thousands of Jews filled in the road behind them and charged up the hill. The shear weight of the mob drove the Arabs back. They fled into the Dome of the Rock and barricaded the doors. Those with weapons prepared to defend their second most holy site with their lives.

Instead of moving in that direction, Shmuel swerved to the right and headed for an opened area on the top of the Temple Mount. He and Amir along with the throng unloaded the two large rocks which had served as the corner stones of the last Temple. It was started, and before anyone could mount an offensive the Temple Mount was under Israeli control and various stones from around the area were identified and by the first evening the first row of blocks for the foundation of the Temple were laid.

The display focused once more on Amir and Shmuel who swigged wine and danced to the music from the minstrels who had come to celebrate the beginning of the Third Temple—or as most called it, The Last Days Temple.

With a motion, the display vanished.

"Where is that young Israeli whose fire burned with his love for the Law, the love for the Land?" Enoch asked.

"Those were easier times. We acted without thinking."

"Would you change what you have done?" Elijah asked.

"Never!" was the immediate reply from both brothers.

"Don't you remember Jonathan; he took his servant and went out to face the enemy that had defeated the army of Israel? He saw G-d answering his prayer and he put the enemy to flight. David slew Goliath and drove the Philistines from the land. Gideon had a handful of men and drove the Midianites from our country."

"You are Jonathan. You are David. You are Gideon. When G-d calls and you answer, miracles happen. Nothing is held back."

"This was all what G-d intended?" Shmuel questioned.

"This is why we are here. You have fulfilled the first part of your mission. We are here to fulfill ours."

"Mission?" Amir was brimming with excitement.

"You are the first two, but there will be others who will be called. We will guide you. We will train you. We will prepare you." As Eli spoke, Amir and Shmuel could see two of the beings of light materialize next to them. This time there was no fear. The two beings stood behind them and laid their hands on their shoulders. Suddenly strength and power seemed to flow into them until they felt they could hold no more."

"How many more will there be?" Shmuel asked."

Enoch chuckled before he answered, "Lots. One hundred and forty four thousand to be precise."

***

"You sent for me, sir?" Ted asked as he lightly knocked on the hospital door, and stuck his head in.

"You're Colonel Ted Brown? Come in." Ipileno responded. He was sitting at a table in the hospital room. He was in his robe, and his head was still wrapped in gauze, but the tubes and IV's were gone. Ipileno's now–dead right eye was covered with an eye patch, and his useless right arm was strapped close to his body with a hospital sling with Velcro straps. Ted stepped into the room, and came to attention.

"Oh, nothing so formal, colonel." Ted heard the electric motor for Ipileno's wheelchair engage as the ambassador used his left hand to maneuver and roll from behind the table. "Come, sit with me for a spell."

Ted moved to the opposite side of the table across from Ipileno. He laid his hat on the table as he sat down. "I've never seen anyone do that before." Ipileno noted.

"What's that, sir?"

"Someone actually sitting at attention."

"Ambassador Ipileno..." Ted began, but Ipileno cut him off.

"Jay."

"Sir?"

"My friends call me 'Jay.'"

"I'm not sure if that would be appropriate, sir. You are the Ambassador from Italy to the New Alliance. You're also the political head of Italy, as well as its religious leader. I don't believe military protocol would recognize such informality on my part."

"Well, if it doesn't; then it's going to be very hard for us to work together."

"Sir?"

"I've put in a request to have you transferred from the New Alliance to my personal security team. I wanted to discuss the matter with you before making it final. This has to be something we both want if it's going to work."

"Sir, I was the head of security that allowed the *Elohims* to take you out."

"I know, I've read the report. From the statements it was determined that your men were not at fault. Your job was to bring me into the building, and then into the conference hall. Colonel Striker was in charge of the actual security of the building. In fact, it was one of your men who caught on to the *Elohims* hidden in the air ducts before they made their move. I imagine if we had not been a little ahead of schedule, his warning would have been enough to save me."

"Still, sir, the assassination was on my watch."

"Theoretically, yes, colonel. However, I've reviewed the reports and don't see anything you or your men did that was inappropriate or undisciplined. Your man actually took out two of the assassins even though he had a punctured lung, ruptured spleen and a bullet in his colon. I also note that he was your brother, but you stayed with me rather than protect your own. That tells a lot about an individual."

"I don't recall all of that being in the report, sir." Ted challenged.

"Not afraid to take the direct approach, either. Another good trait. No, not all of that was in the report."

"Then how did you get the information?...If I might ask."

"I could say that I spoke to your men, or that I reviewed the security films."

"Then I would have to assume that you were lying, sir."

"You're not afraid to put it all on the table, are you?"

"You don't get to be in my position by being bashful about asking the hard questions and confronting the problems."

"Why would you have to say I was lying?"

"The camera that covered that angle of the corridor was taken out in the first volley of fire. The last scene recorded was assassin two dropping to his knee and discharging his weapon at the lens. The camera was not in operation to record the events you are referring to. I've kept track of all my men. None of them has been here to speak with you."

"Perhaps I contacted them by phone. I do have a phone here, you know."

"Which you have used five times. The first time you sought an up-date on the constitutional changes pending in Italy to give you additional power. The second time was to contact a personal friend to let him know that you were all right. The third call was to give a phone interview with the cable news network anchorman. The fourth time was yesterday when you gave instruction to the Vatican to sell off three more masterpieces, and use the money to fund four charities that you have supported for the last ten years. The last call was fifteen minutes ago when you called and asked my superiors to have me come and see you. Also, none of my men would give out any information over a phone line. You never know who is asking the questions, or who might be listening in."

"As seems to be the case with my phone lines, Colonel Brown. I assume that my lines have been tapped?"

"Not 'tapped,' sir. Monitored."

"Is there a difference?"

"It's all in the intent. Something slipped through the last time you were on my watch. No one is going to slip through a second time."

"You're everything I've heard, and everything I've expected. That's why I want you on my team."

"I am on your team, sir. You're my responsibility."

"You're not getting the big picture. The Alliance is just the beginning. There's a greater drama unfolding out there.

Dying taught me that. The time for us all going in a hundred different directions is coming to a close. The petty politics, personal and hidden agendas; it's all got to stop. We need one vision for the entire world. If we're going to make it through the coming months or years it's going to take all we have, working together to get us through."

"I'm sorry sir, but it sounds like you're moving up the ladder faster than I can follow. I work for the Alliance. I've been assigned to you. To that end, I will sacrifice everything I am and have to fulfill that obligation. But now you're talking like someone out to take over the world. That's where I have to excuse myself and put on the brakes."

"I am not talking about taking over the world. I'm talking about saving the world."

"Saving it from what, sir?"

"You have no idea what's coming down, do you?"

"This is a conversation I am not prepared to continue, sir. My security clearance, my knowledge, my understanding of information not available to the general public is an area I do not enter with others, sir!"

"I am not asking you to betray government secrets. I'm asking you to work with me to bring the New Alliance to the position it needs to be in. This New Alliance is only grasping the shadow of coming events. There's more coming that will force the Alliance to restructure in order to survive, or collapse under its own bureaucracy. In order for the world to survive the coming events, it will need a strong central government. It will need one man with vision and faith that we can make it through. Not all of us. Some will not survive what is coming, but if we act now; we can save more through positive action than if no action is taken."

"I'm sorry, Mr. Ambassador, but what you are talking about sounds vaguely like some kind of conspiracy to take over the Alliance. As I said before, I work for the Alliance. I cannot sit here while you make these comments, nor will my oath of loyalty to the Alliance allow me to pretend that these comments were not made." Ted began to rise from the table and prepare to leave.

"What if I told you that I have already made these comments to the Alliance, and that they agree with my position? What if I told you that the Alliance is preparing to restructure under my direction?"

"I would hate to suggest twice in the same conversation that you are lying, sir; but that would have to be my response. I do not know how you could be in touch with anyone in the Alliance without my being aware of it. To date, I have no knowledge of any way you could discuss your position with anyone in the Alliance, much less with those in a position to take action on your recommendations."

"What would you say if I told you that there is a method of communication known to those of us at a certain level of political power that is currently unknown to those at your current level?"

"It would have to be a very good level of communication." Ted suggested.

"Is my room also being monitored for any conversations?" Ipileno challenged with a smile dancing in his one good eye. Ted's cold gaze back told Ipileno it was.

"You might want to check the tapes for the last three days, and review my discussion of the problems facing the Alliance, various options open to the Alliance, and my own recommendations as to the best path we should take to prepare for the coming events."

"My men heard your discussions. They noted that no one was in your room, and that it was their belief that you were alone in your room and possibly practicing a speech you planned to deliver to the Alliance when it convenes next week, or that you were thinking out loud."

"They did not see it as communicating?"

"There are no other listening or broadcasting devices in your room. There was no one else in the room. Their interpretation seemed to be the most logical."

"But, what if I told you that even when you're alone, you are not alone?" The comment made Ted's blood drop several degrees. He remembered what Jim had said before drifting off to sleep. He replaced his hat on the table and sat back down.

"Let's take a few steps back. How did you know about the events in the corridor during the attack? The events you describe took place *after* you were shot through the head." Ted suggested.

"Most call it an *out of body experience*, I believe. When someone is dead, the spirit or consciousness is separated from the body. That is what death is all about. However, that consciousness is still very much aware of the events taking place around it. Take for example the accident victim who watches them carry his body out of the vehicle and work on it. Or consider the person who hovers above his body during surgery, and even moves out into the waiting room to watch how family and friends are reacting to the crisis. You've heard of such things, haven't you?"

"Phantom images." Ted retorted. "Scientists tell us that it's a chemical reaction taking place in the brain. Several chemicals are hit with the last electrical impulses in the dying brain, the chemical reaction still takes place even though the impulse that triggered the reaction is now gone. As the chemicals react to the last burst of energy, they create dreams of what the person would like to see, or expects to see. The kind of experience you are talking about would require the existence of a..." here Ted was suddenly uncomfortable with the topic. It had moved into an area he had avoided for many years.

"...A soul?" Ipileno finished for him.

"Yes, a soul." Ted acknowledged. "However, if you accept the existence of a soul, you open a can of worms that people have been spilling for centuries: immortality, spiritual things, an afterlife, Heaven, Hell, God and the Devil."

"And you do not believe in these things?"

"I don't see how any intelligent person could. These are things that cannot be proven or disproven. They have to be taken on faith, and faith is a personal thing. You cannot take your beliefs, and try to force them on others. That has been the basis for centuries of holy wars, purges, inquisitions and crusades."

"But, I tell you that I have more than faith. I have a personal experience. I am an eye witness to what happens when we die. Yet, you discount my testimony because it does not fit into your scheme of the way the universe works?"

"It is your experience, Mr. Ambassador...Not mine. Until I have such an experience personally, I cannot verify your own."

"Nor can you discount it, either?" Ipileno suggested.

"No sir, I cannot discount it, either."

"Yet, the events I described to you during this *out of the body experience* are accurate. How do you account for that if I wasn't there when they happened? You, yourself, stated that I could not have obtained the information from others present, nor from reports, nor from surveillance films. How did I know these events?"

"Again, I am not claiming you weren't there. You were there, only you were dead. Fading chemical reactions in the brain were responding to information still coming in through various senses. Your ears still heard things. The sounds were transmitted to the brain which was damaged, and operating only in the form of previously triggered chemical reactions. Thus, the chemical reactions heard the sounds, the discussions, and transmitted them into memories being imprinted on the brain.

"This concept has been of particular interest to various security and law enforcement agencies. Some governments have actually conducted research into finding a way to break the code of memories stored in a person's brain at the time of death, and just after...before the chemical reactions cease. This way the killer could be identified through those stored memories. Secrets locked away in an agent's mind who was killed on a mission could be retrieved and the agent's mission completed after death."

"An interesting theory. So, nothing I could tell you here and now would convince you that my experience was the result of my having a soul?"

"I'm opened to any suggestion, but I believe that my theory would cover almost any situation or argument you could raise."

"And so I would have to prove to you that there is a realm, beyond this plane of existence before you would accept my testimony regarding life after death?"

"That would be the point that needed to be addressed, ambassador."

"But, if I could prove this to you; then you would be willing to hear me out on the other issues, the coming events? The changes in the Alliance...?"

"I would at least hear you out. Whether I would believe you, or whether I would arrest you for treason or conspiracy would be a different story."

"What if I could prove to you, right now, that I was in communication with your superiors even as we speak?"

"That would be a powerful position, sir." Ted admitted.

"What if I were to tell you that in three minutes...No, then you would claim that I had previously arranged the event. Pick a time period for me, something in the very near future... let's say no more than ten minutes."

"Alright, let's give it four minutes and fifteen seconds." Ted suggested.

"You do like to be precise." Ipileno smiled. He then nodded as if agreeing with someone who was not there. For a brief second, Ted thought of the old movie *Harvey* with the invisible pooka who was the star's constant companion. He dismissed the image instantly.

"Now, which of your superiors do you want to contact you?"

"How about Stanislov? He's out of the country right now. Getting Stanislov to contact me would be a trick, indeed."

"I see you like to make things interesting. Alright. Stanislov it will be. We're now down to three minutes and ten seconds." Ipileno declared looking at the clock on the nightstand. "What information do you want Stanislov to convey to you?"

"A promotion would be nice." Ted offered with laughter in his eyes. "But to be more reasonable, I would like him to tell me that I shouldn't arrest you for treason or conspiracy to over-throw the Alliance, and that your observations and recommendations for change have been heard by the governing council, they agree with the suggestions, and I'm to give you my full cooperation."

"Done!" Ipileno exclaimed. "You now have one minute and twenty-two seconds. It should be coming in on that phone." The Ambassador motioned to the phone on his nightstand and nodded with his bandaged head for Ted to move over to the phone to prepare for the call.

"This is crazy, sir. There's no way I would get a call from Stanislov in the time we're talking about. He isn't even near any kind of communication device. He's..." The phone rang and cut Ted off. The security man stared at the demanding device.

"I believe the call is for you, colonel. Go ahead and pick it up." Ted's face was already pale, and he fought to keep his hand from trembling as he lifted the receiver and silenced the blaring ring. He tried to keep his voice firm, but it was cracking as he replied.

"Brown here." Ipileno sat quietly, smiling with an inner satisfaction as Ted spoke with Stanislov who told him that the governing council had discussed the proposed changes offered by Ipileno, that they had already informally approved them, that there were some major changes coming in the next few weeks, and that Ted should give Ipileno his full co-operation.

"Excuse me sir. What is the pass code for this date and time?" Ted interrupted.

"You're in London. It's 3:00 to 6:00. The pass code is *Juggernaut*." Stanislov replied. Ted now knew it was not an imposter.

"...And there is no way in Hell you're going to get another promotion so quickly." Stanislov added. Ipileno seemed to know what was said on the other end of the phone, for he raised his left index finger as if to chastise Stanislov for his comment, wagged it twice to rebuke the statement; and stabbed his thumb upward in the air a couple of times as if to indicate raising or increasing something. Stanislov suddenly cleared his throat and added, "Well, we'll look into what we can do about a promotion." Ipileno then wiggled a good-bye with the fingers on his left hand to no one in particular, smiled at some inner joke, and Stanislov excused himself; bid Ted good-bye and the line went dead.

Ted nearly dropped the receiver into its cradle with nerveless fingers. He was in a state of shock. "How...?"

"How is something you will have to accept on *faith* for the moment. Suffice it to say, I have demonstrated that I can communicate from this room, even when I am alone. You set the criteria for the test. I have passed it. For now I need you on board my team. Can I count on you?"

"Yes sir, Mr. Ambassador." Ted stammered.

"I think you need a little time to assimilate all of this. Why don't you take a break? Get a good stiff drink, and something to eat. Sleep on it, and we'll pick this up tomorrow at about nine o'clock."

"Yes sir." Ted agreed. He scooped up his cap and darted from the room faster than he intended, seeking to flee before his own fears could shatter any more of his highly-respected self-control. As he stabbed the button for the elevator he told himself two things: one stiff drink was not going to be enough, and it would take several nights of sleep—if he could sleep—to put all of this into perspective.

Once the Colonel was out of the room, the air shimmered and a dozen EeeDees materialized around Ipileno's bed. He nodded to them, closed his eyes and drifted off to sleep while the extradimensionals stepped out of this plane of existence into the next.

CHAPTER ELEVEN

The Transfer of Power

"Okay, tell me everything you know about ETs." Ted insisted. Jim had put his brother off for two weeks while he was in the hospital. It was his first evening back in his home, and Ted had guaranteed that no listening devices were operating in the room. Jim waited a second as if gathering his thoughts, but his mind was actually performing another task, one he did before he ever approached this subject with anyone. Jim's delaying tactics were making Ted all the more *antsy*, but it needed to be done before they would be safe discussing the matter.

"It began the day the *Rapture Syndrome* hit. Colonel Jackson and I were ordered to Hell's Penthouse for a top level meeting. Nothing in that meeting has been declassified, so I can't tell you particulars, but the President was at the meeting along with *others*. They referred to themselves as Extra-Dimensional, hence EeeDees. They claimed that all the sightings of UFOs, and other unexplained events were tied in to them, and that they had been with us for centuries—as far back as man was on this planet. They claimed they had been working with us to prepare us for this time. They went public at the end of the meeting but wanted people to keep thinking of them as extraterrestrials or ETs. You remember the fleets of UFO and space craft that landed that day? They told everyone they were here to help. In reality, they have been working behind the scenes for centuries."

"Interesting; but it doesn't explain everything."

"Their blogs and news interviews suggest that they travel using ships. They use technology far beyond our own to do what they do. Thousands of the UFOs are parked all across the globe. Has anyone gotten into one?"

"No. Security around their ships is tighter than the security around our world leaders. There have been several accounts and each one has an ET appearing and either stopping or killing the intruder. The stuff in their ships must be pretty valuable and high tech to protect it like that.

"What if I told you that the ships are empty?"

"Empty?"

"It's a sham to keep us from knowing the truth about them."

"And that truth is?

"They don't need tech to do what they do. They can bend the laws of physics personally. They are not teleporting in and out. They are already in the room."

"They're invisible?"

"More than that. The way it was described is that if you are holding a cube in your hand; you can see the entire cube because you are both in the same dimension. But what if you were just a line on one of the squares that made up the cube? You would be unable to perceive the cube. At most, it would only look like other lines since that was all that was visible in your dimension. They are all cubes living in the dimension of cubes. We are the lines or the dots. We are part of their dimension; but we lack the resources to see their dimension. By turning down themselves and reducing themselves to the same dimension as we are in—say they become lines—they suddenly become visible to us. Then they increase themselves back to their true self; and we can't see them anymore. They can be in the room with you; and you would never even know it unless they chose to reveal themselves to you."

"You have no idea..." Ted replied. When Jim gave him a puzzled look, Ted continued. "I didn't see any EeeDees there, but I was given a first-hand demonstration of how they work. Now it makes sense. Ipileno has been in contact with the members of the governing council of the Alliance. It seems that each of them has an EeeDee with them at all times.

They can generate instantaneous communication among themselves without any electronic or mechanical equipment."

"So Ipileno has an EeeDee with him in the hospital room?" Jim asked.

"Yeah. We thought he was talking to himself, but he claimed to be communicating with the members of the governing council. When I confronted him about it, he had me test it to prove he really was in contact. I couldn't sleep for three nights after it happened. Just thinking about it still makes me nervous. I never know if there's one with me or not. How can you tell?"

"You can't. Not unless they want you to know. You always have to assume that there is one."

"It's the ultimate *Big Brother*." Ted noted.

"So what's happening now?" Jim asked to change the direction of the conversation before Ted thought to ask the obvious.

"Three days from now, the Alliance is going to announce it's restructuring according to Ipileno's recommendations. He will become the new head of the Alliance. The governing council will serve as an advisory position only. He's going to consolidate all the nations. He's going to put them under one government, one language, one economic system."

"The governments won't go for it. That's been the problem with the Alliance since the early days when it was just the European Union. No one government was willing to give up its independence. Everyone knew the European Union needed a central government. They all knew it needed a single economic system and policy, but no one wanted to give up what it already had. You remember the flack when they tried to go to Euros rather than country currency?"

"Did you ever realize that the European Union was formed without ever putting it to a vote of the people?"

"Hadn't realized that." Jim confessed.

"It was all done with treaties. Representatives made the agreements. They signed the treaties, and each country was informed of the decision after the fact; but no one was given the chance to have its population vote on it. Same thing with the American Union. Did that go to the people?"

"No" Jim admitted. "Maybe the people have been prepared to accept this?" he suggested. Ted missed the implication.

"The European Union was in such a mess from the countries going bankrupt, scandals, terrorists' attacks; they welcomed the New Alliance."

"But the Alliance is still a young government. Can they handle another change this soon?" Jim asked.

"They will. If not, the governing council has already given orders for the military to move in."

"So you might be shipped out?"

"No, I'm no longer military. Ipileno has me on his personal team."

"*Team?*" Jim asked.

"I'm not quite sure what it's all about, but he's been gathering a team. At first I thought it was just security to protect him from further attacks, but there seems to be more than security and military advisors involved. He's also recruited a number of top research people. Several scientists who were involved with genetics, immune system research, and other fields."

"Genetics? Has he mentioned the immortality gene?" Jim asked.

"Now that's a new one? What's that?"

"It was on the news a while ago, long before the *Rapture Syndrome*. Scientists discovered a gene which, if activated, would prolong the life of individual cells. It had the power to repair or regenerate any damaged area. Someone was speculating that it could create immortality if we could activate this gene in all of our cells. The theory is that when we are in our mother's womb this gene is active and building everything in our body. If we can find a way to activate it outside of the womb, we could replace injured body parts, heal ourselves from all diseases, and stop the aging process."

"Might be what they're working on." Ted admitted. "Most of this stuff is beyond me. I've seen some of the credentials of the scientists. They're good. Most have been ahead of the field in their research, and they have all been working either on gene therapy, immune system reconstruction from the AIDS virus, or other genetic projects."

"Is there a big push on AIDS research and the gay community?"

"There were a couple in there. Why do you...? Oh you think it's because Ipileno is openly gay?"

"No, it's more than that. It's part of the briefing we had at Hell's Penthouse. Technically, everyone who's still here after the *Rapture Syndrome* is gay..."

"Whoa!" Ted raised both hands, palms facing Jim as if to make him back off.

"It's not my theory. Look, I can't reveal what was discussed at that meeting. However, if Ipileno is in contact with the EeeDees like you say; then have him give you a briefing of your own. You're going to need to know these things if you're going to be on his team."

"That would be the best approach. Look, I have discretion in selecting my own team. Ipileno was impressed with your actions during the assassination. He'd like to have you on the team, and so would I. Are you interested?"

"I'd need to think about it." Jim replied. It was obvious that it wasn't the answer Ted was expecting.

"You've gotten gun shy on me?" he asked.

"Hey, having a slug dance around inside of you isn't something I'd want a steady diet of. Besides, I'm still military. I'm still employed by the American Union. I'm only here on assignment. When Ipileno starts doing all this restructuring, the AU may not want to play. I don't want to find myself in the middle of all this. My orders were to serve, but never forget my loyalty is to the American Union. I'm just a visitor here. Whenever I worked on any assignment with you, you knew my loyalty to country came first. Fortunately there was never any conflict. With Ipileno making these moves, I'm not sure. I'd either have to get special permission to join, or renounce my commission, and maybe my citizenship to take that job."

"Politics is sure a pain, isn't it?" Ted retorted. "If you want in, I'll pull what strings I can to get you in. If the AU won't go along; then we can take care of that problem, too."

***

"We need to leave." Eli noted. It was as if he had just read an e-mail or text message, but neither of the men used tech. They were so far off the grid; there was no grid where they were concerned.

"You'll need to get to Tel Aviv airport as quickly as possible."

"Where are we going?" Amir asked dousing the small campfire.

"There's going to be a meeting of the New Alliance Headquarters in three days. There is going to be a change in power. We need you to make contact with someone. He is going to need our help in the coming months; he just doesn't know it yet."

"New Alliance? Sounds serious." Shmuel added.

"It will be. It's one of the events we have been waiting for." Eli explained. "You will need to speak discretely with a man by the name of Jim Brown. He will be at the meeting, near the back."

"That's a pretty common name. Do we have anything else to go on?"

"He'll be in a wheelchair. Be careful. He works for the Security of the New Alliance. His brother is head of security and reports directly to Ipileno."

"Will it be safe to approach him at the meeting?" Amir asked.

"No, but he will eventually be stopping at a small tavern at this address." Enoch handed Amir a slip of paper which he was sure had not existed a few moments before.

"Don't reveal anything more than your names, and make the meeting look accidental. We just want him to be aware of you two for now."

With that Enoch and Eli picked up a few personal items, started to walk down the path leading from the grove; and as they walked they became more and more transparent until they were no longer there.

***

"So what's your decision?" Ted asked. Jim was sitting in a wheel chair at back of the Alliance council chambers. Ipileno had called for a press conference and an emergency meeting of the various members.

"I'm not comfortable with cutting the ties." Jim admitted. "I'd like to be on your team, but only if the AU gives the go-ahead, and even then I won't take part in any mission that endangers the American Union."

"Last we heard, the AU was making a lot of waves. Not just about you're being re-assigned, but about the restructuring of the Alliance, and Ipileno assuming control. Why don't you wait until after the meeting, and then we'll talk once more."

"What's going down?" Jim asked, every alarm in his mind going off. "What's this meeting going to do to change all that?"

"Look, it's best you just watch. When it's all over, and the dust settles, we'll talk." Before Jim could respond, Ted slipped away, and up to the podium next to Ipileno.

Several technicians were making their final adjustments to cameras, microphones and recorders. News photographers were snapping dozens of shots. Finally, Ipileno came to the podium. He arrived under his own power via motorized wheelchair. He did not yet have the strength to stand and walk great distances on his own. His bandages were gone. An eye patch covered his dead eye. He wore a hat so the head wound and current loss of hair would not be obvious. His right arm was still paralyzed and strapped in a sling across his chest. As we wheeled to face the room, the continuing buzz that had filled the meeting chamber for the last half-hour dropped to silence.

"Ladies and Gentlemen. Allow me to introduce myself. For those who have not heard of me, my name is Jason Ipileno. I am the new political leader of Italy, and during the recent vacuum of power in the Vatican since the *Rapture Syndrome*, I am the head of the Catholic Church. I am also the ambassador for Italy to the New Alliance, and was the victim of an assassination several weeks ago.

"You note that I said I was the victim of an assassination, not assassination attempt. To clarify, the attack was successful; but thanks to the efforts of a team of neurosurgeons who were available, I was revived. Death has a way of making us look at things differently. Too many times we are too caught up in our own little petty squabbles, ego trips, and personal empire-building to see the big picture. Death forces us to see the big picture.

"The governing council for the New Alliance has had the wisdom to recognize the importance of a central government to prepare our world to survive the various problems we are currently facing, and which are still to come. They have asked me to assume that role of leadership, and as of midnight last night, I was sworn into office.

"The time has come to put aside the insignificant differences that have separated us, and to focus on those things that unite us. We are a community of nations, but now we shall take the next step into becoming a family of nations. It's going to be like we have all moved in with one another. We are now a mixed family. It's like our children moving back in with their parents in order to make ends meet. We are going to have to make some adjustments with the living conditions, learn to share, trust, and get along. But the various problems that are facing us force us to move in this direction.

"We have been misled by various powers and those in positions of influence. First of all, we have been taught by various religious leaders that man has been basically evil. '*Sinful*' is the word that they have used. We have accepted their estimation of our own nature, and as a result of accepting this concept; we have taught our children that they, too, are basically evil. The result is that our children have grown up believing that they were evil; and have acted accordingly.

"It is this lie which has kept our race from achieving its true Golden Age. It has held us back. It has made us dysfunctional. Man is not evil, but good. Why is it that we feel good when we help someone? Why do we feel good when we succeed at something? Why do we feel good when good things happen? Because it is our true nature to *be* good! Just as we grieve when we see pain and suffering. We hurt when others hurt. We become angry at crime and abuse. It is because these things are contrary to our true nature.

"We have been told that we are basically evil by a system that is the true evil. It is the same system that encouraged child abuse. These are the very ones who told us to beat our children. This is the same system that kept women as little more than domestic slaves. They have plundered the poor. They have protected and shielded child abusers from the law. They have told us to hate those who are different. When did hate become a family value? They did not, would not tolerate differences they saw in others.

"The time has come to recognize these people and systems for the parasites they are. Under my administration, these teachings will no longer be accepted, nor taught. What we do now, and from this day forward we do for our children. This coming generation will be the one to inherit the Golden Age.

"We have seen the ETs among us. They arrived in their ships to help us. They have not been polluted by this religion of hate that has crippled us as a family. The key to curing AIDS would have been available years ago except religion tried to convince the world that this was God's judgment upon my people for choosing to love whom we wanted to love, how we wanted to love. We were punished for loving without restrictions imposed by an antiquated religious system.

"AIDS is not a curse from God. It is a biological weapon. It was created to attack people of color and my own kind. It was an act of government-funded terrorism that has killed millions of innocent people whose only crime was being different. The ETs have shown us how we were meant to be. The key to defeating this biologic weapon is hidden within each one of us. There is a gene in our genetic make up that has the ability to cure AIDS. It has the ability to re-activate an immune system that was rightfully ours until genetically defective members of the gene pool caused it to be shut down.

"Those who were genetically defective have been eliminated. They have paid for their own treachery. Mother Earth has removed them from her. She has expelled those genetically defective members of our race. She called forth our companions the ETs and allowed an act of nature to cleanse our race. We can now regain the paradise that is our rightful inheritance. We can reactive this gene. We can gain immortality. We will make pain, disease, disabilities and death a thing of the past. Under their guidance and work we will reach the potential we have always had within us. We shall be as gods."

The crowd burst into applause and rose to their feet to praise the message Ipileno was delivering. He sat in the wheelchair on the podium, looking almost embarrassed by the sudden attention. He used his one good hand to signal for order and quiet so he could begin once more.

"As we move into this New Age, we must recognize that we have already set into motion events that will cause a great deal of pain and suffering for us: crime, gangs, drug abuse, wasteful spending, excessive taxes, pollution and corruption. We are going to reap the whirlwinds sown by our ancestors. I wish that I could give you greater hope and encouragement; but I will never lie to you. The road is not going to be easy for us. Many may perish because of things we no longer have control over; but if we work together, those who survive will see the kind of future which once was considered to be a fantasy.

But we cannot build this future upon lies and misconceptions. We cannot succeed by giving power to those whose greed made them rich at the expense of others. Their money was their power. Today that power ends! I am declaring a single currency to be used for the New Alliance. Banks have already been given instructions on how to exchange current script for the new system. The wealth of this world will become available to all; and not just to a handful of criminals. I know that some will balk at such a bold change. They will want to cling to the patriotism of local governments. However, the truth is that local governments cannot save us from what is coming. The European Union went through economic collapse before. It has never recovered completely. There is an economic collapse about to hit the world. The financial leaders of the world have known about this for many years. The gold exchange system did not work. It was replaced by the silver exchange system. Then other systems came into play. The truth is that many countries have been bankrupt for many years; but no one held them accountable. Their money is all but worthless. They have made loans to other countries which were never repaid. They sold things without collecting the debt. They gave and they gave until they had nothing left to give. Other countries moved in to claim a share of these countries, only to invest heavily in a system that could not sustain itself.

"The currency which I am creating is based upon supply and demand. It is not based upon gold, silver or other commodities which lose value or can be lost. It is based upon the people. The people have always been strong. The people have always been the true wealth of a government. What we build, what we manufacture, what we grow, or create or develop is our asset. This is what the world wants. In return for what we have, the rest of the world will have to give us what we want. This is the true concept of supply and demand. The system I am implementing is a credit system. Each person will get credit for their work. They can exchange this credit for food, clothing, shelter, entertainment and other tangible commodities. However, it is all based upon the fact that the person obtaining these items must work, must produce something of value.

"Those who do not work will not be able to function in this new system. In the past, the governments have either ignored those who could not, or would not work; or they pampered them. This policy will now change. Each person, still living is valuable and has something of value to give back to the community. We will restructure to find ways to use those skills, abilities and talents so that all who want to work will be allowed to work. Those who do not want to work will no longer be allowed to drain the system."

Again the congress rose as a whole to thunder their applause and approval to the new policies under Ipileno. Ipileno waited patiently for them to finish.

"Our dealings with other countries will be based upon these same criteria. We can no longer allow other countries to continue to renege on debts or pay with currency that has lost its value. I have already begun to work with the banks of the Alliance, and we have joined all of their computer systems into a master system. As of this date, all banks will be operated by the government. We will no longer allow banks to take advantage of their customers with unrealistic charges to access their own funds, nor to use these funds for their own gain and still charge their customers for letting them use these funds. This ends now!

The audience bust into applause a third time. This time Ipileno continued to speak, and they dropped into their seats and sat quietly to hear all that he was saying.

"I have taken these actions to guarantee that we will survive the economic collapse which will hit the world in the next few weeks and continue for several months or even years. No one will lose anything by switching to the credit system. The world markets have seen Japan take serious hits in the stocks in the last few years. Their speculation and long-term spending have been a gamble; spending more than they have in order to reap greater benefits years from now. We would not tolerate this kind of financial spending from the common man on the street. We cannot continue to tolerate it from various countries and governments. Unfortunately this practice has caught up with that country, and they will have a difficult time recovering. The New York Stock Exchange has gone through similar drops in the value of stocks. The governments have taken action to keep the losses from being as severe as they could have been, but our investigations show that it is far more severe than either country is letting on. If Japan and others want to join our credit system, we are willing to make available to them our computer systems and to join their data with our own. Other countries who want to make this change are also invited to work with us to restore the global economy to what it once was.

"We need to set aside those things that separated us. By keeping us separate; governments have kept us weak. The truth is we are children of Mother Earth. This is where our allegiance should lie. We are the Children of Earth. We are citizens of the world. We will no longer allow pettiness to divide us and weaken us. By recognizing our strength as a single people; we take back control of our lives."

Again the applause forced Ipileno to stop momentarily.

"Now, with regards to other issues; we can no longer turn a blind eye to terrorism."

This time the roar and applause was almost deafening, and even when Ipileno tried to speak over it, he was drowned out. Those who knew him could see the annoyance in his good eye, but he waited for the crowd to finish.

"As of this day, we declare war on terrorism, no matter where it might seek to hide. No matter what name is uses. No matter what sheep's clothing it wears; we will destroy it…and destroy it completely." The crowd went wild.

"The destruction of an entire country: Egypt is an act of terrorism we should never have allowed, and once it was committed, we should never have allowed it to go unchallenged. As of this moment, there are terrorist groups in all of our cities. They are known to our police and intelligence agencies, but up until this point they were hindered from doing their jobs through court rulings, politics and red tape. That red tape is now cut. Anyone suspected of terrorist activities is subject to arrest. Their rights are suspended until they are cleared of these charges. We will move quickly, and decisively to wipe this cancer from our streets."

The cheers broke out. Ipileno raised his hand for silence. His face took on a very stern expression.

"Not everyone will greet this news with cheers. Many will scoff at these changes; others will try to undermine them. This is my pledge to you. We will survive!" The crowd started, but Ipileno was ahead of them and motioned silence. "In the past we placed too much emphasis on individuals. Protecting the rights of individuals has cost the countries as a whole too much. The greater good has suffered because of the few who were like dogs in the manger. They barked to keep the others from feeding at the hay; but could not use the hay themselves. Thus, all have suffered. This is my promise: I will do what is good for the whole, not for the few! I will make the hard decisions we must make to guarantee that we, as a whole, will survive. My decisions may not be popular, they will not be easy, but they will be necessary for the greater good. Thank you."

Ipileno then rolled off the platform as the members of the Alliance rose to give him a standing ovation. Jim sat in the back of the room, silent. His eyes gave no hint of what his mind was truly thinking. Amir nodded to Shmuel who was stationed near the rear exit. The two moved out and headed for the tavern listed on the piece of paper.

CHAPTER TWELVE

Wars and Rumors of War

"Why is it that the length of a war is getting shorter, but the death and destruction is still the same?" Jim demanded of no one in particular as he scanned the latest statistics as they came across his desk.

"Who said that wars were getting shorter?" Ted rebuffed.

"No one has to say it. You can just look at the facts. The older wars took years. There was even the Hundred Years War. That lasted generations. World War I and World War II took years. Then in World War II Hitler was known for his lightning wars. The Blitzkrieg took out entire countries in days, not months. Israel went to war and it was so quick, they called it the Six Day War. We then saw Grenada with just a few days. The first Gulf War with Iraq only took hours, not days to execute—even though we did wait around for weeks before doing any land force attacks. And now these wars."

"You're forgetting Korea, Viet Nam, Afghan II and Iraq. They took years to finish, too."

"The first two were police actions. Yes, they are viewed as wars in the history books, but when they were being fought, they were treated as police actions, and so our troops were never allowed to bring things to a conclusion. Politics controlled the time table, and so they took years. Whenever a country determines to go to war, and dedicates its entire forces to it, the wars are getting shorter."

"It's just that our technology is better. It takes less time to defeat the enemy." Ted noted.

"And Afghan II and Iraq?" Jim reminded. Ted just looked at him.

"But look at this. On September twenty-first, Ipileno assumes the presidency of the New Alliance. He declares war on terrorism. On September twenty-ninth, his intelligence force presents evidence that Libya-based operatives were the ones who transported the nukes to Egypt with the help of Iran. On October seventh, all military forces are launched against Libya and Iran. The opposition is disjointed, caught off-guard, and the entire country of Iran falls in thirty-six hours. Libya had been a little better prepared, tried to use several propaganda ploys about attacking civilian targets to gain sympathy, but then the entire structure collapses ninety-three hours later."

"But Libya tried to change its image. Threw out the dictator Gadhafi; tried to set up a new government." Jim added as an afterthought to his argument.

"Still didn't clean house enough. Those who took over still had terrorist ties. Still turned a blind eye to certain groups inside its boarders. No excuse. Both wars only took a little over five to six days. That's pretty impressive." Ted noted.

"But look at these tallies!" Jim shouted, slamming the print-outs onto Ted's desk. "We're talking several million people wiped out. I didn't even know there were that many people in the countries, let alone military personnel!"

"Jim, now you have to realize that in these kinds of countries, everyone serves the military."

"You're telling me that these numbers include civilians? We are targeting civilians?"

"We were targeting terrorists. For every man you kill who's a terrorist, you've got a wife, a brother, a mother, a father, a son or a daughter to take up the cause. Radicals know no sex or age distinction. You can't wipe out terrorism; you have to wipe out the terrorists...all of the terrorists: past, present and future!"

Jim felt his skin begin to crawl. The horror of the operation began to dawn upon him.

"Jim, remember your basic training on terrorism at the Department of Defense. The first thing we had to understand is that for Islamic people, Allah runs each of their governments. They would come to Europe and other countries to become citizens. They would renounce their prior citizenship; but they never did. In order to renounce their allegiance to their country; they would have to renounce their allegiance to Allah. Never happened. Never would. Don't you remember the problems we had in Europe and the old EU? Islam was spreading like wildfire. Governments were afraid to take a stand against terrorism because the population of Islamic people in their country had grown to the point of being a threat.

"Under the guise of religious freedom it went from clothing they could wear, to time off to pray, to not allowing practices belonging to other religions that offended them. The only people who had religious freedom were the Muslims. We could not tolerate any Anti-Islamic practice out of fear of them. They were using our ideals against us.

"Every Islamic person was part of the process to take over the world. Some did it violently through terrorism. Others did it quietly by converting others or increasing the Islamic population until they were the majority; and then they demanded Islamic Law rather that our laws to govern them. No matter how you look at it; it was a coup."

"But women and children?" Jim began, but Ted cut him off.

"It's a cancer. The *Israeli Incident* killed just as indiscriminately. Those troops in the field were killed, but the sulfur bombs in the other countries killed men, women and children. The numbers were just as big back then to break the power of Islam to make war. The strength of the terrorist armies was broken that day; but the seeds are still out there. The seeds are still growing."

Jim began to regret his permanent appointment to the New Alliance. Ipileno had pulled the strings. With his contact through the ETs, and the restructuring of all of North and South America into a single political unit new treaties were created. People were no longer thinking nationally. They were thinking globally. It was no longer the New Alliance or the American Union. They were all different parts of the same government, and slowly all the governments were coming under the control of Ipileno.

When Ipileno exposed the economic secrets of Old America and Japan, both countries began to devour themselves. Riots, panic and looting were nation-wide. Millions had died in both countries; some had set the toll as high as a quarter billion. Technology was smashed back to the Stone Age in some cities and states. With all the destruction in the American Union and Japan, only the New Alliance and their credit-based economic system had held fast. The American Union had sold its soul to join the economic community. It would recover, but it would take many years before it would be the world power it once was. Japan had chosen instead to side with China which had kept its eye on its eastern neighbor since World War II. Now Japan was at the door with hat in hand, signing any treaty China placed in front of it to regain its stability.

Jim knew that he had very few options. He was part of a genocide. It was not against any one race, nor against any one people, but it was a systematic genocide all the same. "What does Geneva say about all of this?"

"What can they say? Geneva is no longer neutral. It's part of the Alliance. Two-thirds of the countries who signed the various Geneva Accords and Agreements are part of the Alliance. They need the Alliance's economic system. They won't say a thing about this."

"And you're going to side with him? You're going to let him wipe out two countries, to crush them and murder their citizens until there's almost no one left?"

"That's the job, Jim! Get with the program. We're taking out terrorism. The terrorists who bombed schools. The terrorists who bombed churches. The terrorists who bombed hospitals, market places, ships, passenger jets and bus stations. It all stops now! No one made them pay when they killed a hundred here, or a hundred there. No one made them pay when they took out five of the world's landmarks and killed sixty thousand people. No one stopped them when they nuked Egypt and made it desolate for the next forty years. Well no more. NO MORE!!" Ted was shouting. "We refuse to live in terror any more. If this is the way the terrorists want to play the game, then it's time they knew what real terror is. There won't be anyone left to strike back in either of these countries. Those who survive will be too worried about where their next meal is coming from to think about killing anyone."

"Sir!" an aide snapped to attention, saluted, and handed Ted another print out. Ted scanned it, passed it to Jim who fought back the tears as he read the words on the page.

"Lebanon?" Jim probed.

"Yes sir." the aide replied. "The holy men of Lebanon have declared a Jihad against President Ipileno and the Alliance. They have opened their borders for all the refugees from Libya and Iran. They have called for all Moslems everywhere to come to Lebanon and strike back." The aide spun on his booted heels and marched from the room.

"Lebanon?" Jim was now demanding of Ted with his tone of voice.

"Yes, Lebanon. Get it through your head, Jim. This is war. It's not clean. It's not nice. It's not pretty. But it is going to be effective. Anyone...and I mean anyone who stands against Ipileno is going to be taken out. He's the only one who can bring about the programs we need to survive."

"Survive?" Jim lashed out. "What good is it to survive, when the entire world becomes a graveyard?"

"We will survive!" Ted caught himself. Thought for a moment, and then backstroked mentally. "Look, if this is more than you signed up for, why don't you take some time off? Take a leave. You came back to work way too soon from your injuries. I'll cover for you."

"Where will I go, Ted? Look out in the streets. Every city is now the site of civil war. We've been cleaning out terrorist strongholds in every city for five weeks. They've dug in, fought back and taken out everything they could before they finally died. We've lost crops, factories, stores, transportation, communications. Don't you see that we are bombing, shooting, burning, and nuking ourselves out of any chance to survive the natural disasters that are coming? When these other forces hit, there's not going to be anything left to save."

"Disasters?" Ted asked.

"Hasn't Ipileno briefed you about them?" The silence was all the answer Jim needed. "Look! I'm breaking security, but that oath was to the United States, and there's little left of it. Go to Ipileno. Ask him about *Wormwood*. Then tell me where I can go to get some rest." Jim snatched his cap off the coat rack by the door and stormed out.

***

Jim motioned for the waitress. "Scotch!" he ordered. A figure at the bar retrieved his drink and worked his way back to the table where Jim had hidden.

"Sounds like a rough day." Amir noted as he slid into the booth across from him.

"Can't talk about it." Jim's mood was more than surly.

"OK. Top Secret. Hush Hush, this is the headquarters for the Alliance. That goes without saying.

"You need to hit something? We can go to the gym, spar a few rounds? Maybe the practice range? Shooting things up always helps me feel better." Amir once more flashed his winning smile towards Jim.

"If only it were that easy." Jim replied. Amir slipped a piece of paper towards him face down. Jim turned it over.

"In the world you will have tribulation; but be of good cheer; for I have overcome the world."

"You?" Jim's voice was incredulous.

"Don't be surprised. There are more of us than you realize. I think your problem is that you feel like you are all alone in this. I know someone who felt like that. His name is Elijah."

"Does he have a last name?" Jim sipped the scotch. It was already hitting his empty stomach.

"No, but I think you might already know him. Seems he was having a bad day, too. He had called fire down from Heaven, consumed the sacrifice, ordered a few hundred false prophets killed, and then Jezebel threatened to kill him"

"Oh, *THAT* Elijah. So what did he do?"

"Believe it or not" Amir added in a disarming tone. "He took off for the hills and wanted to give up, but G-d spoke to him and pointed out that there were still seven thousand men in Israel who had not bowed before Baal."

"Maybe you could introduce me to him. I'd like to hear how he dealt with this feeling of being so helpless to fight the tidal wave that's about to hit."

"If that's what you'd like." Amir smiled once more. Jim nearly choked on his mouthful of scotch.

"Wait a minute. We are talking about *THE* Elijah, right?"

"That's the one. But he likes to be called *Eli.*"

"And you can arrange a meeting with him?"

"Whenever you want."

"Sorry, I'm not into séances." Jim was about to slide out of the booth. He had met Amir and Shmuel a short time ago. They were military. He could tell. But they had respected the fact there were things they could not discuss as they visited; but they seemed to be kindred spirits. The Bible verse quoting Jesus on the paper confirmed what he had suspected, but now his impression of the Israeli went over the top. He chose to break off the conversation.

"No séance, Jim. King Saul learned the danger of that." Jim looked up to see who had just joined them. He was an older Israeli. Jim tried to remember where he had seen the man before. Suddenly his mind connected the dots. He was one of the two terrorists who had detonated the nukes in Egypt. Jim's reflexes were to slide back and reach for his gun, but to his surprise him mind wasn't controlling his body. He slid over to make room for the elderly man.

"Jim," Eli added, "We really need to talk."

***

"*Wormwood*?" Ipileno echoed thoughtfully. Ted could not tell if the President of the Alliance was toying with him, or was actually trying to recall the reference. "Ahhh, *Wormwood*!"

"Then you've heard of it, sir?"

"It's a classified matter." Ipileno countered.

"I know it's a classified matter, but as head of security, I thought that you might want to enlighten me on the topic."

"Do you have a need to know?"

"It's hard to know if I have a need to know unless I know what it is that's being withheld." Ted was tired of the mind games. He always had the feeling that Ipileno was dissecting him for his own amusement. It was like the boy who would tear the wings off of flies, and then watch them suffer for entertainment.

"Perhaps it's time to bring you *into the loop*." Ipileno suggested. "However, once you are in the loop, you will find that it is not so easy to get out of the loop. What I am prepared to reveal to you will make you one of our *inner circle*, what once was called *the Illuminati*—the enlightened ones. With this knowledge comes great responsibility. Any indication of disloyalty or questionable behavior can result in a most unpleasant death. Are you sure you want to take this next step?"

"What are my options if I say '*no*'?"

"Seeing how you already have the term *Wormwood* as part of your vocabulary reduces your options. Enter our *inner circle*, be obedient and live. Betray us and die slowly and painfully. Learn no more, and your death will be quick."

"So my options do seem limited if I want to keep on living." Ted observed, trying to swallow the fear which was rising in his throat.

"This..." Ipileno paused turning to the empty air behind him. "This is an extra-dimensional. An *EeeDee* for short." As Ipileno spoke, the empty air began to quiver, then shimmer and flood with light. Ted covered his eyes, cried out in the intense pain the sudden increase in light caused him. It took several moments for his vision to return, and several more for the flashing lights and phantom images caused by the original light to stop disrupting what he was seeing. It was a creature more majestic than he had ever seen. His knees were weak, unable to hold him. He dropped to the ground, shivering. Slowly the creature before him seemed to become *less* than it was previously. Ipileno had waited for Ted to fully recover from the display of power the EeeDee had just demonstrated.

"Contrary to the popular opinion, these are not beings from other worlds come to save us in our hour of need. They are beings from another dimension, a higher plain of existence than our own. They are not teleporting in as people have been told. The EeeDees are everywhere." Ipileno confessed.

"Angels?" Ted dared to ask.

"That is one of our names." The EeeDee admitted.

"You stand in the Presence of God?" Ted suggested.

"There is no God." The EeeDee snarled. "There are various levels of power among us. Factions war from time to time. New alliances are made or broken to keep the universe in balance."

"And Jesus, Buddha, Mohammed, Moses?" he asked.

"They were men we were working through, except for Jesus. He was one of us. He broke the laws we live by. He made himself known to the world prematurely. He created chaos among the order we were creating for the world. He has been dealt with and no longer poses a threat."

It was too much for Ted's mind to grasp. Everything he had known crumbled. It was harder to accept than the appearance of aliens from another world coming to save them. He diverted his attention from the EeeDee. He could not think about the concepts that had been forced upon him.

"This is how you were in contact with the governing council while still in your hospital room?" Ted stammered, trying to regain some sense of control to his body.

"You are quick to catch on. I like that in you, Ted. Each of us at the higher levels of power in the world governments have at least one EeeDee with them at all times. They are our counselors, advisors, and helpers. They keep things moving in the right direction."

"The right direction, sir?" Ted asked but his eyes were drawn back to the EeeDee who had not broken eye contact ever since Ted was able to look directly at it.

"We are the guardians for your plane of existence. Our nature is such that we are several levels beyond your own comprehension of reality. You are like a speck, unaware that it is part of a something greater. We are aware of all levels of existence. We see the big picture. We are aware of events on other levels of reality which you can never understand."

"Are we talking about Heaven?" Ted dared to ask. The light of the creature increased enough to cause pain, and Ted huddled on the floor.

"That is the wrong kind of thinking. That is the enemy's teachings. We are here to set you free of such influence." the voice sang in his mind.

"Then explain it to me. Help me to understand." Ted asked, daring to lift his eyes back to the creature which was not as brilliant as before.

"We are not the only life form at our plane of existence. We are many, but the many are not one. We are divided into two."

"Good and evil?" Ted suggested trying to grasp as quickly as he could. The light increased causing further pain.

"Good and evil are the enemy's way of thinking. In order to have good and evil, you must have some standard that determines what is good, and what is evil. Something to which you can compare your actions and determine if they are good or evil. There is no such standard. Good is a subjective term, dependent upon who is in power, and which laws have been passed. There is no way to define it, or to regulate it. Thus it is an ineffective term, and is not part of our concepts. We simply recognize that there is our way, and that there is their way."

"And how do we know which way to accept?" Ted asked.

"That is why we are here. All life, on all planes is about choices. We choose what we want to be. You choose what you want to do."

"And there is no right choice, nor wrong choice?"

"There are those choices which comply with our way of acting. There are choices which conform to the other side's way of acting. We are here to recruit all of this world to our way of acting. To make it part of our power base..."

"You see, Ted," Ipileno interrupted as he rose from the desk, raised Ted from the floor, and dropped him into a chair. "These two forces are also at war."

"I thought at some level there would be an end to war. That somewhere along the way war would no longer serve a purpose." Ted offered.

"And that day is coming, but until the war at their level," Here Ipileno stabbed in the direction of the EeeDee with his thumb, "...is over, there cannot be an end of war on our level. This is a chess game being played out on so many levels; the human mind cannot comprehend it. As young children we play checkers, and then we discover chess in which the playing board is the same, but the pieces are different and move in different ways. From there it assumes a three-dimensional level in which the pieces move, the board moves, and everything changes completely with each move. There are so many variables that the mind struggles to plot three or four moves into the future. Take that concept, and multiply it several hundred times. There is no way we humans can even grasp checkers, much less the final confrontation between these beings."

"The other side has misled you for thousands of years. The other side created a written account of what they wanted you to know, but that account is questionable at best, and lies more often. So long as the inhabitants of your world read this account of the issues on our plane of existence and believe it, the other side wins. We, however, do not believe any written account could ever give the true picture. We have chosen to act more directly, to become involved with members of your race on various levels. We have shown them how the written account is weak, ineffective, full of contradictions, lies, and misrepresentations. When you hear only one side of a story, you tend to side with that position. The more enlightened of your race have opened up to us, and allowed us to teach and guide them. They see the greater help in a race willing to interact with lesser races verbally than to set down one written account and leave that account unchanged for centuries. It just can't address all the issues. It cannot stay relevant."

"After my recovery in the hospital, *Abaddon* here came to me to instruct me. I have the remnants of someone else's mind inside of here." Ipileno tapped his forehead as he spoke. "This person had been in constant contact with the EeeDees for most of his life. He discovered that the only way to contact the EeeDees for help was to do the very things the other side was forbidding us to do. It was a massive lie on the part of the other side. They gave us rules, regulations, laws and edicts which were all designed to keep us from making contact with the only other life forms that had an opposing view from their own. Talk about creating a captive audience. I would never have known this except for the person whose brain was used in the transplant had all these memories. As soon as I regained consciousness, my own mind was networking with the new brain tissue, and hooked into these other memories. As soon as I recalled memories of *Abaddon* through this other person's memories, he appeared, helped me recover, and has spent all this time instructing me."

"So where does *Wormwood* come into all of this?" Ted dared to ask. He made sure to direct his question to Ipileno, and not *Abaddon*.

"*Wormwood* is nothing in the great scheme of things. This world is nothing in the bigger picture." It was *Abaddon* who spoke, but Ted kept his eyes on Ipileno. "*Wormwood* is an asteroid coming from outside of your solar system. It will strike the earth. It will cause great destruction, but it is nothing compared to other events which are yet to be."

"Other events?" Ted almost choked the words out of his lips, and was finding himself once more locked into *Abaddon's* gaze as the EeeDee spoke.

"The continental plates that were cracked and torn asunder millennia ago have just about spent their inertia. Before they do, they will strike other plates deeper down and more secure than they. This will begin to reverse the process; driving the continents back into one land mass. This will result in great earthquakes. Pollution will increase. Sunlight will be filtered out. Plant, animal and human life will die; but will not become extinct if the earth follows our plan."

"These are all things that will happen because of events triggered by the other side." Ipileno continued. "The other side is going to wipe out the earth's ability to sustain its life. Our population is far too large to survive when these events hit. We will turn upon ourselves and kill to survive. The EeeDees are guiding us to weed out those in the population now who would hinder our evolution to the next stage. By removing these undesirables now; they will have no place in the aftermath. They will not drain our resources. Our population will be less; but the earth will be able to provide for those who are left. At that point these events will force us to unite and work together for our survival. If these undesirables are not removed before then; they would only tear us further apart and hinder our growth as a race.

"We are destined for greatness. Darwin was correct. We must evolve. But do we let natural selection take millennium to sort out those who are best for our future; or do we speed up the evolution of our race with a conscious effort, and cleanse our race in only a matter of years to bring forth the Golden Age in our lifetime?

"The enemies of the EeeDees have been keeping us weak. They have been using lies to misguide us and keep us under their control. We are the true *freedom fighters,* Ted. We are in a war to liberate the human race from these tyrants. Make no mistake, Ted. They are going to invade earth at some point and try to regain control; to put us back under their rule. They will try to force us to their way of thinking and living. When this happens, the EeeDees who have been helping us, guiding us, will step in. It will be a great battle, but we can win it. Once this battle is won, then Earth will be able to recover from all the abuse the other EeeDees have put it through. With peace on the EeeDee level, there will be peace on our level. We will eventually see the Golden Age our ancestors have tried to create."

"But why weren't we able to achieve this Golden Age before?"

"Every time we came close to achieving the Golden Age, there was the major presence of a gay society accepted and functioning as part of the over-all society. Whenever the Golden Age has been furthest from us, any gay presence is hidden or nil."

"Wait a minute. Are you trying to tell me that gays will bring about the Golden Age?"

"Actually, I'm ready to burst a major bubble you've been hiding in. I know this will come as a shock to you, but there are things about our genetic make-up, the *Rapture Syndrome* and other issues which we need to go over."

Abaddon shimmered out of sight. Ipileno ushered Ted away from the desk, to the table where they would be more relaxed for the rest of the briefing which would take several more hours.

CHAPTER THIRTEEN

Subversion at Home

"We've pretty much wiped out the terrorists, Jason." Ted had grown comfortable with referring to President Ipileno by his first name when they were in private.

"I don't think we've even begun the process." Jason replied as he sorted through several stacks of papers.

"We've crushed Iran, Libya and Lebanon. Our forces have rooted out the strongholds in each of the cities, town and suburbs."

"You're forgetting our Two Israelis." Ipileno snapped.

"What have they been up to this time?" Ted knew that these two men, whom many news sources were now referring to as the Two Witnesses, were a thorn in the president's side. No matter what his men tried; they could never capture them. Those who came face-to-face with them rarely survived the meeting.

"They polluted major water supplies. Tainted them with something that make them look and smell like blood. It's killing what little marine life we have left, and we can't afford to lose many more fresh water supplies. The ecology has done enough damage without them adding to the problem."

"OK. Those two keep getting away. But all of the other terrorist cells and organizations have been quiet...maybe even gone completely. There haven't been any reported terrorist attacks or actions for three months." Ted added trying to bring Ipileno out of his sour mood.

"Just because the viper is silent, does not mean it's gone. We may have taken out the militant forces, but there is still a major faction that remains untouched."

"Untouched? How? We've waged an all-out war against any terrorist group we could find or identify. We've tracked down all caches of weapons and explosives. We've raided their training camps, we've tapped into their computer records, identified their leaders, members and supporters. Anyone who's even related to any member has been identified, detained, sentenced or killed."

"There's a terrorist group we've completely ignored up to this point. I felt it best to wait because this is going to be an even greater war than the last..."

"Greater than the last?!" Ted blurted out. "How? That was probably one of the most costly, one of the most destructive and bloody wars this world has ever seen. After we've tallied all the deaths; both from direct military action, and those who died from famine, disease, and neglect caused by the terrorists; the figures were astronomical. By our calculation twenty-five percent of the entire world's population has died."

"Not all of that was from our personal wars. There was a lot of death in the America Union, Japan and other countries when they suffered economic collapse. Their own riots in the streets, rebellions and uprising accounted for several million deaths there, too." Jason replied in his tone of voice designed to calm those around him who were beginning to lose control.

"We're still talking about over a billion people. One in seven people are dead. How can the next action be greater than that?"

"Ted. This is a weeding out process. When our research finds a way to activate the immortality gene, everyone on the earth will want it. If everyone on the earth gets it, the earth may not be able to sustain us. It may seem brutal at this point, but I would rather identify the dead wood, the malcontents, the sick, and others who would drain our supplies before the immortality gene is activated; than try to deal with people who are immortal, and try to find a way to kill them later."

"It just seems to be a lot killing. When does it all end?"

"When we've removed those from society who will pose a future threat to our Golden Age...Now this should be our last target."

"In Cees?" Ted replied picking up the dossier Ipileno handed him.

"Neo-Christians." Jason explained. "In Cees are just their initials."

"Haven't heard of them. Where are they based? What kinds of numbers are we talking about?"

"We don't have that kind of information. All we know is that they're everywhere."

"What bases have they hit? Which installations do they target?"

"They don't hit installations or targets."

"Then what kind of threat do they pose?"

"The worse kind of threat we know. They don't target installations. They don't hit targets. They recruit."

"Recruit? For what? There has to be some larger objective they're trying to reach."

"Global conquest is their plan."

"But if they're not trying to over-throw anything, how can they conquer the world?"

"It's a battle of ideas. This is the secret arm of the EeeDees' enemies. They have been working behind the scenes. While we have been actively trying to take out the known enemy, they have gone about their work, quietly, secretly. We don't know how many there are. We don't know where they are. All we know is that they are everywhere, like a cancer spreading across the face of the world."

"How do we fight this? How do we stop it? Can't the EeeDees step in? Isn't there something they can do?"

"This is what they have been trying to do for centuries. They have done all that they can do. Apparently, the enemy they are fighting is ruthless. The EeeDees have lost a number of their own to the enemy operatives. Whenever the EeeDees get close to any major group of In Cees, the enemy moves in and the EeeDees never hear from their agents again. They are now forced to take an indirect action through us."

"Won't we be losing people to these enemy EeeDees, too? From what I've gathered, we can never know when an EeeDee is present. If the same is true of these enemy EeeDees, our entire force could be wiped out before we even move against the In Cees. You've seen what happens when we go up against the Two Israelis."

"The Two Israelis are different. They won't be part of this mission. It seems that both factions of EeeDees are governed by, for lack of a better term, rules of engagement. While the EeeDees can be wiped out by their enemies, apparently the enemy EeeDees are not at liberty to take action against us directly. That's the loophole the EeeDees are using. From this point on, it's up to us. We have to take action to physically identify those who are part of the Neo-Christian movement. We have to learn how they recruit, where they recruit. We have to separate them, shut them down, and then wipe them out. Once this faction is gone, then the enemy EeeDees will lose their power base in this world. They will have no choice but to retreat, leaving this world to our extra-dimensional allies. When that happens, then they can help us to reach our full potential."

"So where did they come from? What do we know about them?"

"Most of it is there in the dossier. They emerged after the *Rapture Syndrome* hit. They claim to be the re-birth of the old Christian movement. They claim to be a new faction of that because all the Christians were wiped out in the *Rapture Syndrome*."

"All of them?"

"Yes, all of them. Seems that those who were genetically defective found the teachings, the attitude of the Christian movement fit them perfectly. The EeeDees told me that it was one of the things that worked in our favor. The *Rapture Syndrome* was the first great purge. It took out all the genetically defectives. It also took out the entire Christian movement. Most of those with the attitudes and beliefs of the Christians were gone. It should have been the end of the movement, but we were busy with other matters. We had to turn our attention to economic problems, restructure political empires, wipe out terrorism, and set into motion several programs that will insure our control over the world so we can move it in the direction it needs to go.

"Because we were distracted, several people obtained literature, material and resources from the Christian movement—apparently looting homes of Christians wiped out by the *Rapture Syndrome*, used it for their own purposes, and have begun to spread its lies like a cancer through our entire society. We've uncovered massive hidden libraries, several printing presses and binding machines. So much of the material was on personal computers before the *Rapture Syndrome* that anyone can take it, format it, print it and start the distribution process all over again.

"They've begun teaching homophobia once more. They've taught that man is basically evil. They've discouraged women from seeking to be equal or superior to men. They brought back beating their children as a form of punishment."

"They beat their children? Why?"

"It's part of their basic teachings. They encourage all of their followers to strike, whip or beat their children; to do whatever the parents want in order to force their children into their unnatural way of thinking and acting. Their literature even refers to using rods or clubs to beat their children. In their society, children have no rights. They are little more than property. Women are not allowed to speak out against what their husbands are doing. They can't act without their husband's permission. It's all about a very military, structured discipline that stifles women and children. It makes them less than second class citizens."

"So where do we start?"

"We have several leads. Some of the EeeDees have seen things on the streets. Someone has handed off a pamphlet or book to someone else. People have been overheard speaking about the Neo-Christian doctrines or teachings. We have a list of some potential In Cees, but we need more information. You'll need to move against them, but we have to move quietly at first. You'll need to use only those agents you can trust. Once we have more information, we can move publicly against them; but for now we identify those we can and monitor them. We find out where and when they meet. We try to find their leaders. Then we take them out, one group at a time."

"And this should finish it? This should be the last war we have on the home front?"

"When this movement is crushed, the EeeDees promise me that we can begin to build. Ted, this is something we owe to the children...Not just ours who will inherit the Golden Age, free of their poisonous and self-destructive teachings; but their own children. We have to rescue them from this abusive parenting style. We can't sit back and let the children continue to be beaten, abused and their minds poisoned about their being evil and worthless. We have to move quickly before too much damage is done. With each day we delay, another child is scarred physically, mentally or emotionally. It's going to take a lot of work to salvage these children."

"What about the women in the movement?" Ted asked.

"They went into this knowing what it meant. If they want to surrender their freedom, if they want to sacrifice their free will; we can't stop that. Most of these women are sick. They have extremely low self-esteem and self-images. They have come out of abusive relationships, and they can only function in an abusive relationship. They are a kind of co-dependent. If we take them out of this environment, within a month they will have found someone else to abuse them. We can't think about the women. We can't salvage the men, but we do this for the children. We owe it to the children. We are their only hope. These perverts are twisting their minds. They are preying on the young, the innocent, the weak, and the misguided. They do it quietly so no one notices. Their victims don't know where to turn for help. We're their only hope."

Ted took the dossier with him as he left Ipileno's quarters and went to his own office. Once he had accepted Ipileno's position, he began to move up the ladder of power. Each time he proved himself, he found himself a little higher in the system. Now he was assigned a penthouse office which was half a floor. One entire wall was lined with electrical equipment. Not all of it was for monitoring information. There were a lot of "perks." He had the latest high definition 3D screen television as large as a small theater screen. He had digital recorders, players, surround sound and converters. He could pull up any form of entertainment he wanted from the elaborate control panel on his desk. Another half of a wall was a wet bar. He had any food he wanted, any drink he wanted. He had it all. The view from this office was magnificent. Everything about the position spoke of power, and power was the ultimate aphrodisiac. Women were drawn to him. Women he had never thought to be in his reach were now throwing themselves at his feet. It was not uncommon to come into the office and find several waiting for him, already prepared to entertain him. He had never known such appetites. It had been intoxicating for him. Every fantasy he had ever had, and those he had never even imagined were played out before him, non-stop if he so desired.

Ipileno had told him that everyone left after the *Rapture Syndrome* had the homosexual gene, but he wasn't feeling any desire to move in that direction. Of course he knew that if he did, there was that group of admirers waiting to serve him as well.

This night he had come into his office to find three of his regulars already putting their latest fantasy together and begging him to join them. He had to shut them down, and send them out so he could work. They were too much of a distraction. He had thought how such a life style under the per-*Rapture Syndrome* would have cost him his position, but this new concept of tolerance and acceptance of all beliefs, life styles, and sexual orientation was liberating. No one thought the lesser of him for his indulgences. No one would raise any question, or call attention to it so long as the important work got done. The In Cees were important work.

As the last admirer left giggling at some hidden joke, he locked the door to keep out any further interference. He liked that about his admirers. They respected him. They respected his power. It was understood that when he wanted to work; no one would disturb him. He now sank into the plush high-back chair behind his desk, hit a button on the arm of the chair and the lights were reduced by half. Another button brought up the soft sounds of a waterfall, birds, and other forest sounds. A third button activated the soft jazz which helped him to think.

"Only those I can trust." Ted told himself. He flipped through the dossier, noted about ten to fifteen contacts right in the neighborhood. He checked their photos, background information, and other data. Although the electronic equipment designed to record his own thoughts, observations and words was available to him, he scribbled notes on a pad of paper. He felt a little more in control with his old familiar style of working through problems. He drew arrows from one character trait to another. He wrote questions above each one. He needed to know what kind of team would best slip into the movement without creating suspicion.

As Ted studied each picture, he was surprised at how innocent the people looked. Gazing into their eyes one would never suspect that they were children beaters—wife abusers. That, more than anything else, frightened him.

"You'd think that someone so evil would have it show in their eyes." He then dismissed the though as he recalled several serial killers he had to track down and bring to justice. When he saw them, he wondered if they had some *Dorian Grey* painting hidden away that displayed all of their sins. Most people fell prey to these perverts because they didn't look evil. They looked innocent, helpless, or trustworthy.

It took Ted almost two hours to develop the kind of profiles he needed on the known In Cees. He had pulled up several psychological profiles on the computer. Every known psychotic profile was stored in a vast data base. Top psychiatrists, psychologists, and experts in behavior science and modification had contributed to this program. The official program name had been forgotten long ago. Those in his line of work had simply referred to it as the *Nut Bin*. It was a collection of every nut that was out there, and what similar nuts would do in various situations. Every police agency tied into it found it extremely reliable in predicting the patterns of serial killers, rapists and collectors.

Ted rose from his desk which covered an entire corner of his office, worked his way around to the front of it, crossed to the wet bar, filled a glass with ice; and poured the ancient Scotch over the cubes. They made a cracking sound as the room temperature liquid hit the frozen chunks, the beverage seeping into the crevices. He swirled the cubes around in the glass to chill the entire drink, took a sip, savored the effect; and then swallowed a third of the glass in one gulp. The alcohol hit his stomach which had missed both lunch and dinner. Ted knew what would happen, and he found the immediate *buzz* delightful and exhilarating.

Ted thought about unlocking the door to see which diversion had waited outside for him, but he knew the job was only half over. He carried the bottle, the ice bucket, and the glass to the lush sofa. He dropped into the enveloping cushions, propped his feet up on the glass coffee table, and studied the sky line from out of his window. As the alcohol surged to his mind, he considered the first name for his team. There was only one member he could trust completely. He set down his glass, twisted his wrist around and stabbed the code for his brother's apartment phone into the micro-system. He pressed the audio button and increased the volume of the speaker. The phone rang several times, but there was no answer. After the fifth ring, he could hear it switching him to the message center. He disconnected before it came on line.

Ted retrieved his glass, finished off the contents, and sighed. He wasn't sure what he was feeling. Somehow Jim was closing off to him. He wouldn't say that his brother had become unreliable, nor was his brother a security risk; but there was something there. Jim had disagreed with the policy of the Alliance. Ted had chalked it up to Jim's American ethics. He recalled Jim's resistance to the show of force he had to display at the airport the day Jim had arrived. He was uncomfortable with several other actions the security force had taken. Of course, Ted had to admit, when Jim was needed; he had no problem with killing. He recalled the assassination of Ipileno. He remembered several incidents during the Civil Terrorist War—as it was now being called. His brother had been quick, efficient, and deadly. Jim's actions had taken out several strongholds of terrorist activity. He had saved medical centers, protected crops and supplies. He had killed thirty terrorists on his own in a raid where the terrorists were holding fifty children hostage at a school. No, Jim wasn't gun shy. He wasn't disloyal. Ted wasn't sure what it was, but in the back of his mind he was glad that Jim had not been home. He mentally removed his brother's name from the list of team members.

He was too tired to think any more about the matter. He would be more efficient during the early morning hours. He did his best work in the early hours before dawn. He needed a distraction. He filled his glass with the twenty-year old Scotch, aimed the remote control towards the door, and unlocked it, letting whoever was waiting outside in.

CHAPTER FOURTEEN

Spinning The Web

"These are the only known contacts we have. Now according to intelligence reports, this is a major operation. Don't let their seeming lack of discipline or training fool you. They have operations throughout every city in the world. We are going to be the prototype operation. What we put into effect here will become the template for other operations. Our treaties with other nations will give us jurisdiction to move virtually anywhere, any country, any base of operations, and carry out our objectives with the complete support of any local or national government. Keep that in mind as we put everything together. Don't think locally; expand your thinking to globally. Yes?" Ted responded to a raised hand near the back of the conference room.

"You said 'virtually anywhere.' Which areas are we restricted in our operations?" It was Spencer. He had been chosen for his quick grasp, his attention to detail, and his ability to develop complex and effective strategies in split seconds under pressure. Ted paused for a moment and reminded himself that those were the very qualities he had wanted to add to the team through his brother, Jim. Though Spencer was a second choice, he was still very good.

"Our main problem area will be Israel. When Libya, Iran and Syria were taken out, Israel agreed to work with the Alliance, set up new peace plans; but they still maintain sovereignty in their own country. Although Ipileno has brought peace to the Middle East with the treaties both parties have signed, this was a point of contention with Israel. You might recall from news stories that parts of the treaties had to be re-written to accommodate Israel. Where all the other countries in the Alliance are full members, Israel is only an ally. We may think of them as an Alliance member, but in this matter we need to view them more of a possible *hands off* location."

"They have enough of their own operatives in the field to understand the danger of making such an international agreement." It was Billings. She had been the demolitions member.

"Yes, theirs is one operation we haven't been able to neutralize. Our other limitations are mostly in Africa. We have treaties and agreements with them, but they want to be brought in on any operation we send in. We'll target operations there later in the execution stage. Once we have a proven track record, they will be more agreeable with our tactics."

"What about the oriental block?" It was Dane, the communications officer.

"China, Japan, Taiwan, Korea and the Southeast Asia block have agreed to cooperate fully. Apparently, this Neo-Christian movement has caused a lot of problems in their countries, both before and since the *Rapture Syndrome*. Beijing is more than happy to open the Oriental Block to our efforts. It keeps them from having to use their own resources, and we're the ones who get the blame if something goes wrong."

"Saving face all the time." Dane quipped.

"We have targeted these locations as the most likely places to make contact." Ted clicked the remote control on the laptop computer, and it displayed an area known as *Old Towne*. "We've seen these three people..." Again the computer displayed the images Ted was referring to on the wall. "This is Stacy Adams, Ian Probst, and Eric Hennings. We know that they are contact points for the In Cees. We don't know how high up in the operation they are. They may be small fries, or they may be the key points. We need to find out.

"They frequent this tavern, this restaurant, and this bus station."

"How do we make contact?" Rawlings asked. He was the one who actually frightened Ted. Rawlings was the intelligence gathering officer. *Torturer* seemed like such an ugly word, and Rawlings saw his contribution to the team not as something ugly, but as a disciplined art. He had offered to let others watch him work; he loved an audience. So far most had declined. Those who had attended the private sessions rarely went back for a repeat performance except for Schmidt. She had become a pupil of Rawlings, and the two had formed a close relationship.

"That's the unusual thing about this group. We've tried to find ways to make contact before, but all of our efforts failed. On those few times when contact was made, our operatives left to meet with them, and were never seen nor heard from again."

"So it's a high risk operation?" Spencer asked.

"You wouldn't think so to look at them." Ted observed.

"Those are the ones you have to watch out for. *Still water does run deep.*" Schmidt quoted.

"I once looked like them." Rawlings declared. A quick glimpse at the dead eyes of their intelligence gatherer made everyone suppress a shudder that tried to run up their spines.

"Yes, Spencer, this is classified as a high risk operation. As best we can tell, these contacts make the decision as to whom to approach, and whom to avoid. They're good, very good."

"So what's the plan?" Dane asked. Ted nodded towards Spencer. The tall, lank man rose from his chair near the back of the room. Ted had noted that it was always Spencer's habit to take the chair most distant from the others—even if there was plenty of room at the table, as if it gave him a greater vantage point to observe those he was with. The Norwegian took the remote from Ted and continued the briefing.

"We've gone through several files on this operation. We have tried to identify the kind of person they recruit. This is the profile we've developed." Spencer's chart came up on the wall. There were various codes and marks and numbers scattered throughout the chart.

"They tend to go for the ones who look down–and–out. They avoid those who have a professional look, seem to have money, or have any kind of strong self-confidence. This means they target those who are the most susceptible, those who have nothing to lose, those who are hungry for acceptance or recognition."

"Sounds like the kinds the cults used to target." Billings noted.

"Exactly. That's the kind of targets we are going to offer them. Notice that there have been more contacts at the tavern than at the restaurant, and more at the restaurant than at the bus station."

"So they seem to like to use closed quarters rather than be out in the open." Dane noted.

"Yes. I suspect that they are aware of the danger they are in. They want to keep things unnoticed. This is why they use the tavern more than the restaurant. People are more likely to speak to strangers at the tavern than they would at the restaurant, and no one will think much of it. The bus stop is where people are the least comfortable with new contacts. I would be surprised if there were any first contacts at the bus station. If I were them, I'd start the contact at the tavern; looking for those who are the most vocal against the system— the ones who are willing to talk and listen. From there the second contact takes place at the restaurant, perhaps a free meal. Those who are still hesitant end up at the bus station.

"We're going to place Billings and Dane in the tavern for several nights. We're going to dress you down so you look like people down on their luck." Ted passed two dossiers down to Billings and Dane. "These are your new identities. You don't know each other, and so all communications between you, unless initiated by the In Cees should be avoided. Dane, you're a former business investor who's been wiped out by the new credit-only economy. We think this will make you favorable to them. It will show that you're down–and–out. It will establish that you are hostile towards the Alliance; and your skills in finances will make you valuable to them.

"How will a financier be valuable to them?" Dane asked as he flipped through the papers.

"An operation like this will have to use a lot of money; otherwise, how could they appeal to the down–and–out?" Spencer offered.

"We have long suspected that there is an underground economy." Ted interrupted. "Similar to the kind of underground economy in the American Union; and in areas where the questionable element of society live. They do not want anyone to keep track of them, what they do, what they buy; how much they have. The underground economy is used to avoid taxes; remain undetected. These societies normally use the barter system, or cash. With cash no longer having any value, the underground economy has been forced to find some other form of currency. A person who understands investments, financing and money systems would be valuable to help them build this underground economy."

"Billings, you're going to be a mother of three who is now out on her first night as a prostitute." Spencer explained.

"Shouldn't I be in the *red district*? Almost nobody works taverns or street corners anymore. You can make more in the *red district* or working for legalized houses than by yourself in a tavern." Billings noted.

"Point taken, but this is the very reason we want you in the tavern. You don't know anything about prostitution. You're in the wrong place, doing it wrong, you're desperate enough to sell your body; but not smart enough to make a living at it. We believe this will create a profile that will draw them to you."

"And what happens if someone else moves in on me?" Billings asked.

"Your call. If he looks nice, he's all yours." Spencer joked.

"But do I get to keep the credits?" Billings parried back.

"Probably. It'll be more than you'll get paid for this job." Rawlings cut in. Ted let the banter continue for another few minutes to release any tension; but more so to create a bonding of the team. Humor had a way of doing that. It wasn't just people who worked together who bonded; it was those who worked and laughed together that had the greatest chance of becoming a team.

"Okay. We've got three more days before we set up the sting. Here's the latest information we have on the In Cees. We're going to start working together eight hours a day for the next three days. Get to know each other, recognize strengths and weaknesses. Your individual jobs will be to identify the weaknesses in your partners, and move in to cover them. Their job will be to do the same with you. Strengths have already been worked into the over-all plan. After three days, we're going to place Billings and Dane in the tavern. Dane? You might want to stop by once or twice in the next few days just to establish it as a place you're starting to like. Billings, you avoid it until then. We want you to be a fresh, nervous face when you come through the door."

Ted nodded to dismiss the group. They gathered their papers, pictures, and packets; slipped them into notebooks, briefcases, or pockets and left. Once everyone was out of the room, Ted activated his computer projector once more. He pulled up the tavern from inside and out. He paused at the scenes in the restaurant. A sudden figure caught his eye. Ted slid the keyboard to in front of him and moved the cursor to an area behind the counter where a figure sitting in one of the back booths was barely visible. He zoomed in several times; and had the computer enhance the image with each level. Finally the face was clear enough to make out for certain. It was the one he had suspected at first...

"Jim." Ted whispered to no one in particular. He dismissed it with a passing thought that it must have been a coincident. It was a popular restaurant. It was known for American food. Jim must have been homesick and stumbled onto it. Ted pressed the button to move to the next image of Ian Probst at the bus station. The computer automatically kept the image enlarged and enhanced, and Ted had to reset the image; but his finger stopped just short of hitting the *enter* button. He moved the field a little to the left so the entire face came into view. There was Jim sitting at the bus station a little to Ian's left.

For a brief moment Ted thought the worst. He allowed a coincidence in the restaurant. There were enough factors involved to account for his brother's presence; but not in two places. He scanned the data on the scenes, and saw that both the restaurant and the bus station were taken on the same day, within an hour of each other.

"Maybe he was taking a bus after eating." Ted suggested to himself. However, being the security man that he was, he pulled up every scene in the computer file; even several that were not presented to the team. Ted spent the next several hours going through each scene, field-by-field, face-by-face. When he was done, Jim had not reappeared in any other pictures. Ted breathed a sigh of relief. "Just a coincidence." he admitted, closed out the program, and gathered up his own materials before leaving the conference room.

CHAPTER FIFTEEN

Terror In The Shadows

Schmidt let out one of her favorite expletives. Ted picked it up on the wireless transmitter.

"Something wrong *Snipper*?" Ted asked in the console. During their days together, it had come to be known that Rawlings had given Schmidt the nickname of *Snipper*. Everyone was afraid to ask how she got the name, but it seemed to date back to one of her early sessions where Rawlings had let her take part in an interrogation session.

"Everything's wrong, damn it!" She kept her voice low, but the intensity of her anger was obvious. "We've been sitting here for two weeks, and *zilch*! Billings has been picked up by three guys a night. Dane is using his expense account to pay for his new drinking problem, and the rest of us are getting blisters on our butts from sitting here."

"If you've got any ideas, I'm opened to them." he suggested.

"Maybe it's the wires." came Rawlings' voice. The team had programmed their earpieces so they could hear everything going on.

"What's wrong with the wires? Are they visible?" Ted asked.

"No, they're not visible, but some people just have a sixth sense for when they're being bugged. Maybe if we went without them, we might have more luck." Rawlings whispered as he pretended to drink his beer.

"And maybe we might lose someone. I'm not about to put any team member at risk. If they get out of our sight, they have to have a way to call for help. We have to know where to find them."

"Probst!" came Spencer's hushed whisper. It was the signal that Ian Probst had come in the tavern. It wasn't unusual. He had been in at least two or three nights a week, but every time he had stayed away from the team.

"Adams!" came Dane's voice. It was unusual for both of them to come into the tavern at the same time. It had seemed like they took turns, now both of them were there. A few minutes later, Hennings came in the back way. The trio gave no indication of knowing each other. They sat in different places around the tavern. Probst stayed by the gaming table, watching the chess match which had continued for the last three nights. The players were good, and had taken their time in plotting each move. Someone had commented that Giuerding, the older of the two, had once been a world champion; but that was many years ago. The younger of the two, Wilhelm, was an amateur, but had held his own against Giuerding. The unorthodox, and highly successful moves he had made against his opponent had given the tavern-goers many hours of gossip and discussion.

Hennings took a table in the back, not too far from where Spencer had planted, and called for the bar maid to bring him a glass of white wine. Spencer studied him out of the corner of his eye. He noted that Hennings was taking in the entire room. He was sizing up everyone there. Spencer determined that Hennings must be his counter-part in the In Cees. He would have to be careful since the man had sat so close to him, and obviously paid attention to small details. Spencer made to scratch at his ear, and used the motion to hit the stealth mode button on his ear piece, letting the others know he could not speak, nor should they contact him until further notice.

Adams stood near the door of the bar, not more than a few feet from where she had entered. Her eyes had scanned the room once, then fallen on Billings. Billings had worn a new outfit, also paid for by her expense account. She was enjoying this new role. It was nice to dress up, and have the attention of the men. She sipped at her whiskey, and nearly choked on it when she saw Adams crossing the room to where she sat at the bar. She had expected Probst or Hennings to make the play for her. She wasn't comfortable with Adams.

"Looks like your drink is almost gone. Can I buy to another?" Adams said dropping onto the bar stool next to Billings. A sudden panic hit Billings. She wasn't a stranger to some strange relationships, but she still wasn't ready for this one.

"I'm working." she stammered letting Adams know that she couldn't sit and visit.

"What are you doing, Billings?" Ted snarled into the microphone. "If she wants you, then you want her. Take her up on her offer."

"I know you're working. That's why I'm here." Adams signaled the bartender who brought her a Scotch, and filled Billings' glass. Adams passed a credit chip to the man. "So what are you looking for?"

"Looking for?" Billings was having a hard time regaining control. She had practiced to pick up the men, but this was new territory. "I don't know." She thought for a minute, recalled her cover and proceeded. "I've got three kids. I'm looking for a way to feed them." There! Billings thought. Let her know I've got kids. That should tell her I don't go in for this kind of action.

"I'd like to help." Adams replied. Billings almost let her expletive escape verbally instead of just thinking it. "You like fantasies?"

"Sure, I like fantasies. I like them as much as the next girl." So long as the next girl wasn't into that kind of thing, Billings added in her head.

"Here." Adams offered, slipping a credit chip towards Billings. It was worth three hundred dollars under the old monetary system.

"You must have some kind of fantasy." Billings added, picking the chip up and slipping it into the garter on her leg.

"Come with me, and we'll see if you have the same kind of fantasy I do." Adams offered. She rose from the stool, made her way to the door, and slipped out.

"Do we take her out?" Schmidt whispered.

"For what? Picking up a hooker?" There's no law against that. Billings has to follow through. Billings?" Ted asked from the base.

"She's still at the bar." Rawlings replied.

"Billings! Go after her. That's an order!" Ted barked over the air waves. Two of the team jerked slightly as the intensity of the order stung their ear. Billings gulped down her fresh drink, scooped up her purse, adjusted her low-cut dress and stormed out of the bar. When she found herself in the night air, she suddenly realized that she had left her coat in the bar. She almost went back for it, but a whistle to her left demanded her response. Billings rubbed her bare arms and shoulders with her hands to keep them warm. The backless dress really wasn't meant for the cold nights. The wind also lifted her dress up, and the cold wind made her wish she had worn long johns instead of the more expensive skimpy underwear. The five inch heels didn't help give her a sense of confidence as she stumbled across the cobblestone road.

"I was beginning to wonder." Adams replied when Billings finally made it over to her. "Here, you look like you're freezing." Adams took off her own coat and wrapped it around Billings.

"Thanks!" Billings said. She wasn't sure what to do, nor how to proceed. She pretty much kept quiet while Adams led her further down the street. When Billings was getting concerned about getting out of the range of her ear piece, she finally dared to raise the subject once more.

"What was all that you were talking about in there?"

"We all have fantasies. I have mine, you have yours."

"Yeah?" Billings replied in a non-committal way.

"What's nice is when two people discover that they have the same fantasy." Adams continued. Billing thought a few choice responses in her mind, but kept them to herself.

"So what's your fantasy?" Billing trembled as she spoke. She had opened Pandora's Box. There could be no turning back now. Adams thought the shivering she was doing must be due to the cold.

"You're still cold. Here." and with that Adams, put an arm around her and rubbed her arms to help stimulate the circulation. Billings nearly pushed her away and screamed, but she had to keep the cover. "Now my fantasy is probably the same one as yours."

"I don't know. I've never had fantasies like yours before." Billings countered.

"How do you know until you've heard it?" Adams replied.

"Okay, tell me about it." Billings fought to keep from shivering so Adams wouldn't hold her closer or touch any more of her.

"I used to do your kind of work."

"You did?" Billings wasn't sure what she was referring to. She hoped it was the hooking and not the undercover agent career.

"Yes, I made my living on that same bar stool for a number of years. I kept waiting to find the right person to come along and take me away."

"I'm not looking for anyone to take me away." Billings challenged.

"Not physically, but you're probably looking for someone to take away the fear that's in the pit of your stomach. You want someone to make you feel accepted. Back when I worked the bar, it wasn't legal. If a trick stiffed you, or beat you, or hurt you; it was all part of the trade. You either found a pimp to protect you and take most of what you made, or you put up with it."

"What did you do?" Billing asked.

"I put up with it. I wasn't getting that much for each trick. I'd lost the beauty. I wasn't new anymore. Everyone knew everything about me, what I could do, and what I couldn't."

"No." Billings replied. She looked at Adams and the woman's face and eyes looked soft. She couldn't picture her looking anything but beautiful.

"You're new at this. You're settling into it. You were terrified the first night. I saw that. You're getting comfortable, but in another few weeks the novelty will wear off. It becomes a black hole that starts sucking you dry. You never think some guy won't pay, or that some guy won't stop when you tell him to; but it'll happen. When it does you'll find out that you're not the one in control. That's what makes this all so appealing at first. You think you have power. You're the one who agrees to the deal. You set the terms. They pay you to give them what they want. That's power. Then one night you go with some guy and he wants more. He wants something you don't want to give. He hits you. We're not talking about a slap, either. He'll hit you the way he would hit a man. The first blow will do more than blacken you eye, cut open your cheek, knock a few teeth loose, or break your jaw. It'll prove to you that you aren't the one in control. He's in control and you start to fear for your life."

"What was it like for you?" Billings suddenly forgot entirely about the assignment. There was something compelling about this woman. She had suffered things, been hurt in ways that Billings had only feared. Yet this woman seemed to have risen above it. Billings couldn't put her finger on it, but there was a power in this woman's personality that impressed her. She wanted what this woman had. She didn't even realize that she was out of range for the others to keep track of her.

"It was the most devastating thing. All my confidence was shattered. I wasn't selling my body, I was being raped, and there was nothing I could do to stop it. I couldn't call out for help because I was a hooker. I couldn't tell anyone what had happened because no one was supposed to know what I was doing. I had two kids, too. They stayed with my mom who thought I had taken an evening job at a factory." Adams had a difficult time collecting herself. Billings put her hand on her shoulder to comfort her. "The hardest thing was the following morning..."

"When the bruises showed up? When people began to ask questions?" Billings offered.

"No. It's when I realized that I had to go back out there again the next night and take the same risk of running into him once more, or someone like him. I needed the money to survive. I had to provide for my mother and two kids. We had nothing. I couldn't get a job anywhere that would pay enough to make ends meet. Hooking was good money in a short time. You lie to yourself. You tell yourself a year or more and then you'll be back on your feet, but it's a lie. It becomes a life time."

"How many times were you beaten?" Billings asked.

"I lost count. I learned how to spot the violent...at least I thought I had. There were a lot who didn't show it on their faces. Their smiles would look like angels. They'd flash the money in my direction, impress me, and I'd spend the rest of the night trying to stop the bleeding, or set a broken arm on my own." As they passed under a street light, the harsh glare made two or three of the old scars stand out. The light in the tavern had been softer, and the make-up had done its work to keep it from being obvious.

"Anyway, that's why I'm here. I want to help you. I want to give you an option no one ever gave to me." Adams offered. Her voice was genuine and sincere. Billings couldn't hate this woman. She couldn't fear her any more. She couldn't resist. Something had touched several wounds Billings had hidden inside for many years. All the bravado, wild nights, heavy drinking and loose lifestyle had been her way of pretending they had never happened; making her think she was still in control. Billings knew she wasn't.

"So what kind of offer do you have?" Billings asked, and she honestly wanted to hear the answer.

"Just what I wanted when I was in your place. I wanted it so bad, I would have sold my soul to get it...but I had already done that. I wanted to feel clean inside. I wanted to feel like someone cared for me as a person. I wanted to find a way to hit a reset button for my life. I needed a Prince Charming to come and take me away from everything."

"And did you find this *Prince Charming*?" Billings asked.

"Oh yes!" and the sparkle in Adams' eyes ignited a hunger in Billings she had tried to quench for long years.

***

"Track her!" came Ted's voice to the other ear pieces. Rawlings, Spencer and Schmidt jumped from their chairs in the tavern and headed for the door. Spencer nodded to Dane as they went past.

"Come on, Dane. Our cover's blown." He noted as he motioned with his head to the back of the tavern where Hennings sat smiling as he slowly sipped his drink and watched them all storm out into the night air. He even raised his glass as a kind of salute toward Spencer before he drank.

"You take north. I'll take south." Rawlings barked once in the street. Dane moved in the direction Rawlings had indicated. "You take east." Rawlings motioned toward Spencer, and then pointed to Schmidt. "You go west."

The team split up. Each tried to find some sign of Billings. They stumbled across several people out in the night air, but each encounter was fruitless. Rawlings had rounded several streets when he caught the faint static of conversation. He stopped, turned slowly around in place to see which direction gave him the strongest reading. He finally figured it had to be east from where he was. He tried to signal the others, but they were too far away to hear him. He cursed under his breath, adjusted the gun in his small of his back, and began to run in the direction the static was coming from. He had gone about three or four blocks when the signal began to come in clearer. He stopped once more, reset his bearings and moved further south. He began to move when a sudden high pitched squeal tore into his ear drum. Rawlings pulled the device from his ear and nearly smashed it on the ground. He cried out in pain, tried to clear his ear with his finger, but the ringing continued.

"Damn!" he continued to curse. "Probably ruptured the ear drum." He checked for any signs of blood, and then moved south to try and find a visual fix on Billings. As the information gatherer rounded another corner, the street before him was entirely dark. He drew up suddenly because he could see street lights all around him, he could even see the street lights past the area of shadow, but there, right before him, as if a solid figure waiting for him was a mass of shadow.

Rawlings staggered where he was. He had not known this feeling for several years. He could taste it in his own throat, as if crawling up from the back of his mouth. It was fear. He took several breaths to calm himself, but he began to tremble. The trembling became worse. No matter what he did, he couldn't calm his emotions. He tried every trick he had learned over the years in intelligence gathering. Nothing worked.

The sensation began to grow in its intensity, and Rawlings noted that the blackness was moving closer to him. He stepped back, but the shadow followed him. His mouth was dry, too dry to even curse. His knees began to shake, and he fell hard onto the pavement, tearing the knees in his pants, and scraping the skin underneath. He had a sudden warm sensation running down the inside of his left leg and he realized that for the first time since he was two years old he had wet his pants. At the same moment he began to weep. His body went into convulsions as he sobbed, and wailed in his terror. He huddled on the sidewalk in a fetal position, screaming louder, and louder, and louder as the shadow covered him. At that point, something in his mind snapped, and everything shut down as he slithered into the welcomed comfort of unconsciousness.

CHAPTER SIXTEEN

Fallen Comrades

"Where is she?" Ted was shaking Rawlings and shouting in his face. The information officer recovered his senses with a start, and at that very moment the fear which had seized him so completely hit him hard. He screamed, tore himself out of Ted's hands, and tried to scamper away on all fours like a terrified rat. Dane threw himself onto the man to subdue him. After a few moments, Rawlings realized the animated shadow was no longer there, and his old personality began to return.

"Get the hell off me!" he snapped at Dane, pushing the man to one side.

"Where is Billings?" Ted demanded as Rawlings brought himself to a sitting position on the street,

"I don't know. They got her away from me, too."

"What happened here?" Spencer asked, giving Rawlings a curious analytic once-over as if Rawlings was some kind of microscope slide prepared for viewing. Rawlings became intensely aware of the liquid staining the front of his pants, and of a smelly deposit in the seat of his pants. He cursed loudly, pushed everyone away from him. He saw a clothing store across the street, made for it, found it closed; and kicked the door in. He found the rack with his size pants, snatched a pair and went into the water closet in the back. All the while ignoring the blaring alarm that shredded the silence of the neighborhood.

"Tell the police we're looking for someone. Give them Billings' description, but nothing about the mission. At least *that* should remain classified. Tell them that she's a suspected terrorist, and we need her alive at all costs. That should keep them from shooting her by accident." Ted ducked into the store to recover Rawlings. He found him exiting the water closet wearing the new pants.

"Don't you think the smell and the old pants are going to leave some questions for the police to start asking?" Ted demanded as he confronted the intelligence officer.

"Fine! You want them, you go get them. I took care of my problem. That one is yours."

"No!" Ted retorted, and grabbed Rawlings by the arm. "You're my problem, a missing operative is my problem, and that stench in the bathroom is my problem. I can cover for the broken door and pay for the missing pants, but there's no covering for *that*! Now clean it up, and report outside. I'm building a cover story, and I need your information to make it all fit." With that, Ted stormed to the front of the store. He considered scribbling a note to the owner as to where to send the bills for the pants, and the repair for the lock on the front door; but it would raise questions. *Let him think the terrorist did it. It'll make him even more angry at them,* Ted thought, and then joined his team in the streets in front of the store. The sounds of sirens were growing in the stillness of the night.

"You know, we could be gone before they get here, and no one would ever know." suggested Spencer.

"Except we don't know what all Rawlings touched in there. Any print would make the police start asking questions. It's better to confront this head on, and make it look routine than to make some reporter think he's found a cover-up and start digging." Rawlings joined them just before the first car rounded the corner.

"Good thing there wasn't a real emergency." Schmidt observed. As the first officer emerged from the car, Ted was flashing his credentials. It was obvious the officer was suddenly worried about stumbling onto any operation that involved Alliance security.

"We were following a lead on a known terrorist, someone key to one of our investigations." He flashed a small picture of Billings at the officer. "We need her, and we need her alive and unharmed; but she must be recovered at all costs. We thought she was in the store, but it was a dead end. Put out an all points to have your men comb this area and see if they can find her. If they haven't found her within three hours, contact me for further instructions. As of this moment, this is all an Alliance matter. No reports, no information leaks, and no reporters. If word gets out about this terrorist, someone may take it upon himself to take her out, and we need her alive. Do I make myself clear?"

"Yes sir!" the officer saluted, dropped back into the car with the picture Ted had handed him, scanned it in on the laptop computer; and was broadcasting the description and information printed on the back of the photograph to the dispatcher.

"Come on, we need to talk." Ted moved his team down the street out of the range of any eavesdroppers. "Now! What happened?" He turned hard and suddenly on Rawlings. The fact that the man flinched and threw his hands up protectively told the others something had unnerved him.

"I don't know. I heard a faint transmission in that direction. Suddenly my ear pierce screamed and I pulled it out. When I rounded the corner there was this...this" Here Rawlings was at a loss for words. "Thing!" he finally settled on the term. "It was like a big black shadow, but it seemed alive. There wasn't any shape or form to it, just this sense of complete and total...I don't know what it was. There was a power about it. I couldn't even stand where I was. My legs collapsed under me. I couldn't run. I couldn't speak. I couldn't draw my gun..." At this point Rawlings was trembling and weeping once more. He wiped the tears which streamed down his face with the sleeve of his shirt. Ted motioned to Schmidt.

"Get him to his house. Contact this person," Ted slipped a card to Schmidt. "Tell them to send someone to check him out." She looked at the card, slipped it into a pocket, and helped Rawlings back to the tavern where his car was parked.

"We've got to find her, and find her fast." Ted declared once Rawlings was gone. "He said they were in that direction. Let's move."

"You don't think they're still on the streets, do you?" Spencer countered.

"No, but historically we need to find her within three hours; or we won't find her at all." Ted blurted out.

"So this isn't the first time?" Dane noted.

"We've lost operatives before. None of my operatives. According to President Ipileno, there were four other teams that had gone after the In Cees prior to us. All of them failed."

"Failed?" Dane continued.

"I take it you don't mean just one or two members of the team..." Spencer left his sentence opened allowing Ted the opportunity to complete his thought for him.

"The entire team vanished."

"Vanished?" Dane remarked.

"We're not sure what that involved. Each team went in, had the same kind of contact, walked out of the tavern, restaurant or got on the bus. The contact person was never seen or heard from again. No body was ever found. No evidence of violence or struggle. It's just as if they had ceased to exist. Of the teams, there were one or two who were not contacted, had followed from a distance, and they were in contact the entire time with their base station. One agent managed to stammer about something similar to what Rawlings saw, and was found dead. Coroner said it was severe system shock and failure. Others were just found dead on the street, or not at all."

"You said historically. That implies that someone made it back." Spencer noted.

"One case. The agent contacted by the In Cees came back a few hours later. He told us they talked to him, asked him several questions, but nothing about the operation. They seemed to know the operation was running and chose to make contact anyhow. Our people interrogated him for several days, but nothing new developed. His story was they offered him various possibilities, spoke in vague terms. Nothing solid ever came of it. They wanted to talk to him some more and were going to meet him at the restaurant. According to him, once it was clear he wasn't interested in what they were offering for a life style, they respected his decision; and he found his way home."

"That should have been enough to arrest the members." Dane suggested.

"Oh, we've had enough to arrest any of them; but the problem is we want the operation. We don't know how high they are in the organization. We don't know where they meet. We don't know how they're structured."

"What happened to the agent who made it back?" Spencer asked.

"He followed through with the meeting at the restaurant. We recorded the entire conversation as well as we could. Transmission kept breaking up. We saw them get up, go to the bus stop and get on a bus. Even though we followed it and photographed everyone who got off, our agent was never one of them. When the bus came to the end of the line, two of our people got on as passengers to offer aid, but our man was gone."

"People don't just vanish into thin air." Dane insisted.

"Was there ever a stop where no one got on, or no one got off?" Spencer asked.

"Yes, two such stops." Ted replied.

"Doesn't that seem odd to you? A bus only stops to let someone on or someone off. It must have been one of those two stops where they slipped off without your people seeing them. Were any of those stops around here?"

"No, they were on the other side of town." Ted admitted.

"Are any buses running tonight?" Dane chimed in.

"Not at this hour."

"The light traffic this late at night might work to our advantage." Ted confronted the officer and had him contact the other patrol cars to see if anyone had noticed any traffic in the area, or near where the bus had made its two stops.

"Car thirty-seven saw a car in the area about fifteen minutes ago." the officer reported after jotting notes on all the replies.

"Did they get a description?" Spencer asked.

"White Volvo. Four door. Current model, maybe this year or last year model. Only had a partial plate."

"Partial is better than nothing." Spencer noted and took the paper from the officer. "Let's get back to the office." Ted left a card where the officer could contact him, and instructed the search to move into the area where the white Volvo was spotted.

"It was two hours later when Spencer pushed back from the keyboard, stretched to work the kinks out of his neck and back, and retrieved the print-out he had pulled up.

"There are almost a thousand cars with that partial plate identification. Out of that many, there are forty-three Volvos. Of the forty-three, twenty-six are within the last three years. Of that number, six are white. However, that doesn't mean the In Cees couldn't have painted the car a different color, or even stolen the plate."

"You have a suspicious mind." Dane quipped.

"That's why I do well in this line of work. Do we go for the six?"

"How many are in this area?" Ted asked.

"Four, and there are three of us." Spencer replied.

"Four of us." came a voice from the door. It was Schmidt.

"How's Rawlings?" Ted asked.

"He cried himself to sleep." Schmidt noted.

"Doesn't sound like the Rawlings I know." Dane suggested.

"He saw something tonight. He said the only way he could describe it was that it was like looking into the eyes of the Angel of Death."

"And it unnerved him that much? I thought nothing scared him." Dane challenged.

"It doesn't. He's Da Nishka."

"Da Nishka?" Ted asked.

"Few people ever hear of us. It's an ancient Russian society. It comes from an India name meaning "honest." We will ensure that you get the honest truth from someone we interrogate. Each one is trained by his master in the art of information extraction. It's passed down from one generation to the next. There are probably a hundred members of Da Nishka at any one time. They don't want to be large. They want to be quiet about who and what they are. Their methods of training are brutal. The founder was a Russian Jew. His true name has been lost for ages. He sold out during the Spanish Inquisition and changed faiths to buy his life. He used his new position for the Church to perfect his trade. He also used it to gain his revenge. A lot of people had nothing to confess, but were arrested just because Da Nishka needed more bodies to practice on. The key is to inflict as much pain, both physically and mentally as possible without letting the victim pass out or die."

"Sounds like a lovely order." Dane interrupted.

"I am Rawlings' pupil. I have made it to the tenth level. He's somewhere around twenty or thirty. I've lost count."

"So how do you move up in levels? Based upon how many people you torture or break?" Spencer asked.

"No, it's a training. In order to inflict pain, you have to understand pain. For this reason, each member is tortured by his or her own mentor to push them to their limits."

"That's sick" Dane erupted.

"No more so than sado-masochistic relationships. The body responds to pain in a variety of ways. Most often, it releases endorphins, or some other hormones into the blood stream. They help the body to deal with pain, suppress pain; or send the body into shock when the pain is too great. With practice, the pain releases these chemicals and it can become a high. Sado-masochistic people use this high to increase the sexual pleasure. Many can come strictly through pain without any sex involved."

"And so you inflict pain on each other for the fun of it?" Spencer asked.

"Not for the fun of it, but to understand it. At each level, the pupil has to endure a certain length of pain, certain kinds of pain. The pupil has to know how the body reacts, how to fight it, and how to use it. This way, when we torture someone we can spot how they are reacting. We can know how to adjust the interrogation to keep the victim uncomfortable, make the pain more intense, and extract the information we need. It also means that if we are ever captured and interrogated, we won't break."

"How do you know you won't break? Just how intense are these sessions?" Ted asked. In response, Schmidt raised her shirt. She pulled up her bra; however, only one breast was visible. The right breast was completely gone, and in its place was a horrible scar.

"That was my fifth level. When I took leave a year ago, it wasn't to go on vacation or to visit friends. Rawlings was doing this to me. No pain killers, no chance to black out. No sharp instruments. I had to feel every moment of it. This is where the true students of Da Nishka are born. If they try to back out at this point, their mentors are sworn to kill them even more slowly. If I were ever captured. If I ever talked; I know what they can and will do to me. Each member has sacrificed some body part which isn't needed to do our jobs. People on the street will never know what we have endured. As we go through the fifth level, we have to keep our focus, continue discussing the topic in a level tone. Any loss of control, any sign of the pain affecting us, and the torturer will increase it as a reminder.

"Each level has a rite of passage with some new physical pain, some new level of mental anguish. The entire program is to teach us the true meaning of terror; how to endure it, how to use it. What happened to Rawlings tonight was beyond even his level of control. The terror was so great; all his skills, all his training failed him. I doubt if any of you would have survived the encounter."

The silence hung heavy in the room when she finished. Finally Ted took the list and read off the addresses. He gave

Dane the first address, Spencer the second, Schmidt the third, and he took the last.

"I want constant communication on this. We all have back-ups on this operation. Call for reinforcements the moment anything looks wrong. We don't need any more heroes tonight."

He dismissed the agents, reached into the cabinet, and retrieved four extra ammo clips and slipped them into his jacket pocket. He didn't want to have to admit it, but everything about this night pointed to someone on the inside tipping the In Cees off. He also wanted to check with Ipileno regarding the *Angel of Death* to see if it might be one of the enemy EeeDees. If they were moving openly to work with the In Cees, he might have to ask for the EeeDees to help them out as well.

CHAPTER SEVENTEEN

Dead-Ends

Ted kicked in the door to the apartment. He wasn't sure why he went in without back-up, but he did. He mentally cursed himself for letting himself get so worked up over the assignment that he was getting sloppy. The door jam splintered under the force of his attack, and the wooden door tried to escape its hinges; but instead was guided by the metal hardware so that it slammed into the wall with a deafening "whom." Ted realized that if this were a stronghold for the In Cees, it would be him against the entire squad; and he would be dead in seconds. The echoing of the door told him the room was empty before his eyes adjusted to the faint light.

Sloppy! He told himself. *Follow procedures. Bring in the team; use the high tech cameras to look into the room first. Cover all exits. Coordinate efforts. Move as a single unit. Hell! I'm acting like a bloody amateur! If I was one of my men, I'd be kicking my butt all the way back to the base.*

He pulled out the communication ear piece. Since they were no longer undercover, they could use the more powerful, but less concealable units and stay in touch throughout the city. He raised the wristwatch microphone to his mouth and spoke.

"All units. Negative at my address. Call for back-up before entering any other locations."

"Already in." came Schmidt's voice. From the anger still in her tone, he knew she had found nothing before she even made her report.

"Hell of a time to think of that!" came Dane's voice. "I've just kicked the door in. Too late to back out now...Empty. Damn!"

"Spencer?" It had to be Spencer's location. Three out of four empty. It didn't take a brain surgeon to figure out which address was the right one. "Spencer?" Ted switched his communications unit to the all units mode. "It has to be Spencer's..."

"Call off the cavalry. This place is empty like a tomb. We're doing a once-over before heading back."

"We?" Ted asked.

"Someone has to follow proper procedures. They were designed for a reason, you know."

"Where to?" came Schmidt's voice. She was impatient, and in no mood for casual conversation.

"Meet me at Billings' place. No one goes in until I get there. We do this one by the book." The other members acknowledged his instructions and all the communication units went into stand-by mode. Ted washed the empty room with his flashlight one last time before leaving. He would need to have the *teams* come back and do a careful search of each of the locations. He pulled the wounded door closed after him and sealed it with Alliance Security's red tape.

Ted was waiting for Schmidt to arrive before they moved into Billings' place. He was coordinating the back-up team members into position when Schmidt came out of Billings' front door.

"You're not going to believe this!" she called out and motioned for the others to join her. As they all came into Billing's small house, they noticed the absence of any personal items. The furniture was still there, along with the dishes, but all the clothes, make-up supplies, photographs and other items that make up the fingerprints of a person on a room were gone.

"Any sign of forced entry?" Spencer asked, checking the doors and windows.

"Only where I came in." Schmidt noted.

"You had orders to follow procedures!" Ted tore into her. He had even thought about slapping her hard across the face to drive the message home and to vent his frustration; but he figured she would probably enjoy it, or comment on how poor his technique was. "I don't need a loose cannon right now!"

"I've often wondered where that term came from." Dane suggested. It was probably more to relieve the tension, but Spencer chose to answer anyway.

"From the naval reference, back when the old wooden man o' wars fought the pirates or other ships. The ship would toss and turn to maneuver for a better shot. If one of your cannons wasn't tied down, it could do more damage to your crew or ship than the other side." Ted turned to glare at Spencer, letting Schmidt off the hook for the moment. "Sorry, just a hobby of mine...word origins."

The moment had passed, and beating on Schmidt wasn't going to help. Ted took a mental tally of the data he had, and motioned for his undercover team to join him outside while the back-up teams went to work analyzing Billings' house for clues. "Let's pick this up where it started."

"The tavern?" Dane asked.

"It's the only place we have left." Ted admitted.

As their vehicle rounded the corner, Ted hit the brakes and threw everyone forward. The Tavern was surrounded by police vehicles, lights flashing, and a swarm of patrol men moving all over the neighborhood.

"So much for slipping in nice and quite." Dane observed. The team exited the vehicle, and strode purposefully to the front of the tavern. An officer turned to confront them, and Ted recognized him as the officer who responded when Rawlings had broken into the clothing store. The officer froze at attention and saluted. Ted grabbed the man's wrist and pulled his hand down before the salute was complete.

"You make it hard to remain undercover. What's going down?"

"A kidnapping sir. A man came in a little while ago and began beating up one of the patrons. He then dragged him bodily out of the tavern and into a car."

"Was the surveillance camera on?" Ted asked.

"Yes sir. Our men are going over it now."

"I'll check it out. The rest of you spread out and see who's inside." The team moved into the tavern while the officer escorted Ted to the office where the owner and detectives were reviewing the digital images. Dane noticed Giuerding and Wilhelm seemed oblivious to the entire incident and continued to play their game of chess. As Dane was standing next to the board table, he noticed Wilhelm take his knight and place it directly in front of his bishop, leaving his queen unprotected.

"That was a dumb move." Dane kibitzed. True to his prediction, Giuerding moved his piece to take out the queen. Wilhelm then moved his knight one more time and revealed that the knight's new position put Giuerding's king in check, and could also capture the queen if Giuerding moved the king out of the path of the attack.

"Check!" Wilhelm declared, and then to Dane, "It depends entirely on what you're willing to sacrifice to achieve your objectives." Giuerding studied his only moves and realized any move he made would put the king in checkmate. He reached over and tipped over the king conceding the game.

"Chess is like life." Giuerding told Dane. "It is moves and countermoves. There are captures and sacrifices. Sometimes to get what you really want, you have to give up something very precious to you. If you're not willing to make that sacrifice, then you will never reach your goal."

"What you have to realize is that no piece is ever lost." Wilhelm observed.

"Of course it's lost. You just lost your queen." Dane countered.

"It was removed from the board, but I know where it is. Knowing where something is means it is not lost, just no longer available to you...Like your daughter, for example."

Ted left the police officer at the door, motioned to Schmidt and closed it behind him. He flashed his credentials and everyone in the room became suddenly nervous. "What do you have?"

The detective hit the reverse button on the player, and the tavern came to life in fast motion. People moved in various directions. There was a sudden flurry of even faster activity near the back of the room. The detective released the reverse button and the scene moved to normal time. Ted studied the activity, noticed a man come into the tavern, move to the back of the room, grab the man sitting there and begin to beat him. As several people rose to stop the attack, the man drew a weapon, fired in the general direction, and everyone dropped to the floor, or started to run. The man then slapped his victim several more times, threw him to the floor, kicked him, and then forced him out of the tavern.

"This is now Alliance business." He produced a flashdrive and slipped it into the port on the computer. Schmidt slipped behind the keyboard and typed in the commands so the data transferred to the thumbdrive. Ted nodded and once the data was transferred, Schmidt deleted the files on the computer. Clear your men out and no one is to discuss this with anyone. Do I make myself clear?"

"Yes sir!" came the nervous voices. Spencer was in another part of the tavern. He motioned for him to join him. He kept looking, but couldn't see Dane.

"Where's Dane?" he snapped, anger now filling his voice.

"Dane?" he was right over..." Spencer's voice trailed off when he turned in the direction of the chess game. Dane was no longer in sight, and Wilhelm and Giuerding were no longer at the table. Spencer made a quick scan of the room. "He's gone!"

"What do you mean, *he's gone*? The entire building is surrounded with police." Ted grabbed the police officer who had the misfortune of being the one Ted always encountered throughout the night. "Where's my other man?"

"Your other man?" the officer stammered.

"The one who came in here with me. There were four of us. Myself, this man and this woman. The fourth person is missing. Did he leave?"

"He couldn't have left. We have the tavern sealed..." Ted broke away from the officer even as he spoke, stormed into the office and demanded.

"Are any of the cameras recording?"

"No sir. We had them all down to go over the data. It's an old machine. It can only do one or the other; not both. Everything is off line." the detective reported.

"Damn!" Ted spat as he left the office, motioned to Schmidt and Spencer to fall in behind him. Out in the parking lot, he spun suddenly on Schmidt.

"Your boyfriend was here!"

"Rawlings?" Spencer echoed.

"Yeah. He's on film. He came back here and grabbed Hennings. Where would he go with him?"

"Just leave him alone. He can work this out on his own. By morning you'll know everything there is to know about the In Cees." Schmidt began, but Ted's gun was suddenly pressed against her forehead.

"I've lost two agents, and your *sansei* is holding the only witness I've got. Now where is he?" Schmidt studied Ted's eyes, and knew he had no hesitation about pulling the trigger. Several of the officers had drawn guns and begun to move to protect her, but Spencer was flashing his credentials and shouting,

"Alliance security. Back off. In fact, why don't you all take the rest of the night off?" The officers retreated faster than they had assembled.

"He'd have taken him to the warehouse." Schmidt admitted.

"Then you're going to take us to the warehouse." Ted lowered the gun to make ready to leave.

"Sir! It's a code we live by. He has to be able to do this himself..." The gun was back against her head. "Fine! FINE! I'll take you to the warehouse."

The group didn't say another word except for directions of where to turn, where to continue, and where to park. Schmidt had brought them to the industrial complex near the south side of the city. She went ahead of them to the back door.

"Let me go in first. Rawlings might think it's a rescue attempt by the In Cees, and start taking you all out."

"Is he that good?" Spencer asked.

"He's that good. No one can slip up on him. He can kill with his hands in ways most people can never imagine. He can kill you quick, or cripple you in a second so that you die slowly and painfully."

"Good thing we have you. I'm sure you've had the same kind of training he's had." Ted countered. Schmidt just glared at him, opened the door; and tapped a signal on an overhead pipe. The trio then moved into the darkness. A single light glowed weakly in the back of the warehouse, coming from a smaller office room which had been thrown together. It wasn't much more than three walls propped up against the back wall with a door and a window in them. The ceiling was resting on the top of the walls. Spencer noted several digital cameras through the window. They all had the red lights lit indicating that they were recording.

"I take it that Rawlings is recording his sessions." Spencer noted.

"He records all of his sessions. He's fanatical about it." Schmidt replied.

"Wants to make sure no information is lost?" Spencer queried.

"No, he enjoys his work. Likes to watch it later for entertainment. That's how I got involved with him."

Ted thought *sickos* in his mind, but chose to keep silent. He had two nuclear reactors on his team, and both had *critical* flashing all over them. He wasn't sure how long he could keep them under control. This night was proof of that. As Schmidt tapped on the door, they waited for Rawlings to open it. After a few seconds, Schmidt tapped again; and then burst into the office. The remnants of Rawlings were scattered all over the floor. The torso lay twitching off to one side. Spencer grabbed the trash can and heaved his guts out. Ted wasn't so lucky.

CHAPTER EIGHTEEN

The Immortality Gene

"Rawlings! Speak to me." Schmidt lifted the torso of the information officer and pulled the mangled lump of flesh and broken bones onto her lap. She held his limp head in the crook of her elbow.

"He's alive?!" Ted exclaimed in disbelief.

"Impossible!" Spencer echoed; but Ted was on the communication unit calling for back-up and an ambulance.

"Look at his eyes." Schmidt declared, and sure enough his eyes registered life; although life might be the wrong word. There was fear in those eyes, pain, and suffering; and terror.

"Rawlings! Who did this?" Ted tried to question, but Schmidt cut him off.

"He doesn't even know we're here. I've seen this look before. It's when we've gone too far in a session, and the person is so focused on the pain the rest of the world is blocked off. This is what we try to avoid. Once they're at this level, the mind is gone."

"So he doesn't feel anything?" Spencer asked.

"Oh he feels it. That's all he feels. It's a private Hell. Their whole world is their pain. Even when the body heals, the pain continues. Someone knew how to break him. Someone went further than we'd have ever gone."

"So there's no hope for him?" Ted asked. He was surprised he even had to ask the question. With the numerous parts of Rawlings' body scattered around the office, he was sure the man was already dead, but somehow he had survived. But survival wasn't the right word.

Schmidt lowered the torso and head onto the floor. She drew her gun and placed it hard against Rawlings' head. She squeezed the trigger and the blast from the barrel echoed in the empty warehouse. The bullet tore through the back of the skull, and the sound of the exit as brains and blood sprayed the floor sounded more like a melon splattering on the floor than a life escaping. Schmidt closed her eyes and wept softly for a moment.

"He's not dead." Spencer noted.

"What?!" Schmidt challenged. She looked at Rawlings, and his eyes were still registering the pain, suffering and terror that now possessed him. She drew her gun and fired another bullet into Rawlings' skull. The eyes blinked, but he still was responding to his own Hell. Schmidt emptied the entire clip into Rawlings, hitting the heart and several vital organs as well as the brain, but each time Rawlings—although further mutilated—continued to live...continued to survive, continued to suffer.

Schmidt was nearly out of control as she beat on his body. The rib cage had been shattered by whomever, or whatever had done this to him; and the bones continued to make a *cracking* sound as she beat on him. "What do I do? What do I do?"

"Let it go. He's beyond anything we can do to end his suffering. Run the tapes back. We need to see what happened here tonight."

"I swore to him I wouldn't let him live like this. It's an oath we make. When it gets too bad, when the pain is too much, we end it. It's what keeps us bound." Schmidt was weeping.

"Schmidt, if there was anything more we could do for him, we would do it, but all you're doing at this point is blowing away more of his body." Ted hated to be harsh, but he couldn't handle seeing any more violence right now. He turned to get the image out of his mind, and his foot kicked Rawlings' thigh across the room. He had to fight down the wave of nausea and focus on the screens.

"Look at his head!" Spencer demanded. Ted looked back, and the wound from the bullet had begun to close up. The bleeding had stopped. "How? How can that be?"

"The immortality gene." Ted replied in little more than a whisper.

"That's only a theory." Spencer challenged.

"Immortality gene? What's that?" Schmidt demanded.

"It's believed that we all have the immortality gene in our make-up. Something along the evolutionary line shut it down so we grow old and die. Several scientists believe they can reactivate it. If so, the body would be able to repair itself."

"Even from something this severe?" Schmidt snatched the fingerless hand off the floor and thrust it into Ted's face. Their leader nearly lost it once more. He pushed Schmidt's hand away so he wouldn't have to look at what she held.

"I don't know!" He shouted. "I'm not the one who made this theory up. They say that the body can replace any part of itself if we just know how to tell it to. That's what the immortality gene does. It tells the body to grow a new hand, a new foot, a new organ. So long as the body keeps getting what it needs, and keeps getting signals from the brain to the various cells, it's supposed to keep us living, and eventually replace what's been lost or damaged."

"So how do you kill someone whose immortality gene is activated?"

"I don't know!' Ted repeated.

"Look, Brown!" and it was the first time Schmidt had addressed him with such a tone in her voice. "Death is the only release we have from this much pain. I've got to find a way to kill him. I owe him that!"

"Take off his head." Spencer announced.

"What?" Ted and Schmidt both replied.

"Take off his head. If the brain is sending the signal to repair the body and keep it alive, we have to sever the head."

"But what if it keeps living?" Schmidt countered.

"It shouldn't. According to what Ted said, the brain sends the signal to the body; the body sends the supplies to the brain. Keep the supplies from the brain, or the signal from reaching the body, he has to die."

"He should have died from any one of these." Schmidt ranted motioning to the numerous wounds, amputations and injuries that covered Rawlings' fragments.

"Look! It's the only thing left to try." Spencer insisted. Schmidt went to one of the cabinets, tore open the door, rummaged through various metal objects, and emerged with a machete'. Ted and Spencer chose to look away as she did the deed. When they looked back, Rawlings severed head was off to one side, the eyes now dead and devoid of any sign of suffering.

"Someone is going to pay for this...Big Time!" Schmidt declared.

"I'm not going to have you running off on your own." Ted warned.

"It's not just going to be me. The *Da Nishka* will avenge him. Whoever did this will beg for their death to be as painless and as swift as Rawlings'. Everyone will want a turn."

"Look at this!" Spencer called turning Ted away from the image which fought to get into his mind. Spencer had reprogrammed one of the files. "He brought Hennings here."

On the screen Rawlings was inflicting a deep and painful wound into the chest cavity, but careful not to hit any of the organs.

"This is going to hurt...Of course, that's the whole idea." Rawlings was telling his victim. Hennings lowered his head, fighting back the wave of searing pain that tore through his mind. He began to mumble.

"What's he saying?" Ted asked. In response, Spencer ran the program back, increased the volume, and adjusted several controls to clear up the background noise. It took three or four replays to make out what Hennings was saying.

"He's praying!" Schmidt spat out in disgust. The program continued on. Rawlings went though his usual routine, letting the pain of the chest wound build while now beginning the mental anguish as he described all the things he had planned for his victim. When Rawlings turned around to insert another device into the chest wound, he stopped in mid-sentence. Rawlings tore the shirt off of Hennings shouting,

"Where's the wound? Damn it! Where's the bloody wound?" Rawlings turned back to the camera to retrieve the device he had used to make the first wound, but something passed between him and the camera. Rawlings screamed. Whatever had been there was not registering on the camera.

"Try some of the other monitors." Ted ordered. Schmidt and Spencer ran back all the scans, and Schmidt used the master control to synchronize all of them so they ran at the same time. There was something captured on the recording, but it could only be described as a hole. There seemed to be a hole in space where Rawlings was staring, pointing and screaming. It wasn't a darkness. It wasn't quite a shadow. It was a nothingness; but a solid nothingness—if such a thing were possible. The hole began to speak.

"This is for Cynthia Walker." the hollow voice said in a cold, icy tone. As the voice spoke, one finger after another were torn off of Rawlings' right hand. The information officer tried to control his reaction; but he broke and began to scream. As he collapsed, the nothingness moved over him.

"You do not have the luxury of unconsciousness, nor of death...at least not until you've suffered." The voice continued to list names, and with each name, some new horror was administered to Rawlings' body. By the fourth or fifth name Schmidt was weeping and babbling,

"Oh my God, Oh my God." Which she rambled faster and faster, biting so hard on her knuckle that it began to bleed.

"What is it?" Ted demanded.

"This *thing* knows Rawlings' work."

"What do you mean?" Spencer asked.

"It's listing all the people Rawlings worked on. It's listing them all in order." Schmidt stammered.

"You mean it's someone on the inside? Someone who knows our operation? Has access to our records?" Ted pressed.

"No one could know this much. These are jobs he did that only I knew about. Sometimes things would get slow. Rawlings would need some excitement. We'd go cruising around, find someone and use them."

The voice spoke another name.

"Wait a minute. That's an unsolved kidnapping. Five years ago, she was three years old, and someone snatched her from in front of her house." Spencer turned to watch the monitor and saw brutal acts taking place on Rawlings body. "Is that what that sick bastard did to her?" Spencer screamed, pointing at the monitor and knocking Schmidt against the wall.

"Yes! YES!" she shouted. "The thing is doing to him everything he ever did to any of his victims." The room was suddenly silent; and Schmidt and Spencer realized that Ted had put the entire digital system on freeze frame.

"You and he kidnapped children to practice your craft?" he challenged. She nodded. "You both are nothing more than serial killers, rapists, torturers. My God woman! At least when you're interrogating someone they can give you the information to make the pain stop. How were these people supposed to make the pain stop? How could they make you stop torturing them?"

"They couldn't." Schmidt declared. The horror of it all flooded Ted. He pushed her aside, and went out of the warehouse to get some fresh air. Spencer was right behind him. Once alone in the office, Schmidt looked up at the frozen image on the different monitors. Suddenly the nothingness on the center monitor turned on the screen to face her. She felt her heart crawling up into her throat.

"You're next." the hollow voice echoed.

She stabbed the *pause* button to freeze the image again, but it was obvious she was no longer in control. This was beyond the power of her skills, abilities or technology to stop. Outside the warehouse Spencer and Ted heard the first scream. Spencer turned as if to go back into the building, but Ted caught his shoulder indicating they should not get involved. By the time the ambulance and back-up teams arrived, the screaming had stopped for several minutes. Neither Ted nor Spencer re-entered the building. Neither of them asked to see the final reports on the findings. Ted gave the crew one message before they left,

"Make sure you sever the head."

CHAPTER NINTEEN

Confrontations

"I want answers, and I want them right now!" Ted exploded as he burst into Ipileno's office. If this had been any other intruder, he would have been dead before he cleared the door, but Ipileno sat calmly behind the massive desk that formed a barrier between him and his head of security.

"What sort of answers are you looking for?" Jason replied in a non-committal tone.

"I've lost four agents this night. Two were taken away by the In Cees, and two were killed by something else."

"Something else?"

"I'm laying odds that it was an EeeDee. An EeeDee from the other side." The room was suddenly filled with the presence of Jason's personal EeeDee. Ted threw his hands over his eyes and cried out in pain from the glow. The creature reduced his presence enough for Ted to function.

"An enemy EeeDee involved?" Abaddon inquired. He seemed to float in the air, as if he were not truly part of this world, but were conversing with others around him who were still unseen.

"That's my guess." Ted admitted. "I thought there were rules of engagement between your two sides. I thought you could only work through us, not act directly."

"It appears as if the rules may have changed." Abaddon echoed.

"Well it would be nice if someone would tell me when they do." Abaddon increased his presence enough for Ted to drop to the floor.

"When you can speak in a more civil manner, I will allow you to do so. Do not forget what you are, and what *we* are." the EeeDee instructed. Ted knew that he had no choice but to comply. He fought to hold down his anger and when he nodded, Abaddon decreased enough for Ted to stagger to the closest chair, sweat dripping from his forehead.

"I just came back from the warehouse where Rawlings was holding Hennings."

"He actually captured one of them?" Ipileno asked.

"He saw something tonight during the mission. It unnerved him..."

"For Rawlings to be unnerved it must have been something extreme. Nothing fazed him before."

"He said it was like looking into the eyes of the Angel of Death." A ripple passed over Abaddon at the mention of the mythical creature. "From what I've seen tonight, I believe he was probably correct."

"What happened?" Ipileno leaned back in his chair to wait for Ted's report. The security officer began with the meeting in the tavern, and ended with what they heard before leaving the industrial complex.

"Can they activate the immortality gene?" Ted asked.

"The other side has always had the power to activate the immortality gene. They have just chosen not to until now." Abaddon observed.

"How?' Ted questioned.

"One of the leaders of the early movement had the ability. He was a rebel EeeDee who infused himself with an embryo in a woman's womb. It made him both human and extradimensional. He had a certain mental ability. He could activate his own immortality gene, and when he was in physical contact with others—or close enough to them, he could send the same command on a limited basis to the person he was in contact with. Using this ability he activated people's immortality genes in a limited fashion. He healed the lame, restored sight to the blind, even raised the dead a few times." Abaddon explained.

"Himself included?" Ted asked going right to the heart of the matter. "Are we talking about Jesus here?"

"Yes." came the hollow, drawn-out reply. It could have been mistaken for reluctance to admit such a thing. "You can see how such an ability would give the wrong impression. A person who could heal with a touch or a word, someone who was believed to have been dead, but come back from the dead...Well, he would be seen as a god...or the Son of God. It was his choice. He would be whatever he claimed to be. He saw it for what it was, manipulated the legends, and used them for his own advantage."

"But to allow himself to be killed like that..." Ted noted recalling the stories he had heard in Sunday School when his mother had dragged both he and his brother along while their father went off to the base.

"He did *not* allow that. *We* caused all of that to happen. Despite his lies, he was powerless against us. It was not his choice to die that day. Besides, for someone who can control his own body, repair any damage it sustains; the pain is a minor thing. The minute the injury is inflicted, even as the injury is being inflicted; he could control his immortality gene to activate his healing process. He could leave the outer wounds for last to make it look far worse than it is...And as you saw tonight, the only way to kill a person who has an active immortality gene is to behead them. He died on a cross. There was no damage to his head. Those three days were just the time he needed for his immortality gene to heal the outer damage. It was nothing more than a long nap for him. There's no magic. There's nothing supernatural about it. It's just the manipulation of known laws of nature.

"You will also recall how he left this world...?" Abaddon implied. Ted thought for a minute.

"He Ascended. He rose up from the Mount of Olives and was lost in clouds."

"Exactly." Abaddon confirmed. "Our efforts to shut him down failed. He had to be physically removed from your world. We took him by force. He has been rehabilitated. He has seen the error of his ways. No one else would ever seek to join himself with an embryo and blend our races. It is unthinkable; just as it would be unthinkable for your race to try and produce offsprings with lizards or worms."

"We are really that far below you?" Ted asked.

"I was being kind…" Abaddon admitted.

"So this was one of their EeeDees?" Ted shifted back to his original outrage.

"Yes" Abaddon admitted.

"But now that we know that the In Cees have an active immortality gene." Ipileno noted. "We're going to need to set up some kind of public execution using the beheading technique. The French used the guillotine, didn't they?"

"Are we talking about executions?" Ted asked.

"You didn't think we would slap their wrist and let them go, did you? You've seen what the other side can do, and is more than willing to do."

"I just never thought about it. Once we'd broken them, I thought we'd imprison them or something." Ted stammered.

"Why?" Ipileno pressed. "Do you think being in jail is going to change their minds? These people are committed. Put them in jail, and they just talk to other prisoners. They begin to recruit from their jail cells. No, we can't redeem them; we can't stop them. All we can do is eliminate them. Now go get some rest. You look like Hell."

"I've been though Hell. Is that just a legend, too?" Neither Abaddon nor Ipileno chose to grace the question with an answer. As he was about to leave the room, Ipileno added,

"We know where several nests of In Cees are hiding. We'll start moving tomorrow. I want you and Spencer to coordinate the efforts. I think your experience tonight will make you appreciate what we're dealing with."

"And what if the other EeeDees start to move in again?"

"I don't think they will. Rawlings and Schmidt opened themselves up to the enemy EeeDee by their actions. We will be more careful in the future."

"And if you're wrong?"

"We'll make sure to sever your head as quickly as we can to ease your suffering." The tone in Ipileno's voice was not reassuring. It might have been a joke, but Ted believed it was more of the kind of promise Schmidt had make to Rawlings when they sold their souls to the devil.

Ted dropped into the deep cushioned couch of his office, hugging the bottle of old Scotch as if it were his only means of salvation. He didn't bother with a glass tonight. He guzzled it, downing a third of the bottle in one effort. The door opened, and he shouted,

"I want to be alone!" The door closed, but Ted could tell the person had not left. He leaned forward enough to see who the intruder was before deciding to throw the bottle, or draw his gun. Jim stepped out of the shadows for his brother to recognize him.

"Been out on assignment?" Jim asked.

"How would you know?" and the tone of the older brother was laced with suspicion.

"I know, it's the security man in you, Ted; but you're getting sloppy. You've still got your earpiece in. You only wear it when you're on a mission." Jim snatched a mineral water from the counter, twisted the cap off, and dropped down in the chair opposite his brother.

"Need to talk about it?"

"Yes, but I can't..."

"I know, classified. Well, maybe in general terms. Were you hurt?"

"Not physically." Ted offered.

"Did you have to kill anyone?"

"That's part of it."

"Lost some operatives?"

"Yeah."

"I think that about covers the list. It's part of the job and all the traditional clichés. Any more B. S. I can add?" Jim delivered the lecture with such perfect diplomatic tone that Ted snorted. He wasn't sure if it was the Scotch racing through his blood to his brain, or he just needed some kind of release; but he started to laugh. Jim joined in, and how long they laughed was hard to tell. When the moment had passed, Ted took another swig of the Scotch and added,

"This wasn't the job I signed up for."

"I know. Me neither."

"But we can't quit. We know too much. So we just keep doing the job and hope we survive somehow."

"Me? I like to keep my options open..." Jim began. Suddenly the door to Ted's office burst open. Several guards flooded the room. Filing in behind them was Ipileno, and—in an unprecedented appearance to the general public: Abaddon.

"What the hell?" Ted began, but his speech was starting to slur from the alcohol. He tried to stand, but his legs refused to work. He was about to fall face-first into the coffee table and his only thought was, *Damn! This is going to hurt!* But Jim's hands suddenly caught him, and eased him onto the couch.

"We've found the leak." Ipileno declared, and all weapons locked onto Jim. Ted tried to talk, but the booze was really hitting him and he realized it had been almost a full day since he had kept anything in his stomach. The rush made him feel detached from his body, as if he were only an observer.

"So what makes you think I'm a leak?" Jim confronted.

"For some reason we can never keep an EeeDee assigned to you very long. They seem to keep encountering some kind of accident. You round a corner, and your EeeDee is never seen nor heard from again. That's a good indicator. Tonight when we sent some EeeDees over to check on Ted, they failed to report. Each one we sent over seemed to disappear. That's when we sent in the troops." Abaddon hovered in the air.

"But, if you're right about me; then aren't you taking a chance. If your fellow EeeDees disappeared coming in here, what makes you think that you'd be safe?" The confidence in Jim's voice caught Ipileno and the others off-guard.

"Check your own records, In Cee. You'll find that I am listed there long after this night is over. I serve a purpose, and until my purpose is complete you cannot stop me."

"You might be indestructible, but you're not immune." With those words several EeeDees exploded into this realm of existence. The soldiers screamed and fell to the ground. Ted couldn't tell if they were dead or alive. Ipileno dove out of the room, while Abaddon dematerialized. Ted watched with the detached fascination of someone whose brain was floating in alcohol. He should have dropped to the ground. He should have been in pain. He realized that these EeeDees were more *real* than Abaddon. Abaddon at his most intense was only a shadow compared to these creatures which now hovered in the room. Somehow he was able to function. He wasn't sure if it was the Scotch, or the EeeDees. It was all dawning on him.

"You're one of them!" he bellowed, but his tongue was slurring the words. "You're a traitor!!" He wanted to rise, but his body wasn't working.

"I've never betrayed you, Ted. I never betrayed what I believe in. It's just that somewhere along the way, what I believed in, and what I was serving shifted. I'm here to give you a choice, Ted. I said I like to keep my options opened. They made the same threat to me that they did to you. I found a way to avoid their threats. I found a way to quit playing the game they were playing. If you want, you can walk away from this, too."

"I can't." Ted stammered. "They'd find me. They'll find you."

"Finding me, and beating me are two different things. Life is a series of choices. If you make the wrong ones things only get worse. If you make the right ones; then life finally has a purpose to it."

"It can't be that easy."

"It is. It's so easy that people can't believe it. All of us in the In Cees refused to believe until it was too late. We won't make the mistake a second time."

"I've seen what your side can do...will do. I can't go along with that!" Ted was beginning to feel self-righteous. He liked the feel of it. He was standing up for something. The EeeDees hung silently in the air, witnessing the conversation. They did not make their presence any more intrusive than they had. It seemed as if their only purpose was to give Ted and Jim the chance to talk without being interrupted.

"Our crime is that we have a different set of ideals than yours. In most cases people with different ideals can negotiate and find a way to resolve their differences. But there come those times when the side you are dealing with cannot be trusted. They will not negotiate—or if they do, they do not keep their agreements. At some point, you have to take action to stop the other side. It's not what we want; but it's what we have to do. If we don't stand up, if we don't protect ourselves; your side will wipe us out."

"They're going to wipe you out anyway!' Ted was feeling argumentative now. He was becoming blustery. "We know about your immunity gene..." He thought for a second and corrected himself, "Immortality gene. We know it's been activated. We know how to kill you still."

An EeeDee made contact with Ted's mind. The alcohol dissipated from this brain. Ted downed another swig of the bottle still in his hand. The rush was gone. The harsh reality of his world slammed into him with a reality he could not face. He took another drink, a long one; but it was like drinking water. He turned to face his brother. Jim stepped forward and took the bottle from his brother's hand; placed it on the table in front of him.

"I need your mind clear, Ted. This decision is that important. I can't let booze cloud it or block it. I know where all of this is going. I know it better than you. I know that thousands are going to die by beheading. What happened to Hennings was not the immortality gene. It has not been activated in us. None of us would allow it to be activated. What you saw on the film was the power of God. He healed Hennings. He rescued Hennings and sent him back to us. You won't find him.

"What happened to Rawlings and Schmidt was judgment for their crimes. You were horrified when you realized what they had been doing and whom they were doing it to. God stepped in to stop it permanently. Tonight Da Nishka ceased to exist. There are still seventy-three members lying in their hidden torture chambers with wounds they inflicted on their victim now inflicted on them. Their immortality genes were activated. Death was removed as an option. The other twenty-five were found by others just like Rawlings and Schmidt. Those others figured out what to do to end their lives; but not their suffering. In answer to your question to Ipileno about Hell; yes it is real. Very real. But there Rawlings and Schmidt's minds will not be broken. That escape will also be lost to them."

"What happened tonight?" Ted almost sobbed. He struggled to get hold of his emotions. He wasn't drunk. He could not blame it on the booze.

"Two of your people are now my people. They realized they did not like their life the way it was. They wanted to change it. We gave them the chance to do so. It's why I'm here to offer the same chance to you. With regards to Rawlings and Schmidt, it was a judgment long-time coming. It was the Angel of Death they both encountered. Their sins found them out. God's judgment is coming. Upon Da Nishka tonight; upon the entire world in the years ahead."

"Ipileno's going to hunt all of you down. He's going to wipe you all out." Ted snatched the Scotch off the table and took another swig. Still nothing.

"I know. That's why I'm here. Tonight was my last night to see you before I went away. Even if they hadn't discovered me, I would have gone away. I'm the leader of the In Cees. Don't know how it happened; but one thing led to another, and here I am. We're both in positions of power; but we're on opposite sides. I want to give you the chance to come with me."

Ted thought about it for a minute, but a minute was all the attention span he had left in his mental state. Images of Rawlings flashed through his mind. He tried to block them out. He took a deep drink, finishing the bottle. Waited for the rush that never came. He looked about his office and realized all that he'd be giving up.

"No!" he shouted. He threw the empty bottle at the closest EeeDee. It passed harmlessly through the creature and shattered on the wall. "I won't go. I won't betray my trust. I've given my oath of allegiance..."

"The country you gave your oath of allegiance to doesn't exist anymore. It was sold out. All the ideals and dreams are gone."

"But I promised. I gave my word...you gave your word."

"That's Dad talking, Ted. Dad sold his soul to the military. He never thought it through, never asked the hard questions. In this world, you have to ask the hard questions. Come with me." Jim extended his hand, and for one brief moment, Ted considered taking it. But he realized he was in the headquarters of the New Alliance. It was the seat of power for the world. There were hundreds, maybe thousands of security men between him and the front door. Jim would never make it. If he went along, he'd be throwing his life away, too. He wanted to live...oh God how he wanted to live. He knocked Jim's hand aside with the back of his hand.

"If you change your mind, I'll do what I can. But it's never going to be this easy again. Are you sure this is what you want?"

"Go on. Get out of here!" his hate-filled voice echoed in his ears. Jim turned, and the EeeDees escorted him from the room. Ted kept waiting for the sounds of gun fire which would cut his brother down; but it never came. He tried to keep track of time as to how long until they got to the front door and the last line of troops would take them out; but the alcohol was returning to his bloodstream pumping back into his brain. With the EeeDees gone from the room the protection from the alcohol was gone; he dropped into the dark abyss he had sought to escape the images of Rawlings on the warehouse floor.

CHAPTER TWENTY

The Purge Begins

Amir hugged the wall of the alley. Behind him twenty men and women were gasping from the distance they had just run. Behind them they heard the sounds of guns and cursing. Shmuel looked at his brother and saw the concern in his eyes.

"Just like Damascus, heh?" he quipped.

"Damascus didn't involve civilians. It didn't involve leaving anyone behind." Amir whispered back.

"We can't save them all." Shmuel reminded. That was the message Eli had given them when they were sent out two weeks ago to find the various In Cee strongholds and start bringing believers back to Israel. They were given names and descriptions to ensure they brought the right ones back. At first it was a simple choice of just meeting with the "Chosen Ones" and convincing them to go with them. But since the Purge had begun, there were several times when Amir and Shmuel were only minutes ahead of Ted's troops. Then it was difficult. Then you grabbed and ran. Then you had to leave others behind. Neither of the brothers liked this. For the twenty they slipped through the Alliance's net, they had left behind fifty-three more.

Enoch was suddenly before them. Eli guarded the flank. As troops rounded the alleyway, fire dropped from the night sky and filled the entire area. Several troops began to scream, but the heat cut their lives short in mid-scream.

Enoch stepped forward and disappeared as if stepping out of this world. Amir and Shmuel began to usher the survivors through. There was no portal. There was no door. It was just a point in the air where on one side you were in the flame-drenched alley and the next you were in Ein Ghedi, Israel. As the last survivor went through, Eli pushed Amir and Shmuel ahead of them. Already troops were coming down a different path. Bullets ricocheted off the brick walls, but the last three were also gone.

"That was close." Amir noted. He slipped his gun into his belt in the small of his back.

"The enemy is getting more aggressive."

"And what about the ones we could not save?" Shmuel asked. Enoch looked to Eli. Eli nodded for Enoch to take the survivors off to get food and rest.

"They will die." Eli confessed.

"Why couldn't we bring more?" Amir demanded. "Why are there just certain ones that we are allowed to save? With your abilities we could bring back more, many more."

"Because it is the Will of G-d." Eli noted.

"That sounds like a cop out." Shmuel declared. He did not want to fight among themselves; but it bothered him that they had to save some and let other die.

"This is the Purge spoken of in Scripture. The Dragon has declared war on the saints of G-d." The *Dragon* was their code word for Ipileno. "The Scripture tell us that all believers except for the One Hundred and Forty Four Thousand shall be martyred. G-d is allowing this. He is bringing them home. He is taking them out of this world because their work is coming to an end; and soon your true work will begin."

"But why this way?"

"I do not understand; NOR DO I QUESTION THE WORKING OF G-D." Eli began. His voice was firm and full of command. Amir and Shmuel realized they had been about to cross a line that was not permitted to be crossed. "When we question G-d; then the enemy has gained a foothold." Eli's voice was softer now.

"Enoch and I know what awaits them in the Kingdom. We know the glory waiting for them. They will have a special reward. Giving their lives for their G-d carries a special blessing. I wish we could reveal to you the things of Heaven;

but it is not lawful for a man to see these things and speak of them. Because the enemy fears the Immortality Gene, they are executing our brothers and sisters quickly; and in a painless manner. They will not suffer. If the enemy believed the Immortality Gene was inactive; they would torture them and make their deaths slow and painful.

"G-d is calling them home. He is giving them the strength to bear their trial. He is not giving us the strength to bear their trials because it is not our trial to bear."

"And how many will eventually fall into the hands of the enemy?" Shmuel asked.

"All...all save the Hundred and Forty Four Thousand. The enemy calls it the *Purge*; G-d calls it a *Transition*. He is shifting His work from them. They are being called to their reward and rest. You and your brothers and sisters will be stepping into their place. You will be the final evangelists. You will be G-d's Final Message to this world."

"And when will Jim join us?" Amir asked.

"Soon. He is doing all he can to save his flock; but it torments him that he cannot save them all. It breaks his heart that his own brother is the source of this death and killing. He does this as much to save his flock as he does trying to atone for the sins of his brother."

"And will he be one of us?" Shmuel asked.

"No," Eli whispered. "He is not one of the Hundred and Forty Four. His work, too, will be coming to an end. As will ours."

"What do you mean?"

"Our work is only given a short time to complete. Three and a half years. That is all." Enoch declared as he returned to the group. Obviously he and Eli could hear and know what the other was hearing and seeing.

"Three and a half years? That is too short a time. We won't be ready." Shmuel challenged.

"Three and a half years was all G-d the Father gave our Messiah to prepare His followers. All Yeshua had was three and a half years to train and prepare His Disciples. It was enough then. It will be enough now."

"But you are not Messiah. You are not Yeshua. Can you do as much as He in such a short time?" Amir added.

"Perhaps that's why God the Father sent two of us in place of only Him." Eli joked.

CHAPTER TWENTY-ONE

The Foundations of The Earth

"This is the man we're after. Former Major James R. Brown," Ted announced to the room-full of operatives. He flashed the image of his brother on the wall and the computer rotated the image and changed between various poses and possible alterations. "Don't be taken in...We were. He's dangerous, very dangerous. He was a mole in our operation for over two years. He knows our entire operation. He knows all of our agents. He helped to design several procedures and departments for us."

Ted paused. It had been six months since Jim had last been seen. During that time his teams had uncovered hundreds of In Cee strongholds, dragged most of the members into the streets and executed them on the spot. There had been some protests at first, but when the word got out who and what these people were; neighbors, relatives, and co-workers began to provide tips and leads to find other In Cees. The operation had been going almost non-stop for four months. They had broken the power base of the In Cees in the Alliance cities. Now they needed to spread out to other countries. It still galled Ted that his own brother had been the head of the In Cees, and he had never noticed. Of course, now that Jim was exposed, Ted could go back and see the clues, put the pieces together; but the damage had already been done.

"We've also got the green light to terminate these two on sight..." Ted pulled up the codes on the keyboard and the man who had appeared in the Jewish home on Passover night replaced Jim's for the room to see. Ted let it rotate and morph into possible disguises. "His name is Eli. That's the only name he seems to use."

Ted hit the keyboard again and a second face appeared. Where Eli was mostly bald, this man had a full head of white hair. His eyes were a piercing blue. The shoulder-length white hair was pulled back in a ponytail in the first image. He had a well-trimmed beard in the next, and in the third morph his hair was cut to modern fashion and he was clean-shaven.

"This is the other. He goes by the name of Enoch. No last name. No aliases currently on record. You know these last two as the *Two Israelis*; some are calling them the *Two Witnesses*. They first appeared as a team during the *Israeli Incident* and were responsible for setting off the nukes in the Egyptian mosque. They keep showing up throughout the world. Every time they do, they announce new disasters. They've polluted major fresh water sources. Wiped out entire crops. Whenever they are confronted, they kill everyone. To date, no survivors. They are extremely dangerous. We are changing our tactics concerning them; but we can't use those tactics unless they are found. We've been flashing their images along with Brown's on every vid, internet screen, personal computer and cell phone for the last eight weeks."

The briefing lasted another half-hour as various questions were asked and answered. Ted outlined various strategies and procedures. When he dismissed the operatives, Spencer came to the front of the room and handed him several reports. Ted glanced at them.

"We're increasing the number of executions." he noted.

"About eight percent. It's been climbing at this rate for the last six days."

"Any sign of it tapering off?"

"Not if people keep giving us leads."

"Better order another three portable guillotines to keep up."

"The men enjoy the chance to execute the In Cees personally, but it's starting to wear them out, and slow down the over-all operation. They'll be happy to hear the news."

Spencer paused and looked at the image of Jim which still *morphed* on the main wall. The image changed to that of Eli. "Still no word?"

"Oh, we have lots of words. His face has been plastered on every television, newspaper, web-site and magazine across the continent. All it does is make us look bad. Since we know who the leader is, the public thinks we should have had him in custody before the end of the week. Every lead we get is a dead one."

"Probably in Israel." Spencer suggested.

"Any special reason?" Ted asked.

"Outside of the fact that most of Israel openly accepts Jesus as their Messiah?"

"Where did you hear that?" Ted challenged. Spencer looked at Ted with his *You've Got To Be Kidding Me* look.

"That's why Ipileno was able to get them to stop the daily sacrifices after the *Rapture Syndrome* hit. From the High Priest down it seems like everyone woke up that morning and suddenly realized Jesus was their Messiah. Once they accepted that, they no longer needed the daily sacrifices. The whole country went In Cee on us; or as they like to call themselves, *Messianic*." Spencer noted.

"Israel has been opposed to the executions. They see it as the same kind of genocide they endured during Hitler's War. They've become a sanctuary for In Cees around the world.

"We keep uncovering the smugglers bringing them into Israel, but for every three we find it looks like ten more get through. Israel is becoming the world's In Cee state."

"You know they are the same movement as the In Cees, only using a different name. The only difference between the two is that the Messianics have an entire nation protecting them. At some point we are going to have to move against them if we want to crush the movement completely." Spencer suggested.

"Does Israel pose a threat to the Alliance?" Ted asked.

"My first gut feeling would be *no*. I don't see Israel attacking the Alliance. But it may pose a threat to our agenda. They won't let us in to take out any In Cees in their boarders. The

In Cees and the Messianics are joining together. They are teaching the same things. All our work in the streets of the Alliance are worthless to stop the movement if we let one country continue to generate more In Cees…and Messianics." Spencer added. He had been pressing Ted for weeks to get some confirmation that the Alliance was going to move on Israel, but Ipileno wasn't moving that way, yet.

"I wish they would just openly oppose Ipileno. It would make the job a lot easier. Let Israel get in our way and then we can move in with an army and wipe them all out." Ted noted as he handed the reports back to Spencer.

"It's that damned Temple. Ipileno never should have let them build it." Ted continued.

"He really did not have much choice in the matter. They were getting everything ready for it back in the 1980's. They found genetic markers for everyone of the line of Cohen— the last of the priestly line. They had replaced the Menorah, the Table of Show Bread and several other items. The Temple Mount Faithful had reclaimed the cornerstone of the original Temple and had it sitting at the base of the Temple Mount since the beginning of the twenty-first century. All they needed was permission to start rebuilding." Spencer noted.

"What was that memo that started the whole thing?"

"The Red Heifer. It's a breed of cows that's been extinct for thousands of years. Then one was born in the old United States, and then several were born in Israel. They needed to kill one and burn it; then mix the ashes with water and sprinkle it on the Temple to dedicate it. They've been ready to build for years; but there was no red heifer…well, there wasn't a priest who would certify one for the sacrifice. Then during one of the religious holidays one rabbi certified a red heifer and now every rabbi in the country is certifying everything."

"Still can't believe they had the Ark hidden away all these years."

"They found it in a chamber under the Temple Mount. Arabs tried to fill the chamber with cement to keep them from getting it; but they had already moved it by then."

"Damned Israeli efficiency." Ted spat the words out of his mouth as if it were leaving a bad taste in it.

"Oh." Spencer added as if suddenly remembering something. "There's also some other information coming out of Israel..."

"Other than the Messianics?"

"I think it's part of the movement. Seems the *Two Israelis* have become the leaders of the Messianics. They've got a permanent platform for making quite a stir. Seems our green light for *shoot on sight* might be yellow turning red."

"So they now have the protection of the Israeli government? Ipileno needs to seek extradition of those two back here."

"They may not honor it. If our reports are correct, the *Two Israelis* have been working miracles."

"There are no such things as miracles." Ted declared. "Everything follows the laws of nature. Charlatans just manipulate them to their own end."

"Maybe, but people are starting to believe. There are still the reports of their turning water to blood, keeping the sky from raining, calling fire from the sky."

"It's all a bag of tricks!" Ted dismissed the entire affair with a wave of his hand as he descended the platform and headed for the door.

"Maybe, but how do you explain the lack of rain world-wide since they showed up? We've lost a lot of crops. Famine is spreading. The plague and disease is not far behind. You can explain the water to blood trick with chemicals. The fire from the sky might be a new weapon; but no rain world-wide except for in Israel for over two years is where your argument falls apart."

"What are you suggesting?" Ted confronted without stopping his stride towards the exit.

"Are you sure it isn't EeeDees from the other side becoming involved once more?" Spencer shouted after him. Ted was back in his face in an instant with his gun under Spencer's chin.

"Where did you hear that?"

"Ted, I was there that night. I saw the image on the film in Rawling's torture chamber. Call it an Angel of Death. Call it supernatural. Call it what you will; but I pay attention. I read the reports. I fill in what's missing between the lines. THAT'S why you put me on the team in the first place. Don't act dumb with me." Spencer used his index finger and pushed the gun barrel away from his chin.

"That term. That information is classified high above your pay grade. Never mention it. Never write it. Never think it until I give you permission." Ted's eyes flashed nervously around the room. The EeeDees were still confidential. Those in the direct protection squad of Ipileno knew about them. He knew about them. The heads of governments knew about them; but no one else. He was surprised they had not filled the room when Spencer mentioned their name.

Spencer's suggestion had been one he had tried to avoid. He thought for a moment, re-holstered his weapon and added;

"Let me check on it." and then he left the room.

He was barely out of the building when a strange rumble began to build. He scanned the sky for signs of planes that might be bombing any near-by installations. He could feel the roaring in the ground, coming through the concrete. What was probably the most frightening aspect was that it seemed to be coming right for him; but there was nothing visible. Spencer was suddenly at his side.

"Earthquake!' he shouted above the building roar. Before Ted could ask any more, the ground began to shake. The first hit felt like a rolling wave where the ground actually rose and dropped three times. Things began to crack and crumble. The building they had just been in began to shake. The ground rocked and became more violent.

"It's a big one. Got to be an eight or greater!" Spencer shouted above the sounds of crashing buildings and screaming metal support beams bending under the weight which was thrown out of kilter. The ground thrust up like a see-saw and then dropped Ted and Spencer unceremoniously to the ground as it plunged.

"My God!" Spencer screamed above the noise. "It's heading for a nine. Any reports of Elenin?" His reference was to the celestial object sometimes called a comet that been sighted when major quakes had hit a few years ago. Although never proven, some believed its gravitational field caused the quakes. Ted tried to recall any briefings on the object. All he could do was shake his head because the roar was so great it drowned out anything else. Ted had no idea how to measure quakes. He hadn't been raised in California the way Spencer had been. He couldn't measure the intensity of a quake by just the feel. If Spencer had pegged the first few seconds at an eight, and then jumped to nine; this one had to be more. The Indonesian quake was deep and the tsunami did the real damage. Chile had the 8.8. New Zealand was up there. Japan's level was never final but the experts put it up between 8.0 or 9.0. The debate was if the quake or the tsunami did the greater damage. Ted was glad they were nowhere near a shoreline.

When he tried to get to his feet, he was tossed about like a rag doll. He finally chose to lay flat on the ground and press himself against the earth in hopes to stop moving; but the entire ground was churning, lifting, falling, rocking and shaking; and taking him with it. He had never experienced the sensation of falling off the ground, but it was very close to what he was feeling right now. He was disoriented. He felt a wave of vertigo and nausea came over him. There was no way to regain his sense of balance or his dignity.

Explosions began to roar above the sounds of breaking glass, car alarms, crumbling buildings, and screams as bodies and buildings were crushed. Ted rolled over on his stomach, and he and Spencer tried to get to their knees to ride the tremors out. To the south several mountains were actually erupting, spewing rock, smoke and lava into the air. Walls of scalding, super-heated air and smoke were driven down the mountain sides. They were too far from the range to worry about the steam clouds; but still the sky was growing dark from all the smoke belching into the air. Flaming rocks began to plunge from the sky all around them. There was no way to predict where they would hit or how many there were.

For what seemed to be an eternity, the ground rocked, the mountains spewed, and the world seemed about to tear itself apart. Then the noise began to drop. It fell quickly; and suddenly there was silence. It was an eerier silence. Ted could still see the mountains erupting. He could feel the rumbling in the earth, but somehow all sound was being suppressed. The pressure of the air became so great it blocked all sound waves. His ears began to ache with intense pressure. His head felt like it was tearing in two. He tried to grab for his ears; but dropped to the ground unconscious before he could complete the motion.

Even though he and Spencer were oblivious to their surroundings, the silence continued for another half-hour as the air was compressed by the super-heated waves of gas and clouds, and the inversion layer of cooler air above. The two weather fronts collided across the landscape. The first sound which was finally able to be heard was the crashing of thunder as lightning raked the ground. Despite the thunderstorm, no rain was produced. It was the faint stinging of dying embers floating to the ground and hitting his face that woke Ted with a start.

CHAPTER TWENTY-TWO

Survival of The Fittest

Ted and Spencer were directing rescue operations trying to dig out the people who were still trapped in the collapsed buildings on the base. It had been a treacherous effort. The debris shot into the upper atmosphere by the erupting mountains had begun to fall, and had been falling in an almost steady barrage for the last four or five hours with no sign of it letting up. The rock had been propelled so high that it had almost escaped the Earth's gravitational pull, but as it fell back to Earth, the rocks were heated and either burned away to nothing leaving the impression of thousands of shooting stars visible both in the daytime and the night, or they made contact; causing greater destruction and death wherever they hit. As an added danger, the eruptions threw moisture into the air in the form of steam, and when the moisture rose high enough in the sky to be cooled, it fell as hail. Some of the balls of hail were the size of a man's fist; and further damage, injury and death grew in the wake of the continued storms. Ted noted hail was falling; but the much-needed rain was nowhere to be seen. As they worked they listened to reports, mostly from private radios; but their transmissions were breaking up from all the electrical storms caused by the super-heated air of the eruptions. The lava wasn't always cooled when it fell, and the magma that was spewed outward instead of upward struck the ground igniting everything it touched. Forest fires, brush fires and fire storms littered the landscape. In towns and cities where fire departments had survived the quake, the firemen spent all their time moving people to safety, and had abandoned structures to the unquenchable flames. The bleak crops—as pathetic as they were—were burned to ash; and with it the hope of communities to hold off starvation for the coming winter. As Ted listened to varied reports, it seemed as if the entire world had burst into flame and everyone who could see it spoke of it looking like the mouth of Hell itself.

Ted cursed the sky. It had been over two years without rain. No one had believed the Jewish fanatics when they made that decree; but even when colliding weather fronts should have produced torrents of rain, all they got were hail and ash. It was unnatural. Now the fires were draining what little water they had left for drinking.

Ted was atop the rubble breaking up the concrete slab with a jack hammer while others used sledge hammers or pulled the smaller sections away with lifts, ropes, or by hand. Although it was high noon, or mid-afternoon, lights had to be set up to illuminate the work area. The sky was black with smoke, thicker than any cloud cover. Ash was drifting down around them as they worked, and everyone wore either a dust mask or some kind of cloth over their nose and mouth so that they could breathe. Those who had goggles to protect their eyes wore them, but most had to stop and wipe the tears out of their red, irritated eyes where ash had settled in them. All wore some kind of hard hat even though it would offer little protection if one of the falling rocks struck them. Because they fell with such fury, they would tear through any structure, and being inside was no safer than being out in the open. Some of the men had commented they felt safer where they could see the rock missiles coming and the whine of displaced air heated by the rock's passing gave some brief warning before impact.

The faint image of the sun which filtered through the smoke was weak, but the temperature where they were working seemed at least ten degrees hotter than when the earthquake had first hit.

"Green house effect." Spencer noted as he tore a section off his t-shirt and tied it around his forehead to soak up the sweat while he worked. Once the sweatband was in place, he repositioned his hard hat.

"Green house effect?" a man next to him asked.

"It's the same principle as a green house where they grow plants. You can put one of those things up in the winter, and it will stay warm enough inside to grow tropical plants. The sun light passes through the glass. The glass filters out most of the levels of radiating light, and all that gets through is the stuff that makes things hot. It gets held inside and heats everything." Spencer explained as he swung his hammer against the concrete barrier.

"Kinda like why you get a sunburn at the beach when the clouds are covering the sun?" the man asked once more.

"Yeah. That's the idea." The man then pulled his shirt back on.

"I burn easy." the man replied and started back to work. The whine of a falling rock tore through the smoke. All eyes turned to the sky, saw the burning ember spat out by the heavens streaking to the north of them. The whine died before it struck. There was a feeling of a group exhale, and then they turned back to the task before them. Two yellow orbs emerged from the distance. As the objects came closer, Ted could see they were headlights of a jeep; but the smoke and dust in the air between them turned the normally powerful white lamps to faint yellow glows as the light fought to pierce the pollution. A battered jeep that was attached to the lights finally came charging up to the edge of the debris and the driver called out,

"Colonel Brown! President Ipileno wants to see you immediately." Ted cut off the jack hammer, and climbed down from his position to hear the man better. "President Ipileno wants you in his office now!" the man called out above the continued sounds of the rescue operation. Ted motioned to another man to take over his place. He signaled Spencer that he was leaving and he was in charge. The head of security then climbed into the jeep. The seat had debris on it and the driver swiped it off with his hand before Ted was all the way into the jeep. The windshield was cracked, the metalwork dented in numerous places. The paint job was obviously shot, and there was still a lot of dust, dirt and rock on the floor and back area. The speed with which the driver had traveled seemed to have blown off any dirt on the outside of the jeep.

"Where was the jeep?" Ted asked the driver.

"Near the barracks." the driver replied.

"How bad?"

"Pretty bad. Fortunately most people were out on assignments. We estimate about fifty...maybe sixty were still inside."

"How are the rescue operations going?"

"There are no rescue operations." the driver replied.

"They're all dead?!"

"No sir. We can still hear some of them under the rubble."

"Then why is there no rescue operation?!" Ted was becoming angry at the driver's attitude. "Do you need equipment? Men?"

"President Ipileno will explain it to you sir. That's why he sent for you."

Ted was in no mood to be civil when he entered Ipileno's office. He was hot, thirsty, dirty, and his eyes were burning. He found it painful to take a breath because of all the dust, ash and pollution he had been breathing. The information the driver had revealed hadn't helped. Despite all his raging anger, Ted had learned his lesson and stood at attention, hard hat under his arm, waiting for Ipileno to speak. Abaddon was with him. The EeeDee had begun to be present all the time since the night Jim had been exposed. However, when Ted inquired of others who had seen Abaddon, they reported the EeeDee looked like any other man, they just couldn't agree on a description of him. Ted assumed it was some trick the EeeDee was playing with their senses. He wondered how many tricks the creature had played on him. Ipileno turned his executive chair slowly around to face Ted.

"There will be no rescue operations, colonel. Is that clear?"

"But sir, there are people trapped under there. We can hear them calling for help."

"'No rescue operations.'" the president repeated. "What part of that command do you not understand?"

"The basis for such an order, sir." Ted replied. Ipileno looked as if he were becoming exasperated with his head of security. Ted knew that his own position had been precarious at best since it was revealed that his brother was the security leak. It had been one of the reasons he had worked so hard to wipe out the In Cees and to find his brother. He saw it as a way of vindicating himself before Ipileno. This order, however, wasn't making sense. The president had turned his chair away from Ted as if the audience was ended. Ted waited for an answer. Finally Abaddon walked *through* the desk to come face-to-face with the colonel. The head of security fought to keep control of his reaction since it was scaring the hell out of him.

"This is only the first quake. An even greater one is coming in a very short time."

"Weeks? Days?" Ted interrupted. If it were possible for annoyance to become a solid thing and hang in the air, it did as Abaddon studied Ted's face.

"Hours." the EeeDee revealed. Ted wanted to burst from the room and begin to make preparations but Abaddon's presence was making it clear such actions were not an option for him. The EeeDee turned away from Ted, walked back through the desk and noted,

"Colonel Brown seems to have been a good boy lately. He has put in long hours to erase the In Cees from the cities under your control. Perhaps we should humor him and let him in on the situation." Ipileno thought for several long moments. When he turned his chair back to face Ted the president's face was as pleasant as if he were trying to win over the one vote he needed for re-election.

"Sit down, Ted. What we've just experienced is the beginning of a series of quakes." The whine of another incoming rock grew in intensity. Ted involuntarily fingered his hard hat as if it might offer some protection. The scream grew and was replaced by the sound of it impacting into the ground, the force of the hit driving dirt and rock into the air. The explosion came to the west. As soon as the noise died down, Ipileno continued without even making inquiry as to the damage or loss of life. "What makes these quakes so strong and so different is that they are world-wide. This was just the first."

"World-wide?" Ted echoed more out of shock than disrespect.

"When a comet struck the earth many centuries ago and nearly wiped out all life at that time, the impact cracked the continental plates. Before that time all land was a single mass. The fury of the comet striking cracked the ground down to its deepest level where the land mass floated on the molten core of the earth. Oceans rushed in, struck the lava, exploded into steam which further drove the continents apart. The steam then fell as torrential rains for weeks. Most of the energy of the impact and the steam took about a year to dissipate. The continents settled into position, but always moved, ever so slightly. Now the continental plates have begun to make contact with each other." Abaddon explained.

"The comet struck, cracked the land mass, and drove the continents apart creating the Atlantic Ocean. The continental plates are making contact in the Pacific Ocean." Ipileno continued. He stabbed a button on the control panel on his desk. A flat-screen TV as large as the entire wall descended from the ceiling and flickered to life. It was a news channel, probably one of the few still operating. The reporter was obviously bobbing up and down in rough seas as the cameraman tried to keep an image centered on the screen. It was a great mountain jutting up from the ocean. What terrified Ted even more than its size and the churning sea around it was the fact that he could actually see the mountain continue to grow.

"This is where the plates are colliding." Abaddon spoke over the reporter's voice. "The plates are crumbling at the point of impact, and are pushing up the debris. Before it is done, this mountain will rise above the waters higher than Mount Everest. If you measure it from the ocean floor it will be ten times that size." The EeeDee paused to let the image sink in.

"What is going to happen is this..." The screen went into fast-forward motion. Ted for a moment thought it might be a digital image, but no video tape had ever moved so quickly. The mountain grew to even greater heights. It began to shake. For all of its mass and bulk it actually rocked back and forth. Each side of the mountain was shoved higher than the other; then the shorter side would scrape along the massive fault in the mountain, pass the previous peak and jut higher than before. Tons of rock broken loose by the action tumbled into the sea around it. Then the process would repeat itself. The mountain rocked, it shook, and then it exploded. Ted leaped back as if the eruption might come through the screen. The molten rocks sprayed the news crew, cracked the camera lens, and melted the camera housing while several holes were burning into the cameraman's face, chest and skull. Abaddon had pulled the image back so Ted could see the agonizing death of the news crew and seamen who had manned the once great vessel. It was bombarded with thousands of small natural rock-mortars, shredding its deck and hull. The boiling water poured into the broken wreck and dragged it with all hands beneath the waves. There was no camera to film the scene, but the images continued to be displayed on the TV.

The entire mountain became fire as lava spewed into the sky and flowed out of the broken crater that had once been its peak. Steam began to rise around the shore of the new mountain-island. Abaddon waved his hand and the steam no longer obscured their view. Ted shivered as he realized that somehow Abaddon was creating the image of things which had not yet taken place. The mountain-island continued to explode. The entire mountain was hurled into the air. Abaddon slowed the image showing the flaming mountain as it plunged back into the waves. The mountain sank leaving a great hole in the ocean which the waters sought vainly to fill. Ships that had survived the rain of burning rock and numerous tidal waves since they were miles off shore when the first quake had struck were sucked into the hole that was filling with steam that exploded from the hole. Even though the section of sea floor which had collapsed was massive, the heat was boiling the waters, turning them to steam, and the steam was expanding at such a rate it couldn't be contained in the cavity. As it was driven out of the crater in the sea, so much air was displaced at such force, and at such a speed, that a roar began to build and was so loud Ted had to plug his ears to keep from being deafened by the noise. Abaddon took pleasure in watching Ted squirm in pain, and then reduced the volume before inflicting permanent damage.

Finally the waters had cooled the molten lava at the bottom of the hole enough to stop boiling away into steam. The hole then filled, the waters crashing into each other and massive tidal waves began to spread out from the point where the mountain had sunk. The walls of water grew higher and higher. Ted looked in the direction of Abaddon.

"They are already a mile high. When they reach the shores of the continents they will be almost three times that size. They will destroy all islands in their paths, and bury the coastlines in water as far in-land as a hundred miles. All ships in the Pacific Ocean will be wiped out, that would be almost a third of all ships in the world. Most sea life in the Pacific Ocean will be destroyed." The scene continued to play out before the head of security. It was more than his mind could grasp. As the seas and waters began to settle, he noted that the blue-green of the ocean was replaced by a color of reddish-brown, making the sea look like a spreading pool of blood. He didn't even know where to begin his questions. He sat and let it play before him, praying that somehow his mind would go numb, or his eyes explode so he wouldn't have to see this anymore. On those occasions when he closed his eyes, the horror continued in his mind and he realized that there was no escaping the scenes, the memories, or the fear that clung in his throat. Finally Abaddon motioned and the scene on the TV shifted to a string of islands.

"This is what the last quake looked liked from this point of view." The image zoomed in and all the trees, mountains and buildings were clear and precise. The picture shook as if the image had been a car in slow motion colliding with a wall. The trees, mountains and buildings not only shook, but literally moved several feet. The trees swayed with the impact, the buildings collapsed, the mountains began to crumble or erupt. Ted was reminded of the videos of the Japanese quake. Beautiful farmlands turned into debris in only a few seconds.

"This is what the next quake will look like." Abaddon lectured. Here the motion was three or four times more obvious. Trees snapped or were up-rooted trying to compensate for the sudden shift in position. There were no buildings, and the last of the mountains exploded and crumbled as lava poured forth.

"There will be no rescue operations." Ipileno repeated in a cold voice, any trace of warmth or friendliness gone from his eyes.

"As you can see, our resources will be severely depleted because of this. Every person we save is a person who will eat our food or drink our water. It may sound harsh. It may seem cruel. But for the good of the world as a whole; there will be no rescue operations. All of this is a weeding-out process. If the immortality gene were activated today, within twenty years the world could no longer support us. We must let those who will die from these events die. When the world has recovered from all that is going to beset it, and only those who are the strongest and the most fit have survived; we will activate the immortality gene. Then, and only then will the ratio of life and supplies available be balanced. Only then can life go on. Until that time each person is on their own." Abaddon related.

"Even me?" Ted asked with little more than a whisper.

"Even you." Ipileno noted without the slightest hint of regret.

"There will be those who won't give up on others. They will try to rescue them." Ted suggested.

"If that is what they feel they have to do, then fine. However, they will do it on their own time, and with their own equipment. Anyone caught disobeying this order will be shot. We will need all of our energies and supplies for the greater disasters ahead."

"And will we perform rescue operations at that time?" Ted asked rising from the chair.

"No." came the ice cold voice of Abaddon. "From here on out, it is the survival of the fittest."

"So I'd better make sure I'm fit." Ted remarked; but there was no humor in his voice. When Abaddon lowered his presence and Ipileno rotated his chair back to the broken window that covered one whole wall of his office, Ted realized the meeting was over and began to slip out of the room. He wondered why it was he felt more dirty than when he entered. In the distance the whine of another in-coming rock's shrill scream grew; and Ted thought for a moment that if it struck him, it would be a blessing. It burned out before striking the Earth. At the threshold, the head of security stopped. Two questions seemed to be in his mind. He turned back and cleared his throat. There was almost the sound of a muttered sigh from the high-back chair as it turned back around.

"Just a couple of points I need clarified..." Ted began. It was Abaddon who motioned for him to continue. "What caused the loss of sound and the intense pain in our ears we all felt in the last quake, and will it be that bad during the next?"

"The loss of sound was caused by instantaneous compression of the entire Earth's atmosphere. With the pressure change came the pain in your ears as they tried to adjust. The entire atmosphere of the earth was compressed because as the continental plates collided, it actually altered the rotation of the entire planet. For that half-hour, the ground moved one way, and the atmosphere went another. It has compensated.

The length of days will be altered. Seasons will be altered. Weather patterns will be completely unpredictable. However, when the next quakes hit, even though they are larger—more powerful—the direction of the Earth's rotation will not be affected." Abaddon replied.

"And the last point...What are we going to do about *Wormwood*?"

"*Wormwood* is still on course for Earth. We cannot allow it to strike because then *all* life would be wiped out. We have defenses already set into motion. *If* you are still alive when the time comes, I will let you see what we have planned." Ipileno offered. It was the tone when Ipileno spoke the word *if* that made Ted's blood drop several degrees. The head of security chose to leave at that point knowing it would increase his chances of being alive when *Wormwood* arrived.

CHAPTER TWENTY-THREE

In The Shadow of The Temple

Jim stood on the top of the Mount of Olives as he watched the noon-day sun turn the city of Jerusalem to gold. The once-powerful sun, weakened as it was, filtered through the perpetual smoke and pollution in the air; and tired as it was in these Autumn months was still strong enough at this time of day to create the effect. It had once been a sight tourist could only see in the early morning or the late evening when the sun struck the city at an angle and painted it with a yellow-glow. Now it happened only at noon; but the sight could still make one breathless. The buildings, both old and new that spread out before the Temple, like bowing subjects; glowed golden for these few minutes each day. The entire world seemed to pay homage to the Temple of G-d.

The Mount of Olives was only a short walk across the street from the Eastern Gate, up the road from the Garden of Gethsemane. Years ago it had been little more than a dirt path, but when Israel did a major facelift for its Year of Jubilee the road had been paved. Jim thought it took something away. It had been the same path Jesus and millions of others had traveled; but it was hard to imaging Jesus walking down a paved road.

The Golden Gate was across the street from the Garden of Gethsemane. It had been sealed many years ago to keep the Jewish Messiah from passing through it and fulfilling prophecy. A cemetery had been created in front of the gate to keep law-abiding Jews from even walking close to the wall for fear of becoming unclean. Unfortunately, all these precautions to keep the Messiah from entering the city through this gate and fulfilling the ancient prophecy were doomed. They were doomed because the Messiah had already made the predicted entrance on Palm Sunday as part of the Triumphant Entry of Yeshua—Jesus. All the efforts on the part of those trying to prevent prophecy only fulfilled a second prophecy which said that the gate would be sealed after the Messiah had passed through it.

It had been a debate that lasted the entire time the Temple was being rebuilt: *should the gate be re-opened?* It was the same arguments that had been debated when Israel captured Jerusalem many years ago. The hard-line Jews had insisted that it be opened so that the Messiah—when He comes— could pass through it. Others claimed that if He truly was the Messiah then He would open the gate for Himself. And so the debate had continued. Those who favored the gate remaining shut had to do nothing to win; those wanting it opened had to be the ones to generate activity.

Finally, both sides did agree that a law-abiding Jew could not walk through a cemetery because he would become unclean, and the Messiah could never be unclean. Thus, began the effort to move the cemetery away from the Eastern Gate. At least they could agree on that one point. Of course, the Jews could not do the actual work themselves, or they would become unclean. Therefore they had to hire others to do it for them, and these others had charged a great deal for the work.

The Temple with its golden doors glistened in the yellow noon-day sun. On the various Holy Days such as this, the smell of the burnt offerings would drift across the Kidron Valley and towards the top of the Mount of Olives. This was the third Yom Kippur celebration since the *Israeli Incident.* The fourth time Israel had celebrated their Day of Atonement with a completed Temple. The smell of the offerings kept Jim thinking of a perpetual Bar-B-Q.

The fact that the Temple was still standing for this Yom Kippur celebration was a miracle. It was a miracle everyone recognized. When the massive quakes had begun to hit, and entire mountain ranges crumbled, the structures of Israel remained safe and intact. The ancient ruins remained where modern structures in other countries collapsed. Jim smiled as he thought of the protective hand of G-d. The world was in ruins, but Jerusalem was still Jerusalem. It was still the City of G-d.

His focus shifted to the right of the Temple. Even the area where the Dome of the Rock once squatted off to one side of the Temple Mount glistened in the noon-day sun. Although the Dome of the Rock as a structure was destroyed by sulfur bombs during the *Israeli Incident*, the rock it had enclosed remained undamaged, and was clearly visible in the bottom of the crater next to the Temple. It was believed to have been the very rock where Abraham had offered Isaac as a sacrifice. The Muslims insisted Abraham had offered Ishmael there, not Isaac; and so it was their second most holy site, surpassed only by Mecca.

Jim's eyes followed the walls of the ancient city. Jericho's Road ran along the outside of the city walls. Despite it being an important route through Jerusalem, it still remained a two lane road through the Kidron Valley. It was a mixture of ancient and modern. He could spot those tell-tale stones of Herod's addition to the wall by their beveled edges. The smaller stones were later. From his place on the Mount of Olives he could point out half a dozen sites of historical important and recite the information about each as if he were a tour guide.

Jim had learned more in his few months in Israel than he would have imagined. This was a land of rich history; and you could not turn around without bumping into it. Excavations were everywhere. When he met with the others who had lived here most of their lives; they were bubbling with excitement and pride; and would spend hours sharing their treasured memories.

Jim hated to admit it, but Ipileno had worked a miracle here. For generations any talk of re-building the Temple was doomed to failure. Not just because of the protests of animal rights activists who even now marched and picketed in the Western Wall area vainly trying to keep animal sacrifices for Yom Kippur from taking place; but the Muslims would not let anything happen to the Dome of the Rock. Israel had made a serious mistake turning the Temple Mount over to Islamic control when they captured Jerusalem in the Six Day War of 1967. For years it was a tourist site that any could go and visit. They even let non-believers into the Dome if they would remove their shoes. However, touching between sexes was carefully monitored and not allowed. Yet when the Temple Mount Faithful began to suggest and then demand rebuilding the End Times Temple—as most were now calling it; the Muslins shut down the top of the Temple Mount and if you could make it to the top; you could not preach or pray there unless you were Muslim. One Passover several years ago a group of rabbis actually slipped onto the Temple Mount and performed a Passover sacrifice and filmed it. It made the rounds on the internet.

There had been recent talk of allowing the Dome to be rebuilt. It was Ipileno who had pointed out that the Dome sat squarely in the Court of the Gentiles. He had been the one to support building the entire Temple but leaving off the Court of the Gentiles. As far as the Jews were concerned; that wasn't an issue. Let the Gentiles do what they wanted in the Court of the Gentiles. Jews did not go through it unless they had to.

Of course, although Ipileno had been credited by the world with the rebuilding of the Temple, he did not initiate the rebuilding. That was something that grew on its own. The Day of Atonement took place several years ago along with Succoth. The city was charged with the energy of every Jewish-born male coming back to Jerusalem to present himself before the Lord as G-d had required three times a year in the Law of Moses. For some reason, every Jew felt the calling this year more than any year before. The hard-line Jews built their dwelling places out of the traditional kinds of branches. The modern Jews had his portable plastic and PVC pipe Succoth Huts that he could set up anywhere. Traffic came to a standstill as every road in Jerusalem was closed off. Succoth structures filled every yard, rooftop, field, street and opened space. The only way to get around in the city was on foot; even motorcycles or scooters were hard to navigate among the crowds.

At the end of the seven-day celebration, the eighth day of the feast had something as a spur of the moment event. It was like a national consensus that it was time. In the midst of the celebration of the last day of Succoth someone made a suggestion. Before you knew it, someone moved a truck and crane next to the cornerstones that had been left at the foot of the Temple Mount years ago. Within half an hour the Jews had taken the Temple Mount and were laying the cornerstones. Other stones were identified and retrieved. The Arabs tried to storm the Temple Mount by force to stop the construction, but there were more Jews in the city than Arabs that day. The sheer weight of the mobs held them back. No one could gain access to the Temple Mount except the Jews. The Arab nations threatened an all-out invasion to retake the Temple Mount. The United Nations held emergency sessions. America had a fleet in the Mediterranean Sea. Russia was threatening an invasion.

All the while the Jews began to recover blocks from the original Temple left strewn about the area by the ancient Roman army. Before the week was out the foundation was in place. The bronze altar was in place, and the daily sacrifices resumed. It was into this chaos that Ipileno appeared and made his observation that the Dome of the Rock was in the Court of the Gentiles. No one had touched the structure to rebuild the Temple. It was still unharmed. He negotiated a treaty between Arabs and Jews that day so both could have what they wanted. The efforts fell short of making Jerusalem a universal city; but the Jews would let the Arabs return to the Temple Mount and visit the Dome of the Rock. However, the work would continue on the Temple. This time Israel did not surrender the Temple Mount. They had military might there to protect their project and workers. The Arabs protested and shouted, but none would try to stop the work. After a few weeks, the protestors slipped away.

Once the Jews had regained control of the Temple Mount, this only left the problem of the Temple treasures. The Ark of the Covenant, which had been built by Moses in the Wilderness, was needed for the Holy of Holies. The Altar of Incense, the Menorah and the Table of the Show Bread were also needed for the Holy Place. The items were believed to have been lost centuries ago when Babylon invaded Israel and carried off everything to its own capital. Some taught the items were returned when Artaxerxes allowed Nehemiah to return and re-build the walls of Jerusalem. Documents showed the cups were still stored in Babylon before the return because when the king drank out of them to false gods, a hand appeared and wrote on the wall; pronouncing the doom of the king for such a sin. Thus the Temple treasures were in Babylon, and then all record of them was lost.

When Rome burned the Temple in 70 AD, it created such heat that all the gold inside melted and oozed between the cracks in the floor. Thus, the Romans left no stone in place when they literally dismantled the Temple to steal the gold. Most believed that the replacement Temple treasures were destroyed in the fire, melted down or carried away.

To the non-Jew this didn't seem like such a problem. All the Jews had to do was make new treasures for the Temple. The Temple Mount Faithful took up the call. They recreated the Golden Menorah. It stood across from the Western Wall for several years. The Table of Show Bread, the Altar of Incense and even the Bronze Laver had been replaced and stored.

The garments of the High Priest proved a little more difficult. The snails needed for the purple dye were believed extinct. The moths for the crimson red color had not been seen for centuries. Then some Israelis in Greece noted certain snails in the flowerbeds in an outside cafe there. A million snails disappeared almost over night. Greece noted something that big disappearing; but the problem was solved through prosperous negotiations.

A scientist stepped out his back door and found the moth on a tree in his back yard. They suddenly reappeared. It was as if G-d were telling His Chosen People that now was the time for the Temple to be rebuilt. The Temple Mount Faithful did all the preparation. They even found members of the Tribe of Levi and trained them in the Laws of Moses concerning sacrifices. But replacing the pieces would not be enough. They had to be consecrated according to instructions from G-d.

According to Mosaic Law the ashes of the Red Heifer were needed to complete the consecration ceremony. Israel needed the original items or the Red Heifer. There was debate by the legal scholars for years over this one issue alone. It would have made things so much easier to simply use the original pieces. In the middle of all these preparations by the Temple Mount Faithful there came the report that a Red Heifer had been born in the United States. Jim snorted to himself. It would never be the American Union to him. It was always his home—the good old U.S. of A. The heifer was defective, and while the rabbis were examining and buying it, other red heifers began to be born in Israel. Each piece could be replaced and consecrated according to Mosaic Law; but the purist wished the Ark had not been lost.

It had been at the Yom Kippur when the cornerstones were laid when Rabbi Gobbles certified the first Red Heifer as qualified for the sacrifice. It was at that point that there was no holding the fanatics back. Once the foundation was laid, the location of the bronze altars was identified. They were moved into place and the Red Heifer was sacrificed outside of the city according to the Law of Moses. Its body was burned and the ashes mixed with water. Before the day was out, the bronze altars were being consecrated with the ash and water mixture. The following morning the daily sacrifices began. There was cheering throughout the city. Shofar horns could be heard blaring the ancient call to worship from several high rise buildings surrounding the Temple Mount area.

However, as the construction moved forward, Israel revealed its greatest secret: the Ark of the Covenant had never left the Temple Mount. The works of art depicting the Menorah being carried off to Babylon never depicted the Ark among the treasures. Priests had carried it deep under the Temple Mount and placed it in a chamber directly under the Holy of Holies. If God was looking down from Heaven, the Ark would be in its original place—just a few hundred feet lower than before.

During the earlier excavations under the Temple Mount the chief rabbi had broken through into one of the chambers. He saw an object the size and shape of the Ark covered in animal skins. There was just one problem: he was struck mute by the experience. Just like the father of John the Baptist, he could not speak for several days after the experience. When his voice returned; he would not shut up about the find. Muslims heard of his find, drilled down from the top of the Temple Mount and poured in enough cement to fill the entire chamber. For years afterwards, worshippers would go under the Temple Mount and place their prayers on paper and slip them into the cracks in the wall that now sealed the chamber that was believed to mark the place of the Holy of Holies.

However, even though the chief rabbi could not speak, did not mean he could not write. A secret band of ceremonially-clean rabbis, following the Laws of Moses had slipped into the chamber that first evening. They placed the Ark on their shoulders and carried it to a safe location. As all the other pieces of the Temple were assembled, the Ark was brought forth covered in its proper newly-restored skins and carried on the shoulders of Levites to add to the Temple Treasures.

It had been a national day of rejoicing when the Ark was presented and carried through the streets around the Temple Mount. Devout Jews wept openly. Shofars blasted for hours as it made the rounds. Groups broke out in traditional dancing and songs all along the parade route. While many tried to get as close as they could, and waved their Torah or Tanakh in the direction of the Ark and kissed them repeatedly; none would dare to get close enough to touch it. Only the Levites bearing the treasure on their shoulders could make contact with the precious Ark.

Although it would have been faster to load the Ark onto a cart and wheel it out; the Ark was presented to the world clothed with its proper covering still intact after all these centuries. The poles were put into place, and those of the priesthood who could trace their lineage back further than anyone else were given the honor of carrying the treasure out of the chamber, along the tunnel and into the open on their shoulders. No one would even consider it being moved in any other way. Whenever someone not familiar with the death of Uzzah suggested some other way of moving the artifact, those more learned referred them to the Second Book of Samuel to enlighten them.

The Temple Mount Faithful had begun the process generations ago of tracking down those who were of the tribe of Levi. Cohen had been believed to be a variation of Kohath—the family in the tribe of Levi who had been responsible for moving the Temple Treasures in the wilderness after the sons of Aaron had covered them. Other names had been identified from ancient records and documents to find those who could trace their lineage back to the actual priestly tribe. Members of families had been contacted and recruited to begin training. Some had been in training for three or four generations, passing the skill down from father to son. The Temple Mount Faithful had undertaken the task of recreating the garments for the priests, the tools the priest would use. When genetics and DNA testing had been perfected, it was discovered that those of the Tribe of Levi had a genetic marker. G-d had "marked" His Chosen tribe. All those who had believed they had been of the Tribe of Levi had to undergo the test to be sure. Those who did not pass were barred from the priesthood. Thus when the Temple treasures were uncovered, and the plans approved, these priests came forth into the spotlight to begin their roles.

When the foundation was laid for the new Temple, the entire nation had celebrated. There had been concern that the more militant factions of the Muslim and Arabs races would take advantage of the celebration to attack, and so those who attended came with a prayer book in one hand, and a rifle in the other. However, Ipileno's treaty was honored by all; whether because it offered true peace for the region, or out of fear for what would happen to anyone who broke the treaty.

Ironically, the Temple was completed on the anniversary of Yom Kippur. It had taken a full year. The dedication was scheduled as part of the Day of Atonement ceremony. As the Temple was being dedicated, the *Israeli Incident* hit. Although there was death and sulfur bombs dropping everywhere, the Jews seemed protected. They completed their celebration.

At the end of the seven days of Succoth, the eighth day feast offered another miracle. It was on this day that Jews would eventually admit that they came to realize Jesus—Yeshua—was their Messiah. No one came forward to make an announcement. Each Jew thought that it was something that had happened to him or her alone. It was as if a light came on, as if a blindness had ended. All the prophecies came to mind. All the arguments suddenly made sense. But none would admit this openly. Many went into their homes, into private rooms and wept when the realization hit them. They had missed so much. How could they have been so blind? Each one feared what would happen to them when they admitted their change of faith to others.

It was at this time that Ipileno returned to try and bring an end to the animal sacrifices. From the moment the first row of foundation stones were laid and the bronze altar filled with sacred fire, the daily sacrifices had been performed. Ipileno now wanted to ease the growing tension with the animal rights activists. To his surprise, he did not meet with the fanatical resistance to his idea as he expected when he met with the High Priest. In fact, the entire Sanhedrin which had been restored and now guided Israel on religious matters as the Knesset guided the nation in political matters seemed more than agreeable to end the daily sacrifices in exchange for some hefty consolations. After meeting such light resistance to the idea of ending the daily sacrifice, Ipileno thought he could go after all animal sacrifices, and this is when the fanatical force of the Sanhedrin came to bear on him. He left Israel with a treaty to end the daily sacrifices, but the High Priest and Sanhedrin would not budge on the Holy Day sacrifices. He counted it a small victory for the animal rights activists.

It was at this time that it slowly came out that many no longer saw the need for the daily sacrifices. They were expendable, not just to the High Priest and the Sanhedrin; but to the Jews on the street as well. As discussions began one or two confessed that they no longer saw the need for a daily sacrifice, just the Holy Day ceremonies. When pressed on the subject, Rabbi Swenson was the first to confess his change of faith. He was still a Jew, but he now recognized that Yeshua was the Messiah they had been waiting for. Once his confession was public others came forward. It was as if the entire nation—the entire faith world-wide—had come to this realization at the same time, on the same day and in the same way. A few fanatics held out; but even they eventually saw the truth of their Messiah.

Now it was the Fourth Yom Kippur under the Temple Era. Jim looked out over the areas around the Temple. Already the numerous sects had set up shop in the various courts. Each Rabbi had his own following and had sectioned off a part of the court where he and his students would meet for lessons.

There had been some issues raised about women wanting to be recognized as Rabbis and given a place to teach; but the priests had been firm on the issue. Finally the priests allowed the women to be teachers, but they were forced to stay in the Court of the Women to teach. It was not an easy compromise. There was the Court of the Women on the outer rim of the Temple. Next came the Court of the Men, and every level inward was for a more sacred use until the Holy of Holies where the Yom Kippur ceremony to atone for sin was performed once a year and then only by the High

Priest. There had been a lot of politicking involved as to which priest would qualify for the position.

"Wormwood is coming" Dane said, and Jim had momentarily forgotten the man had been standing with him. He had almost forgotten that several were on the Mount of Olives. In response to Dane's observation, Jim looked into the sky and saw the red orb of the sun filtered through tons of volcanic ash, dust and steam. It was about the size of his fist. To the left of it shone Wormwood. It had become visible to the naked eye about two weeks ago. Those who had not heard of its coming were panicking. Now it was visible in the day time as a separate star, probably about the size of a dime in the sky. It was not just a point of light, but an orb like a small moon glowing orange through the haze.

"So it is." Jim acknowledged.

"What do you think they'll do about it?" one of the In Cees asked from the back of the group. Jim motioned for them to move over to a grove of olive trees. There were Churches scattered throughout the mount, a couple of hotels and restaurants on the peak, but olive trees were plentiful. Israel had learned to use tourist money and a tourist labor force to re-foliate their nation. Whenever tourists came to Israel, they were allowed to pay for a small sapling or some other kind of tree, they would be bused to a grove or field, and everyone would plant their tree. A certificate was given to commemorate the planting and the name of the person who had planted it. The years of effort had paid off with numerous trees throughout the nation. Even on the Mount of Olives there were several groves that were public and free for anyone to use. Jim led his group to one of these and everyone sat on the ground or rested against a tree. When everyone was comfortable, Jim began.

"The Bible tells us that a star is going to fall into one third of the rivers and the fountains of water. It will turn the waters bitter and millions will die from drinking the waters. The Bible also calls this star *Wormwood*." He paused to let the thoughts sink in.

"But how could the Bible know the name of the star when it wasn't even named until a few weeks ago?" Someone asked from the left side of the group.

"It had been named that several years ago. What is unusual is that the name was given to it by people who had no knowledge of its coming being listed in the Bible. When it was first reported years ago, the nations kept it quiet. They worked in secret to build tunnels and compounds under the mountains to survive if the asteroid ever hit. Those who worked the projects noted that the mountains of the world would soon look like wormwood from all their tunneling. The project came to be called *Wormwood* unofficially, and then the name was transferred to the asteroid. As for how the Bible knows the name..." Jim paused for humor. "Well, look who wrote it. Nothing has been a surprise to Him." A ripple of laugher passed over the crowd.

"What are we going to do?" someone else asked.

"We wait. And we trust God." Jim replied. It wasn't blind faith that guided him. He had been in contact with Amir and Shmuel who had kept him advised of events, had guided him to move most of his operation to Israel to survive the purge his own brother led. Through the twin brothers he had met Enoch and Eli. Where once his faith was weak; now it had been tested and proven strong.

"I can tell you this," Jim continued. "The nations of the world have been working on this for several years now. The arms race was set aside. We thought the nuclear missiles were being dismantled and destroyed, but a great percentage of them were sent into orbit to prepare for the coming of Wormwood. About a month ago, the nations began to coordinate moving all transmission and spy satellites to the far side of the Earth. They will be protected from Wormwood by the planet. At this moment several thousand nuclear warheads are in place and about to be launched towards the asteroid."

"We've all seen the disaster films, Jim. What are the odds of their pulling it off?"

"Pretty good. According to reports, Wormwood is about half the size of Manhattan." Several gasps sounded around the group. "That actually works in our favor. It's large enough to have its own gravity and gravitational pull. We've seen the tide pretty high lately. That isn't just because of New Everest sinking in the Pacific. Wormwood is close enough, and large enough to add a little extra to the tide. Because of that pull, all we have to do is get the missiles in the general vicinity, and then Wormwood will pull them in."

"Any idea what will happen?"

"Wormwood will be blown to pieces. Unless the debris is parallel to the Earth, the atmosphere will either burn it up, or deflect it back into space. A small percentage of the debris will hit the Earth head on. A lot of that will burn up before it hits."

"So this isn't an E.L.E.?"

Jim and several others laughed when they recognized the reference to a summer blockbuster movie from several years ago. He knew it had to be Ben who was obsessed with old films and had vids and DVDs of everything he could get his hands on. He was probably their only source of entertainment. Ben had raided numerous homes of Christians after the *Rapture Syndrome* hit, looting them for a number of things. Unfortunately, he wasn't a believer at the time and had taken electronics, computers, and entertainment equipment. He had stashes of these things hidden all over the planet right now. Whenever they needed something, Ben always seemed to have it or knew where to get it. For this reason most had forgiven him his obsession.

"No, Ben." Several chuckles passed over the crowd and the speaker blushed to be recognized. "This won't be an extinction level event. None of these will ever get to that level. It *will* get bad. There will be a lot of lives lost, but God tells us that there will be people left. People will still be making war up to the minute when He comes back. He will put things back. He will clean things up. He's going to make it all work the way it was supposed to. That's a promise He gives us." Jim held up the battered Bible he had salvaged years ago before he left the base. He couldn't count all the times he had blamed himself for not saving more of them. With their scanners, computers, printers and other equipment, they were lucky enough to reproduce the Bible through an underground market. A lot of Neo-Christians recognized the *Rapture Syndrome* for what it truly was. They had gone to homes, stores and other sources and purchased, or stolen every copy of computer programs for Bible, videos, cassette tapes, and actual Bibles that they could before the ban went into effect. They knew who the Christians were who had been sharing with them up until even the day before. They had refused to listen on the last day, the following day they wept for their mistake; and went to homes and stores to get everything they could on Christianity and the Rapture. There were hidden libraries around the world, carefully guarded, copied and preserved. Several times Ipileno's men had broken in. Jim had tried to warn his people, but some Neo-Christians gave their lives just to buy time for another box of Bibles to get spirited away to safety.

The meeting settled into a less formal gathering. They broke up into groups to share or visit. Dane made his way to Jim. He had been dealing with the loss of his daughter for several years. He had blamed himself for her death. When Giuerding and Wilhelm had begun to share with him about life after death, he saw that his daughter was not lost to him unless he messed up. The chess players had maneuvered Dane out of the tavern by the back way, taking great care to move in a casual manner so none would notice them. Once outside, they waited until a commotion called one of the officers away, and then they simply walked away. Now Giuerding and Wilhelm had become two of his closest friends. He had not truly realized how skilled the pair were at chess. He thought they had merely played a game as a diversion, but they had actually designed their game to give signals to the various operatives in the tavern as to when it was safe, who should make which move and when they should remain still and silent. They had to make the moves up as the game progressed and still give the codes to Neo-Christians in the tavern. Dane had watched them now understanding what they were doing and he was amazed at their skill.

"You put a lot trust in that book." Dane commented nodding at the Bible in Jim's hand.

"It's more than a book..." Jim began.

"I know. It's God's Word. It's His message to us." Dane repeated. He had wanted so much to believe, but he was still young in his faith. This was all new to him. Jim smiled. Dane was reciting lessons to him. They still were not his own beliefs; but the beliefs of those around him.

"Actually, this is a legally binding contract between us and God." Jim observed. That had been a different way of looking at it for Dane. Jim could tell the concept of a legal contract was an area of interest to the man. He may have been the communication officer for Ted, but he dabbled in law.

"So how does it work?" Dane asked.

"Like any contract. It first has to establish the legal authority. Is this a contract controlled by the laws of the United States? Is it a contract which is only effective in California? New York? England? Or some other province? You have to know the legal authority so you know which laws control it."

"So what's the legal authority here?" Dane asked picking the Bible up and flipping through it.

"It's like a copyright law." Jim noted.

"Copyright?" Dane's face took on a quizzical look.

"Just like a writer applies for a copyright to protect his work, this is like God applying for a copyright on the entire world. He starts off by making His claim as the Creator of the universe. When a writer files for copyright, he claims he created the work. It belongs to the author. God created the universe, it belongs to Him."

"And what if you don't buy that Creation stuff? What if you still believe it's all Evolution."

"Then you don't recognize God's legal authority. If God is not the Creator; then He has no legal right over us. Any attempt by God to set standards for us, control us or judge us are nothing more than the actions of a tyrant who should be opposed and fought."

"You're saying we should fight God?"

"No, but if you follow the teachings of evolution to their logical conclusion; that's what they are teaching. That's what Ipileno is going to declare. He will present himself and his armies as the ultimate freedom fighters. They will be fighting for freedom from the ultimate despot—God.

Creation gives God authority over us. He has the right. Evolution denied that claim of God and demands we fight Him for our freedom."

"I always thought Creation versus Evolution was just a philosophical debate." Duane confessed.

"Which is just what the enemy wanted you to believe. Evolution pretended to be the thinking man's answer. Creation was the response of the unthinking. No self-respecting person would seriously consider Creation. So it was dismissed without knowing why."

"The Bible starts with copyright law. '*In the beginning God created the heavens and the earth...*' Then God takes the stand the way an author would take the stand and tells the jury all the details of how the work was created. Then God makes His claim to have made man and woman. Genesis Two gives us the details of how He did it. These first two chapters are God's claim to have legal authority over us as our Creator.

"But you said the Bible was a contract. Contract law is not the same as copyright law." Duane reminded.

"It builds. As our Creator God has the right to set standards for us. He also has the right to hold us accountable for those standards. When we fail; He has the right to punish us."

"So where does the contract come in?"

"When Adam and Eve broke the law: '*Don't eat the fruit!*' God had no choice but to follow through on the punishment: '*You shall surely die.*' That's where the contract comes in. God offered our race a deal. Rather than punish us, He will accept the punishment and pay it for us; but it's not an automatic thing. That's the contract. The Old Testament tells us who this Messiah is going to be who will pay for our sins and save us. The New Testament documents that Jesus is the Messiah and fulfilled the contract."

"You make it all sound so simple." Duane replied.

"It has always been simple. God made this contract with Adam and Eve. He then confirmed it with a man called Abraham. It was passed down to his children, and his children's children."

"The Jews?" Dane asked incredulously.

"They were the ones that God would use to restore the relationship..." Jim began, but a new voice cut him off from behind.

"But the Jews misunderstood. They were the ones G-d would use to fulfill His contract, but they began to love the contract instead of G-d." Jim jumped up and embraced the man before seeing him.

"Eli!" Jim shouted.

"Jim!" the man greeted, held him at an arm's length and hugged him once more. "So this is Dane?"

"Yes. This is Dane." Jim echoed as if the man had been the subject of conversations between them.

"He seems smart enough." Eli joked. "Were you giving him your famous *the Bible is a contract between G-d and man* lesson?"

"Yes he was." Dane replied with a hint of irritation in his voice.

"Oh, so just because you're not the first one to hear it, means it isn't true?" Eli countered.

"Well...no." Dane admitted after thinking about it.

"It is true...and it's a good comparison. I was impressed with it when he first shared it with me."

"When did you join the movement?" Dane asked as Eli sat down between him and Jim. Jim laughed a short laugh as if there was more to the question than was public knowledge.

"Let's just say I've been a member for a long time. But as I was saying. The entire system of laws set up by G-d for the

Jews was a picture of what He was going to do to restore the relationship between Him and us. Unfortunately, my people fell in love with the system. We missed all the images of the Messiah; and when He came, my people refused to recognize Him. G-d did what He promised. He found a way to do the impossible. He found a way to let man come back into His presence and fellowship with Him."

"Jesus?" Dane asked. It was still more of a question than a declaration. Jim knew he was still learning. He still had doubts and questions; but there wasn't anything wrong with that. When you asked questions until you had the truth, until you understood; it was good. It's only when you stop asking the questions that you have a problem.

"Yes, Jesus. Or Yeshua, as we call Him. Can G-d make a rock so big He can't lift it? Only by limiting Himself. Jesus was G-d limiting Himself. Yeshua was G-d becoming man to do the impossible; to do what was otherwise impossible for G-d or man, but finally possible for the G-d-man."

"Your people?" Dane suddenly remembered the words of Eli.

"Yes. My people." Eli admitted.

"So you're a Jew?"

"I prefer to think of myself as a Messianic." Eli admitted. "Some used the term, *Completed Jew* and I don't have a problem with that. It's a good description. We were never complete until we put Yeshua into our system of laws. Once we recognize Him as the Messiah promised centuries ago, it all makes perfect sense. So I'm a Completed Jew who sees Yeshua as my Messiah—hence, Messianic."

Eli?..." Dane thought out loud. "You're not...?" but Eli cut him off.

"You are quick. I think he'll make a good student." Eli observed to Jim.

"I've always thought so." Jim admitted. Eli laughed a very contagious laugh, clapped Jim on the shoulder, squeezed Dane's as he rose and went to speak to some of the others around the grove.

"He's one of them?" Dane asked.

"Depends on which *one* you're referring to." Jim toyed.

"Not just a completed Jew. Not just one of the hundred and forty-four. He's one of the Witnesses."

"You've heard about them?" Jim asked; his voice not completely without humor.

"He and the other were responsible for stopping the rain, calling fire from the sky. They've even turned water to blood according to some people."

"Then if that's the *one* you're talking about, yes, he's one of them."

"But he seems so...normal. So human." Dane observed.

"You were expecting a long robe, full beard and a walking staff?" Jim joked.

"Well, no. But to be all that he's supposed to be. I just expected more."

"Than an older Jewish man walking around in jeans, Reeboks and a t-shirt that says *my parents went to Israel, and all I got was this lousy t-shirt*?"

Dane suddenly realized that Jim had almost described Eli, except for the slogan on the t-shirt. There was no slogan on it. And Eli wore a yamaka and wrapped a prayer shawl around his waist; but it was the best way to describe Eli. Dane started to laugh, and Jim joined in. Those close to them had no idea what the humor was; but the pair had a contagious laughter and others joined them. Eli turned from the far side of the grove with a knowing eye, and he laughed louder than anyone else.

CHAPTER TWENTY-FOUR

Death From The Skies

Ted heard screaming from off to his left. He had made it a point not to get involved unless it was part of his assignment. Good Samaritans were easy targets for gangs. The violence had grown over the last few months. With the extermination of the In Cees in the cities, it seemed as if certain groups had become more active, more bold. He was in one of the neighborhoods not far from his house. The screaming was coming in his direction. He knew that he would be in the middle of whatever trouble was coming down. He pulled his gun, checked the clip, and loaded a bullet in the chamber just as a man came running around the corner. Ten men of various ages were not far behind him. The victim saw Ted, recognized the uniform; and ran straight for him calling for help. The gang trailing him didn't seem the least bit intimidated by an Alliance security officer becoming involved.

"Help me!" the man gasped. "They're trying to rape me!"

"Rape you?" Ted echoed in disbelief. The fastest of the group was now almost to Ted. The head of security spun on his heels, planted the muzzle of his gun against the man's forehead, and the others finally stopped. "What's this all about?"

"They're trying to rape me." the man repeated.

"Well?" Ted pressed the gang in front of him. He watched for any signs of movement to warn that someone might be going for a weapon. No one was moving.

"He's a homophobic." one of the men shouted back. Ted noted that the man had a fascination for leather and chains.

"What makes you think that? Did he say anything to you?"

"He didn't have to."

"And what's that supposed to mean?"

"He's a homophobic. He doesn't like queers." another member shouted.

"You all keep saying that, but no one wants to give me any evidence. Did he attack you? Did he speak out against you? What's his crime?"

"He's homophobic." The man with the gun to his forehead replied.

"Okay. Maybe you can fill me in. What happened?" Ted asked of the man cowering behind him.

"I was at the depot. They came up to me and started poking me. Asking me to go with them. I told them *no*. They asked what was wrong with them. I told them they were gay. I then said that there wasn't anything wrong with that. That's when that man," here the victim pointed to the man in leather and chains, "Said if there wasn't anything wrong with it, then why wasn't I one of them. I told them I didn't want to be gay. That's when they told me they could change my mind...show me how good it felt. They told me once I had done it with each of them, I'd feel different about it. That's when I started running, and they came after me."

"Is that the way it was?" Ted asked. No one responded. "I'm just going to say this once. While alternate life-styles are endorsed by President Ipileno, and protected by law, rape is not. Now unless you want to find yourselves in jail, or the morgue, I suggest you leave."

When no one made a move, Ted pulled the hammer back on his pistol. The man he was holding gave him an icy stare. "You're one of them."

"What do you mean, *I'm one of them*?" Ted countered. "Who's this *Them* you're referring to?"

"A homophobic. If you're here, then you're queer. Stop fighting it." Ted flinched at the comment. Ipileno would not reveal the defective gene basis for the *Rapture Syndrome* publicly; but he was spreading it freely among his own people. Soon it would be common knowledge. The hidden information was making the militants more bold.

The man noticed Ted had been distracted mentally and lunged toward Ted in a threatening manner. The sound of the bullet discharging into the front of the man's skull was a muffled sound, but the scream as the blood and brains sprayed out the back of the man's head was not.

"Now you know the law. Anyone who tries to assault or threaten any member of Alliance security is shot on sight. That means any one of you. I suggest you move on while you can."

"You've only got eight bullets left. There's still nine of us." one of the men declared. Ted shifted the aim of his weapon, fired a second cartridge, and the man dropped like a marionette whose strings had been cut.

"Maybe so, but that doesn't do you any good. Who's next?" The crowd broke and started to run. Once they were gone, the man who had been chased kept telling Ted *thank you* over and over. "Here, let me walk you out of the neighborhood. Which way do you live?"

"Over there." The man replied. "Shouldn't we call the police? Make a report?"

"Don't need to. I'll send a memo over to them tomorrow."

"But there are two bodies back there..." the man began.

"And it could have been us. You have a problem?"

"No, no. It just seems so different now-a-days. People seem so expendable."

"Right now, they are."

"Those gangs. They seem to be showing up more and more." the man observed in an effort to change the conversation. "If you're not with someone of your own sex, it's like they think you're an easy target."

"Maybe you just shouldn't be out by yourself at night. The police force is pretty thin with all the problems we've been having lately. Stay inside and make their job a little easier." Ted suggested. The man nodded, commented that this was his building, and went inside. He took one look back, and then scurried into the sanctuary of the security gate.

Ted sighed. He hated the paper work. He half-considered just heading home and letting the police try to figure out what had just happened, but he knew that office and inter-departmental politics would be a bigger pain than the paperwork. He headed toward the depot to catch the late train back into town.

"So you had an incident last night." Ipileno noted. Ted had been called into the president's office to watch *Project Wormwood* on the big screen TV. With all the natural disasters, television transmissions were poor even with the best equipment. The Alliance had several direct satellite feeds, and so the picture was passable.

"A rape gang tried to hit on this one guy." Ted offered as explanation. He really wasn't in the mood to talk about it, but Ipileno seemed determined.

"And so you blew two of them away?"

"Only when they tried to threaten me."

"Oh, well, that's a different story."

"Wait a minute!" Ted snapped. "I thought rape was still a crime."

"Technically it is, but you know how things have been lately..."

"You mean we now allow rape?"

"Well the man was a homophobic. He probably had all the wrong indoctrination about alternate life styles. Most of those kinds have to be forced into the right kind of situation. Once they've experienced it for themselves, they change."

"From what I've seen, most people who are victims of the rape gangs are either dead, or they go home and blow their own brains out."

"Then they weren't mentally strong enough to deal with it."

"So they've been weeded out." Ted finished for him. He turned his attention back to the screen which was showing the asteroid tumbling slowly toward Earth. The missiles had been fired about three hours ago. By the count-down clock in the bottom right of the screen, there was another twenty-three minutes until impact. The head of security rose from the plush couch, crossed to the sliding glass door and went out onto the balcony. An electrical storm was ripping apart an area several miles to the south. Ted scanned the dense smoke and cloud-covered sky. The sun was orange and hanging a little past mid-way. *Wormwood* was a red color now. It had glowed like a star for several weeks, became a *fuzzy* orb looking more like a comet for another week or so. Now over the last few weeks, it was like an egg in the sky.

Ted wasn't sure why he had come outside. It certainly wasn't for a breath of fresh air since the ash and dust in the air were already making his lungs ache. But somehow it seemed less polluted out here than in the room. He heard Abaddon's voice coming through the opened sliding glass door.

"The others are now concerned." Abaddon reported.

"Concerned?" Ipileno replied.

"Yes. It seems they have figured out the same things we did, but now it is too late to change it. Some of the other countries—the America Union in particular—are trying to find some way of speeding up or slowing down the missiles." At this point Ted re-entered the room.

"Why would they want to do that?"

"It seems no one else had the foresight that we did. It seems that their EeeDees failed to advise them as well as Abaddon advised us."

"Concerning...?" Ted let trail off.

"When the missiles hit the asteroid, it will pretty much turn it into so much rock, debris and dust."

"So it's not going to hit?"

"It will hit, but not as a single object." Abaddon offered.

"The rock and dust will strike the Earth, and so depending upon when the asteroid is destroyed, that part of the Earth facing the dust and rock cloud will be the area affected. No one thought about that until just recently."

"The last half hour to be precise. Now they realize that we will be passing through the cloud. If we destroy the asteroid sooner, one part of the Earth will be spared, and another section of the world will be in position when we pass. The same if we slow down the missiles and it's destroyed a little later. Now everyone is jockeying to change the time and place of *Wormwood's* destruction to protect their own country."

"Can they?" Ted asked.

"No, it's all up to gravity at this point. There's no fuel left to speed the missiles up, and no way to slow them down. Events have been set into motion that cannot be changed." Ipileno declared.

"So which section of the Earth gets hit?"

"They won't be hit. There's no real danger of impact once the missiles do their job. But there will be meteors, many of which will make it all the way to the ground. The biggest problem will be the dust. It will settle across most of the Western Hemisphere—the American Union. The winds will carry it further south...maybe as far as New Zealand or Australia depending on the air currents and rotation of the earth." Abaddon noted.

"So the biggest threat is dust?" Ted's voice was incredulous that so much concern was being raised over dust settling on the Earth. Tons of dust fell to earth all the time. "What's the big deal?"

"The big deal is that we are using nuclear missiles to destroy the asteroid. Thus, the rock and dust will be radioactive. No one thought of that until just now." Ipileno retorted.

"How bad? More weeding out?" Ted confronted.

"The problem will be with the water supplies. They will all have radioactivity in them from the radioactive dust. People will be drinking their own death and not even know it. The weaker ones will die within a few days. Others will succumb to cancer or other disease related to radiation over the next few months or years." the president replied without the faintest hint of concern in his voice.

"Thousands?" Ted asked.

"More like millions." Abaddon corrected.

"But there is an up-side to all of this."

"An *up-side*?" Ted asked.

"Yes, when this passes, we should be able to activate the immortality gene."

"We know how?" Ted asked, all but forgetting the death warrant that was already signed for half of the world.

"We've known how to activate it for some time now. We just didn't want to because our resources wouldn't be able to sustain such a large population." Ipileno announced.

"So what's involved? How long will it take?"

"We found the procedure while doing AIDS research. We have developed a genetically-mutated bacteria which attaches to the intestinal track. Its function will be to break down those agents we ingest which weaken the immune system. We follow up with injections that contain the substance needed to trigger the immortality gene. Once the immortality gene is active, it will begin to heal and replace damaged cells in the body."

"So soon you will have your eye sight back, and be able to use your right arm again?" Ted asked trying to put all of this into a more positive, personal triumph.

"Unfortunately, I already have the immortality gene activated. According to our experts, because the blindness and paralysis is due to the brain damage, and the need for the transplant, the immortality gene can't repair that. The brain transplant is causing a lot of problems they did not foresee. It's a different kind of DNA mixing with my own DNA. However, we have tested it on some people, and it proves quite impressive. Ahhh!"

The exclamation from Ipileno turned Ted's attention back to the screen. The first wave of missiles was making impact. The nuclear blasts in the vacuum of space were almost like something unnatural. The exploding mushroom clouds were distorted and short-lived in the airless environment. What made the effect even more eerie was that it all was happening in absolute silence. Ted tried very hard not to think about the fact that several million people were now going to die, and there was nothing they could do to save themselves.

CHAPTER TWENTY-FIVE

The Fallen One

"He's here." Eli said to no one in particular. Those who were gathered with them all seemed to know something that Dane was missing.

"Who's here?" Dane asked looking around to see if he could spot someone just entering the area. They were in a hilly region of southern Israel. *Masada* was what several had called it, but it was actually the plain beneath the ancient fortress. Off to the left was the area once known as the Dead Sea. The quakes had broken up the southern end of the sea, and water was flowing out of it. This change was altering its entire make-up. The Dead Sea had been known for its high salts and chemical composition caused by all the water flowing into it with no way to flow out. The waters evaporated over the course of centuries in the hot desert sun, and left behind the chemical deposits. Now the aftershocks were breaking the deposits loose so that the waters that were now passing through the sea were slowly washing the pollutants and salts out of it; but it would still take years to undo all the damage in the Dead Sea.

The dust from *Wormwood* had further polluted the air throughout the world. It was nearly ten o'clock in the morning before the sun was strong enough to light the world in other countries. By four in the afternoon, it was as dark as sunset. For all the pollution, though, the rains had not fallen as expected. Many scientists had predicted that after several rain storms, the pollution would be washed from the skies, except for that which was too high in the atmosphere. Unfortunately, there had been no rain.

However, this was not a world-wide phenomenon. It still rained in Israel. Not enough to cleanse the skies, but enough to provide water to the Jews and their crops. Although Israel had shortened days and polluted skies; the skies cleared enough to let enough light through for more of the day to salvage the harvests. For the rest of the world, the drought and darkness continued with no end in sight. The reason for the state of the world's ecology now sat before Dane.

Enoch and Eli appeared in Israel first. Then during the *Israeli Incident* they appeared in Egypt. Next, they appeared in London. They began to proclaim Yeshua as the Messiah the Jews had been waiting for. They declared that He would be returning to claim His throne. Police tried to drive them out of the area, but fire came down from Heaven at their command. Rather than consuming the soldiers, it formed a wall between them and the two men until they had finished making their various declarations.

Enoch had declared that the skies would not rain until they had given the word. Those in the streets around them began to laugh. Eli raised his hand, and fire fell from the sky consuming those who had dared to laugh. When additional police and troops arrived to surround them, the two walked through them. The troops did not have the strength to stand before them. The pair began to appear throughout the world, in all major cities. The message was always the same. The response was also always the same.

After several weeks without rain, people began to wonder if these two had some power or hidden knowledge. After six months, police and troops gave up any hope of arresting them or killing them as all attempts had ended in disaster.

They stood before presidents, tyrants and rulers. No world leader was exempt. They openly declared the secrets these rulers tried to hide from their people. Assassinations, black mail, rapes and other crimes were laid bare along with the cry to confess and repent. Their appearances further destabilized all that Ipileno had tried to build. Jim had even heard that several times they stood before Ipileno and openly declared him to be the Anti-Christ. Even Abaddon fled the room at their command.

After their message of no rain, and months later when water had become scarce, the two had touched several major water sources, and the waters had turned thick and red as if now blood. They repeated this action in Germany, Russia, China, South America, Canada, Australia and New Zealand. All sea and river life died in the red currents. The rotting fish had raised a stench that even today lingered in many parts of the countries.

Between the loss of sunlight, the lack of rain and the polluted blood water crops died, famine swept the land. Only in Israel did the rain appear, the crops flourish and life was spared. People began to die throughout the world. Unburied bodies brought plague and more death. The Witnesses continued with their cries to repent; and still the world defied the power of G-d, and continued to die in their sins.

Dane gave up on spotting any new faces to the crowd. The entire plain was a sea of people. There were thousands of them there. Some said it was all of the hundred and forty-four thousand. Others said that it went beyond that number since those In Cees who were not part of the select group of the Hundred and Forty Four were also there. Jim had said it was the largest gathering of believers the world had ever seen...at least since the *Rapture Syndrome* had hit.

"Who's here?" Dane asked of anyone who would listen.

"The Fallen One." Enoch replied.

"*Fallen One*?" Dane asked once more.

"They'll explain." Jim offered. He had been with these two men for almost a year now. It had been months since *Wormwood* had been destroyed. The Alliance was advertising their latest creation: the immortality gene. People from all over the world were flocking to Europe for the chance to under-go treatment. However, the treatment had a price tag. Most never gave it more than a passing thought, but those gathered here knew the price was their immortal soul. Enoch and Eli had shown up here two weeks ago. They had sat here at the base of Masada all that time in prayer and fasting. Jim had feared for their health for going so long without food, and taking so little water in such intense heat, but neither man showed the slightest sign of strain.

Once Eli and Enoch were here; the others began to come. Most seemed to know they were supposed to be here. The Hundred and Forty-Four were the next to come. They had heard the *calling*. The others came because Eli and Enoch were here. Some came because they were curious. However, those not dedicated had left when the heat continued to climb in the Israeli desert. This had been the first words Eli or Enoch had spoken since they came here. Jim had come with them since he was now their servant and student. They had taught him a great deal during the last year. Dane and a few others came early because Jim had come.

"The *Fallen One* has been cast out of Heaven." Enoch confirmed. "He has been removed from the Presence of G-d, and is now bound to the Earth. He knows that his time is short, and so he comes to personally direct his war against the believers, and against Israel, G-d's Chosen."

"Is he talking about whom I think he's talking about?" Dane whispered to Jim, but Enoch chose to be the one to reply.

"Satan has been cast out of Heaven."

"But I thought he had been cast out a long time ago." Stacy Adams asked. It had been the kind of sessions they had been used to: asking questions and discussing answers. Somehow the fact that over a hundred thousand people were part of the group didn't seem to change anything. The desert air and the perfect acoustics of the rocky mountains turned the plain into a vast auditorium. Whenever Enoch or Eli spoke, everyone was able to hear them.

"Lucifer was cast out of Heaven centuries ago, but he came back to accuse the brethren. For centuries he has stood in the courts of Heaven before the Presence of G-d and accused the believers of crimes; seeking to turn G-d's favor from us. He has failed. G-d will no longer hear his lies, and so Lucifer has been driven out by force. He and all of his followers have been driven out of Heaven and down to the earth. It is here that they will stay."

"A great war is coming." Eli continued. "It will be the final war until *His* coming. In preparation, we must prepare to leave, to spread out unto all the corners of the earth one last time to share G-d's message. We do not need to leave at once; but you will know when the time comes. When it does come, you will have to leave; and leave quickly. It is better to prepare now than to have to leave important things behind."

"But before we leave this place, we give you the gift of spiritual vision." Enoch declared. He passed his hands over the entire gathering, and cries and exclamations erupted throughout the sea of people. Jim had the experience of seeing another world super-imposed upon the one he was looking at. It was as if someone had taken a clear sheet of plastic and placed it over his eyes. However the plastic was not entirely clear, but had small images painted on them. Thus he saw the world as he was used to seeing it; but there was more there than when he had last looked. He blinked, rubbed his eyes, and looked around. When he looked at those in the gathering, he saw each one wore a mark on their foreheads. It had not been there before, but now it almost seemed to glow.

Amir and Shmuel's marks seemed brighter than all the rest. Their street clothes were now white and glowed from an unknown source.

"It is the mark of G-d, His seal set upon all who believe and are to be given special protection." Eli declared. When Jim turned to the speaker, he saw that they were in robes of pure white, so white it would almost hurt normal eyes to look upon them. They were ancient, but not in a feeble sort of way. They were full of wisdom and power, the kind of wisdom that comes from living many lifetimes, and the power that comes from being chosen of G-d. However, Eli and Enoch were pointing in a different direction; diverting the attention from their own glorified images. Jim turned in the direction they were pointing, and nearly collapsed.

Surrounding the entire gathering were EeeDees, an army of angelic beings of intense light. They had not reduced their Presence as they had done on previous encounters, but with the new vision he had, his eyes did not sting and ache from the sight. Each EeeDee hovered in the air as if on unseen wings of light. Each one held a great and powerful sword. Each one was directing the attention of the crowd even further to the east.

Although there were miles of mountains and hills between, with this new spiritual vision they possessed, each observer had no difficulty seeing what the EeeDees were pointing to. A great pit was being opened, a pit so deep, so vast that it seemed to have no bottom. When Jim looked, he could only think he was looking into the darkest corner of Hell. Over the opening he saw a figure. Where once it had been awe-inspiring, when now seen with Jim's new eyes Abaddon was more to be pitied than worshipped. He was still a being of great power, but there was an emptiness at the core of his being which could suck everything of worth and value in and destroy it without ever easing that tormenting void.

Abaddon held a great key in his hand with which he had just opened the bottomless pit. While Abaddon and several other EeeDees stood back, a black smoke poured out of the opening in time and space itself. The plumes of smoke tumbled high into the sky, further blotting out the sun; but that no longer mattered to Jim and the others. Their new eyesight was great enough to still see it all.

Something emerged out of the smoke. At first Jim thought it might be some new one-man helicopter because of its size and shape, but as his eyes made the adjustment, he could see it was a living thing. Obviously it was shaped like a helicopter. Its sides were like plates of armor or the glistening finish he had once admired on a June bug. Where the helicopter would once have had the windshield, there was actually the large, rounded face of a man, if something so hideous could truly be a man. It had long flowing hair trailing back from its head flowing upon some unseen supernatural breeze. It raised its face toward Abaddon, and smiled, revealing a row of sharp teeth, the kind a carnivore would use to rip its prey apart. The creature hovered in the smoke-filled air, dipped its front section lower in order to bow to Abaddon; and then its wings began to beat with a rhythmic pounding that grew to a deafening level. Jim then noticed other similar creatures emerging from the billowing smoke. He also noted what looked like a lance or spear protruding out of the tail of the creatures.

"For those who have not met him," Enoch announced in reference to the EeeDee, "His name is Abaddon. In the time of our Lord he was called Apollyon. In all tongues which gave him name, his name means *Destroyer*; for this is what he has lived for. These locusts coming out of the bottomless pit cannot be seen with human eyes. Humans will not see them, nor hear them coming; but they will feel the pain of their stingers."

"And what will happen?" Dane asked. Eli responded to the question.

"They will seek out those who do not have the Seal of God on their foreheads. They will run them through with their great tails, piercing all the way to the very soul. The pain will be great. It will be so intense that it will be more than human mind can bear. Many will find their minds broken from the torment. Other, unfortunately, will not. The Anti-Christ has activated the immortality gene. He and Abaddon have sought to remove what G-d held back from Adam and Eve in the Garden when they had fallen. *And G-d said 'Behold man has become as Us, knowing good from evil, and now lest he put forth his hand and eat of the Tree of Life and live forever, We shall put him out of the Garden.'* And Ipileno and Abaddon have tried to give back what G-d in His love and mercy took away: eternal life in this body. To remind man that death is a gift of G-d, to bring an end to pain and suffering, G-d has allowed these creatures to be released from the pit. They will sting those men not protected by G-d, and those men shall suffer the torment of the damned for five months. For five months mankind will seek death, but death will flee from them."

A shiver crept up Billings spine.

"Will we be protected?" she asked.

"This is the judgment of G-d. He will not judge us because His Son has already paid the price. Thus, no. They will not have any power over us. But woe to those who fall under their control."

Dane stood with a confused look upon his face. He did not have the spiritual vision and so he did not see what the others were seeing; but at this point he was not sure that he wanted to see that they were describing.

The gathering took one last look in the direction of the bottomless pit. The sky was blotted out above it, not so much from the rising smoke, but from the millions of supernatural locust which now hovered in the air before Abaddon.

CHAPTER TWENTY-SIX

The Torments of The Damned

Ted heard the screaming as the figure fell head-long off the skyscraper. It was a common sound as people who had taken the immortality gene treatment tried to find some way to end their agony. When the body struck the pavement with a bone crunching *thud* the screaming didn't stop as one would expect; but it only increased. This was something they didn't tell you when they promised you immortality. All the experts were unable to find the connection between the treatment and the disease; but there was a connection. All of those who had taken the treatment—had activated their immortality gene; were suffering. Ted rolled over in his bed, fought to hold down the scream that wanted to tear from his throat. It was as if something were inside of him, tearing him apart; but the immortality gene was healing it as quickly as the damage was done. However, the inner wounds were continuing to occur immediately after the healing was begun.

Of course, there were not any physical wounds inside. They had all been tested for that; but it was as if some huge jagged stake was tearing into them over and over again. Fire burned in their veins as if some venom were coursing through them. Every organ inside of him was on fire. His mind was exhausted from the long days without sleep. There was no escape. The drugs normally used to treat pain and suffering were countered by the immortality gene. His nervous system would not shut down. He would not fall into a deep sleep. There was no escape from the torment. He prayed and screamed for God to drive him mad so he would no longer be aware of his condition. Even that was denied him.

He had seen it all as part of security. People had done everything they could think of to end their torments. He thought of Rawlings and Schmidt who had their immortality genes activated. They had been driven to the breaking point; but were not allowed to die. He had never thought it would happen to him.

People had begun to go insane; ran through the streets screaming their pain. They tried to blow their brains out. They had leaped from the tallest building around. They had tried to crush themselves. Some had even commandeered the guillotines used to kill the In Cees. He was sure that would have worked, but no. For some reason the neck muscles, skin and vertebrae of the neck were too strong. No matter how sharp the blade, no matter how high the blade was before it fell, it couldn't sever the head. Those who tried to crush themselves broke everything in their bodies except those organs and bones needed to sustain life. They were deformed, crippled, mutilated; but they would not die. Their bodies would eventually repair even that extensive damage, but the pain would not go away.

He pulled hard at the ropes, shaking the entire bed, screaming at the top of his lungs. It was all he could do in his hopeless frustration. The fire coursed through his heart, stomach, arms, legs and mind. He kicked, twisted and screamed. On the other side of the room Spencer stood, silent. Spencer had seen what was happening to others who had taken the immortality gene treatment. The entire world was at a total stand-still because there weren't enough people left like Spencer who could function. And so everything shut down; governments, transportation, stores, and hospitals. The world was effectively driven back to a stone-age lifestyle until this disease could be cured or until it passed.

Spencer had worked with Ted. He had seen the fear building in the head of security as more and more people became infected. Ted knew it was only a matter of time before he experienced the same pain and torment. Spencer had waited until the first signs of the pain struck Ted. He then knocked the head of security unconscious, tied him to the bed, and cared for him every day. It was all he could do for his commanding officer. Ted cursed Spencer for tying him there. Begged him to end his life. He screamed and cursed Ipileno and Abaddon for ever activating the damned immortality gene. He cursed until his throat was too raw to scream any more; and then he sobbed until he had no more tears left.

Jim read the reports. His people had kept an eye on things happening in the Alliance capital. His agents had told him about the side-effect of the immortality gene activation and that his brother was infected. Jim and the others knew what the true cause of their pain was. The locust had spread out across the earth from the bottomless pit. They had affixed themselves to their victims, inflicting pain and torment on them. There were no physical wounds or scars. Everything pointed to a mental problem; but all the tests failed to show why the body was registering such intense pain. They looked everywhere except to the supernatural.

Jim knew that Abaddon was enjoying the scenes of agony. He was the one who had released the locust. Yet he had remained adamant that he was at a loss as to how the disease spread or how to cure it. The head of the In Cees picked up another report. Scientists were working on a way to de-activate the immortality gene. According to the information smuggled out, they hoped to have a protocol in place within two weeks. Jim realized that it would be the five-month mark since the locust had been released. He found it amazing that a book written two thousand years ago had predicted this curse and even identified the time span for it.

"They will de-activate the gene. There will be a greater demand for the de-activation of the gene than for its original treatment." Enoch noted.

"It's just a matter of a few weeks. They will push the torment to the back of their minds. They will use drugs and strong drink to make believe it never happened; but they will still wake up in the night screaming." Eli observed.

"And what will they do, Eli?" Jim asked.

"They will realize that Israel did not have anyone suffer these torments. They will become angry at us. We were too smart to activate the immortality gene. We rejected their offer; scorned their gifts. And now they will realize we were smarter than they." Enoch replied. "It will make them angry, and so they will come to vent their anger."

"They will attack Israel?" Dane asked.

"They will try." Eli admitted. "They will amass a great army. It will be an army of those who hate Israel and all it has stood for. Up until this point, many followed the Anti-Christ thinking he was a great world leader. They followed him because he was charismatic, and offered them hope. But that is about to change. *The Fallen One* has woven his web of deceit; but now he is about to reveal himself. He is about to show all who and what he is. The hearts of those who serve him are now prepared to accept him openly. When they come against Israel it will be because they hate us, and serve him with full knowledge of their fate. It will be an army of sorcerers, murderers—those who have worshipped his false gods of gold, and silver."

"Surely people do not actually worship false idols in this day and age?" Stacy suggested.

"We are too civilized, too advanced for all of that?" Enoch suggested with mock seriousness in his voice. "When the angels of the Lord went into Sodom and Gomorrah to investigate the sins of the city, they found men willing to rape angels. *We would never commit such an act!* And yet rape gangs roam the streets of most cities. If an angel were to take human form, they would not hesitate to try and rape him. They would desire the angel all the more because of the beauty of such a creature."

"When Moses brought the Israelites out of bondage, and Joshua led them into the Promised Land, the tribes in the land of milk and honey sacrificed their new-born babies to their gods of pleasure. Yet now the world serves the gods of sex and pleasure. When a child is conceived as a result, people demand the right to speak to those people and try to convince them to sacrifice their children before they are even born." Eli added.

"As for worshipping gold and silver. Man has always worshipped gold and silver. They sacrifice their families and health upon altars of careers. They sacrifice their integrity, their honesty, their dreams—all to move up that corporate ladder. Idols take on many forms; but this world has fallen prey to them all. There is no false god they have not bowed to. Now they will bow down to the father of lies. They will know him for what he is; and serve him all the same."

"So the time has come for us to leave?" Jim asked.

"No, not yet. G-d has not yet delivered us into their hands."

"But if the Alliance comes with all of its armies and weapons, if Satan draws all of his servants to make war against us; what chance do we have?" Dane asked.

"The chance that we have always had. Do not believe the lies of *the Fallen One*. He has tried for years to convince the world that he is equal to G-d. He is not. He is nothing more than a creation, like us all. He is subject to G-d the same as we. He cannot do anything which G-d does not allow. The Creator can destroy him and for all his screaming, boasting, or lying; he cannot stop Him."

"So what will happen?" Stacy asked. In response, Eli motioned towards the east where the River Euphrates still flowed. It, too, was a river of blood like all the other major water sources. The world was now convinced that the lack of rain, and the rivers and seas of blood were the results of Eli and Enoch. Newspapers and broadcasts cursed them, defamed them. Rewards were posted in every city for their capture or death. Each person who did not believe in the Messiah of the Jews cursed their names at least once a day. They were, for all intents and purposes, the most hated men in the entire earth. But for all of *the Fallen One's* efforts, they could not be found. When they appeared in public to preach and condemn, no one could lay a hand on them. When asked about this phenomena they would simply say, *It's not yet our time.*

As Jim and the others looked in the direction Eli indicated, their spiritual vision revealed the river separating. The waters parted down the middle, creating a doorway that opened up. Out of the opening came four angels. The EeeDees were larger, and more fearsome than any Jim had seen before. Although it seemed a physical impossibility, each angel held in his massive hands the winds of the world as if they were sheets blowing in a strong gale. The winds whipped about them, and the angels wrestled with them as a man might wrestle with a spirited team of horses by pulling the reins and holding them back. As they did so, the angels laughed as if it were all but a sport to control such natural forces.

"They wear swords, but do not seem to draw them." Jim observed.

"When the time is right, they will draw their swords, "Eli announced." And when they do, one-third of the Alliance forces will die within a single hour. They will not draw their swords until they have been commanded by G-d to release the winds. The winds will tear through Ipileno's armies, tearing their skin like massive sand blasters as the sands of the deserts are hurled at them by the winds. Tanks and equipment will be torn apart. While the armies are battered, wounded, blinded and confused; the angels will draw their swords and strike."

"And one-third of the Alliance forces will die?" Stacy asked.

"At first, but once the armies have been broken and routed, these angels will go forth with their swords and winds, breaking open the bowels of the earth even more; and the fire, smoke and brimstone which spews from the new volcanoes, fissures, and craters will kill one-third of all mankind."

"A third of everyone? How can God be so cruel?" Dane asked though he still could not see what the others saw. "I though He was a God of love."

"He is a G-d of love. This is a world that has rebelled against Him. This is a world trying to kill those who love Him. He has offered this world His love. He has offered this world His

Son, and this world has spat in His face. We are not dealing with a G-d of love at this point. This is a G-d of justice. This is a G-d of righteousness. In His love He took those who were His own out. What is left are those who deserve His judgment. And this is His judgment." Enoch declared.

"But," Eli interrupted. "Even in His judgment G-d is merciful."

"How?" Dane asked.

"When G-d judged the world centuries ago by flooding it with water there was no hope for those who had rejected G-d. Now there will be seven years of judgment. Not all life will be wiped out. And mankind will have seven years to change their minds and turn to Him."

"And will they?" Stacy asked.

"Some will. You are one of them. Many will not. And it will not be because they are ignorant of G-d. Nor because they are deceived. When this next war begins, everyone will be on the side he or she has chosen. Those who serve *the Fallen One* will serve him knowing full well who and what he is. They will attack the Chosen of G-d, knowing full well who we are, and who G-d is."

"They will know they are following Satan in an attack against God, and will do so willingly?" Jim's voice was incredulous.

"The folly of man knows no limits." Eli noted. Jim turned his attention back to the four angels whose forearm muscles rippled as they reined in the supernatural winds which howled on a level most could never imagine.

CHAPTER TWENTY-SEVEN

The Power Behind The Man

Ted slid the computer card over the sensor. The locking mechanism buzzed as the bolt pulled back to allow him access to his apartment. The sensor in the ceiling registered his movements and the lights came on in the room. As the lights came to life, a screen on the coffee table also flickered to life.

"Hello, Ted." It was the voice of Jim, and the image came into focus. For a brief moment, Ted thought to see how Jim's people got into his apartment, but he knew it would be fruitless. He even thought for a moment about tracing the signal, but on previous occasions it had proven a waste of time. Dane was good at this work. None of Ted's men could match him for his creativity. The last time he had sent his team scurrying to triangulate the signal they found it coming from the headquarters of the New Alliance itself. It was all too much for Ted to overcome. He hated to admit defeat; but he was too tired to go through the motions already knowing the outcome.

"You seem to have a habit of leaving messages for me." Ted noted. "You must have a pretty good income to keep throwing these lap tops away like this."

"Not at all," Jim replied. "Take a look. Every one of them is Alliance equipment. Why should I waste my resources when I can waste yours instead? You know the two things terrorist guard the most: the location of weapons and equipment; and where the money is hidden. I've learned a lot studying the terrorists over the years. It helps keep me ahead of your men."

"So you admit that you're terrorists?" Ted asked with a faint hope of some small victory.

"Terrorists? No, we have no political agenda other than survival and sharing our message. If people refuse to listen; then we leave them alone. If they accept; all the better."

"The Alliance has classified your movement as a terrorist faction." Ted countered.

"Then we are a very unique terrorist group. We do not use terrorism to spread our message. We do not force people to accept. We do not kill except in self-defense. The only thing that makes us a terrorist organization is how the Alliance treats us."

"So, does this message have a point?" Ted interrupted.

"Just wanted to make sure you were still okay. There were a lot of casualties in the last invasion attempt. I wanted to make sure you weren't one of them."

"How touching. Why do you care about me? You know that if we ever come face-to-face, I've sworn to kill you by my own hand...That is unless your immunity gene is active..." Ted let his voice trail off to turn his statement into a question."

"No. I never activated my gene. In fact, Eric Henning never activated his gene, either. The truth is, all the healings you've seen and heard about are the result of our EeeDees taking an active role in our movement."

"Some day we will perfect the immortality gene. It's just a matter of time." Ted challenged.

"Actually, there was nothing wrong with your immortality gene program. It was sabotaged."

"By who?"

"Whom." Jim corrected. "...Abaddon."

"That's crazy. He's been behind us all the way."

"He is nothing more than a glorified servant. He has his own agenda. He brought forth his own resources to torment those with the immortality gene activated for his own personal reasons."

"What do you mean, '*Abaddon is only a glorified servant*?'"

"He serves another. His master is now on earth with him. They are amassing their forces."

"If that's true, then you have reason to be afraid."

"Not really. Abaddon serves his master; but his master is limited in what he can do."

"Are we back to this *higher power* crap again?"

"There is only one who is in charge of all of this. He has given each group room to make their own decisions; but even those decisions are forced to be within limits set down. For all of Abaddon's power he can only do what his master allows him to do. For all the power his master displays he can only do what he is allowed to do."

"If this supreme power is so great, then why does He allow all of this to take place?"

"Because man has rebelled for centuries. This is all the just desserts the world deserves for all it's done. It's not anger; it's justice. He even set down what He was going to do centuries ago."

"You don't believe that, do you?"

"Why shouldn't I?" Jim countered.

"You've only got one side of the story. You're only listening to what He wants you to hear."

"Your side has been saying a lot of things over the centuries, too. It's just that what they've been saying hasn't stood up to scrutiny. It's full of holes. It's not credible. Everything they've said has fallen by the wayside; and people stopped believing it. Both sides of the argument have been presented. Right now, only one version can be believed."

"Your version?"

"The version I follow. It's not my personal version. I've joined it, not created it. I'd like you to join, too."

"We've had this discussion over and over. It's not going anywhere."

"What's it going to take to convince you?" Jim's voice was firm, his eyes determined. It caught Ted off-guard, and for a moment he gave it serious consideration.

"Let's face the facts, Jim. Here's what you believe: You believe that I'm serving a man who is called the Anti-Christ. You believe the EeeDees helping us are demons. You believe the ultimate source of all this power is Satan. You believe that you serve God, and I serve the devil...don't you see? These are labels created centuries ago to misrepresent the issues and players in a war fought on more levels than we can even begin to grasp. What makes you so sure you're right?"

"Abaddon has said that there are rules of engagement. They cannot do certain things, like activating the immortality gene, right?"

"Yes. He's said things like that." Ted admitted reluctantly.

"He's told you that if all the believers on my side are removed, then my side cannot operate in this world. If they cannot operate in this world, then your side wins...right?"

"That's the way it works." Ted agreed.

"Why?"

"What do you mean, *Why*" Ted snapped.

"Why does it work that way?"

"I don't see where this is going."

"It's going to the logical conclusion. If that's the way this whole system works; then why does it work that way? The logical conclusion about having rules of engagement is that there must be a higher authority that made these rules. There must be some court of appeal where violations can be presented and the rules enforced. If there is no higher court of appeal; then these rules of engagement are just agreements. Either side can break them when they wish without fear of retribution. If it is just an agreement; then why follow them? If winning is what matters, and you can win by breaking these rules of engagement; why not break them? Why not do what you want to do—what you have to do—in order to win?"

Ted hated to admit that he didn't have a response to Jim's position. He also hated it when he realized he had been silent too long and Jim knew he had no valid response.

"Abaddon has made it clear that their forces cannot take open, active part in the conflict. They have to work through you. Why?" Jim waited a few seconds and then answered the question Ted could not. "Because there are rules of engagement. Wouldn't it be faster for the EeeDees to take part, move openly and destroy the followers of my side? Yes, it would. Why don't they? Because of the rules of engagement. Why do they obey the rules of engagement? Because they have to; not because they want to. Why do they have to? Because there is a higher power over them; a power they cannot disobey no matter how much they want to..."

"Alright!" Ted cut his brother off. "You've made your point. But what proves that this higher power is on your side? Your side has been putting rules and regulations on mankind for centuries. It's labeled everyone as sinners. It sends everyone to Hell. What's so great about that?"

"Because that isn't the true picture. Take away our side. Remove everything that makes up the Neo-Christian movement, even the Christian movement; and you have the same results: we're all sinners. We're all in violation of the laws set down by the higher power. We're all doomed to go to Hell for these violations. That's there without Christianity. Christianity simply says you don't have to suffer that fate. Christianity offers an escape from this destiny. That's all."

"Well, Abaddon says that we can take our fate into our own hands. We can over-throw these forces that want to send us all to Hell."

"So you have been listening to him. He has been feeding you bits and pieces."

"He tells me that if we don't stop your movement, we will go to Hell. He's shown us images of it. It's not a place I want to go."

"Then don't. All you have to do is accept what Jesus did. Let Him protect you; and you won't go there."

"He's the one sending us there!" Ted shouted. "Abaddon tells us that if we stop your movement, break the power your EeeDees have in this world by removing all of their followers; then we become the power in charge. We can stop your side from sending us to Hell. We can create a paradise right here... on earth. No more sin, no more guilt, no more damnation."

"Just because the warning sign isn't there any more; doesn't mean the danger is gone."

"What are you talking about? What warning sign?"

"That's all we are, Ted. We're like warning signs posted in this world to warn you about Hell; to warn you about the judgment already assigned to you. To show you how to avoid that fate. Remove us, and all you are doing is tearing down the warning signs. So you still go to Hell; it's just that you won't know it's coming. Even with your immortality gene activated, sooner or later you're going to die. It might be centuries instead of years; but you're going to die. And when you do, you leave this plane of existence and enter the realm of the EeeDees. Once you're there, you are still subject to that higher power that controls them. That higher power will still send you to Hell."

"Not if we take out the higher power!" Ted challenged. He felt beads of sweat on his brow. His mouth was dry, and he was uncomfortable with the entire direction of this conversation. He needed to respond. As soon as he blurted out the words, it all made perfect sense. For the first time the confrontation on so many planes of existence came into perfect clarity. This is why the war was waging. This is why the movement had to be stopped. It wasn't going to be enough for Abaddon to block off access to this world to the other side; they had to take out the higher power. They had to defeat God.

"Exactly what we intend to do." came the voice of Abaddon behind him. Ted nearly screamed due to the sudden appearance of the EeeDee. "He makes others believe He is powerful, but His power is in the number of followers He has. Break His power base, and He cannot stand against us." The EeeDee was speaking to the screen. Ted hated to admit that he was impressed by the calmness still possessing Jim's features. The head of security had been hardened by countless conflicts, and he nearly lost it by the sudden appearance of the supernatural creature. Jim showed no more reaction to Abaddon's appearance than he would have to someone walking into the room and joining the discussion.

"You are not part of this conversation." Jim replied in a quiet, firm voice.

"I can be part of this conversation if Ted wishes." Abaddon suggested.

"Do you want to see how powerful this EeeDee really is?" Jim asked of his brother. "Don't let him be part of the conversation." Jim suggested.

Ted struggled with his decision. He saw the anger churning in Abaddon's eyes. He did not believe he had the strength to deny the EeeDee. Suddenly there was a sense of conviction coming over him. He glanced toward the computer screen and noted Jim's head was down, eyes closed as if in prayer. He looked at Abaddon and replied,

"I'd like to finish this up in private."

"I insist on staying." Abaddon pressed, moving closer toward Ted to intimidate him. Jim's voice came over the satellite link,

"You heard the decision, Abaddon. Your invitation does not exist. In the name of Jesus...go away."

Abaddon howled in rage, turned as if to attack Ted; but caught himself. "I will abide by your decision, mortal...but take care in what you say."

With those words, Abaddon disappeared from the room. Ted wasn't sure if the EeeDee was actually gone, or if he had simply closed off any evidence of his being there.

"He is gone." Jim confirmed. "He could not stay."

"He chose to leave." Ted suggested.

"He tried to save face, to make you think it was his decision. If they are so sure of their ability to over-throw God; then why do they still obey the laws He set down?"

Ted reached over and closed down the connection. The screen went dark. His moment of clarity was still there in his mind. He hated to admit that everything was the way Jim had described it. He sought for another point of view...a different perspective, but there was none. He now knew it was all a question of which side was he going to believe; which side was he going to follow. For all of Jim's arguments, Ted couldn't believe it could all be that easy. If Jim was wrong, or if Jim's side lost and Ted went with them, he was lost, too. With Abaddon... (Here Ted corrected himself. He now knew the power behind their movement. He now dared to call it by name)...with Satan, at least he had the ability to take actions into his own hands. He could make his own future happen instead of trusting it to someone else. He didn't like the choice he was about to make, but it was the only one that still left him in charge.

CHAPTER TWENTY-EIGHT

Revelations and Deceptions

Ted sat in his office, looking out over the scenery. The crumpled remains of most of the complex reminded him of the months of stench from the crushed unburied bodies. The rats and bugs that fed on the bodies eventually removed the stench; but then the plague and other illnesses had followed. It had been one disaster after another. One more weeding out after another. Once the scene had been breathtaking, now it was a dismal reminder of the destruction their world had endured at the hand of a vengeful God. He knew it now. He had all the goodness burned out of him. It was all about survival of the fittest—his survival at any costs. It was now him against God and the forces of Heaven. Only by defeating them could he survive. Most had come to realize it. Whenever anything else happened, people began to curse God. They spoke openly now of Ipileno as an Anti-Christ, rallying to his support all over the world. Ipileno stood for all those things they hated in Jesus and Christianity: the rules, restrictions, hypocrisy, condemnation. They saw Ipileno as a refreshing leader. He was a man of the people. His creed was freedom, indulgence, pleasure and self. Man was the center of his universe, not God. This was the Age of Man: the New Age. The Age of Man with man serving as his own god. The world had been prepared, and now was ready to storm the very gates of Heaven, drag God from His throne and establish their own order—Ipileno's order.

The once impressive skyline which heralded the growing technology of Europe seemed little more than rows of broken, shattered teeth. Through the earthquakes, the eruptions, the burning hail and meteorites that had rained down for weeks; not a building was left in its original state. The tallest of the skyscrapers had been snapped off the way a giant might snap a match stick between finger and thumb. The smaller buildings had broken and crumbled. Where once eighty-storied mirrored structures had reflected back the glory of man's accomplishments; cracked glass, empty sockets of deserted offices stared blindly back. A cold wind howled the pain of the world as it passed through these wounded edifices.

"You now understand." Abaddon offered.

"What's to understand?" Ted asked back.

"Whom you are serving." the EeeDee continued.

"I am serving Jason Ipileno, the Anti-Christ. He and I serve you, Abaddon lord of demons. We all serve Satan. Is that clear enough for you?" The human spat out.

"Very..." came an ethereal response, reverberating so that the newly-replaced glass of Ted's office shook so violently that it threatened to shatter. "...but how do you feel about it?" It was the voice of Satan. Ever since Ted's last meeting with Jim, the EeeDee behind Abaddon's forces no longer sought to hide his presence nor his identity. He seemed to gloat in it, revel in it. He wanted the entire world to know. It was as if it gave him the greatest pleasure to have those of the inner circle openly acknowledge whom they served.

"Angry." Ted replied.

"Angry at me?" Satan asked. It had been a tone that would have made lesser men cringe and tremble; but Ted had gone far beyond that. Something had been dying inside of him from the moment he had begun to work for Ipileno. The thrill of such power and status had been so overwhelming that he had failed to notice that feeling within him begin to wither. Now that power and status no longer impressed him, he was all too aware of the aching emptiness where his soul should be. He was a man with few options, little to lose and much to gain. It made him reckless.

"Angry at God, if you must know. He was there all the time. He could have revealed Himself at any moment. Yet He chose not to..."

"It just shows that He does not care about you. That He has lied all these centuries..." Satan began, but Ted actually found the inner strength through his anger to cut him off.

"Bull! Look, you've got me. Don't try to sell me anything else. I'm here because it's my choice to be here. I have no illusions about this. We're all damned to Hell. We're going to burn for all eternity...unless we can stop Him. I want my freedom. I want my right to choose. That's why I'm here. I'm not buying what He's selling, and I'm not buying you, either! If His side wins, I lose. If you win, then we have a chance...if you want to impress me; then convince me that you can take Him out."

"An interesting offer." Satan mused. "What if I were to do something He has never done?"

"That would be impressive." Ted admitted. "What do you have in mind?"

"Has He ever made anything inanimate speak?" Satan suggested. Ted picked his brain, but he couldn't think of any incident. He remembered once where someone told him that God had made a donkey speak, but the donkey was alive. He couldn't think of any story where God made something inanimate speak.

"Not that I can recall. Is that what you're going to do?"

"Yes, but not here. Not now. We must make sure it is where everyone can see and hear. It will have to be an event of world-wide importance. Give me just a little more time."

"How much more time?" Ted asked.

"Enough time to capture Jerusalem. I think the Temple will be the best place to perform this miracle."

"We tried to take Jerusalem once before. Got our butts whipped good. Lost most of our men, a lot of our weapons. No one's been able to take Jerusalem since the *Israeli Incident*."

"Well, let me try one more time." Satan offered, a strange smile breaking across his unreal face.

CHAPTER TWENTY-NINE

The One Hundred and Forty-Four

Jim scanned the print-out he had just been handed. "Rumor has it that Ipileno is going to try and take Jerusalem."

"It's about time for that." Eli noted without much surprise in his voice and pretending to look at a watch he never wore as if he knew the exact moment all of this was going to take place.

"It's coming?" Jim asked looking up from the message.

"Yes. There will be the invasion of Jerusalem. The Abomination will be set up in the Temple. Then there will be the Mark of the Beast." Eli confirmed. "Of course if you get the Mark of the Beast on the back of the hand, it will still work; but Ipileno will always consider you a second-class citizen."

"Those with the Mark on their foreheads will have a special status." Enoch agreed.

"Yes, but back of the hand or forehead will still do what it's supposed to. There's a tiny computer chip inserted under the skin when the Mark is imprinted. Everyone will have the same mark, but everyone will have a different computer chip code." Eli observed.

"I don't see how you do that." Dane interrupted.

"Do what?" Eli asked, sipping his coffee from a paper cup. "This is really good." he declared to Jim.

"How can you see all of these things take place, and accept them so calmly? Don't you understand what's happening out there? If Ipileno invades and takes Jerusalem thousands will probably die. Don't you care about the loss of human life?" Dane confronted.

"Dane, human life is never lost. Nor does G-d allow it to be wasted. He is keeping track of each one. He knows what is coming. When someone dies in this life, they are born into the next. Pain and suffering cease. True life begins. So human life is never lost. It merely moves from this world to the next."

"How can you be so sure?" Dane challenged.

"You do not believe. We understand that. How do we handle it? Only by the grace of G-d, Dane. G-d gives us what we need when we need it. Do not try to carry a burden that is not yours. Do not try to bear a weight before G-d gives it to you." Eli counseled.

"As to why we are so calm about this, why should we act surprised over something that has been predicted for centuries? What? We didn't see it coming?" Enoch replied. "G-d told us what was going to happen. It's finally happening. Why should that be so surprising? It not happening? Now that would be a surprise!"

"Look, you might be used to all this hocus pocus stuff. But it scares the hell out of me."

"I should hope so." Eli added with a smile.

"You want me to be scared?" Dane countered.

"No...I want the Hell out of you. Dane, you've stayed on the sidelines, but you've never gotten into life. You've found it hard to believe that the laws of physics and nature can be altered, even suspended. You know there is something big coming down; but you can't comprehend it. You keep trying to see with your physical eyes."

"*Let go and trust the Force, Luke.*" Dane quipped back.

"Nothing that easy." Enoch added. "All that involved was Eastern Mysticism: stop thinking, don't pay attention to conflicts or contradictions, and just accept. We're asking you to use everything that G-d gave you. To ask those hard questions. To seek. To search. To challenge. You've been on the verge ever since you came to us. You saw something here that was more than you could hope for...but you've refused to accept what your mind tells you is real. You won't take advantage of what's right in front of you."

"Why is it so easy for all of you? Why can you believe?" Dane challenged.

"For us," Eli smiled, "It's not about believing. It's not even about faith. It's about knowing, experiencing. I can tell you this coffee is good—we never had anything like this in my days—but until you put it into your mouth, taste it for yourself and swallow it; you'll never know. You'll just have to take my word for it. It's taking the chance. Committing. Like stepping out of the plane and praying to G-d the chute really does work. It changes your life. You're committed. You can't get the taste of coffee out of your mouth. You can't climb back into the plane. There's no turning back; and that's what you're afraid of." To add emphasis to his words, Elijah stretched out his hand and offered the cup of coffee to Dane.

"*Taste and see that the Lord is good.*" Enoch quoted.

"It can't be that easy?"

"Oh it can," Enoch declared. "But once you've done it, there's no turning back. Life doesn't come with a *re-set* button like your fancy computers. You can't *delete* and start over. Getting in is easy; it's the following through that gets tough. You might want to give up, but G-d won't let you."

"The Psalms refers to Him as the Hound of Heaven. He won't let you get away. He'll track you down wherever you run." Eli suggested.

"Why, to punish me for my sins?" Dane snapped back.

"No, to love you." Jim added. It was the quiet confidence in his team leader's voice that always seemed to hold him when he wanted to run.

"Why is it so easy for you? Don't you have your doubts? Don't you question everything?"

"I'm security. I question more things than you...but once I've gotten the answers I'm looking for, I act on them. That's also part of being security. Not just doubting, but trusting your own judgment enough to follow through. Any security officer who keeps refusing to believe all the evidence won't commit to taking action and can never do his job."

"What do you need to believe?" Eli offered. "I am now authorized to give you, or show you, or tell you what you need in order to believe."

"Why am I that important?"

"Everyone is that important." Enoch suggested.

"Alright. Here's what I want. I want to believe. Oh God how I want to believe." There were actually tears beginning to well-up in Dane's eyes. "You tell me to trust. You talk about faith. I don't have that kind of faith. I can't generate that kind of trust."

"Which is where the problem lies." Eli observed. "Faith is not something we generate. Faith does not come from within us. If our faith is what got us through, none of us would make it. Faith is the gift of G-d. He gives us what we need to believe. He gives us enough to meet the task ahead. It is not what we think it is."

"For too many centuries, charlatans have used faith as a club to beat up those who did not get well when someone prayed for a healing; when someone couldn't experience a miracle." Enoch noted. "This is faith, true faith: *when all the events have played out, all the lives been lived, then each of us will have played his or her part in the great confrontation...be it great or small, each action and decision we have undertaken will fit together—our successes and failures—will accomplish what He intended. All things work together to bring everything to the end He has promised.* It won't heal those who need to be lame. It won't take away the pain we need to grow, but it will bring us to G-d."

"Why is it so easy for you?"

"Oh sure...now it is easy!" Eli remarked letting the Yiddish stereotype accent he joked with slip into his voice. "But at first it was hard. That first step out of the plane is the hardest. Once you've done it enough times, people watching you think *you* make it look easy."

"And how long have you been doing this?" Dane confronted. He had heard rumors; written it off as legends or gossip.

"Did you know that the oldest man who ever lived, died before his father did?" Enoch asked. It seemed like he was changing the subject, and anger flared in Dane voice.

"What?"

"Did you know that the oldest man to ever live, died before his father did?"

"No! I didn't know that...How could that be possible? If the oldest man who ever lived died before his father did, then he wouldn't be the oldest man to ever live. What does all of this have to do with how long you've been doing this?"

"Everything. I just find it an interesting riddle." There was a sparkle in Enoch's eyes which kept Dane from blowing it all off.

"The Bible tells us that it's appointed unto man once to die, and then comes the Judgment. Even our Lord Jesus had to die since He had become human." Eli picked up the conversation.

"So what does this have to do with my question?" Dane was becoming annoyed once more. He felt as if they were deliberately avoiding him.

"Did you know that there were two men in the Bible who did not die?" The calm, conversational tone of Eli's voice forced Dane to set aside his former question and respond to Eli.

"Everyone dies. You said that yourself. It is appointed unto man once to die."

"Yes, it is appointed," Enoch agreed. "But for these two, their appointment with death just hasn't taken place yet."

"One of these men was the prophet Elijah. He was taken up into Heaven in a whirlwind." Eli continued.

"I thought it was a fiery chariot." Dane corrected.

"No...There was a fiery chariot involved, but it kept his student Elisha from getting to him. It was actually a whirlwind that picked him up and carried him to Heaven. Check it out."

"I keep getting Elijah and Elisha mixed up. Why did they have to have such similar names?" Dane was flustered that he hadn't actually checked it out for himself but had listened to stories his mother had told him long ago. Of course, he didn't believe the stories, so why was it important to get them right?

"The oldest man to ever live was Methuselah." Enoch returned to his little riddle, much to Dane's annoyance. *Would Enoch ever get off that subject?* "Methuselah lived nine hundred and sixty-nine years before he died."

"But he still died before his father did." Dane observed with the annoyance back in his voice.

"Yes, he did. You see, Methuselah's father never died. He was the other one to be taken bodily into Heaven." There was almost a regret in Enoch's voice. "Did you know who Methuselah's father was?"

"No. I never checked that one out, either." Dane began to wonder why he was even hanging around with this group. He had one brief flash of considering leaving, just leaving; but he knew if he did, he would always feel empty inside. He didn't have what these people had, but he knew it was what he needed to fill that emptiness.

"His father's name was *Enoch*." Jim noted. Dane was instantly focused on the three in front of him.

"You were named after Enoch?" Dane asked.

"Actually we were named at the same time." Enoch replied with a smile filling his face.

"Whoa! Time out." Dane took a step back. "You're *the* Enoch. And I suppose Elijah is really Eli...jah." He paused and his voice cracked. "No! No way! You've been around for thousands of years?"

"Actually, we've just got back." Elijah smiled. "Like I said, we didn't have this in my days." He took another sip from the paper cup, filled it from the camp stove pot, and filled a second cup which he passed to Dane. Dane took a sip from it trying to clear his mind.

"That wasn't hard, was it?" Elijah commented on Dane drinking the coffee, and Dane recalled the previous analogy Elijah had presented.

"No, but I've drank coffee before."

"And we've trusted G-d before. It was hard for us when we took that first step in trusting G-d, but He brought us all the way through. It's not faith for us at this point. We've seen Heaven. We know what is there, and what lies ahead. Watching G-d work for a few thousand years gives us a unique perspective."

"Look! I want to believe. I really do. It's just getting weird... actually weirder. Look at the world. It's going to hell in a hand cart. How can God allow this sick behavior?" Dane pointed to several magazines which showed Ipileno with the EeeDees. "How can God let the world get so messed up?"

"What you are seeing is the world under Satan. This is what he will make of the world. This is his territory now. We are literally behind enemy lines. The fallen one will challenge everything G-d stands for. G-d has allowed this in order to make it clear to both sides what they are choosing. The shades of grey are now gone. From this point on, there will be either light or dark. Everything their side does offends us; that's what Satan wants. Everything we do will tick their side off. These life-styles are not compatible. There is no longer any point where they mix and coexist. Everyone who will eventually take the Mark of the Beast rejects G-d knowingly. They accept Satan with open eyes. They do it knowing it is an abomination to G-d. That's what makes it so exciting to them. It's not the act, it's the attitude. They know that by doing this, they ally themselves to Satan and stand against G-d. The time for delusions and illusions are gone."

"I don't want to go back to that." Dane admitted. "I just don't know how to go forward. Help me." His last words were little more than a plea. In response Elijah and Enoch stepped forward. They took Dane by each elbow, closed their eyes for a silent prayer. Dane closed his eyes out of respect, and while his eyes were closed, he felt some kind of energy begin to fill his body. He was stronger than he had been a moment ago. It was like a new life was flooding the hidden chambers of his body, soul and mind. When he opened his eyes, his breath was caught away as he saw a world superimposed on his own. He looked out over the camp which had been filled with the refuges from all over the world. There had been more than he could count; more than he believed they could support or hide. But the camp was even more crowded now than it had been moments ago. Next to each of those in the camp stood a powerful figure, even next to Billings. Each was a mighty warrior, easily twelve or fifteen feet tall. Their robes and hair fluttered in an unfelt breeze from some different plane of existence. Each figure was standing guard over someone in the camp. There was a pairing of warrior and refugee. On the forehead of each refugee there was a glowing symbol.

As Dane looked at Elijah and Enoch on either side of him, they had transformed, too. They were young and ancient at the same time. Their eyes blazed with wisdom and their arms and hands that supported him were as strong as steel. Dane looked at Jim and was surprised to see that Jim did not have such a mark on his forehead. Although Jim seemed confident and sure, he had no special warrior bonded to him. Dane's confused and elated expression was all the question that Elijah and Enoch needed.

"These are the hundred and forty-four thousand." Elijah declared, encompassing the entire camp with a wave of his hand. "These are those from the Children of Israel who have been set aside for this final confrontation, sealed by G-d and empowered to do His will. Twelve thousand from each of the twelve tribes."

"And why is Jim not one of them?" Dane asked.

"He is not from the lineage of Abraham. These have all been carefully prepared by G-d from one generation to the next. He has kept track of who they are and preserved them. Even they did not know they were part of the chosen until G-d revealed it to them." Enoch offered.

"But aren't you part of the hundred and forty-four?"

"No. We serve a different purpose. One that is coming to its close. We are the Two Witnesses. We are here to prepare the hundred and forty-four, and it is almost complete."

Dane noted a lone spirit warrior standing off to one side. "What's left to be done?"

"This one is for you, Dane. You are the last of the hundred and forty-four. You are the last of the chosen. This is why we worked so hard with you. This is where your destiny lies. This is the choice you have to make." Enoch replied, but it seemed his voice was different. His was the voice which spoke, but the words seemed to come from another.

"But I'm not Jewish." Dane suggested.

"You know all of your ancestors?" Elijah quipped in his stereotype Yiddish accent.

"And if I choose not to...?" Dane suggested.

"You know that you will." Elijah joked, and Dane knew in that moment Elijah was right. *This* is what he had been looking for. This is what would make him complete. He had one last concern.

"But what if I fail?"

"When G-d is involved, failure is not even a possibility." Elijah added. Dane looked at Jim who was beaming with joy for him. Jim was not one of the hundred and forty-four. He knew that, and it didn't bother him. He was excited for Dane, and everything finally made sense. He nodded his acceptance, and the lone spirit warrior came forward to embrace him with G-d's love and power.

CHAPTER THIRTY

The First Strands of The Web

"You have been going about this all wrong." Abaddon declared. He, Ipileno and Ted sat facing each other in one of the side conference rooms. Hovering in the air above them was an image of Jim. It was produced solely by Abaddon's power without the aid of any technology. Several months ago Ted would have been impressed with such accomplishments, but now it was commonplace and had lost its charm.

"How am I going about this all wrong?" Ted challenged. "My men are covering all major exit points from Israel. His face is plastered on every wall, paper, vid screen and broadcast."

"You are not going to get him by looking for him." Abaddon observed.

"What is this bull? More of your Eastern Mysticism? I won't find him until I stop looking for him?" Ted mocked.

"If you want to find him, you must first find these two." Abaddon continued ignoring Ted's remarks as if they were less than nothing. It aggravated Ted when he was treated this way. The image in the air rippled and then crystallized into two different faces.

"The Israelis?" Ted asked recognizing the faces from countless briefings with his men.

"Enoch and Elijah." Ipileno announced.

"Enoch Who?" Ted quipped. "And there are several thousand Elijahs in Jerusalem the last time I checked..."

"*THE* Enoch, and *THE* Elijah." Abaddon interrupted.

"*The?*" Ted asked. "What do you mean, *the?*"

"Simply that." Ipileno interjected. "The Enoch and the Elijah. Enoch, the father of Methuselah. *He walked with God and was not for God took him.*"

"Took him?" Ted echoed. He hated when they did this to him and made him look ignorant. "What the hell are you talking about?"

"From ancient times. Enoch never died. He was taken bodily into Heaven."

"And this is him?" Ted retorted. "He looks pretty good for a guy who's several thousands of years old. And what about him?"

"Elijah...He, too, was taken physically into Heaven."

"He never died, either? I thought everyone died." Ted blurted out.

"There are a few exceptions." Ipileno noted.

"So if these guys went bodily into Heaven, where do I begin to look for them...with a telescope?"

"They are in Jerusalem. They are the Two Witnesses who have been guiding the Neo-Christian movement for the last three and a half years."

"I thought they were in Heaven?"

"They came back." Abaddon replied. The offended tone of his voice told Ted that he had pushed the Extra-dimensional to the verge of losing his temper. It was a small victory, but Ted took sadistic pleasure in such accomplishments.

"They are in Jerusalem, and if you want to find your wayward brother, you need to find them. Our sources tell us that he is never far from them." Ipileno added. Ted was suddenly focused on the mission. If these two were the contact he needed to find Jim; then he would find them.

"There's just one point I don't understand..." Ted began. Ipileno's face took on an exasperated expression while Abaddon drifted near the back of the room, all but turning his back on Ted. Ted knew he was expendable. He knew he should have been struck dead on any one of several previous occasions. He wasn't sure why they hadn't killed him, but his soul was so cold inside of him that the only pleasure he had in life was pushing the envelope a little further.

"What point is that?' Ipileno sighed.

"You keep talking about your forces, and your sources. However, when it comes to the actual action, you always come to me or my men. Why is that? If you know where they are; then why don't you send in an army of EeeDees and take them out."

"We can't." Abaddon admitted from the back of the room. He did not turn to face Ted as he spoke.

"What do you mean you *can't?* The reason we are on your side is because you promise to beat this other side out. If you can't take them out; then why should we stay with you?"

"It's not as easy as all of that. There are laws, older than the world. These laws govern the actions of the EeeDees."

"Why? Why do they govern them? If this is a rebellion; then why obey the rules? In rebellions rules are meant to be broken. You go out of your way to break them. The EeeDees are playing by the rules and leading a rebellion at the same time?" Abaddon dissolved at Ted's comments. He did not want to respond or even hear the debate. It would be between Ted and Ipileno from this point on.

"God has agreed to not become personally involved with the conflict so long as both sides obey the rules." Jason explained.

"That's stupid. He's going to sit back, let us take out more and more of His forces, build our power base, and He won't do or say a thing so long as we *'play by the rules'*?"

"That's the size of it."

"Why? Why would He sit back and not do anything?"

"Because He has promised."

"That's it? *Oh, I know you're planning on taking out my entire army. I know that you're going to kick my butt off the celestial throne. I know you're going to try and kill me and take over, but so long as you do it without breaking my rules I promise not to stop you?"*

"Like I've always said, God is dumber than we think. Satan learned this several thousand years ago. He's used this stupidity against God since man was created. It's been a major flaw that we have been able to exploit. So long as the EeeDees abide by the agreement and work through us, God is keeping a hands off policy. He's the ultimate Boy Scout. He plays by the rules. He helps old ladies across the street. He makes me sick; but if He's stupid enough to sit back and let us grow in power and reduce His power base; then let Him. He deserves to lose His throne."

The head of security took one long last look at Enoch and Elijah as their images drifted on the air between them. The fact that their images were still there told Ted that Abaddon may have left the room, but he was still monitoring it. Ted left the room without a backward glance and headed for the privacy of his office.

He would push them too far some day. On that day he would be a pile of ashes, which was going to be his destiny. He knew it, but no longer seemed to care. This lack of caring gave him an inner strength. There was nothing to gain; so there was nothing to lose. All he sought now was revenge on his brother for the bitter betrayal and humiliation he had experienced. Ipileno and Abaddon were willing to give him what he needed to fulfill this revenge. He used them as much as they used him. Neither trusted the other. Neither cared about the other.

Ted activated his personal computer and display system. Enoch and Elijah now hovered before him thanks to technology and not extradimensional forces. He studied the images before him. He highlighted several pictures, diagrams, and files for printing. As the pages printed out, Spencer came into the office.

"Looks like you've been burning the midnight oil." Spencer observed. "Something big coming down?"

"No more than usual. I just needed to put together a report for Ipileno. He's chewing my butt out again." Ted shifted the papers so that Spencer couldn't get a clear look at them. It had been gnawing away in the back of his mind. Every time his team went into action, they were normally too late. It had been months since they had made any real progress against the Neo-Christians. Ted had thought that Dane had found some way to break into their security computers and tap information. For the last several missions, Ted had tried to plant incorrect information in the computer files or to keep any information out of the computers altogether. If Dane had broken the codes and was tapping in from that source it should have increased their success ratio. But to no avail. Spencer had even suggested that the Neo-Christians' extra-dimensionals were the source of the leak, but there was no way to test the theory. Ted was now working on the assumption that someone inside his operation was the leak. Even though Spencer had been with him for a long time, Ted had made up his mind that no one was going to be above suspicion.

Ted stuffed the printouts into a briefcase, re-enforcing the impression the papers were not a final product nor overly important. He slipped out of the office leaving Spencer on watch. Ted took note of the various cameras around the facility. He identified the ones placed in the open, and those which were hidden from view. He ran the pattern through his mind and recalled the ones that were broken and had not been repaired lately. Using this knowledge, he plotted his exit along the only path not monitored by security. His path brought him to the armory. A quick scan of his retina gained him access.

It had been a while since Ted had actually gone undercover. The technology had changed a lot since then. He began to collect various tracking devices. He noted that they were small enough to fit into a shirt button, but powerful enough to be picked up from ten miles away without running it through the satellite link. Listening devices came in a wide variety. Ted also selected several uniforms, clothing and stealth wardrobe which suppressed body heat from infra-red or heat seeking monitors. He noticed several tubes of similar make-up and contact lens to complete the camouflage.

Several other hi-tech, compact devices were slipped into a backpack along with three extra pistols and four boxes of ammunition.

Ted slipped out of the armory and continued his effort to wind his way out of the building without being spotted by any passer-by or monitors. Spencer sat in the command chair of security, adjusting several cameras only he knew about, locking onto the movements of his superior officer. Once Ted was out of the building, Spencer called for Carlos to relieve him at the center.

* * *

"What your brother doesn't seem to understand is that for all of his efforts to remain undetected, he sticks out like a sore thumb." Enoch observed as they stood on the balcony watching the crowd in the streets down below. One figure tried to blend in. Jim had to admit that the outfit was perfect. Ted looked like any other low life gathered on the street below. Ted had finally managed to work with his hair to get rid of the clean military look that had always been a problem for him. With so many gangs shaving their heads, the bald look added to the image. Of course Ted's head was not symmetrically shaped and so it detracted from the hard-guy image he was trying to portray, but the clothes, the chains and the tattoo were all good touches.

Unfortunately, while Ted slouched with the proper amount of disdain for those around him and tried to appear disinterested, a large EeeDee stood next to him and kept waving to Jim and pointing with exaggerated motions toward Ted. Ted was unaware of the motions as were those on the street around him. However, those on the balcony smirked as they sipped their drinks.

"So long as Jubal follows him around, I think your brother is going to have a hard time being inconspicuous." Eli added.

"He seems determined to make us believe that he's not who he is; that he's not really there." Jim agreed and nearly sprayed his drink as Jubal began to use his fingers to make rabbit ears sprout up from his brother's head. "Does he have to do that?"

"That's just his nature. Jubal has always enjoyed humor and jokes. He keeps things interesting for us." Enoch noted.

"But this is a serious situation. My brother has tracked us down." Jim's attention was drawn away as Jubal pretended to be about to drop a flower pot on Ted's head. "He should be a street mime."

"He was. Jubal has the gift of humor. He uses it quite well." Elijah replied.

"I just can't think of angels as having such a sense of humor...Of playing..." Jim searched for the word but Enoch completed the thought for him.

"...Practical jokes?"

"He should be serious." Jim was adamant, turning his back on the EeeDee so he couldn't see what other shenanigans Jubal was performing on his brother.

"He is serious. Don't let his manner fool you. If we were in any danger, those nimble fingers tickling your brother's ears would grasp his sword in a moment and his eyes would burn with such fire that few could stand before him."

"I just can't see him as such a warrior." Jim confessed. Instantly Jubal was before him, his eyes blazing with power and Jim had to catch himself before his glass dropped from his fingers.

"We are not in any danger...at least not for the moment." Jubal declared. "Your brother is simply watching. His demons-in-attendance have been bound and dragged off. He is making no plans to contact Ipileno or Abaddon. This is between the two of you. He has gone to a great deal of trouble to get here, used up a lot of his personal cash, was in danger of having his throat cut twice; and once was barely missed when a sniper took a shot at him."

"I thought that you might like one last chance to speak to him. Face-to-face is always better than over those lap top contraptions you keep using." Elijah suggested. "Jubal kept track of him for the last two weeks. We thought it might be nice to help him along."

Jubal's form dissolved into bubbles, fizzled into nothingness before Jim and reassembled next to Ted. This time the angel held a sign visible only to those on the balcony. It read, "I'm an undercover spy. Ignore me!" with a little arrow pointing to Ted.

"Ted thinks that he is a spider weaving his web, but the truth is, it is our web he is balancing upon." Enoch chuckled at the antics of Jubal and poured another drink.

"But we are going to be in danger." Jim suggested.

"It depends on what you call '*danger*'" Enoch replied.

"I call it danger that you two have a price on your heads bigger than mine. There have been three near misses in the last week-and-a-half. Ted's men have tripled their efforts to find you and kill you; and now he's less than three blocks away." Jim noticed that Ted was laughing about something. "What's going on?"

"Jubal has altered his listening device. Your brother has been monitoring our conversation since he set up camp. He's got three cameras recording our activities. One's on that roof. The second is across the street and the third is in his sun glasses. Jubal has been letting him listen in, but he's hearing things completely different from what we are saying. I imagine that Jubal has provided him something funny to listen to."

"But he's here. Within gun shot. What's to keep him from pulling out one of his pistols and taking one or both of you out?"

"If he did manage to get his pistol out of his shoulder holster, and he could get the safety to release, Jubal would have already removed the bullets from the clip. He would have to reload. Any of those actions would give us more than enough time to leave the balcony and remove the target."

"But the time is coming." Jim suggested.

"Coming? No, more like it is upon us. Soon it will be over." Elijah confessed as he sipped the last liquid from his glass. He sucked the remaining taste from an ice cube in the glass.

"Soon?! We should be getting out of here."

"But this is where it is going to happen." Enoch observed.

"All the more reason to flee." Jim declared.

"Flee from the will of G-d?" Elijah's voice was incredulous.

"That wasn't what I meant. Why stand here and wait for death?"

"It is appointed unto man once to die. It's an appointment. I hate to miss an appointment." Enoch smiled. They had beaten the horse to death more than once. Each time Jim found himself frustrated. He could not convince Enoch or Elijah to take greater precautions, nor remove themselves from the coming disaster.

"If you die, the hundred and forty-four will scatter." Jim suggested.

"That is what they are supposed to do. We have given them all we can. They are ready to take up their roles. They cannot do that while we are still here..." Elijah began, but it was Enoch who completed the observation.

"...And so we must leave."

"So leave, but there's no need to die." Jim begged.

"What's so terrible about death?" Enoch chided.

"Stop it!" Jim shouted. "I care about you...both of you. You've been the source of strength I was missing for so long. Do you know how hard it was for me those first few years when I was on my own? We heard rumors about you. We knew something was going on; but I was in the thick of it. My people were being hunted down and killed without mercy throughout all of Europe—all over the world. I couldn't keep track of how many I had worked with who were dragged from their beds screaming only to be killed by the mobs. They were strapped into the execution machines and people laughed at them and cheered that they were going to die. I nearly gave up. I nearly ran away. I didn't have the strength to keep going. Then Amir and Shmuel came to me. They introduced us. I wasn't alone anymore. I wasn't the one everyone came to for decisions. For help. For protection. I don't know if I can take that again."

"You won't have to, Jim." The tone of Elijah's voice made Jim stop for a second. He pointed to himself. The pair nodded in agreement, but it was Enoch who spoke.

"You are the last of the Gentile In Cees. You are the last of those who came through the Rapture and believed. You will be the Last Martyr. Now G-d is fulfilling His promise. When Yeshua entered Jerusalem that day on the donkey, He fulfilled several prophecies. In short, He declared Himself to be our Messiah. The priests rebuked His followers and rejected Him. They activated an older prophecy; one Moses delivered while our people were still in the Wilderness. *'They have made me jealous with other gods; and I will make them jealous with a people who are not a people.'* A gap took place between the Sixty-ninth Week and the Seventieth Week of the prophecy of Daniel as G-d turned from His Chosen People and turned to your people to spread His Word."

"Now G-d has grafted our people back in. We are assuming the final mission. We will anoint the Most High. Your calling home is soon, Jim. It is time for you and us to rest; and to entrust the work to other hands G-d has appointed." Elijah completed. Jim stood stunned for a minute. He had dreaded what would eventually come. He had run from it. He had cheated it at every turn. But now Elijah and Enoch were about to embrace their destiny. He now knew he would share their destiny. There was no more fear. There was a sense of relief. A weight was being lifted. He found himself looking forward to it.

"The hundred and forty-four are prepared. They have been identified and sealed by G-d. When we are gone, they will be greater than we ever were. Ipileno thinks he has problems now with just the two of us. Imagine how he will be when we are cut down and he discovers that a hundred and forty-four thousand clones of us spread across the face of the earth."

"I imagine he will try to hunt them down and kill them." Jim suggested.

"He will try, but the only reason he will kill us is because our time is complete. Our mission is over. Today makes the one thousand, two hundred and sixtieth day. Three and a half years by the Babylonia calendar. The exact day revealed to John in the Revelation. It's time to move on. But the Hundred and Forty-Four will have the same protection we had. He will not be able to kill them, nor even find them. They will carry on the next phase of our work."

When Enoch finished speaking he noted that his glass was empty. The sun was still hot and so he turned to go back into the apartment for a refill. As he turned his back on the balcony, Jim saw a mischievous look dance in the Witness' eyes. Enoch turned back to the street, leaned over the balcony and waved deliberately to Ted before crossing back over and into the apartment.

CHAPTER THIRTY-ONE

The Final Meeting

There came a rapping at the hotel door. Jim opened it and found Ted filling the door frame. Behind him stood Jubal.

"Come on, give him a hug. He is your brother." Jubal encouraged. Ted was oblivious to the voice of the EeeDee behind him.

""Jubal!" Jim chided. "Not now. This is serious." Ted looked around to see to whom Jim was speaking. Jubal acting as if his feelings were hurt slipped between them into the room.

"Come on guys. I think they want to be alone. This is what they call a *Kodak moment*."

"In a minute, Jubal." Enoch countered. "You've come this far, Ted. You might as well make it the rest of the way over the threshold."

"How did you know I was watching you?" Ted challenged as he thrust himself into the room. "And who are you talking to?"

"In answer to both your questions..." Elijah began, "... Jubal."

"Jubal?" Ted echoed.

"I think they mean me." Jubal replied, suddenly making himself visible to Ted. Even though the head of security had been in the presence of other EeeDees, and had been through countless battles, he started at the sudden presence.

"You're using EeeDees?" Ted demanded.

"We work with them." Enoch corrected.

"So you're breaking the rules..." Ted accused, but Jim cut him off.

"Rules?! What rules?"

"The rules of engagement." Ted countered. "The EeeDees don't become involved in the conflict. They work through us."

Elijah took a slow sip from his drink, keeping his eyes trained on Ted. The head of security actually felt himself grow nervous for the first time in many lifetimes. When Ted was sufficiently uncomfortable for Elijah, the Witness replied; "I don't believe there are any such rules."

"Of course there are! Abaddon told me all about it. So long as we play by the rules; then God won't get involved." Ted flushed as he suddenly realized he had given information to the enemy. He cursed under his breath.

"Careful" Jubal cautioned. "Otherwise I'll have to wash your mouth out with soap." Ted hesitated for a moment as he tried to determine if the EeeDee was serious or not.

"There are no such rules of engagement." Enoch replied. "The calmness in the Witness' voice made Ted give him his full attention. The anger he had known a moment ago was gone.

"There is an agreement between God and Satan, that if Satan does not directly employ his angels; then God will allow him to continue to build his power base. However, the angelic hosts are very much a part of our work, and God is very much involved. Do not foster the belief that we are powerless before you." Enoch nodded to no one in particular and slowly row upon row of angelic forces began to materialize in the room. They never became solid, nor attained their true glory; but appeared as only a shadow of their true potential. Ted had no idea how anyone could move without touching one, and still they continued to multiply. The Witness nodded once more, and the army faded from view; but Ted had no illusion that they were actually gone.

"How long do we have?" Elijah asked Jubal who had not faded along with the other EeeDees.

"They are in the city. Twenty minutes...maybe thirty." Jubal noted. The tone in the room tried to become depressed, but Enoch smiled broadly and slapped Elijah on the shoulder.

"Maybe now is a good time to look upon the Temple Mount."

"Yes..." Elijah replied after a moment of consideration. "That is a good spot. If you'll excuse us for a few moments, Jubal." In response to Elijah's request, the EeeDee made a soft popping sound and was replaced with smoke wisps that drifted out the window and were gone.

"He always likes to show off." Enoch observed. The Witnesses stepped up to Jim. Their eyes met and some unspoken message was passed between them.

"I should go with you." Jim offered. Elijah held up his hand in mild protest.

"We will be together soon enough. This is our path. Yours is here. Are you ready?"

"I don't think we're ever ready." Jim answered.

"Here." Enoch offered and touched Jim on the shoulder. Ted wasn't sure what was going on, but he could see that Jim seemed to have some new reservoir of strength. The depression that had hung in the room and tried to drop on them was evaporating like a vapor of steam. Enoch then wrapped his fingers into the sleeves of Jim's shirt, pulled him to him and hugged him as if he were falling and only by clinging to Jim could he keep upright. When Enoch released his brother. Ted noted tears in the Witness' eyes.

"Don't be mistaken, my son." Enoch confessed to Jim. "These are tears of joy. I know what's waiting for you. It's glorious... glorious..." The last word was a whisper choked off by the excitement that made Enoch's body quiver. Enoch regained control of himself, smiled with his entire personality, and added; "You're going to love it!" He hugged Jim one last time.

Elijah embraced Jim, and rubbed his back with his massive hands. Ted had never noticed such large hands before. There were powerful hands. Elijah patted Jim on the back several times, savored the moment, released him and then whispered in Jim's ear, "Baruch Ha Shem."

Elijah retrieved his glass, raised it to Enoch who lifted his own. The two drained the liquid in one long refreshing draught, tossed the glasses in the fireplace and let go with a rich contagious laugh. "On the other side, Jim!" Enoch declared. Without any further ceremony the two moved out of the room with a sense of purpose that Ted had always desired in his own life. They took nothing with them as if they had no further needs in this life.

"So these are the nuts you've linked up with?" Ted criticized.

"I don't think that is why you came." Jim suggested. His brother broke eye contact with him; something Ted had never done before. His brother rubbed his hands together, shifted his weight from one foot to the other trying to find the words to say.

"You want to know if you're making the right choice." Jim announced. Ted would never have put it in those words; but once it was voiced, he knew that was exactly the reason he was here. Jim answered the question for him, "You're not!"

"What do you mean, *I'm not*? Just like that? No need to discuss the issue? No different point of view?"

"Okay. Let's pretend that it's not obvious. What makes you think you're on the right side?"

"We have power, Jim. For the first time in my life, I am in charge. When I walk into a room, my subordinates don't just obey me. They don't just respect me. They *fear* me. They want what I have. They want to be where I'm at. I have reached the top."

"And where do you go from here?" Jim countered.

"What do you mean, *Where do I go from here?* Where's left to go? I can finally relax."

"No you can't. You talk about power, but power is an illusion. For every time you walk into a room and see people fear you; you've had to submit to others over you to get it. And when you come into their office, you have that same fear you see in your subordinates' eyes. That power is only there because they keep you in power. If Ipileno or Abaddon kicked you out tomorrow, you'd have nothing. You can't hold onto that power. It's there only because they give it to you. There nothing you can do to force them to keep giving it to you. You're climbing up a ladder of smoke. It can't last, and it can't hold you up. There's no security in that."

"And there's security in this?" Ted challenged sweeping his arm out to encompass the entire room.

"Not in this. But in this" Jim answered thumping on his chest over his heart. "This is all going to burn. You've only seen the beginning of all of this. The worst is still to come!"

"Then why do you keep trying? What's going to be left to save?"

"Because all of this is nothing more than birth pains. A new world is coming. A new order is coming."

"The kingdom of Jesus?" Ted snarled. His stomach actually tensed when he spoke the name.

"Yes, the kingdom of Jesus."

"And what if our side wins? Then what becomes of this new world. This new kingdom? The only way it can come to be is if we fail."

"Do you really think that winning is a possibility for your side?"

"We have as much chance for winning as your side. In fact, we have more chance of winning than your side."

"How?" Jim countered. Ted nearly blurted out something about their strength and forces, but caught himself. He couldn't believe that he was slipping. He was making the kinds of mistakes an amateur would make during interrogation training. His silence prompted Jim to pick up the line of reasoning.

"There is one point you've over-looked in this great scheme of yours."

"What's that?" Ted couldn't believe that his brother would reveal something so strategic, but it looked as if he would. Ted decided to let him ramble for a time and see what he could learn of the other side's plans.

"The point that you're missing is that your leader is a created being."

"What?" Ted blurted. It wasn't the response he was looking for. It didn't make any sense to him.

"Satan is not God's equal. It's not like they both existed before the world, put this together as a battle ground and to the victor go the spoils. This world, this universe, all the EeeDees and your boss, Satan, were created by God. *If*—and this is a really big *if*–*if* Satan somehow was able to defeat God and kill God, how do you think all of this will continue?"

"What do you mean?"

"God is the source for all of this. God is holding it together. Think of this universe, your body, Ipileno, Abaddon and Satan as nothing more than the flame over a Bunsen Burner. Turn off the gas, and it's all gone. If Satan can kill God, then all he does is destroy everything. God is the ultimate *Dead Man's Switch*." Jim made reference to a terrorist tactic of preventing a bomb from going off so long as the terrorist was alive and keeping the bomb from blowing. "Kill the terrorist, he drops the fail safe, the connection completes; and the bomb goes off. Or in this case, the universe ceases to exist."

"You're lying!" Ted countered.

"Now that's a good comeback." Jim noted. "Anything more concrete? Anything to suggest I'm wrong?" Jim paused. When Ted was silent he continued. "Ted, you're on the side that can never win. Even if they could win, they lose. Your whole movement is a lose/lose situation. If you don't defeat God then you go to Hell. If you do defeat God then everything disappears back into nothingness. What do you hope to gain from all of this? Power? You only have power because someone gives it to you."

"Freedom." Ted snapped. "That's it. I'm doing this for the freedom."

"*Freedom*? What *freedom*?" Jim retorted.

"Freedom to live my life the way I want. I can make my own choices. I can do what I want."

"Ted? Is this the life you've wanted? Is this what you wanted to do and be when you were a kid? Is this what you wanted to be doing when you were in college? In all of your life, have you ever sat down and said to yourself, *this* is what I want to end up doing?"

"No..." Ted almost choked on the admission. He was suddenly so tired. He was confused. He had no more energy to fight. He looked around him and realized that he had fought all these years and was no closer to what he truly wanted. All the drinking, all the fighting, all the sex was to fill something which was missing inside of him. Even as he realized the emptiness inside of him, the horror of what he had done to himself; he knew that Jim was right. And as Ted realized the hunger in what was once his soul, he saw it as the weakness he had always feared. With that sudden revelation came an anger at himself which quickly turned to a rage; a blind, unthinking, all-consuming rage. The focal point of that rage was the person who had opened the old wound, revealed the weakness he had fought for so long to control. In almost a blind panic, Ted forgot about all the EeeDees who had filled the room only moments ago. He drew his gun from where it had been tucked in his belt against the small of his back.

"You've almost got me believing!" Ted screamed so loud and so hard his vocal cords felt as if they were tearing. Jim never made any attempt to move out of the line of fire. Ted told himself it was because his movements were too fast, but deep inside he knew that Jim had no fear of dying. He saw this as his own fate and did not flinch nor shirk from it. Ted's shout turned to a scream, a wail of the damned as he fired the first round. The powder exploded in the chamber, driving the slug forward, spitting it from the barrel and the pistol jerked in Ted's hand. The metal tore into Jim's chest. Blood sprayed out his back. Ted's finger kept squeezing the trigger; and round after round erupted in smoke, fire, and a thunder which couldn't silence the desperation inside of him. Five of the bullets slammed into Jim as his body fell. The sixth shattered the sliding glass door behind Jim. The remaining slugs hurled over the balcony into the streets of Jerusalem.

Ted had no idea how many times he had pulled the trigger for the hammer to beat on spent cartridges, but he kept hearing the gun shots. It took him several minutes to realize that it wasn't his gun making the sounds. The sounds of more powerful weapons and automatic rifles were coming from several blocks away. The realization brought Ted to his senses. He raced to the balcony. Below him several Special Forces operatives were running down the street. He recognized them as his own men.

"Grains!" he barked. The man stopped, spun and had his rifle trained on Ted before the echo of Ted's voice faded from the streets. Ted had his hands raised, the gun hanging limp from his finger. Grains recognized Ted.

"Sorry chief!" he called back and lowered the rifle.

"What's happening?"

"I thought you knew." Grains responded. Ted shook his head no and his subordinate continued. "We've got the Witnesses. Both of them. They were on the street in front of the Temple Mount. Everyone hit them. You never saw so many bullets tear into someone. Several In Cees took off running in different directions. We're tracking them down as part of the clean-up operation. Looks like it's all over. All the leaders on the In Cee side are dead, except for your brother."

"He's dead, too." Ted offered.

"You, sir?" Grains asked. Ted nodded. "Good job, sir!" Ted motioned and Grains continued to join the team as they swept through the streets. The head of security walked slowly back into the room. As he stood over his brother's still body, Abaddon spoke from behind him.

"So it all came together."

"What do you mean, *came together*?" Ted asked without turning to look at the EeeDee.

"We knew that once you found your brother, we could move in and take out the entire movement. Good work."

"So it's over?" Ted asked turning to face Abaddon.

"We've killed their leaders, broken their power base, scattered their forces. They can't recover from this. We are the seat of power in this world." Abaddon faded from view. Ted turned back and knelt beside Jim's body, closing the eyes which had continued to stare at him as if challenging Abaddon's claim that it truly was all over.

As if to confirm the Witnesses were truly dead, the skies began to rain. Not just here in Jerusalem, but throughout the entire world. Ted could not tell if the skies were rejoicing in their freedom to rain as they had wanted to for so long to cleanse the air; or if they were weeping for the deaths of those now lying in the street before the Temple Mount.

CHAPTER THIRTY-TWO

Prophecies and Promises

Ted looked at the note in his hand. It was written in Spencer's penmanship on a scrap of paper. Ted had wondered what had become of Spencer. He had not seen his second-in-command since the day he left him in the control center back at Alliance headquarters. The note had only five words and a time scribble underneath: "Meet me at the bodies."

Ted knew what Spencer was referring to. With the execution of the Witnesses, the entire world had broken out in celebration. The world was breathing a sigh of relief. The wars were over. The power of God had been broken. No more In Cees were left to carry on the struggle. Their forces had been scattered. Their leaders dead. For the last three days the entire population of earth had been conducting an all-out bash. Drinks, drugs, sex, song...it was all non-stop. Ipileno sent presents to all the men who had taken out Elijah and Enoch. It was a gold bar for each bullet they had fired into the two bodies; over two hundred by last count. People everywhere were sending gifts. Bars were pouring free drinks, restaurants catering to the masses, musicians in the streets. All the long years of fire, flood, drought, plague, disaster and earthquakes were all–but forgotten. The two who had brought all of these things upon the world lay dead before Ted.

Ipileno had set up a display on the street corner where Elijah and Enoch had been taken out. Cable networks were covering it non–stop. It was actually the most watched program for the last year...maybe even in the history of cable. Everyone wanted to see the dead bodies, the bullet holes and especially the blood. The blood soaked the clothing, ran onto the sidewalk and stained the concrete. Ipileno had placed a barricade around the Witnesses so no one could drag the bodies off or steal any body parts. They were to lay there until he decided what to do with them.

He had spoken in private of publicly ripping the heads off of both bodies, giving the honor to those who had served him best and broadcasting the scene to the entire world. He then was going to mount each one on the arm rests of his throne when he set up his headquarters in the Temple. He planned to have the High Priest crushed with others under his throne when the final invasion of Jerusalem took place, and the heads of the Witnesses staring out with their dead eyes and sagging mouths looking at anyone who stood before him as he held court. It would be the perfect symbol of his complete victory over God.

Those who fired the first shots were plastered on every website, vid, paper and magazine. They were the heroes of the day. They could write their own ticket. Get anything they wanted. No one would dare say no to them. They felt like gods of a New Age.

Ted had positioned himself out of the line of the automatic remote cameras. He, too, had become one of the most famous celebrities in the world. Not only had he been head of security, not only had his men taken out the Witness with an unauthorized raid the Israelis never saw coming; but his killing his brother had been the final deliverance of the world from the In Cee plague. He was literally being called the New Messiah.

"Not a pretty sight, is it?" Spencer's voice came from behind Ted.

"I don't know. There are some who think this is the most beautiful sight in the entire world. This is the freedom we've been fighting for." Ted declared turning to meet his second-in command. Ted's eyes locked onto Spencer's forehead. For a brief moment there seemed to be some mark glowing in the center and then it was gone.

"What was that?"

"I'm an In Cee. You thought it was Neo-Christian. We changed it to 'In Christ.'"

Ted fingers snatched the gun from its holster preparing to eradicate the last of the movement. Instantly Ted found himself hanging in the air, the pistol dropping from his nerveless fingers as Jubal jerked him off his feet and dangled him in the air. The motion threatened to dislocate his arms from their sockets and tear his limbs from his body. The smoldering eyes of the EeeDee locked onto his and the rage burning there caused Ted to lose control of his bodily functions.

"Not this time!" Jubal snarled. "I had to let you the last time; but never again. It ends here." The EeeDee dropped the head of security unceremoniously to the pavement, slamming his knees onto the concrete and twisting his ankle as he hit. Spencer stepped forward.

"It's not over, Ted."

"Of course it's over. The Witnesses are dead. Jim is dead. And in a short time you're going to be dead." As he spoke, Ted kept an eye out to see if Jubal made any further motion in his direction. The EeeDee was keeping his distance. So long as Ted made no threat or movement toward Spencer Jubal seemed content to let Ted live.

"Then you do not know the prophecies." Came a voice behind him. Ted thought he recognized it; but it was impossible. He twisted around to see Enoch standing up. Even though he had lain dead on the street for three days, he was now fully healed. The wounds were gone. The blood stains on the concrete burned away. Even more so, Enoch was almost glowing. There was a glory, a majesty about him so powerful it all but blinded Ted. Enoch reached over and took Elijah's hand as he rose from the pavement. Ted had to turn away because the combined presence of the Witnesses was more than his eyes could stand. Spencer stood still, unaffected by the glow.

"You never read the Bible, Ted. This was predicted thousands of years ago. You were a fool. It was all laid out in careful detail. The earthquakes, the fires, the plagues; the death and resurrection of the Witnesses. Some security man you are. It was all right there, and you ignored it. You played right into G-d's hands. You did everything like some puppet." Spencer observed.

"I'm not a puppet!" Ted roared, but he was in too much pain to move. His knees and ankles were bleeding and swelling. His armpits throbbed and made his hands weak. Ted tried not to think that he did look like some marionette whose strings had been cut as he sat crumpled on the sidewalk.

"Whatever. Keep deluding yourself. The night Rawlings and Schmidt died, my eyes were opened up. I vowed never to come to their end. I sought out your brother. I joined the In Cees and was their mole for years. You have no idea how hard it was for me to supervise the deaths. It was just a matter of time before I was exposed."

"But you were one of us. You turned in the In Cees. I saw your reports." Ted stammered in disbelief.

"No. Others did all of that. I stole the credit for it. Those who had their successes snatched out from under them and I took the credit hated me. They thought I was working my way up the corporate ladder at their expense. I did it to convince you I was one of you. But I never was. Not since that night with Rawlings and Schmidt."

"We'll track you down, Spencer. We won't let you become the new leader of the movement." Ted threatened. Spencer laughed in reply.

"Me? I'm not the leader. Ted, how stupid can you be? I tried to warn you, but you never listened. The leader of the movement is not one person. There are a hundred and forty-four thousand of us...and each one is protected by an EeeDee. I never realized until I met Elijah and Enoch that I was one of the Hundred and Forty-Four Thousand mentioned in Scripture. Let me repeat that for you, Ted because you seem to have this on-going problem of hearing what we say. THOUSAND. A Hundred and Forty-Four THOUSAND of us.

"I hate to burst your bubble, but it isn't over. It's far from over. This is just the first three–and–a–half years. We have three-and-a-half to go. It's going to get a whole lot worse than this before we get done with you."

The light from behind Ted grew even more brilliant. Spencer waved to someone behind Ted. Shielding his eyes from the glare, Ted looked around and saw Enoch and Elijah literally rising into the air as if under their own power. The cameras which had been on automatic were continuing to follow them as they rose higher and higher. Soon they were out of sight. Although Ted was half a world away, he could hear the wail of raging anger in Ipileno's soul as their victory was snatched from them.

"I will see you at Armageddon..." Jubal promised Ted. The EeeDee was suddenly in his face. "...and it will be my pleasure on that day to kill you for what you did to Jim and all the others. On that day, you will have to account for them all. Try not to die until then...please." The EeeDee dematerialized leaving Spencer alone with the head of security.

"It's not over, Ted...it's far from over." Spencer reminded his former boss. He then turned and walked down the street until he, too, was out of sight.

END

Author Notes

(Or What Was I Really Trying To Do Here)

I can't believe I am back at this again. You don't know, because you have the luxury of reading the finished product. My wife and friends know that this is about the sixth time I've gone back to rewrite this story. God gives me so much, and then lets me think I'm done; but He keeps me from publishing this work. Then months or years later He reveals something else; and I sit down and start again. From hand-written sections, to manual typewriters, electric typewriters, a Brothers word processor, four personal computers and now lap top; this story has been told and retold.

The last time I thought I was done. I always think I am done. I made several copies, gave it to friends to proof and we even had a dinner get together to discuss the story. They all told me what I didn't want to hear: there has to be a sequel. I was adamant. This is it. I'm done. Telling and living the first three-and-a-half years drained me each time I went back in. This is probably why God had me take so long finishing this project. I made it clear there was no sequel. Then a few weeks later I scanned several folders in my G Drive and saw a title that made me realize that there probably will be a sequel—if God permits—and I had already titled it and started it many years ago.

With that realization I knew I had to come back and re-write the story one more time and introduce several characters. So now I have finished the sixth re-write; and I am back to my Author Notes section—hopefully for the last time.

As I said in the introduction of the book, this was originally all part of the introduction, but was moved here so as not to spoil the surprises in the book. If you're reading this before reading the book, this the ultimate SPOILER ALERT. So go back and read the book first. I want you to enjoy the unfolding of the story as a first-time reader.

In this section I would like to make a few comments about the manuscript and its beginnings. I'd like to mention how I first came to hear about the Rapture. My father had been called to the ministry when I was about thirteen—yes, I am a PK [Preacher's Kid]. And, yes, I've heard the song, "SON OF A PREACHER MAN" so you don't need to sing it for me. My father was called to the ministry, but for some time he just taught classes in our Church. He was the first one to talk about the Book of Daniel and Revelation. Then Hal Lindsey put out a book called THE LATE GREAT PLANET EARTH. That pretty much pushed the Rapture into the public domain.

Then Calvary Chapel of Costa Mesa got started and a company called Maranatha Music began to release record albums of rock and roll type music but with Christian themes. To be honest, these were almost considered an underground kind of music and were strongly discouraged by the Church leaders where I went to Church.

Fortunately I had a friend who had connections, and he bought a few of these records and introduced me to them when no one else was around. My first session was at his house listening to a song called, I WISH WE'D ALL BEEN READY written and sung by Larry Norman. He was not on the Maranatha Label, but other record companies had jumped on the bandwagon. It was a song about the Rapture.

About the same time I was just out of high school my friend's parents had just gotten divorced. He and his sisters were living with his dad. Yes, this is the one with the smuggled Maranatha Music record albums. His mom took everything out of the house...and I do mean everything. When his father had to go back east for a family emergency, the house was left pretty much to us. We made a trip to every

Christian bookstore, every Church member's home, and every personal library we could plunder. We ended up back at his house with a mountain of books on two subjects: the Gifts of the Spirit, and the Rapture. As there was no furniture in the living room area, we spread out sleeping bags, broke open bags of chips, and stacked the books around the room according to category.

We each picked a book and began to read. We read the book, we searched the Scriptures, we stayed up until two or three o'clock in the morning, woke up at six or seven, threw together a quick meal; and started back in again. When we finished a book, we discussed it, debated it, pointed out its strengths or weaknesses according to the Bible; and then either accepted its teachings or threw them out. We did this for almost a week. Needless to say, we could only hit up the drive-thru windows at fast food places since we hadn't stopped for personal hygiene. At the end of the week, we were probably better versed than anyone else in the city when it came to the Gifts of the Spirit and the Rapture; but no one could come near us until we took a bath.

Looking for an outlet for all this studying, I put together a short play for our local Church. In this play, we were showing slides from the moon landing. My father had worked for *Rocketdyne* which was part of the space program, and he had purchased a set of slides of the first moon landing for me. One of the slides was the landing craft on the moon. The lights were hitting it, and the metal foil it was covered in caught your eye. As I studied the slide, I created the story that the protective covering had a small tear in it. Given all the emphasis on quarantining the astronauts for several days when they came back from the moon because there might be some germ they picked up, I chose to focus on that as the basis for the story.

That had been my plan, but then reality set in. Instead of having all the space program props and scenes with an actual moon landing on stage, I had to find a cheaper way of presenting my story. After all, we were on a very small budget—mine, and I was unemployed. I finally worked out a cheaper way to present my theory on an alternative explanation for millions disappearing other than the Rapture. I could by-pass the sets, props and costumes needed to depict the moon landing, and just display the slides I had on the subject. I wanted to do a debriefing scene where someone showed the slides and discussed how the germ made it back to Earth, and all the damage the germ did once here. However, even that went by the way-side...we didn't even have a slide projector.

What we came up with instead were three students sitting around talking about the Rapture. Two are saved, the other is not. After all the debate about the Rapture to educate the audience on the topic, the two Christian students go out to get some food. There's a long wait for them to return. They never do. A police officer comes to the door. Our music director was a highway patrol officer, so we drafted him; after all, he already had the uniform so it was cheaper that way. He told the non-Christian that the Christian's car had just slowed and stopped in the middle of the street. The strangest thing was that when they looked inside the car, there was no one there, but the seat belts were still buckled.

The original idea of the space program bringing back a germ was still something I liked, but I couldn't put it all into a play, and it never seemed right for a puppet script. Thus, I decided to break down, and put it into a book. There had been a lot of books at that time about the Rapture and the Tribulation Period, but they all seemed to lack something. Most were simply a way for someone to stand up on their soap box and preach the Rapture. Characters were stereotypes at best. Several books were not even based upon Scripture, and no one had taken a look at it from a non-Christian's point of view. Thus, I felt it would be better to try and make the book as realistic as possible, come at it from the non-Christian point of view, and explain away everything the Christians were pointing to as an act of God and proof that He existed.

I started writing the book after I was married in 1976. I guess if I had to point to one event triggering the book, it would have to be a comment made by Greg Laurie during one of his sermons at Calvary Chapel of Riverside (now known as *Harvest*). Greg was always putting humor in his sermons, and this one about the Rapture (or *the Great Escape* as Greg liked to call it) was no different. He started spewing out all these off-the-wall explanations the government would give to explain the Rapture away. I'm sure he didn't mean any of them to be taken seriously, but that little memory in the back of my head was knocking—actually pounding—on my creative center's front door. Why not do a book trying to seriously explain away the Rapture? Someone was going to have to do it once the Rapture took place. You can't have several billion people look around, see millions disappear in the blink of an eye, say, "Hmmm, must have been the Rapture" and not panic and run screaming into the night. If everyone believes it's the Rapture, then no one is going to let the Anti-Christ take over...So somebody has to explain it all away in a logical, believable way.

With Greg's jokes in mind, came the realization that when the *Rapture* does take place, the world is going to have to explain away a lot of things. Thus, the book took on the form of a government cover-up about the *Rapture*. (Keep in mind that Watergate had just taken place, and government cover-up stories seemed pretty popular.) The argument which came to mind was the old slide from the moon landing, and the torn foil covering of the space craft—thanks Dad!.

From there I put together that it would probably be seen as some kind of biological organism which got out of control. It only affected certain people and then mutated. (Yes, looking at it now several years later, it may seem that I was influenced by Michael Crichton's *Andromeda Strain*, but it wasn't his work that gave me the idea; it was the moon landing slide and the quarantining of astronauts who had been to the moon.)

I used the space program instead of a biological weapons lab as the source in order to show how bad the environment would be when the Rapture took place. Also, at that time, moon landings were becoming a thing of the past, and there was talk of building a space station.

A THIEF IN THE NIGHT was one of the first movies about the *Rapture*. It was predictable, but we all watched it several times. What bothered me as much as the bad acting, was that it still had a wonderful world with green fields and blue skies, and fresh water. I thought the world would be much more like it was portrayed in the movie *SOYLENT GREEN*— which I had seen the night before my first viewing of *THE THIEF IN THE NIGHT.*

Once I had men in space, I had to address the theological question of: "if men were away from the earth by being in space when the *Rapture* took place, would they still go?" Not wanting to touch that one with any length of pole, I waited until they entered the Earth's atmosphere, and were technically part of the world once more. From there the government explanation of the *Rapture* actually being an organism brought back from space, touching the oxygen-rich atmosphere, spreading instantly all over the world, completely breaking down victims to their cellular-level so nothing is left but clothing and personal items was too good a story line to pass up. As it was going to be blamed on a germ, I came up with the title for the book.

I had been hearing about Churches and Christian broadcasting companies preparing the "Doomsday Message" to the world. When everyone disappears, all these secular stations have been paid to play certain messages. Personally, don't waste your money! When everyone disappears, and the world is in mass panic, the last thing the government will let us do is add to the panic by broadcasting messages of doom and gloom.

I had started *THE RAPTURE SYNDROME* with one character in mind. However, after a few chapters, I couldn't have my character remain a non-believer and still be respectable to the readers or me. Thus, I created his brother. This gave me the perfect way of contrasting the sides during the Tribulation. One brother will be a believer, the other will serve the Anti-Christ.

When I wrote the book, it was rather strange. I got the idea of doing a partial brain transplant for the Anti-Christ as a revolutionary new treatment for the fatal head wound he received. I then added memory transferal from the donor. The deceased donor had been a Satanist whose memories were of Black Masses. After I had written the story, I found an article in a magazine about partial brain transplants on mice, and how it had a high potential of success, and seemed to suggest that some memories could be transferred. I thought it was something I had made up as pure science fiction. Now it may be common-place in the future. In fact, as I was correcting a prior final copy of this manuscript, my wife pointed out an article in the local paper, *The Press Enterprise*. It was a story about using the brain cells from aborted fetuses to treat Parkinson's Disease [*Fetal Tissue Helps Parkinson' Victims* Thursday, April 22, 1999, page one and twelve]. The partial brain transplant is no longer a thing of pure speculation.

I also used a laser for the surgery, and after the story was complete, I found an article in a magazine about doctors now using lasers for this kind of delicate surgery. Twenty years later, it seems only logical to use lasers in this kind of surgery, but when the book was first written, lasers were still something you would use for a ray gun or light saber, not a surgical device.

The final shock came several years later. In my earliest draft of the story, I had the astronauts using the Centaur rockets on their shuttle craft. Now years later I was working as a claims adjuster, and was investigating a claim at a lab we insured. I came to the office of the employer, was waiting in the lobby and saw a picture on the wall of the Centaur rockets used on the shuttle. I was a space program buff, but I never knew there were actually rockets on the shuttle called Centaur rockets. I had used that term because I loved mythology and was looking for a mythological creature to use in the book.

One other point: when I was writing about the Israeli's cutting up the plywood tanks and weapons for firewood, I suddenly stopped myself. "That can't be right," I told myself. I went and looked up the actual passage from the Bible, and was surprised to see that the Bible tells us that the weapons will be cut up and used for firewood.

In 1998, I returned to THE RAPTURE SYNDROME and began to rewrite it. Not because I thought it might be out of date, but I just wanted to have it on computer disc. However, as I've discovered with other works I was putting onto computer, manuscripts have ways of taking over and forcing me in directions I hadn't considered previously. I had only worked on the first two chapters, and the manuscript took over.

In the 1960's the concept of there even being a Gay Movement was unheard of. In 2011, anyone who even refuses to embrace the Gay Movement is in danger of being arrested for Hate Crimes. So before someone tries to claim that I am committing a Hate Crime by making the Anti-Christ openly gay, let me point out that making the Anti-Christ gay was not my choice. It comes from a prophecy in the Old Testament. The Bible tells us that the Anti-Christ will not be *"a lover of women."* Scholars take this to be a polite King James term for the Anti-Christ being gay. The actions and attitudes he portrays in this book are because he is the Anti-Christ, not because he is gay.

When I began to rewrite the manuscript into the computer in 1998 I realized I would have to deal with this prophecy in order to make this account of the Tribulation Period as realistic as possible. The Gay Movement would have to grow in size and power in order for someone who is openly gay to be voted into an office that controls most of the world. Thus, I tried to look at the world as it was in 1998 and extrapolate where it would be when the Rapture took place.

Having watched television and movies for many years, you can see the subtle reconditioning taking place. Many years ago, *Soap* had the first gay character on television. He was a comic figure, and was used through a kind of "reverse humor" to show how stupid many of the beliefs people held about gays appeared to the gay community. Someone would be uncomfortable around a gay man, and say or do something that showed how stupid they really were. Now many years later, gays are on most shows as serious characters. A majority of movies have gay characters or a gay scene in them.

If you have any sense of writing, you can see how some of these scenes or characters don't belong in the story line, but seem to have been forced or added for no other reason than to attack homophobia. The idea is that if we are exposed to gay thoughts and lifestyles enough, we will stop being afraid of them. When we stop being afraid, we will start looking at them. When they have been presented in countless stories as victims of hatred, and a minority that has been persecuted, we will feel sorry for them. From there we will protect them, support them, and even fight for them.

Notice how the media referred to those with AIDS when it first began to report on the illness as *AIDS Victims*, not patients. It generated greater sympathy.

I grew up during the Women's Liberation Movement. Television and Hollywood tried countless times to do role reversal in science fiction shows. The women were in charge, and the men were subjugated. They were trying to change our way of thinking. It was terrible writing. Bad logic. But it was trying to make a point. However, by the time Hollywood and Television turned their efforts to the Gay Movement, they were much better at subtle reconditioning techniques. Only the earliest Television shows were obvious in their efforts.

There is something that people need to realize about bigotry. As long as we feel the need to make the distinction, you still have bigotry. Unless there is a reason to point out a distinction in a scene or story because it is part of the plot or character development; you should be able to fill that part for a movie with any person of any age, race, religion, sex or sexual orientation and make it work.

We had a woman in the Church I grew up in who made this point in an explosive way. Each time the minister mentioned the race of someone—specifically African American—she would slam the hymn book on the tile floor for all to hear. Negative reinforcement. In the 1960's we were trying to deal with the equality of women and script writers went to great extremes to push women into scenes or role to counter the stereotypical women roles. It had just the opposite effect. It made the distinction more obvious. It wasn't until J. Michael Straczynski produced his television series of Babylon 5 that I realized how to do it. He wrote powerful characters. The character fit the scene. The character was essential to the plot. It just so happened that the character was a woman. THAT's when women had been treated equally in the media.

So when approaching this subject of a gay character, I tried to give it the same treatment as Straczynski. It was essential to note because it was a prophetic fulfillment. After that, there was no need to keep calling attention to it or beat it to death. The scene with the gay rape gang attacking Ted was essential to show how the message that only gays survived the Rapture Syndrome was getting out to the world. Not through the media, but through the more militant of the movement who wanted to shove someone's face into it.

The scene was also to show that with each movement, when given political power or support there is the danger of the extremes in that movement abusing the power. The scene was also used to show the logical conclusion of the automatic response created by Television and Hollywood. Every time someone noted that a person was gay, the automatic response was, "Not that there's anything wrong with that." It was such an automatic response it became a joke by itself. So the logical conclusion of the automatic response of "Not that there's anything wrong with that" would be, "If there's nothing wrong with it; then why aren't you part of it?"

So with this realization that the Anti-Christ will be gay as part of a fulfillment of prophecy, in THE RAPTURE SYNDROME I sought to take the trends being presented in

1998 and follow them to their logical conclusion. The Gay Movement will be common place during the Tribulation Period; so common place that a gay man will be accepted, loved by the world, and given more power over our lives than anyone in all the history of the world. There will not be a need to keep calling attention to it unless it somehow furthers the character or the story. But for it to be possible for the world to embrace a gay man as a world leader, the Gay Movement will have to be a prominent party and political force.

Back in the 1998 era gossip sheets would throw the question out on the headlines: "Are they, or aren't they?" There were actresses and actors on the front page with that headline and each would have had the "gay label" placed on them, but they denied it. The militant faction of the Gay Movement would attack them openly saying, "You're gay! Come out of the closet!" Thus, I took what I was observing in the world at the time I was putting this manuscript on computer (1998), and moved it along its logical course.

The world will accept gay as a way of life. It will stop attacking it, and will embrace it as common and acceptable. From there the militant faction will push further. When major movements in gay rights pass courts or Congress, we see on television the more militant members of the gay communities coming onto the streets to celebrate. Invariably someone will sing for the camera "We're here. We're Queer... And we're not going to disappear. Get used to us."

As I was rewriting the manuscript in 1998, I did one thing different. I added the claim that it was the gay gene that made people immune to the Rapture Syndrome. If it was a biological organism that wiped out millions of people in a second; then why did some disappear and others did not? There had to be something that made survivors immune. It had to be something that is in the genetic make up. It had to be something that was vague and undetectable at the time. Otherwise, all African Americans would have disappeared. All women would have disappeared. Everyone with red hair would have disappeared. It had to be a genetic trait that you could not put your finger on and identify with just a quick glance at the survivors versus the victims.

The Gay Community has been claiming for years that it was a genetic trait that made them gay. They had been seeking for it for years. It wasn't found when gene mapping was finished; but what if it was something we couldn't spot right away? What if we just missed it? Thus, to say that this gay gene provided protection for the world would give the gays a great propaganda weapon.

From this belief, it would follow that everyone left after the Rapture had the gay gene in his/her chromosome make-up. The militant faction of the Gay Movement would then be able to say things like "If you're here, then you're queer!" Everyone left must be gay; and those who don't practice it are either fighting it or hiding it. Those fighting it need to be nurtured and brought into the "fold." Those hiding it must be pressured into being honest about their hidden feelings the way militant gays pressured celebrities to come out of the closet willingly or be exposed. The gay gene being the reason for your salvation would be a recruiting tidal wave for the Gay Community. It would be a call to stop fighting it and embrace it so it can unite the world rather than divide the world.

I know dealing with the Gay Movement in a Tribulation World might make some readers uncomfortable. Acknowledging the strong gay influence in the world during the Tribulation Period should not be seen either as a personal endorsement or attack on my part. It is an effort to try and predict what the world will be like as honestly as possible, and it was a factor I could not choose to ignore.

There will be some political changes which I think we will see. The Bible speaks of Russia attacking Israel. They use wooden weapons and tanks. Given the fact that the Israelis burn the weapons for seven years, I suspect the attack will be at the time of the Rapture since the weapons are available to burn for seven years. Russia is almost destroyed as a political power. It will ally itself with other countries for Armageddon, but as a single power, it has lost a lot of its might.

There is no reference to America during the Tribulation Period, at least not by terms we would recognize. Some suggest the Babylon of Revelation is America. As the new Babylon is destroyed, and merchants weep from afar over its loss they suggest this is America. Believe me, when the Trade Towers fell on 9/11 and you could see the smoke rising from the harbor, it reminded me of the description of the destruction of the new Babylon. I did go back and do a lot of research just to make sure I hadn't missed something in my view of the End Times. I don't see America as a major power in the latter half of the Tribulation Period. Either we cease to exist, we are destroyed, weakened, or become an isolationist nation.

I believe that China will eventually become democratic. The reason for this belief is that God does not hold people accountable for things they are not responsible for. If the Anti-Christ were a dictator, and had ruled through conquest, those under him would not be responsible for following him. They were forced to do it. I believe all the major powers will eventually move toward democracy, at least for the purpose of electing the Anti-Christ to rule them. Once he is in power, he will be able to become the dictator with people's consent. Thus, people will be responsible for following him because they chose—at least initially—to follow him.

Also China will either break up into smaller countries, or will ally themselves with other Asian countries. I say this because the Scriptures speak of the "kings" of the east. This is plural, not singular. The kings of the east mass an army to come against Israel. The size of the army sounds like China, but China has a single ruler. Therefore, China must either break up, create a multiple-leader government, or ally itself with others. There should also be a combined power growing in Africa with several rulers involved because again the Scriptures speak of the "kings" of the south coming against Israel.

I found a reference in Ezekiel about Egypt being desolate for forty years. Some Bible scholars claim that this already happened when Egypt was conquered by Babylon. Its people were scattered. However, the situation the scholars speak of does not fulfill all of the facts concerning the prophecy. It says that no one shall live there, and that no animals will be there, either. Forty years is the approximate time frame before people can move back into an area hit with a nuclear bomb. This would keep people and animals out; or they would die. Thus, I believe Egypt will be struck with some kind of nuclear disaster, either a bomb, a terrorist attack, a reactor, or an experiment gone wrong.

As the current Mid-East Crisis is growing, I have added another thought to the nuclear blast in Egypt. Egypt has become the location for peace talks and discussions between Israel and the Palestinians. Should the leaders come to Egypt, what better way to destroy the negotiations than to have a suicide bomber walk into downtown Cairo with a portable nuclear bomb in his back pack, hit the button and waste everything within several miles? You don't have to even be close with a nuclear blast. Suicide bombers have been used several times in attacks on the enemies of the terrorists. Each time a new peace talk comes to Egypt, I actually find myself holding my breath and waiting for the news story to hit.

I have one other concept I put into the book, and when I mention this one, people think, "Well, he's been spending too much time with his puppets. His brain has turned to foam rubber just like theirs." But let me present it to you, and see what you might think. Going back to the passage which says that the world shall be like it was in the days of Noah, I started thinking. Prior to Noah, people lived for hundreds of years. Scientists have speculated that with the water canopy encircling the globe at that time, solar radiation was filtered out more efficiently than just the ozone layer could on its own. If cellular damage is slowed down—say by removing this additional solar radiation—the body can replace or repair most of itself. When the cellular damage speeds up, the body can't fix it.

Also, the body has the ability to build any part of itself. Lizards can re-grow tails after they drop them off. What we are seeing now among the medical profession are new techniques where the physician is asking, "How can I tell the body to grow this, or fix that?" Inside the womb, the embryo takes material provided by the mother, and grows every part of the body; everything from skin to complex neural pathways. If physicians can find the *"trigger"* to activate this growing process used by the embryo, they can direct the body to grow a new arm, to repair broken spinal cords. In short, the body would become almost immortal. On television in the late 1990's, scientists were excited to discover a gene that made cells live longer. They seem to be getting closer. I believe that AIDS research will find the key to activating this *"trigger."* The immune system defends the body from attack. It protects the body from germs. AIDS blocks the immune system so it cannot function. At some point the research is going to find a way to reactivate the immune system, and I believe that this *"trigger"* to activate self-repair of the body may be closely related.

To cite some sources to give this credibility you might remember the late Christopher Reeve. He was a quadriplegic due to a horse accident. He was bound to a wheelchair or bed. He wanted to walk once more. He had lobbied for Congress to pass legislation that would let medical experiments be performed on aborted fetuses. Why? Because they believe that this is where they will find the code to tell the body to grow or repair the spinal cord. One year he was part of an advertisement showing his standing up and walking once more as he came forward to personally thank someone who had donated to the research that allowed him to be healed. Thus, I'm not out in left field when I suggest that the body can repair most injuries if this *"trigger"* is activated.

Now I had to deal with a passage from the Bible which talks about the Tribulation saints being martyred. The method of execution is beheading. That seems like a lot of effort to kill someone. A shot to the brain is faster and takes less effort. To create a guillotine, heft an ax, or some other method takes a lot more time and energy. So why go back to beheading?

Given the above theory, it would make sense to decapitate as a form of execution. If the body's *"trigger"* has been activated, then most injuries, even fatal ones, could be repaired given time and care. I believe that if the *"trigger"* has been activated, then only a complete beheading, severing of the head from the body would produce complete death. The brain would not have the blood, oxygen and nutrients needed to grow the damaged body part. The headless body would not have the instruction to repair its damage. Thus, beheading is the only way to guarantee death by execution.

Also, one of the judgments is that men will seek death, and death will flee from them. The pain they will be going through will be more than they can endure, but death is no longer an escape for them. Thus, I believe that at some point mankind will learn how to activate the *"trigger"* to an on-going repair system which will make death an impossibility. It may not be the way I'm picturing it, but there has to be some form of immortality or extended life for those in the Tribulation Period for this Scripture to be true.

Lastly, I address the issue of UFOs. I spent many years as an avid fan of UFO-ology, and was heavily involved in research on the subject. My studies led me to expand my focus into other areas of unexplained phenomena which included psychic abilities, astral projection, curses, witchcraft, demonology and ghosts. I finally came to realize that there was something out there. Everyone couldn't be the victim of hallucinations, delusion, or practical jokes. However, I did notice one common theme: whenever contact was made with aliens in these accounts, the message given by aliens always challenged what the Bible taught about God, man, and the universe. I had to believe either the Bible, or the aliens.

I finally had to come to the conclusion that all the UFO sightings, contacts, etc were appearances by something or someone that wanted us to stop believing in the teachings of the Bible. Since all the various "new teachings" these aliens gave us contradicted each other, I knew they couldn't be true. It was a time of restoring my Christian faith. I had to denounce the doctrines of aliens and psychics, and cling to the teachings of the Bible. This brought me to the final position that UFO's, ghosts, and other unexplained phenomena were attempts by Satan to lead us away from God.

Scriptures tell us that demons can create their own form of miracles, signs, and wonders; and that they will try to deceive the entire world. Combining what I knew of UFOs, psychic powers, ghosts, and others unexplained phenomena I saw this as part of Satan's plan to lead us away from God. The Bible also tells us that men will give heed to the doctrine of demons in the last days. Putting all of this together, I used this in the book to show how demons will reveal themselves openly during the Tribulation Period. However instead of being extraterrestrials (ETs), they reveal that they are extradimensionals (EeeDees). As creatures with advanced technology, different ways of looking at the universe, and an alternative to the teachings of God and the Bible, leaders will listen to their advice. Given the increase in the New Age movement where people are seeking a religion without God, and their focus on unexplained phenomena as revelations about the true nature of the universe, I chose to use this in my book.

What surprised me so much was that many years ago I was listening to a cassette tape by Dr. Walter Martin regarding UFOs. He made some comment about Satan using aliens to deceive us in the last days. Personally, I thought he was off his rocker. Intelligent, mature adults would never seriously listen to aliens. However, after many years, we have seen movies about aliens. *The X-Files* had been the hottest TV show around. People have been seeing angels everywhere. New Age teachers are blending aliens and angels as guides to help us through our troubled times. Everything is in place, and it just takes a couple of pieces of solid documentation to put it all together.

When I had finished writing Chapter Four, I was actually frightened. In one fell swoop I had pulled several pieces together and in addition to wiping out millions of people in a plague I had discredited Jesus, trashed the Bible, turned Christians into the enemy and made homosexuality the norm for the entire world. I gave serious thought to burning the copy, deleting it from the computer, and putting something else in its place. I gave it to my wife, and she was frightened. It was too terrifying to think of all this coming together in such a neat little package, but she said "*keep it.*" My daughter read it and had the same terrifying realization. Everyone who read it was frightened by it, but everyone saw that it could happen that way, and in fact it seemed to put all the pieces into place, and give a very believable prediction of how Satan will twist things when he is no longer hindered by Christians. Thus, Chapter Four stayed. Remember, this is from the 1998 re-write. It is now 2014, and it is no longer so hard to believe.

I did pause in the writing to go back to Scripture and try to put everything into a kind of time line for the Tribulation. What I realized was that there was a lot of death and destruction in just seven years. Some suggested this become a series, others said edit it down or ignore a lot of it. My feeling was, "Wow! How am I going to put all this doom and gloom into one book?"

In response I was tempted to do another series, but after working for thirty years on *THE DULAN ARCHIVES*, I wasn't ready to start another series. Plus, Tim LaHaye was doing a series on the Tribulation Period back in 1998, and I tried very hard to avoid any other works by other authors in my research and writing of this one. Thus I am hard pressed with the task of putting it all together in one book without making my readers suicidal. [Note: these are my comments from 1998, not 2014.]

I also realized that several of the judgments coming are similar to disaster movies coming out at theaters *DEEP IMPACT* and *ARMEGEDDON*, and I wanted to get my version done before I saw theirs. I did not want to be tempted to use their vision to make my job easier. So when I was doing the re-write back in 1998, it all had to come together in about four weeks because that's when the first movie came out, and I didn't want to miss it.

When I finished Chapter Four, I found I needed to go back and change the ending just a little. I needed to foreshadow the coming comet that would crash into the earth. The Bible calls the comet "Wormwood," and so I saw no reason to change the name, but to use it for the story.

Revelation tells us that there is going to be seven seals which are broken in Heaven after the Rapture. Each seal brings a doom upon the earth. The first seal reveals the Anti-Christ, and so he had to be my first focus after the Rapture. I needed to get him into place. I believe he will rise to power through political election, but once in power he will extend that power through brutal wars. I get this from the Book of Daniel which shows the beast—symbolic of the Anti-Christ—holding three ribs in his mouth. Scholars believe three countries will be broken and crushed by the Anti-Christ as he extends his power.

When the seventh seal is broken, we see seven angels coming forth to blow trumpets. Each angel brings another judgment upon the earth. When the last trumpet sounds, we see seven more angels coming out with bowls of judgment which are poured out on the earth. With the last bowl being poured out, we see the Second Coming of Jesus and the Battle of Armageddon. There are a lot of disasters to cram into seven years. In fact, they seem to come during the last three-and-one-half years of the Tribulation Period. It's like "How much pain and suffering can the world—and my readers—take?"

We see earthquakes. We see a volcano erupt. We see a comet hit the earth. We see meteor storms, we see the death of all sea life, the destruction of one-third of all plants. We see wars which kill five-sixths of the Russian army, wars which kill one-fourth of a 200,000 man army. We see 7,000 die in an earthquake. We see all mountains moved, and islands are no longer visible because of earthquakes. All water is polluted so it appears to be blood. We see sores that are painful and "noisome." How a sore can give off a noise I'm still working on that one. We see hail and fire falling to the earth. We see hail so large it becomes fatal when it strikes people. We see darkness, days shorted to one-third their normal length, cloud coverings that make the sun black and the moon like blood. Then we see the covering ripped away, and the sun becomes so harsh it scorches men caught in its direct contact.

The high death tolls in quakes seemed staggering until the Indonesia quake and tsunami killed over 100,000. Now some of the figures seem tame to me. But back in 1998 I could not grasp such destruction.

With all of this as the backdrop, how much do I put into the book? When does the disaster take center-stage and the characters fall into the background? Are there areas of over-lap in the judgments so I can make it easier to write about and not get depressed? But then I remember the Scripture which tells us that all this is like the birth pains of a woman in labor. When these pains are over, we have a new world order. Jesus will physically rule from Jerusalem for a thousand years. After that, there is a new Heaven and earth. The key is to look toward the end, and not just the path set before us.

How am I going to pull all of this off? I really wasn't sure when I started the re-write in 1998, but you're reading the end of the book, so I must have done something. I just hope that Jesus takes over at the right point to make it all as accurate as possible. Just keep one thought in mind: I'm not claiming to be a prophet. I'm just looking at prophecies and letting my imagination and prayer take over to tell a story. If it doesn't work out just this way, don't show up with rocks at my front door to stone me. After all, this is supposed to just be a story.

It's hard to make sure I've considered every prophecy. I had one scene that was great: the Invasion of Jerusalem and the Mark of the Beast. Then just before our get together to discuss the proof reading of my manuscript I came across Daniel Chapter Twelve. There the Angel tells Daniel that from the time the daily sacrifices end and the Abomination of Desolation come is one thousand two hundred and ninety days. WHAT? That's thirty days after the death of the Two

Witnesses, and the Death of the Two Witnesses is the end of my story. To be faithful to the prophecy, I had to pull the scene out and rework the manuscript. So I started with a simple rewrite to correct for the prophecy from Daniel; and then thought I was done. I sacrificed the Invasion of Jerusalem scene.

Again, I was wrong. The scene demanded to be told, and with the folder in my G Drive already setting the stage for the last three and a half years I surrendered and agreed to consider a sequel. When I finally committed to writing a sequel, I had to put everything on hold and go back and start with a Prologue and then had to rework each chapter to fit with it and the coming sequel.

Just one final point to make in closing. I think I've finished this manuscript several times. Several times I thought I was done; only to have God pull me back in. Here is it, January of 2014. Hopefully the story is finally finished. Hopefully God will let me send it off. If not, I'll be back adding some more to it.

I know the book doesn't paint a pretty picture of the Tribulation Period, but I do hope it paints an accurate one. It's not a place you want to go to or live through on purpose. That's why God offers His salvation free to anyone who wants it. All you have to do is ask. God's message will have been presented to the entire Earth before the Rapture takes place. Everyone in the world when the Rapture takes place will have been given the choice of accepting Jesus as their personal Savior. Those who have accepted God's forgiveness and salvation will be snatched away before it gets bad; those who are left will be there because they chose to be there. I hope you choose to accept what God offers, and are spared from this seven-year period of judgment. I believe in the Rapture. I believe in the Tribulation Period. I believe in God's love, grace and mercy. I believe that God can forgive even the most horrible of sins if we let Him. Why? Because of the same faith which guided me in writing this book the way I did: I believe the Bible to be true.

The Bible has always given us an accurate picture of the dealings of God with man, even when they aren't pretty. We have seen our saints fallen at some point in their lives. We have seen them restored and/or still used by God. God is not looking for perfection. He is looking for our love. That has always been the motivation of God: "For God so loved that He gave..." The Rapture is God's love for His Church. The Tribulation Period is God's love for those left behind. This is the Rapture and the Tribulation Period, as realistically as I can make it given my imagination and study of Scripture. It may be right, it might be wrong; but it's my best attempt to give you the chance to glimpse the coming events on God's calendar. I hope it speaks to you. I hope it gets you to start thinking. Even more, I hope it gets you to start praying. I hope it makes it all a little more real for you. I hope that God uses it according to His will, and not my own. However, being the writer that I am, I also hope that you enjoyed it.

Don't forget:

"Rapture practice at 2:00 tomorrow. Be there!"

"How will we know it's a practice?"

"If we come back down it's a practice. If we keep going; it's the real thing."

If you need an example of what to pray to accept Jesus as your Savior, let me suggest the following. However, anything along the same lines will work:

"Jesus, I recognize my need for you. Forgive me of my sins. Be my personal Savior. I accept your offer of forgiveness. Come and live inside me and make me one of Your own. Amen."

Author's Notes originally written 4/15/98 by Dennis Knotts

[Revised 8/27/2011] [Revised once more 4/2/2012] [One more time 6/23/2012] [And again on 1/25/2014] Will this ever get done?!

CPSIA information can be obtained
at www.ICGtesting.com
Printed in the USA
FFOW03n1349240414
5018FF

9 781628 578690